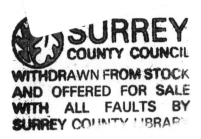
Eldred Jones, Lulubelle & the Most High

Also by Clare Nonhebel

FICTION
Cold Showers
The Partisan
Incentives
Child's Play

NON-FICTION
Healed and Souled
(by Ashuli: co-written with Joseph Stefanazzi)
Don't Ask Me to Believe

Eldred Jones,
Lulubelle &
the Most High

CLARE
NONHEBEL

A LION BOOK

This book is a work of fiction and the story is
entirely a creation of the imagination. No parallel
between any events or persons is intended.

Published by
Lion Publishing plc
Sandy Lane West, Oxford, England
ISBN 0 7459 3812 4

First edition 1998
10 9 8 7 6 5 4 3 2 1 0

A catalogue record for this book is available
from the British Library

Printed and bound in Great Britain by
Biddles Ltd, Guildford and King's Lynn

Chapter One

Eldred Jones taught himself to read at the age of five. This would not have qualified him as a child genius, except for three significant facts: Eldred had spent the first five years of his life in an oxygen tent; he had not spoken a single word since birth, and the book he was reading was a medical textbook.

His parents, Edgar and Mildred Jones, had even thought that Eldred might be retarded, that his brain as well as his poor little inadequate lungs might have been damaged at birth.

Mildred used to suffer sleepless nights, wondering if it was her fault, whether she should have given up smoking or dosed herself with megavitamins during pregnancy. It distressed her to see little Eldred, blue around the mouth and gasping for breath, looking at her and beyond her with sad eyes that seemed to expect no help from anyone.

Eldred would survive, the consultant assured her; he would outgrow his need for the oxygen tent and for the hospital that had been almost his only home for five years; his resistance to infection was increasing as the months went by. There was no reason to believe that Eldred would not turn out to be a normal healthy child.

'But why isn't he talking yet?' Mildred asked Mr Jennings the lung specialist, Mr Abdul the paediatrician, Dr Thompson the registrar, Dr Ahmed the house doctor, the day and night ward sisters, the nurses, the auxiliary nurses, the cleaners, the hospital porters, the neighbours, the people she met on buses, in shops and in the launderette, and anyone else who would listen to her. 'He seems quite an intelligent child,' she said. 'I'm sure he's taking in most of what we say. Why doesn't he talk?'

The nurses talked to Eldred, read him little stories about talking animals, ferocious monsters and eccentric magicians, and sang him nursery rhymes, clapping and miming the words while five-year-old Eldred watched them with solemn dark brown eyes.

A retired teacher came to the ward four mornings a week and

showed Eldred alphabet books and counting games and how to make little figures from non-allergenic modelling clay, naming the colours as she tried to interest the child in red cats and blue snakes and green dinosaurs.

Eldred watched politely but wouldn't join in. Miss Dalrymple left the hospital every week more and more discouraged. Like Mildred, she was convinced that Eldred understood. So why didn't he respond?

He was beginning to make Miss Dalrymple nervous. Was the child secretly laughing at her? Was he bored? Autistic? Deaf-mute? But the child had been tested for everything under the sun and apart from a hard-to-diagnose lung condition he seemed perfect.

Once, reading Eldred a story about a wriggly worm that ate everything in its path and turned into a very outsize worm whose wriggly mum had to put him on a diet, Miss Dalrymple glanced up and caught Eldred watching her with an expression in his eyes that she couldn't fathom. She searched for a word to describe it, out of her schoolteacher's wide vocabulary, and failed.

Only later, while a solitary Miss Dalrymple was eating her mushroom omelette in front of a 'Survival' programme on mountain gorillas, did the answer appear in her brain like one of the flash cards she used to use for her reception class. The word was pity.

It was during the following week that Edgar Jones, making his routine Sunday visit to his silent little son, heard Eldred speak.

The hospital lifts were out of order and Edgar had climbed the five flights of stairs to Eldred's ward, stopping at every floor to calm the wheezing of his weak chest that his son had probably (so Mildred told the doctor) inherited.

So Edgar entered the ward short of breath and approached little Eldred's oxygen tent without his usual greeting – the hearty, embarrassed, 'Hello, little man; how goes it today?' that announced the start of Edgar's weekly half-hour attempt to find something to say to his child.

Eldred didn't hear his father coming. Inside the oxygen tent, his thin shoulders were hunched over a thick volume that the house doctor had left behind that morning when he was called away suddenly in the middle of sounding Eldred's chest.

The child was so absorbed in the text that Edgar, forgetting his bedside manner, said in the tone he would have used for a normal person who was not his son, 'What's that you're reading?'

'Pulmonary malfunction,' murmured Eldred, without thinking.

The shock hit them both at once. Father and son, each suddenly aware of the other's real existence, stared into an identically startled pair of brown eyes.

'You spoke,' said Edgar stupidly. He sat down, pulled out a tissue and wiped his brow. Then, 'You can read,' he said. Eldred didn't reply.

'You can read textbooks on lung disease,' Edgar said accusingly, reaching into the oxygen tent and examining the title of his five year old's reading book. His eyes filled with tears. 'Why?' he asked. 'Why this book? We've given you piles of storybooks.'

Eldred hesitated, his expression anxious and compassionate. 'They didn't interest me,' he said finally.

'And this one does?' Edgar said, turning the pages in perplexity.

'Oh, very much,' said Eldred. 'I've found the remedy for my disease.'

C h a p t e r   T w o

It was probably psychosomatic in origin, Eldred explained to Mr Jennings, Mr Abdul, Dr Thompson, Dr Ahmed and a crowd of medical students. 'Very difficult for you to diagnose,' Eldred said sympathetically, 'especially as the resultant symptoms are typical of at least three types of organic pulmonary disease.'

Eldred's doctors were not delighted with him. 'We arranged an appointment for you with one of the most eminent child psychologists in Europe,' Mr Abdul pointed out. 'Why didn't you speak to him?'

'I didn't want to speak until I was sure of my findings,' Eldred said. 'An article in the October '73 issue of *Clinical Psychologist* warned against prematurely publicizing the results of insufficient research.'

One or two of the medical students started to giggle. Mr Jennings' neck pinkened above his red and white striped collar.

'If you are going to be a psychologist, sonny,' he said, 'one thing you will have to learn is the value of the expert's superior knowledge. If you had answered Jason Wilbrahim's questions he would have arrived at these conclusions years before you.'

Eldred looked reproachfully at him. 'Would you confide your intimate pre-birth memories to a man who made sexual overtures towards a male student nurse in the presence of a child?' he enquired.

The press loved Eldred. The hospital authorities were not so loving. Within a week, Eldred was giving interviews not from his familiar oxygen tent in the fifth floor ward but from his parents' home on an outer London housing estate.

Asked how it felt to be home at last, Eldred replied, 'Psychologically it will require a period of adjustment, but physically I am suffering no ill-effects, since my symptoms abated as soon as I had identified the source of my condition.'

It turned out that Eldred, while he was living in his oxygen tent, had regularly disconnected himself and escaped at night to scavenge the hospital for reading material.

He had educated himself with the aid of medical textbooks, scientific periodicals, psychology students' unfinished theses, biographies, travel books, novels, puzzle books, computer users' journals, newspapers, women's magazines, children's comics and men-only magazines.

Back in his tent, wheezing and gasping after these forays, he would reconnect himself to the apparatus and allow himself half an hour to recover his breathing rhythm before devouring the contents of the papers and books, using a speed-reading technique learned from a self-help book he had borrowed from a patient's locker.

Then he would detach himself again from his cocoon and return each book to its rightful place (having memorized this by visualization techniques perfected in five days from a book called *A Photographic Memory in Only Six Weeks*).

Eldred's picture appeared in every national newspaper, with features in a range of magazines. The journalists had no need to follow their normal practice of plumping up the quotes or converting them into artificially grammatical language, as Eldred spoke fluently and grammatically on any number of subjects.

The only topic on which he was uninformative was the pre-birth memory which he claimed had caused the trauma that led to his lung damage.

'This is now irrelevant, since the condition is cured,' Eldred told the press politely but firmly. 'I have already erased it from my memory bank.'

Eventually public interest was sated and died down. Eldred's life settled into a new routine. He attended school, joining the six to seven year olds' class rather than the five year olds' as a concession to his advanced standard of education in some areas.

At school he learned to join in activities which didn't interest him, such as the class project (a Plasticine model of the Lake District), playground fights, organized games (running along benches and throwing beanbags), and homework (a list of six objects found in a kitchen and ten sums involving numbers under twenty-five).

Eldred found this good training for joining in activities which didn't interest him at home – going to the launderette with his mother Mildred and watching children's TV with his parents rather than the Open University programmes he had video-recorded.

He was no trouble at home. Edgar and Mildred, who had been afraid that their child prodigy would be a handful, were relieved to see the child accept a normal life.

'All that funny high-falutin talk was only because he was stuck in that oxygen tent,' Mildred told her husband. 'I wouldn't wonder if all that pure air didn't hype up his brain. It's not natural for a child, is it? Now he's home he'll become normal. Have you seen this lovely picture of a house he's brought home, Daddy? The teacher said he couldn't do it at first, kept asking her peculiar questions about architecture, but when she showed him the other children's drawings and told him to copy them he managed fine.'

All in all, the Joneses were satisfied that little Eldred, despite his five years of deprived childhood, would be able to keep up with his parents' lifestyle.

Edgar even began to consider moving back to his native Ipswich, now the family no longer needed to be within visiting range of the big London hospital. But here Eldred unexpectedly put his foot down.

'If it wouldn't be too much trouble to you and Mum,' he told his father, calmly but with a determined expression on his five-year-old face, 'I would prefer to continue living here, within easy reach of adequate reference-library facilities.'

Chapter Three

Eldred was learning. One of the things he learned was that not everything can be learned from books. He began to study people very carefully. He learned then that people don't like being studied. And that taught him to be more subtle in his research.

He learned too that people don't like success, except within certain limits. And that taught Eldred to be secretive.

He learned that when someone asked him, 'How did you know that?' it was acceptable to say, 'I read it in a book' or, 'I saw a programme on TV,' because second-hand knowledge was not suspect. What people could not accept was that some of Eldred's knowledge arose from Eldred himself.

'Where do you get all your ideas from?' Edgar's aunts would ask the child.

In the early days, soon after his homecoming from the hospital,

Eldred would reply, 'Ideas arise from inspiration working through information acquired and selected for retention by the individual mind.'

Now, at the age of six and a half, he was becoming worldly-wise. He knew people wanted to believe that ideas were something acquired, like facts from an encyclopaedia or tins of tuna-fish from Sainsbury's – commodities which had been prepared by other people and only needed to be taken off the shelf and claimed as their own.

'I could have been a scientist,' Eldred's father occasionally sighed, 'only I never had the education.'

'I could have been a writer of children's books,' Mildred would chime in. 'I was always writing stories when I was a little girl. Eldred gets all his scribbling from me. I could still do it now, if only I had the ideas.'

Little Eldred took his parents seriously. On one of his frequent visits to the local library he spent some time in the reference section and returned with a sheet of carefully copied information on adult education science courses for his father.

He also, for the first time, used his ticket to take out eight storybooks from the children's section. 'You need to study the market,' he told Mildred. 'I only selected books with recent publication dates. The senior librarian told me that trends in children's publishing change very rapidly.'

Mildred, to Eldred's surprise, became angry. 'If you think I've got time for all that stuff, you can think again,' she said. 'I've got a house to run and a family to look after. By the time I've turned round in the morning, it's time to fetch you from school at quarter past three.'

Eldred was concerned. 'Shall we make alternative arrangements for fetching me?' he enquired. 'With another parent perhaps? I wouldn't like to be the cause of your failing to fulfil your ambition to write.'

'I didn't say it was an ambition,' Mildred said, growing flustered. 'I said it was something I could have done at one time. I'm too old to learn new tricks now.'

'From the neurological and psychological reports I have read,' said Eldred helpfully, 'I gather that brain cells do die, or at least become inoperative, in old age, but they can be regenerated in cases where people have the motivation to extend their mental horizons. So the willingness to learn can in itself re-stimulate the capacity for learning.'

Mildred sent him to do his homework. It didn't take him very long, but instinct warned Eldred to stay out of his mother's way for a while; she seemed angry about something. So he sat at his little desk and pondered her reaction to his helpfulness. The conclusion of his pondering made him sad.

When Edgar came home from work, Eldred hid the information about science courses under his bed and went to talk to his father in the kitchen first. Something told him that this seemingly innocent subject of his parents' unfulfilled ambitions hid a minefield.

'How was work today, Dad?' Eldred asked, when Edgar was installed at the kitchen table with a cup of tea in front of him. 'Did you sell much insurance?'

'Quite a few enquiries,' Edgar said. 'I doubt they'll come to much, in the present recession.'

Eldred was interested. 'Won't the effective value of the policies when they reach maturity repay the sacrifice in income invested in them now? Or could it be that the rate of environmental damage to the planet makes people dubious about the validity of a future to insure against or provide for at all?'

Edgar frowned at him. 'What do you mean? People are always going to need insurance.'

'Don't bother your father now, Eldred,' said Mildred automatically. 'He's been working hard all day. He doesn't want a lot of questions.'

Eldred refrained from telling his mother that medical research provided evidence that a change of mental activity actually rested the brain. Tact was a lesson he was trying to learn. Instead he said. 'Do you ever wish you had taken up some other kind of job, Dad? Like, say, writing books? Or science?'

Edgar pulled himself to his feet. 'My job's as good as anybody's,' he said. 'Books and science are no good when someone's house burns down, are they?'

'So,' said Eldred cautiously, 'you feel more needed as an insurance salesman than you would as a scientist?'

'Feelings have got nothing to do with it,' said Edgar irritably. 'It's facts I'm talking about. You stick to facts, son.'

'You've gone and upset your father now,' said Mildred, as Edgar took his tea into the lounge/dining room.

'Yes, I can see that,' said Eldred. He went back to his room, tore up the pages of carefully copied information about adult education courses and wrapped the pieces in an old newspaper before putting them into the bin. He stayed in his room until called to join his parents in front of 'The Paul Daniels Magic Show'. He was learning.

Chapter Four

By the time he was eight years old, Eldred had mastered basic calculus, designed a computer program for cross-checking the claims of different scientific research establishments, and was reading everything he could find on the application of psychology in town planning.

He had also discovered that his father considered it normal for him to spend hours at the computer, as other kids did. Edgar somehow managed to turn a blind eye to the fact that while other kids used their VDUs to zap aliens and rescue treasure from secret dungeons, Eldred was currently using his to plot graphics for an organic waste recycling system.

Mildred was not so happy for Eldred to sit in front of a computer screen for so long, but she considered it normal for him to go out on his bike with his friends or to play football with them in the park. She might have been less happy if she had heard the conversations that Eldred had with those friends.

Eldred was information-gathering. He had realized that spending his first five years in hospital, surrounded by adults anxious about his health, had deprived him of valuable early experience of normal life. So he gently but persistently pumped his friends for anecdotes about their young lives and asked penetrating questions about their impressions of their families.

He was popular. Edgar and Mildred were relieved about this. They assumed it happened naturally because Eldred was learning to become more normal, and making friends was a sign of normality. But Eldred was not normal. He was simply getting cleverer at appearing normal, as he was getting cleverer at everything else.

Eldred knew that you do not make friends by gaining high marks in every school subject and coming first in every test. So he made a few deliberate mistakes. He also discovered that children didn't mind another child excelling at some things, as long as he was useless at something else.

So although he made studious efforts to discover what seemed to make one child good at sport and another hopeless, he did not exert himself to overcome his own deficiencies in physical coordination and willingly let himself be classed among the 'two-left-feet' footballers.

Unlike the other two-left-footers, however, Eldred didn't refuse to play football out of school. He played, and let the other kids in the park gloat over his stumbling attempts and call him a wimp. It made them feel superior.

Eldred's teacher was not fooled.

'You're capable of far better work than this,' Mrs Garcia told Eldred severely, when he handed in a higher than average spelling test or an only moderately accurate rainfall chart. 'You're just being lazy. I won't have any child in my class doing less than their best.'

But it was the same Mrs Garcia who looked at Eldred with unveiled dislike when he put his hand up to answer too many questions. 'Give somebody else a chance, Eldred Jones,' she said. 'You're getting too big for your boots.'

It was Mrs Garcia who, in the school quiz, asked eight-year-old Eldred's ten-year-old classmates questions from the seven year olds' sheet and set Eldred questions from the eleven to twelve year olds' category.

It was Mrs Garcia who, when Eldred was still winning every round of the quiz, refused three of Eldred's correct answers and deliberately misunderstood a fourth one, so that he only tied in first place with one of the top-formers.

And it was Mrs Garcia who doctored the class averages so that, at the end of term, another child collected the form prize. The other children, who hadn't detected Mrs Garcia giving wrong answers in the quiz, noticed this.

'Eldred always comes first,' they told Mrs Garcia. 'He's cleverer than Samantha. Why didn't Eldred get the prize?'

'It may look as though Eldred always comes first,' said Mrs Garcia firmly, 'but we teachers give marks for every separate piece of work and then we calculate the averages. You haven't learnt about averages yet. Don't judge what you don't know about, children.' But the children knew about truth and about adults lying, and they continued to mutter.

'Perhaps,' said Eldred, trying to be conciliatory, 'there are other factors taken into consideration, apart from just marks.' He had, without being conscious of doing it, memorized all his marks as the term went on and recalculated the average each time. And last week, when he had caught sight of the book of class marks lying open on Mrs Garcia's desk, he had, just as an exercise against boredom, memorized the averages of every child in the class, in alphabetical order. At this stage of his school life, Eldred had not yet learned that a teacher's judgment may not be impartial.

'What factors exactly did you have in mind, Eldred?' Mrs Garcia asked, narrowing her eyes.

Eldred considered. 'Social factors, perhaps?' he hazarded. 'Samantha's always well-behaved. She helps you carry your books and she's the first to offer to stay behind after class to clean the board. And her mother is a divorced parent who is anxious about Samantha doing well at school, to show she isn't disturbed by the breakup of the marriage.' (Samantha nodded at this.)

'And I have come first every other term,' Eldred continued meditatively, 'which has meant that some of the others, who are bright for their age, have unfairly got into trouble with their parents for not winning the prize.' (Several small heads nodded here.)

'And you think,' said Mrs Garcia with dangerous reasonableness, 'that I might have compensated Samantha and placated the other parents by giving her higher marks, even though the standard of your work was of course far better than anyone else's, Eldred Jones? Are you saying that the teacher – the teacher – cheated?'

The children began shifting in their chairs, becoming nervous. Eldred registered this. He had noticed that other children's instincts were often more reliable than his own in detecting what would annoy adults.

In fact some children, it seemed to Eldred, modelled their whole life around avoiding causing annoyance. In the presence of adults they acted a role all the time, playing at being children of the kind that adults liked: naïve, dependent, unperceptive and easily pleased. Only when they were alone or with other children, unobserved, did they behave with their natural shrewd intelligence.

When the children all held their breath, as with Mrs Garcia now, Eldred respected their instincts and knew he had to tread carefully in answering Mrs Garcia.

'No,' he said. 'I'm not saying it.'

The look she gave him made it clear that she knew he was thinking it. 'Open your reading books,' she said. 'Page eleven.'

Eldred learned two new lessons that day. The first, which saddened him, was that a teacher can be unjust. The second, which encouraged him, was that his classmates did not only like him when he pretended to be less intelligent than he was.

Darren gave him some bubble gum. Leroy whispered, 'She's an old bitch!' And the prizewinner Samantha herself said audibly as Mrs Garcia left the class, 'I know you got higher marks than me all term, Eldred, but my mum's going to be ever so pleased with me. You don't mind too much, do you?'

Eldred found that he didn't. That evening, instead of going home to work on his latest computer program, he stayed in the park until late, playing football with some of the children.

When he got home late, muddy and tired, Edgar spanked him for worrying his mother by missing tea and staying out after dark, but Eldred didn't mind that either. He had scored a goal at football, for the first time ever. And the other children had cheered.

As he went to bed hungry, Eldred knew he had never felt so happy in his life.

Chapter Five

Eldred's ninth birthday was one that his parents would never forget and Eldred himself didn't like to remember.

For a start, he had flu.

'You're staying in bed,' said Mildred, but Eldred had one of his rare moments of stubbornness. (Mildred wouldn't have said they were rare, but then she didn't know how often Eldred struggled with inner protests and yielded to her way. Her requests were always quite reasonable, so she had no way of knowing they caused her young son such agony.)

'I have to go to school,' said Eldred. 'I'm going to school.'

'I'd have thought you'd be glad to stay at home on your birthday,' said Mildred, 'even without a temperature like this.'

'It's the class trip,' Eldred reminded her.

Mildred was immediately suspicious. 'Where to?'

'A farm,' he said.

'Oh, that's all right,' said Mildred, relieved. 'I thought it was something educational.'

Eldred got out of bed and began looking for socks. 'Why don't you like things being educational, Mum?'

Mildred pushed him away from the drawer and took out the socks herself. 'I want you to grow up normal, son,' she told him. 'People can make life miserable for anyone who's that bit different. You can learn too much and become too clever for your own good.'

'But everyone is different,' said Eldred. 'Unique. We were told that in Religious Ed. at school,' he added hastily, in case Mildred suspected him of being original. 'Each person is different from everyone else. They might pretend not to be, if they want popularity.'

'Well, pretend, like everyone else,' said Mildred. 'You don't have to be that different, do you? Moderation in all things.'

Eldred's sigh was huge.

'What's wrong with that?' Mildred demanded. 'I'm telling you how to get on in the world, that's all.'

Eldred put on his socks, took them off again and put them on the other feet. Catching his mother's eye, he excused himself, 'There's a slight difference in the design. They don't fit so well the other way round.'

'You're changing the subject,' Mildred said, 'just because your dim old mother has said something sensible.'

'You're not dim,' said Eldred kindly, 'but I didn't follow your argument. How could I be moderately myself and moderately pretending? Surely I could only be Eldred if I was Eldred all the time, not pretending some of the time to be someone else? It's all one life, isn't it?'

'Hurry up, if you're going to school,' said Mildred. 'You should have reminded me last night about the trip. I'll put some cartons of squash in your bag. With a fever like that, you'll be needing a lot of cold drinks.'

'Thank you,' said Eldred.

On the coach, Eldred was so excited he could hardly wait to arrive at the farm. He did equations in his head to calm himself down. The other children were equally excited. They threw sandwiches and squirted drinks, stuffed crisps down each other's sweaters and screamed, and were reprimanded by Mrs Garcia.

The farm was a large, modern and highly mechanized one, owned by a consortium. The children were met by the farm manager, a farm mechanic, and the stockman.

'We'll divide you into three groups,' said Mrs Garcia, 'and these men will each take one group and show you their particular area of work. Then we'll change you round.'

Most of the girls volunteered for the stockman's group, wanting to see the animals. Most of the boys ran towards the mechanic, hoping for a chance to drive the tractors and combine harvester. The teacher firmly equalled out the groups. 'You'll all get a chance to see everything. Be patient.'

Eldred, who stood a head shorter than the others in his class, stationed himself beside the farm manager. 'If you don't mind, I'll come with you,' he said.

The man grinned. 'Bit small to be interested in management, aren't you?'

'I thought it would be more appropriate to start by getting an overview of the running of a farm,' Eldred explained, 'before studying the details such as care of animals and maintenance of machinery, important though those matters undoubtedly are.'

The grin dropped from the man's face. He looked at Eldred more closely. 'Well, well,' he said. 'An overview, eh? Then you've picked the right man for the job.'

'What I'm particularly interested in,' Eldred confided, as the first group moved away, following the stockman towards the milking parlour, 'is the recycling of organic farm waste.'

'Are you indeed?' said the manager. 'I have a special interest in that myself. The problem with a farm of this size, you see, is the quantity of waste it generates and the space required to store it while it's being converted into a usable form. It's all useful stuff, no doubt about that, but it's the time taken, see, to reduce it. Can't use the space for nothing else, all that time.'

'And how long precisely would it take,' Eldred enquired, 'to reduce, say, a metric tonne of raw slurry to usable manure? And how long to produce silage from waste vegetation? Is there a time difference between maturing it in a closed container and out in the open? Would there be an appreciable difference in quality between these two methods? Are chemicals lost, for instance, by exposure to the elements?'

'I'll show you how we deal with this at the moment, and what the chief disadvantages of the different systems are,' the man promised. 'Follow me.'

By lunchtime, Mrs Garcia was seriously annoyed. The children in farm manager Bruce Mackeson's group had all run off and were playing in the hayloft, while Eldred and Bruce were locked in a conversation that seemed to be, from what she overheard, on the subject of decomposition of cow dung.

'We got bored,' the other children said, when she told them off for straying.

'I'm not surprised,' said Mrs Garcia tartly.

She redistributed the groups, forcing Eldred to go and watch hens' eggs being collected and Bruce to answer another group's questions about the difference between hay and straw and whether veal was an animal.

'When we're back at school tomorrow,' Mrs Garcia announced at the end of the day, herding evil-smelling children on to the coach, 'we'll start to use our new knowledge in a little project. How many of you think you can now draw a good tractor for me?'

Amid cries of, 'Me, Miss!' and a sea of waving hands, Bruce Mackeson boarded the coach, stamping most of the mud off his boots first and, ignoring Mrs Garcia, strode to the back of the coach. She watched him with narrowed eyes as he handed Eldred a slip of paper. 'Let me know,' he said, 'as soon as it's ready.'

He returned to the door of the coach, where Mrs Garcia shook his hand and thanked him politely for all the trouble he and his colleagues had taken with her class. As soon as the coach was out of the farmyard, she made her way down the aisle towards Eldred. A girl put her hand up, stopping her. 'Please, Miss...' and while her attention was distracted, Eldred crumpled up the paper and threw it out of the window. Mrs Garcia saw him. 'What was that he gave you?' she asked.

'Nothing,' said Eldred, watching it blow away. Rage rose in him and he tried to rationalize it away: Mrs Garcia couldn't take Bruce Mackeson's phone number away from him; he had memorized it. It was good to have an ally who was so interested in his design for a waste recycling plant and had promised support when Eldred's work was completed. It was not a bad birthday present. He had no reason to feel angry with Mrs Garcia for asking a perfectly normal question. His disproportionate rage with the world frightened him at times. Mrs Garcia had already turned away.

It may have been anger with Mrs Garcia that fuelled Eldred's rebellion that day, or it may simply have been a flood of enthusiasm for his own personal project and an impatience to get on with it now that he had some evidence of its potential usefulness. Whatever it was, it impelled Eldred to get off the coach when it stopped near the school gates, rather than stay on it to be dropped nearer home with the other children who lived on the same estate.

The unknown force – anger or enthusiasm or a mixture of both – sent him running through the open door of the high school, where first-schoolers never ventured, and up and down corridors.

The classroom doors were all closed; there was still another half hour of the high school day to go. Scurrying through the empty corridors stirred memories in Eldred's heart of his early forays in search of knowledge in the hospital, and he felt the same mix of emotions: excitement, apprehension, and loneliness.

He located the computer room on the third floor of the main building. It contained fifteen VDUs and no people. Eldred went in and shut the door behind him.

Switching on the nearest computer and inserting a spare disk, he noted with satisfaction that the machine was a more sophisticated model than his own computer at home. It would give him more scope. The software was unfamiliar, though. He would need time to assimilate the different programs before he could begin to apply the new information gleaned at the farm to the model he had been working on at home over the past few months. The dimensions of the plant and the equations associated with its chemical process were fresh in his mind, but it would take time to key in the information. He wished he had brought a floppy disk with him when he left home this morning.

Seizing a software manual from one of the desks, Eldred retired to an alcove out of sight of the door, sat down cross-legged and began to read. When the school bell rang at four o'clock he didn't move, although by now he had memorized the procedures he needed. He was waiting for the duty teacher to put his head round the door prior to locking it for the night.

The idea of being locked in the computer room till next morning troubled him briefly, then he dismissed the worry. He rarely felt hungry while he was working; he still had a carton of squash left in his bag; if necessary, he could pee in the metal waste bin. There was no problem.

He gave brief consideration to his parents' reaction but reasoned that their anxiety would soon give way to rapturous approval when they saw what he had designed and heard that an expert like Bruce Mackeson had described it as exactly the breakthrough the agriculture industry needed. Also, it was his birthday and he hadn't been consulted about what he would like as a treat (his father having decided that a football would be an appropriate gift for a normal nine-year-old boy) so surely Edgar and Mildred would concede him a choice in the use of the rest of his day? He had been very patient with all their restrictions until this time, but he was nine now.

His own reasoning satisfied him, so when he heard the key turn in the door no qualms inhibited Eldred from installing himself on a chair in front of one of the computer screens, propping himself up to the right height with a couple of large books, and getting started.

Nine years old today, and the whole night ahead to work on a quick-conversion recycling plant for organic waste: what more could Eldred Jones' heart desire?

Chapter Six

The circus was on the move again. Lulubelle was relieved; she hated staying in one place too long. Most of all she dreaded the winter quartering. Sometimes the circus could still get bookings: there were enough people willing to sit in a draughty Big Top, coaxed in by the promise of heating – though the reality was noisy blasts of hot air which both deafened and roasted those in the immediate vicinity and left other people windswept without being much warmer. And, at least in the smaller circuses, the generators seldom worked perfectly. So all in all, in the winter months, people preferred to stay at home.

People said that circuses were dying: animal acts were cruel, and there were better variety acts on TV. But enough folk – adults as well as children – were still seduced by the excitement. Lulubelle loved the publicity parades. Some circuses simply stuck up posters all over the next town they were visiting, and arrived in anonymous vans.

That was one advantage of being with Mannfield's (though there weren't many, Lulubelle considered): at least they knew about publicity. They used her for all she was worth, parading her through town on a trailer decorated like a carnival float, waving and smiling, posing in her briefest and most glamorous sequinned costume, with spangled antennae sprouting from her headband. The music was so loud that all the shoppers turned to see where it was coming from, and once she had their attention, Lulubelle would perform slow handstands, while the trailer halted for her at green traffic lights and all the cars behind hooted.

Lulubelle loved being the centre of attention. She resented her craving for it, as an addict resents his need for the drugs he lives for and despises, but the attention she yearned for was also the attention she earned, she told herself. She deserved every bit of applause. She was the best. Not the best in the business, she had to admit. Not yet. But then, she was only ten.

When she pictured the world, she saw it as a giant circus, with each person rehearsing their particular act, and on the poster advertising the world's finest attractions there was a gap. Above the gap was an arrow, pointing down from the heavens, and on the arrow was written: LULUBELLE LACOSTO IS ON HER WAY: WATCH THIS SPACE!

'Get out of the way, kid!'

She jumped. Eight men were dragging the edges of a tarpaulin outwards, like fishermen spreading a net, and one of them had almost stumbled into her before she had noticed. That was what came of daydreaming, as her mother was always telling her: 'Head in the clouds again, girl! Come down to earth like the rest of us!'

'Sorry,' she mumbled, and fled for the caravan. Almost there, she paused, turned three consecutive somersaults in the air, and landed at the foot of the pull-up steps. 'Mum!'

'What?'

The bunk was still pulled down. Her mother was lying across it, painting her nails.

'You haven't packed up,' Lulubelle said. 'The first vans are moving out.'

'There's not much to pack, is there?' said her mother. 'Let me finish the other hand.'

'We can't move like this!' Lulubelle said. 'It'll all get thrown around again; you know what happened last time. Everything got broken.'

'That wasn't my fault,' said Lucinda.

'I never said it was,' Lulubelle said. 'But we don't want it happening again.'

She began tidying up, moving a greasy pan off the top of the stove. 'Fold the bed up, Mum,' she said. 'I need to get to the sink.'

'In a minute.'

'We've got to get moving, Mum! You know what Mr Mannfield said!'

'Sod him,' said Lucinda. 'Throw me a tissue, Lu; I've smudged my thumb. Look what you've made me do, with all your nagging.'

'We can't afford to lose another job,' said Lulubelle. She handed her mother a tissue. 'Sit in the window seat,' she coaxed her. 'I'll make you a coffee if you get up.'

'I've run out of fags,' Lucinda grumbled. 'I can't drink coffee without a ciggy.'

'I'll get you some,' Lulubelle promised. 'When I've cleared up – all right?'

Swearing under her breath, Lucinda shifted her body sideways off the bunk, levering herself upright at the last minute as though lifting an enormous weight, though her frame was slim enough. She stretched out one leg and inspected it. 'I'm sure I'm getting veins.'

Lulubelle steered her towards the window seat. The caravan in front of them was already trundling geriatrically across the rutted surface of the field. Jake, who would be towing their van, was standing a hundred metres away, dragging on a cigarette and chatting to Sam. Lulubelle prayed that Sam's conversation would distract him. Once Jake sauntered over to their van, he'd start shouting at Lucinda about not being ready again, and Mr Mannfield had a habit of appearing out of thin air if he heard shouting.

She ran to the bunk, folded the bedding roughly and stowed it in the cupboard overhead, tugged the rusting legs of the bed till they folded flat, and kicked the bed into its storage space in the wall of the van.

'Yoo-hoo, Ja-ake!' Lucinda was rapping on the window to attract his attention.

'What are you doing?' Lulubelle demanded furiously. 'We don't want him to see we're not ready!'

'I need a ciggy, darling,' said Lucinda plaintively. 'He might have a spare one.'

'And he might have a spare black eye in his fists,' Lulubelle said. 'Give me a hand here, Mum!'

'Don't call me that,' Lucinda said. She turned away, her back hunched. It was a sign, Lulubelle knew, that she did not intend to be co-operative. It was going to be one of those days.

'Jake!' It was Mr Mannfield's voice. 'Get that caravan on the towbar and get it moving!' He hammered on the door as he opened it. No one ever knocked and then waited to be let in.

Lulubelle bounded towards the door. She gave him her brightest smile. 'Mr Mannfield!' she said.

He was momentarily diverted. Lucinda, behind her, moved out of sight, bunching herself into the corner so that he wouldn't notice she was still in her negligee, with her hair in curlers and yesterday's mascara smudged.

'All ready?' he said.

'Just waiting for Jake,' said Lulubelle demurely.

'Jake!' he roared again, without bothering to turn his head. Lulubelle flinched.

'Coming!' Jake responded sulkily.

Mr Mannfield stepped backwards heavily, taking the three steps with one stamp of his boot. 'Get moving,' he told him.

Lulubelle pushed the door half-shut after him. Lucinda stood with one hand to her heart, theatrically. 'Whew!' she said. 'Thanks, darling!'

Lulubelle turned on her. 'Get dressed!' she said. She threw the dirty frying pan into the bin on the inside of the sink cupboard door and began fastening the covers on the sink and the cooker.

'Don't do that!' Lucinda protested. 'Dumping the pan in the bin! That's dirty, that is!'

The look Lulubelle gave her was withering. Lucinda heaved a deep, injured sigh and began to get dressed. 'That daughter of mine's turning into a real old nag,' she said, under her breath.

Lulubelle went on stolidly stowing piles of Lucinda's belongings into cupboards and securing the doors. There were tears in her eyes but Lucinda didn't notice, and Lulubelle was hardly aware of them herself.

Chapter Seven

Mr Abdul was glad he'd changed hospitals now. He'd been keen to move away from the area but hadn't known whether he'd be ridiculed if he applied for another job, even though it was a few years now since the Eldred Jones episode. Would any reputable hospital want to employ him? Thanks to his photo appearing in all the newspapers, he was now known as the paediatrician who had not only been unable to treat successfully a lung disease which, once diagnosed, had cleared up overnight, but who had been previously heard to refer to the child patient who carried out his own diagnosis and apparent cure as 'possibly slightly retarded'.

Fortunately, his new employers had reacted good-humouredly

and he had been able to play it down. When they mentioned Eldred at the interview, as he had known they would, it was clear they regarded the incident as a good joke – a joke at Mr Abdul's expense, of course – but he had laughed along with them and then, modestly, turned the story to his own account.

He didn't say very much, just let it be known by the lift of an eyebrow, a gentle shrug of the shoulders, that professional discretion prevented, of course... 'But there's always more to a patient's history,' murmured Mr Abdul, 'than one is permitted to discuss, least of all with the gutter press. And the patient's family, of course, will not divulge any history of deeper problems... What can I say?'

The atmosphere changed. No, no, they all assured him: he was not required to say any more. Naturally, they understood. And they themselves, as fellow professionals, had never believed for one minute the ridiculously distorted version of events offered by the popular press. Mr Abdul's silence on the evident psychological problems of his young patient was entirely to his credit... and of course no one would dream of probing any further...

Since he had become officially an employee, a few of his superiors had appeared to change their minds about this, and hinted that – solely among medical colleagues who wouldn't dream of breathing a word – it might be acceptable, and even obligatory, in the interests of medical knowledge, for Mr Abdul to be a little less discreet about his former patient. But Mr Abdul had so far escaped the pressure to confirm that he had been in control of Eldred's case all along, meeting each enquiry with an enigmatic smile, an expressive spreading of his hands, and the words, 'What can I say?'

By now, his colleagues seemed to be getting the message that what Mr Abdul could say was nothing at all, much as his apologetic air seemed to suggest that he would like to, if only medical ethics permitted. This was gaining him a name for being a good chap, though one rather incapable of discerning when it was quite safe to bend the rules. Mr Abdul didn't mind being seen as a stickler for the ethical rule-book. Anything was better than being known as the child-expert who had been outsmarted by a five year old.

He still felt a slight sense of unease as he entered the ward at the start of each new day's shift, so it was always a relief to him when work began with a problem he could deal with easily. Keith Harper was a straightforward case. He was a hospital regular, a fourteen-year-old boy, disabled from birth, who looked much younger than his years and could therefore be addressed with the same level of paternalistic kindness that Mr Abdul would use towards any child – any child, perhaps, except Eldred Jones.

'Now, Keith,' Mr Abdul greeted him warmly this morning, 'I see you're back with us once more.'

The small hunched figure in the child-size wheelchair craned his head to peer up at him crookedly. The gaze from his blue eyes was unexpectedly shrewd.

'I haven't met you before,' the boy pointed out.

'Not me personally, no,' said Mr Abdul. 'When I said "back with us", I was speaking on behalf of the hospital.' He felt suddenly foolish.

'You're the new paediatrician?' Keith asked. 'Mr Gannet told me last time that he was leaving.'

'I am Mr Abdul,' said Mr Abdul, drawing himself up to full height. This meant the boy had to crane his neck even more to look up at him. Mr Abdul pulled up a chair and sat down.

'I'm here to discuss your operation with you,' he said, clearing his throat. 'I see that you are no stranger to surgery, Keith, having had no less than thirteen operations before.'

'Fourteen,' said Keith apologetically. 'This will be the fifteenth. If I have it done.'

'If?' Mr Abdul looked up from Keith's notes. This was a problem within his field. He was notoriously good with children who lost their nerve before surgery. He was a master of reassurance. 'It's natural,' he said soothingly, 'to feel afraid, Keith.'

'It's not fear,' said Keith. 'I've done it before, fourteen times. I'm just wondering if there's any point in it.'

'Ah,' said Mr Abdul. 'Now there I can help you, Keith, and that's what I'm here to do: to explain to you exactly what this operation is for and what it will do for you. I usually find it helpful to draw a diagram – that's a kind of picture – of your bones. Do you know what a fibula is?'

Keith pressed a knob on the control panel of his electric wheelchair and spun himself round. One shaky hand reached towards a large book on the bed. 'Would you mind passing me that book?' Keith asked politely. 'I can't quite reach it.'

The book was open, Mr Abdul saw, at a complex diagram of the human skeleton showing some of the tissues as well as the structure of the bones. His heart sank. Was this another Eldred, lecturing to his doctors from a pilfered medical textbook?

'I'm not an expert,' Keith said modestly, 'but naturally you want to find out as much as possible about your own condition, don't you?'

Mr Abdul did not agree. Patients were, by nature, intended to be passive recipients of the hard-earned fruits of medical expertise, not co-workers with their doctors. Amateurs should not be encouraged to meddle in what was best left to professionals.

He laughed tolerantly, to show that his words could not convey any offence. 'Sometimes,' he said, with one eyebrow raised humorously, 'the patient is the person least equipped to comprehend the detailed analysis of his own malady. We experts may take quite a different view from a lay person.'

Keith's eyes widened. 'But in the end, the only purpose of an operation is to benefit the patient,' he said, 'isn't it?'

'Among other things,' Mr Abdul conceded, 'but we professionals have the authority and the responsibility – which of course we don't take lightly – to decide exactly what will benefit the patient and what will not.' He glanced at his watch discreetly, and smiled. Take your time, he conveyed to the child, but not too much time.

The child was not smiling.

'What other things?' he asked.

'I beg your pardon?' said Mr Abdul.

'I said the purpose of an operation was to benefit the patient, and you said, "Among other things",' Keith reminded him. 'What other purpose could there be?'

'It's imperative, of course, and very natural,' Mr Abdul assured him, 'for the patient to think first of his own interests – though as I say, he can only decide in the light of professional guidance in what respects his own interests consist...' He was becoming ungrammatical, he noted with annoyance, as well as slipping into using the longer words he would normally only use with adults; this boy had somehow influenced him to relinquish his usual tone for addressing sick children and was making him defensive.

He cleared his throat again, rustled his notes, and stood up. 'But there are other things involved,' he said, 'such as the effect on the patient's social environment and relationship with the family, who have to facilitate his attempts to live with his disability...' He was doing it again. The child was watching him, with eyes that were strangely unchildlike. Mr Abdul blotted the innocent gaze of five-year-old Eldred Jones from his memory, and continued, '...and of course the contribution to medical research and the knowledge we acquire which enables us to offer help in similar cases...'

'You mean,' said Keith, 'you would ask me to have this operation to further your research or to make my body easier for my parents to lift and dress – even if I decided it wouldn't make life any easier for myself?'

There was definitely something of Eldred Jones about this case, Mr Abdul felt. He moved backwards a couple of steps.

'None of us can decide to do something,' he said, 'merely on the basis of what suits ourselves, Keith. And, as I say, we are not always in the best position to decide what would most benefit ourselves. I will leave you to think about it, Keith, and I am here for you to discuss your doubts with at any time – I want you to know that. But, as your consultant, I have no doubt that this operation will be in your best interests, and I promise you that I myself will give you the very best of my skill to ensure that your surgery is successful.'

'It won't make me walk,' said Keith simply.

'No,' said Mr Abdul.

'Then I don't believe,' Keith said, 'that another operation would benefit me.'

A whirring noise from the wheelchair signalled that the child's clawlike hand had selected reverse gear again on the control panel, and Mr Abdul found that he had been dismissed from the conversation, as the chair bore the small crippled body away from him.

Chapter Eight

It was unfortunate for Eldred but merciful for Mr and Mrs Jones, sitting at home with a gift-wrapped football, a birthday tea table, two aunts and a policewoman, that Charlie Austin was driving his girlfriend home at midnight and noticed a light on in the school.

As Charlie was the computer science teacher and there had been several recent break-ins at the school, his natural first thought was that local youths were after his precious computers. He slammed on the brakes and flung himself out of the car, shouting at Mandy to stay where she was, and ran to the phone box by the school gates to call the key-holding member of staff and the police.

Mandy, having been reared on solid feminist doctrine, ignored his command to stay out of the action, such as it was, and joined him. After a few token curses to establish his manhood, Charlie went back to lock the car and agreed to let Mandy stay with him while he pursued the dangerous course of standing at the gates, staring up at the lighted classroom window and speculating about who might be in there and how they had gained entry.

When she had said, 'Probably some kids playing Terminal Terror Targets' three times, Mandy fell silent. Charlie advanced other theories, contradicted himself, then finally they both said at once, 'Have to wait for the police,' and laughed.

Two police officers and the school's deputy head arrived simultaneously. Charlie and Mandy followed them up the stairs.

'Stand back and leave this to us,' hissed the younger policeman as they neared the computer room. 'Surprise is the essence.'

Scorning the key held out to him by the deputy head, he hurled himself against the door, surprising himself with a sore shoulder that became worse, not better, over the next few days. His second surprise was that the door did not give way. Silently, the deputy head pushed him aside and unlocked it.

The five of them stood looking at the small hunched figure of Eldred Jones, seated in lonely silence in front of a bright computer screen, typing furiously. He turned and squinted at them, blurry-eyed from concentration, then reacted fast, punching the relevant keys to close the document, but Charlie moved faster still.

'I'll have that,' he said. 'Confiscated.' He whipped the disk out of the machine and pocketed it.

Eldred screamed like a wounded animal.

Mandy flinched. 'Give it back to him, Charlie,' she said.

'It's school property,' said Charlie.

'Don't delete it!' Eldred begged. 'It's my program!'

'You've no right to be in here,' Charlie said, 'making up computer games on school property. How did you get into the building?'

'We'll do the questioning,' said the younger policeman, rubbing his shoulder. 'Come along with us now.'

'Hold on,' said his colleague. 'Could this be the boy reported missing this afternoon?'

So it was that Eldred was returned to 43 Cottrill Court, Aylmers Road, to end his ninth birthday in disgrace.

Edgar and Mildred were to remember the day chiefly for the hours between 6 p.m. and midnight when they sat, first expectantly then with mounting panic, in the open-plan living room at the table with its tuna sandwiches and iced birthday cake in the shape of a clown's face, staring at the present they had told Eldred he wanted.

In between phone calls to schoolfriends' parents and the police, they took it in turns to say, 'If anything's happened to him, I'll never forgive myself,' and to reassure one another that neither had ever done anything to Eldred that needed forgiving. In the end, when their son was restored to them safe and sound, it was Eldred they couldn't forgive.

Eldred's chief impression of the day was of elation in writing the program, followed by despair and terror in the sleepless small hours of the morning alone at home in bed: a waking nightmare that Mr Austin might wipe the disk without first printing out the contents and that he, Eldred, would never get access to a machine on which to reproduce the graphics so accurately, even if he remembered them.

In later years he was to recall few details of his parents' reaction, but only that it was the occasion of a change of climate in family relationships – a change from chilly to icy.

The elder police officer's memory of that day died as soon as his shift ended. A missing youngster had been found playing computer games in a local school and had been returned safely to his family. The event was logged in a couple of lines for the record and the officer saw no need to allow it to occupy space in his mind as well.

The younger officer remembered the incident, not with his mind but with his sore shoulder.

The high school's deputy head was to enter Eldred's name in her mental records as a troublesome child who got her out of a warm bed to open up the school doors late at night. Being a vindictive person, she began to plan complicated forms of revenge for the time when Eldred would be old enough to enter the sphere of her full-time persecution, and was seriously disappointed when health problems caused by excess acid forced her to take early retirement before that date.

Mandy, Charlie Austin's girlfriend, was haunted for a few days by Eldred's scream and the anguish on his face when Charlie took the disk away from him. The vision soon faded but years later, married to a fast-food franchise holder, she was to find herself being unusually considerate in giving her children time to finish their activities before calling them for tea or bathtime or bed.

It was only Charlie Austin whose memories of Eldred's ninth birthday were entirely positive, for Charlie, staying behind in the computer room while the police escorted Eldred out, inserted the disk and began to scan its contents.

What he saw made him remove the disk again very quickly, allowing no one to see it, and return to school early the following morning.

Slowly scrolling the text up the VDU screen, he read and re-read Eldred's project. When he reached the unfinished appendix and found pages of almost completed computer graphics, a beautifully detailed cross-section and accurately scaled diagrams of a time-saving design for a waste recycling plant, he pursed his lips and let out a stream of expletives.

'Fucking Henry!' he concluded. 'We've only got a sodding genius in the school!'

Chapter Nine

Being recognized as a genius was a mixed blessing, Eldred found. Just as the press had rallied round his hospital bed when a junior nurse had tipped them off about the amazing five year old who read medical textbooks, now there was a bevy of informed adults who, in acclaiming Eldred's expertise in inventing a new machine, also seemed to want to acclaim themselves as experts on Eldred.

He became a discovery and, once discovered, everyone wanted to discover something new about him that no one else had yet found. And every new discoverer claimed Eldred as their own.

There was the problem with the waste recycling machine. Charlie Austin held the computer disk and was in a strong position; he told Eldred that he himself would take the necessary steps to get the design developed for industrial use.

But Bruce Mackeson the farm manager had already offered to help Eldred launch the design; he had the contacts, he said. He had given Eldred his home phone number for this purpose and was waiting to hear from him any day now.

Eldred told Mr Austin about his dilemma and Mr Austin dismissed it. Eldred was the school genius so naturally the school was responsible for his achievements, especially as the machine had been designed on the school computer, and that was that.

'But I didn't gain the information at school,' Eldred pointed out.

'You gained it on an educational trip organized by the school,' countered Mr Austin.

'No, I'd been working on it for ages at home before that,' said Eldred. 'The one who helped me the most was actually Terry Smith.'

'Terry Smith?'

'In the reference section of the borough library,' Eldred explained. 'He's really good. He finds me all the right books whenever I want to look up anything.'

Mrs Garcia was another contender for ownership of Eldred's brain.

'I've nurtured that boy's intelligence,' she said, 'guided him, watched him since the first day he joined my class. He's not one of your pupils, Mr Austin. He's not even at high school.'

'He probably should be,' Mr Austin asserted. 'The boy's wasted among those babies. He must be bored stiff.'

Mrs Garcia drew herself to her full height of five foot two. 'Not in *my* classes,' she said.

Eldred was an unwilling witness to this debate, which took place in the staff car park beside the playground, where the two teachers' cars were parked in unfriendly proximity.

As he tried to edge away from Mrs Garcia, who had commissioned him to carry a pile of books to her car for her, Mr Austin turned to him.

'Shall we let Eldred be the judge of that, Mrs Garcia?' he suggested. 'Are you bored in class, Eldred, doing simple arithmetic and spelling tests and projects on dinosaurs?'

Eldred gulped and shuffled the gravel with his feet. He wished he was somewhere else, even a place with dinosaurs in it.

'He's no better than average in most of those subjects,' said Mrs Garcia. 'Just because he has a flair for one thing doesn't mean he doesn't need to be taught. His concentration is appalling and his handwriting's illegible. Isn't it, Eldred?'

'Boredom!' said Mr Austin triumphantly. 'Lack of stimulation. Leads to apathy.'

Eldred looked at the horizon. He wondered how they would react if he dropped the books on the ground and ran away. He didn't seem to be necessary to the discussion.

'Eldred!' said Mr Austin. 'How would you like it if I could arrange with the Head for you to join my information technology class with the fourteen year olds?'

Eldred looked from Mr Austin to Mrs Garcia and didn't like what he saw in either face. He had a flash of inspiration.

'I'd have to ask my mum and dad,' he said. He deposited the pile of books on the bonnet of Mrs Garcia's car and fled for home.

Mildred and Edgar were surprisingly unhelpful to Eldred. Considering that they had always insisted on him keeping a low profile and concealing his intelligence, they greeted Mr Austin's assessment of Eldred's genius with enthusiasm.

'Well,' said Edgar, when Eldred told him the news that Mr Austin wanted him to join a class of fourteen year olds, 'this is quite a feather in our caps, Mother, isn't it?'

Mildred, wiping her hands on a teatowel, agreed. 'We always knew he had it in him, didn't we, Dad?'

'I don't want to be in an older class,' said Eldred. 'They might make me be there for other subjects as well, if I do all right in computing, and then I won't see my friends.'

'You could see them at playtime,' said Mildred. 'Anyway, you'd soon make new friends.'

'People who are fourteen won't be friends with people who are nine,' Eldred told her.

'You mustn't be ungrateful, son,' said Mr Jones. 'It's very kind of Mr Austin to take an interest in you like this.'

'Very kind,' Mildred echoed.

There was relief in both their voices. Eldred realized that, after all the years of embarrassment about his unusualness, they were happy that somebody wanted to own him for precisely that reason. They were no longer required to bear the burden of Eldred alone. Mr Austin could take the blame when other parents made jealous remarks about special treatment and favouritism. The Joneses were tired of being disapproved of, by doctors, neighbours, family and friends; of the implicit accusations of arrogance in daring to have a child whose intelligence did not match the national average.

Now they would be approved of, at least by the school authorities, for letting the school take the credit for Eldred's intellect.

'I have to go to the library,' Eldred said.

'You'll have your tea first,' Mildred told him, but Eldred said, 'They'll be closed by then, Mum!' and she gave in.

He needed to talk to Terry Smith. Terry was a thin young man, prematurely balding, whose ambition had been to become a research scientist. His widowed mother, who was not in the best of health, took illicit cleaning jobs (unknown to the Department of Social Security) to equip her student son with new clothes when he was offered a university place.

Then, in Terry's second year as an undergraduate, his mother was diagnosed as having leukaemia. Her only son spent one sleepless night in his hostel room struggling with ambition and conscience, then packed his suitcase and informed his tutor he was returning home to look after his mother.

Very few people knew Terry's history, apart from his physics tutor, who remained in occasional contact with him, and Eldred. To anyone else, Terry Smith was an amiable but aimless young man who was helpful if you had any difficulty in finding the right reference book but who was obviously not the type to achieve much in life. Terry's social activities revolved around visits to the hospital, where his mother spent increasing periods of time, trips to the launderette with his own and his mother's washing, and take-away meals – mainly burgers – on the way home.

Terry sympathized with Eldred's situation. 'You ought be allowed a choice in what happens to you,' he said, 'but unfortunately, because you're a minor, it's technically your parents' responsibility to make all the decisions for you.'

'It's my machine,' said Eldred. 'Bruce Mackeson said he knew some people who could construct a prototype for me. I want to see it working.'

'Of course you do,' said Terry Smith. 'But you've got to be

cautious. Who's to say which of those people might do the dirty on you?'

'Do the dirty?' queried Eldred. 'How do you mean?'

'Who's going to believe a sophisticated piece of machinery was invented by a nine year old?' Terry said. 'Anyone you hand this design to can just pass it off as their own idea, and what's to stop them?'

'What can I do?' Eldred asked him.

Terry thought about it. 'Get the press behind you,' he said. 'I'll dig out those old newspaper cuttings on you when you were five and show them to a friend of mine on the local rag. 'Nine Year Old Invents Ecologically Friendly Waste Recycling System on Home Computer'. That'll get them on your side. Not only a genius, but Green as well. The press'll love it. You'll have the nationals down here in no time. Then you've got it in print, confirmed as your own invention.'

'I don't think my parents would like all the fuss,' Eldred said.

'You might be surprised,' said Terry sagely. 'Reflected limelight, all that. Bit of excitement in their lives.'

Eldred recalled his parents' reaction to Mr Austin calling him a genius. If established authorities approved of Eldred, it seemed to be all right. He wasn't sure whether journalists counted as respectable authority figures exactly, but his father did place great faith in what he read in the paper.

'How would I go about it?' Eldred asked.

Terry winked. 'Leave it to me,' he said. 'One phone call is all I need.'

Chapter Ten

The vehicle which was used to tow their caravan was the cab of a lorry to which any kind of trailer or truck could be attached. On its own, it looked strange, Lulubelle always thought – like a giant head without a body.

Coupled to one of the trucks which carried fairground equipment or animal cages, the head gained a matching body, like Arto the strongman whose bulging biceps and muscled torso were matched by the almost square head, the dimensions of a compressed cannonball, which arose from a neck the same width as the head, balanced on shoulders like steel girders.

There was special status attached to driving the lions' trailer. Most circuses nowadays had given up having wild animal acts. Mannfield's had given up elephants, because of the expense, but kept the lions. Public reaction to lions was love or hate. Many county councils and city boroughs played it safe and wouldn't book circuses that brought lions into their territory, even though the cages had strong bars and an outer cage of reinforced steel mesh.

Even in a motorway crash, there would be little risk of an escape. But it was that tiny element of risk that captivated audiences, and even the circus staff themselves. Sitting up in a big lorry cab, king of the road, driving the King of the Jungle, had to be more exciting than towing a generator or scaffolding.

Towing Lucinda Lacosto's small battered caravan was especially undignified and the lorry cab looked as out of place as Arto's head would look on Lucinda's narrow shoulders.

Jake the driver felt it an insult to be allocated this job so Lucinda made an effort to be specially nice to him. And it was an effort this morning, with her head aching and Lulubelle getting on her nerves with all her nagging. Children had no right to speak to their parents the way that Lulubelle did; she seemed to think she was the mother and Lucinda the troublesome child.

Lucinda snuggled up to Jake on the split leather cab seat. She liked sitting high up like this, with a view of the road, and liked the travelling, once they got going. Sitting leaning against a man's solid body, smoking cigarettes she had wheedled out of him, and gazing sleepily at the cars on the motorway, so far beneath them, was preferable to a work day any time – all that endless rehearsing and exercising, trying to limber up when her joints were stiff with cold – and less supple with every passing year, she was forced to realize.

Lucinda tuned the radio to the country music station.

'Oh, Mum!' Lulubelle protested.

'You don't appreciate good music,' Lucinda said. 'Does she, Jake? The old-timers are sometimes the most romantic.' She wriggled against him slightly and he half-smiled. His bad mood would evaporate by the time they hit the motorway. She knew how to get through to him.

'I've got stomach ache,' Lulubelle complained.

'Have you, love? Take an aspirin out of my bag,' Lucinda said. Jake revved the engine and they moved forward, the little caravan lurching as it left the rutted mud of the field and turned sharply on to the road.

The locals always complained that the circus left the roads in a state, covered with mud and remnants of branches ripped from the overhanging trees by the huge vehicles. But the local farmer was well paid for the use of his field and had few complaints, and the council could afford to clean up the roads. It was a small price to pay for the magic the circus and fairground folk brought into the drab little lives of these townspeople for a few days. The children would talk about it all year, till the circus came back again – if it was allowed to; if the local complainers' committee didn't prevail.

Lulubelle's knowledge of the geography of the British Isles was different from the geography she learned in the many schools she belonged to for a few weeks at a time. Her map was dominated, not by major cities and centres of industry, but by towns that were welcoming to the circus people and towns that were hostile or cold, clinging to their routine lives and unwilling to be seduced for a few days by supergirls in tutus who performed impossible contortions with ease and grace, seals that danced and balanced plates on their noses, lions that threatened to devour their trainer alive, and trapezists who defied death every night.

What Mannfield's, and the other circuses she had belonged to since the day she was born, offered to people was a glimpse of another world, a world where every fantasy came to life. How could they be so chained to their environment as to worry about mud on the roads and the odd episode of being overcharged by Saul on the roller-coaster? Even if Mannfield's charged them a thousand pounds, could any cost be too much? Was it too great a sacrifice for the circus people to camp out in muddy fields, shivering with cold when the generators broke down, going hungry when they arrived in a town late at night and found all the take-aways closed?

Lulubelle sometimes imagined what it would be like to live in one of those little houses whose lighted windows punctuated the anonymous streets the circus trucks rumbled through in the dark early winter nights. Boring, said all the circus people. No business like showbusiness, duckie. They'd all tried the settled life, if only for a few months in the winter down-time. It was all right at first, they said: solid walls around you, good TV picture reception, warm fires or central heating, no tiresome assembling and taking down of the giant marquees – often in driving rain – but instead hot water for baths, regular meals, a quiet routine and a chance to get your washing dry... oh, it was fine for a while.

Then they would start to miss one or two of the good things about circus life: the nightly applause, the gasps of incredulity at a spectacular part of the routine, the look on the children's faces, as though they'd been transported to a land they'd only known about in dreams...

Then they'd wake up one morning and find themselves missing some of the things they complained about. Living cheek-by-jowl with the same people they worked with and could never escape from was suddenly remembered as the warm camaraderie of circus life, rather than one of its major annoyances.

The secure and solid walls of their own little house would begin to close in on them. When the wind howled outside without sending the pans hanging on the wall clattering to the accompaniment of the rocking of the caravan, it no longer seemed a relief that the house stood firm against its buffeting, but a strangely unnatural lack of reaction. A life so safe and impervious to the elements began to seem lifeless.

The day would come when they found themselves fondly recalling the rows between the animal trainers and the clowns about who came first in the billing, and feeling a glow of affection for the tyrannical ringmaster, so full of himself in his tailcoat and boots and drooping Victorian moustaches and so ordinary in the cold light of day, unshaven and in his shirtsleeves, chivvying the men as they battled to fold the vast tarpaulins in an autumn gale.

Then they would know they were lost souls: enslaved to the merciless spirit of circus life that forced them to extremes of endurance, whipping them into a frenzy of overachievement, demanding miracles of them night after night, tiring quickly of their superhuman accomplishments and requiring ever more dangerous and difficult feats, and rewarding even their greatest success by kicking them out of town and on to the next before daylight.

A gust of rain showered the windscreen and Jake switched on the wipers, smearing mud across his field of vision. He swore under his breath, pumping the windscreen wash button which yielded no more than a helpless trickle of fluid. Lulubelle, peering through the side window which was equally spattered with mud, noticed a girl of her own age, in school uniform, hurrying across a footbridge to join a group of her mates. She wondered what it would be like to have a whole day of school ahead, knowing it would be part of a whole term, a whole year, a whole school-age lifetime without the responsibility of a career until she was sixteen or seventeen, or more maybe.

To go to school and be taught, and be fed a meal at lunchtime, and be loosed on to a sports field once a week to run around playing some game as part of a team, pretending it was important that you won but knowing it was only a game and nobody's livelihood depended on it, before returning to the same home every day, with homework time and tea around a table with a father returning from work...

She wasn't envious, she told herself. Certainly the children in the various schools she'd attended had envied her, so probably the circus people had got it right and within a week she'd be bored with that kind of life. But she wouldn't mind a chance to be somebody else for a while, someone whose mother didn't get drunk and risk losing her job and jeopardize her daughter's dreams and hopes of a promising career. She sighed, rocking herself forward with both arms clasped across her stomach.

'Still got the tummy-ache?' enquired Lucinda.

'There wasn't any aspirin in your bag,' Lulubelle told her.

Lucinda slipped an arm around her shoulders. 'I'll get you some when we stop,' she promised. 'You all right, Lu? You're white as a sheet – isn't she, Jake?'

'I feel a bit funny,' Lulubelle admitted.

'Well, cuddle up to me,' Lucinda said. 'Nothing like a cuddle to make everything right.' She looked at Jake and winked but he didn't notice. She leaned forward and turned up the radio. 'I like this one,' she said.

The truck pulled out onto the motorway, cutting in front of a Porsche which swerved into the outside lane and sounded its horn. Jake squared his shoulders, appeased by his truck's show of strength, even if it was only towing a caravan. The windscreen wipers squeaked and the sky was darkening.

'Stand by your ma – a – an!' Lucinda sang.

Chapter Eleven

The Special Needs teacher was ill, so the Special Needs group joined Mrs Garcia's class, which included nine-year-old Eldred. Because she considered teaching children with learning difficulties to be a slight to her status, Mrs Garcia was giving a sharp lecture on equality.

'There's no cause for anyone in this class to think they're anything special,' she said, her eyes roaming round all the desks impartially. 'Everyone is special in some way.' Her gaze fixed itself momentarily on Jilly Martin, thirteen years old with the IQ of a child of seven, and quickly moved on.

'Everyone in this class has talents,' said Mrs Garcia, 'and individual qualities.' This time her roving glance lighted on Matthew Evans, who gave her one of his individual quality bold stares. Matthew was playground champion of staring people out. His gaze never faltered.

Mrs Garcia looked round for help. Unconsciously she looked in Eldred's direction. Eldred was drawing diagrams with his finger in the air just above his desk.

'Eldred Jones,' said Mrs Garcia, 'what do you think you are doing?'

Eldred froze. 'Nothing,' he said.

'Exactly,' said Mrs Garcia. 'Nothing is what you are contributing to this class. But you're not meant to be doing nothing, are you, Eldred? You are meant to be listening to me.'

'I am listening,' said Eldred.

'Then tell me what I have just said,' challenged Mrs Garcia. Her discomfort with Matthew Evans' stare was finding a familiar release. At the same time, she was annoyed with herself. The last thing she had intended to do this morning was single out Eldred, a child who attracted far too much attention outside her classroom to merit much of her notice within it. The boy could be very irritating.

'You said that everyone in this room is special and has special talents and qualities,' Eldred recounted.

'And do you believe that, Eldred?' asked Mrs Garcia.

'Oh yes,' said Eldred simply.

'Then I'm sure you will be able to tell us about them, won't you?' she said.

Eldred hesitated.

'I see,' said Mrs Garcia. 'You don't really believe it. You think nobody has any talents except Eldred Jones.'

Jilly Martin's face bore an expression of acute anxiety and distress. Mrs Garcia grew more irritated. Mixed ability teaching was all very well, but there should be limits. Putting children like Jilly and Eldred into one group, even for a day or two, was ludicrous. What was she expected to teach them? What on earth could such extremes of the national average have in common with one another?

Having Eldred in her class was bad enough – out of his age group and often, she felt, out of her control – but Jilly! If the parents were unfortunate enough to have produced a child who was so slow-witted that she gazed in incomprehension at the simplest remark, at least they could have had the good sense to have her adenoids operated on, so that she would close her mouth while she gazed.

'No,' said Eldred. 'That's not it.' He wriggled in his seat. Jilly exchanged glances with him. Her eyes were brimming with tears. Matthew Evans looked at Eldred and mimed an enormous yawn. Eldred giggled, and Jilly's anxiety lifted. She giggled too. Mrs Garcia felt the class was ganging up on her. The only way she knew how to nip that in the bud was to single out one child and make an example of him. It obviously wouldn't be fair to single out Jilly, so she chose Eldred.

'As you find this funny, Eldred, you can come and stand out here until you can tell me one talent belonging to a child in this class apart from yourself.'

Eldred's brow cleared. 'Oh,' he said. 'I can do that. I thought you wanted me to say everybody's.'

'You mean to say you couldn't?' said Mrs Garcia with heavy sarcasm.

'I would have had to think about it,' said Eldred seriously, 'and it would have taken rather a long time.'

Mrs Garcia could never be sure, at such times, whether Eldred was taking the mickey. She could, of course, put him to the test by making him go through every child in the class, systematically naming each one's strong points, but if she called his bluff and Eldred was able to do this, she would have let him show her up.

'Nonsense,' said Mrs Garcia firmly. 'It certainly would not take all that long to name each child's good points, Eldred, but in fact all I am asking you to do is name one, apart from your own, to prove my statement that no child is more special than any other.'

'Danny Goldberg is conker champion,' said Eldred.

The class cheered. Danny Goldberg stood up and clenched his hands above his head in a victory salute.

'Hardly a matter of great significance,' said Mrs Garcia, as Eldred moved to go back to his seat. 'Now it's quite clear, Eldred, that you do not listen to me, because you rushed to answer then before I had told you which child's special gifts I wished you to name.'

Tension emanated from Mrs Garcia in small staccato bursts, communicating itself to the children. The bolder ones smothered laughter behind cupped hands and kicked each other's legs under the desks; the more sensitive ones quivered. Little Jilly Martin with the ever-open mouth and ever-drooping socks on skinny legs, quivered more than all the rest. She dreaded trouble in class even more than she dreaded going home and being asked, 'What did you learn at school today?'

'Jilly,' said Mrs Garcia ruthlessly.

Jilly jumped. 'What?' she said.

'Eldred will tell the class Jilly's talents,' Mrs Garcia said.

'That's not fair,' said Matthew Evans.

'Thank you, Matthew,' said Mrs Garcia. 'When I need your opinion I will ask for it.'

'Please Miss,' said Danny Goldberg, 'Jilly's educationally subnormal, her mum told my mum, and it means she doesn't have talents so it's not fair to make her the example.'

'It certainly does not mean she does not have talents,' said Mrs Garcia, 'and I am the last person in this class who would make an example of Jilly. So, Eldred, we're all waiting. Stop fidgeting and speak up so everyone can hear you.'

Eldred moved over to Jilly's desk and took her hand. He waited. Mrs Garcia folded her arms and pursed her mouth. The ticking of the clock on her desk was audible.

'Ah-huh,' said Mrs Garcia, satisfied.

'Jilly has a gift for sensing atmospheres,' said Eldred, coming out of his reverie and speaking rapidly and without expression, like someone reading from an autocue, 'which is why she is shaking so much at present. She also has the gift of sympathy for anyone who is down, and the gift of accepting people as they are.

'Jilly doesn't put up any defences to protect herself and shut people out but lets everyone affect her. She has a gift of gentleness and doesn't ever want to hurt anyone; she would rather get hurt herself than hurt anyone else. She loves everyone even when they're not nice to her. She understands love. If someone talks to her without love, she doesn't understand what they're talking about, but if they talk to her with love, she understands everything. This probably means that she has perfect understanding.'

There was a brief silence, then Matthew said wonderingly, 'Yeah, that's right,' and Sunil added, 'Right on, Jilly!'

Jilly smiled, a wide open-mouthed smile, her eyes bright.

'Sit down, thank you, Eldred,' said Mrs Garcia. 'Now perhaps we can get on. We've wasted enough time for one morning. Come in!' she shouted, unnecessarily loudly, as there was a knock at the door.

One of the high school girls entered. 'Mrs Garcia, the Head says Eldred Jones is to come and join Mr Austin's class for the next double lesson of computer studies.'

The children gasped. Eldred sighed heavily.

'Quiet, class,' said Mrs Garcia authoritatively. 'Eldred, go quickly, please. Stop fiddling about with pens; you won't need anything.'

'Do I have to go?' Eldred appealed.

Mrs Garcia raised one eyebrow. 'If the Head says you go, you go, boy.'

Eldred left. The children muttered among themselves. Amazement and envy mingled in their reactions. Only Jilly Martin sat looking at the door through which Eldred had gone, with sadness in her brown eyes.

Chapter Twelve

Mr Austin's computer class was not one of Eldred's successes.

Towards the end of the lesson, Mr Austin told him, 'Go up to the staff room and wait for me there; I'll see you when the bell goes for break.'

Guiltily, Eldred stood up and left the class. He didn't know where the staff room was. He didn't know whether Mr Austin meant him to go into the staff room or wait outside. He didn't know what he had done wrong. Tears gathered in the corners of his eyes.

'Looking for someone?' asked a woman emerging from a door marked 'School Secretary'.

'The staff room,' whispered Eldred.

She took pity on him. 'I'll show you.'

They went up several flights of stairs and down a couple of long corridors. Waves of boredom, anxiety and frustration billowed like smoke from the cracks under closed doors of classrooms. Eldred shivered.

'Who do you want to see in the staff room?' the school secretary asked, tapping on the door.

'No one. I have to wait for Mr Austin.'

She opened the door and looked round it. 'Nobody in there. He'll be along when the bell goes. He's always first in line for coffee! Take a seat here.'

'Am I allowed?' asked Eldred fearfully.

She ruffled his hair. 'They won't eat you.'

Left to himself, Eldred did as he always did when he was worried: he gathered information. Some of his best researches had arisen from reading at random in the public library when parents or teachers were annoyed with him for something he had done, or not done.

He thumbed through a few piles of exercise books awaiting correction, mentally filing away the contents and comparing the inconsistencies in different pupils' accounts of the same historical battle, till he was almost certain where the errors lay. Discarding the errors, he memorized the facts. This took him about five minutes. Eldred looked around for something else.

Heaps of periodicals hung off the edges of shelves. Gingerly, Eldred removed the top dozen or so, without toppling the whole stack. Most were educational supplements, teaching journals, newspapers open at the 'Situations Vacant – Educational' section;

there were several publishers' brochures and advertising leaflets for audio-visual aids. Eldred scanned them all, committed them to memory, replaced them and took down another pile.

The bell rang, making him jump and causing a cascade of magazines from the shelf. Some fell on his head; the rest scattered on the floor around his feet. Flustered, he gathered them up, clutching them to his chest. Another pile sighed and subsided gracefully from the far end of the shelf, just as the door opened and three teachers entered, one of them Mr Austin.

'What's this?' said Mr Austin, putting his hand to his head theatrically. 'I told you to wait for me, child, not to wreck the place.' The other teachers laughed.

Agitated, Eldred looked down at the brochure on top of the pile he held. He blinked, photographing the words that would later be developed in his sleeping brain, then looked back at Mr Austin, who was unaware of this process.

'What happened to you in my class?' Mr Austin said.

'I couldn't do it,' said Eldred.

'If you could design a waste reprocessor, you could have done the exercises I set the class today,' said Mr Austin. 'Are you ready to tell me the truth now?'

'Pardon?'

'I won't be angry with you,' said Mr Austin. 'You found the design lying around the farm office, didn't you, and brought it home to copy?'

Eldred was speechless. He blushed deep red.

'I thought it was something like that,' said Mr Austin. 'I knew there was no way a boy of your age could design something like that.'

'It's not true,' Eldred whispered.

'Oh yes, I did know,' Mr Austin averred. 'We teachers get quite good at assessing a child's ability, you know. I suppose you thought you'd get into trouble. Well, you've had your telling off for being in the school building after hours and using the school computers, and if you run along back to your class now, you'll hear no more about this from me. But in future, tell the truth – all right? It gets you into less trouble in the long run. And if you haven't returned the original design yet, you'd better send it back to its owner, pronto, or you will really be in trouble – appropriating someone's invention for your own nefarious purposes.'

Eldred's brain registered 'nefarious' – initial letters probably n-e-f, or n-e-p-h; possible meanings 'unworthy' or maybe 'shady'. Later he would look it up in a dictionary. Another part of his brain informed him that he had lost all his work on the reprocessing plant, and something inside his heart began to weep.

'Please,' said Eldred. 'Please, can I have my disk back?'

'*Your* disk?' said Mr Austin. 'The disk you stole from the school computer room?'

'Can I copy it on to one of my own disks? Or pay for it out of my pocket money? Or at least have one last look at it?' begged Eldred.

He had done the last part so quickly, when he had heard the police coming down the corridor and trying to push down the computer room door, that he hadn't memorized the precise dimensions of the important second chamber of the plant.

Mr Austin took a cup from beside the coffee urn. 'If you don't convince me of your intention to put this matter right immediately,' he said, 'I really have no other option than to speak to the Head about this. Is that what you want?'

'No,' said Eldred, with a shudder.

'Then return the original to wherever you got it from – by post, anonymously, if you want – and forget about any plans to copy it. All right?'

Eldred didn't think it would help to say that the disk held the original design and there were no copies. 'What will you do with the information on the disk?' he asked.

'Erase it,' said Mr Austin.

Eldred ran.

Playtime was in session in the First School compound. By the gates, watching everyone, was Jilly Martin. Her nose was running. Eldred, who was making furtive use of his handkerchief, offered her a wipe. She sniffled into it happily.

'I thought you'd gone,' she said.

'I'm back.'

'Didn't they want you?' asked Jilly.

'No.'

She nodded. 'Couldn't you do the work?'

'Oh,' said Eldred, 'the work was easy enough. But I couldn't do it there.'

'Why?'

'Nobody wanted to be there,' said Eldred. 'They were all thinking really loudly about all the other things they wished they were doing instead. They're better at that than us. They're fourteen, so they've had years of being forced to do things they don't want to do, and thinking of something else. I couldn't do it. It was tiring.'

'I get tired at school,' said Jilly.

'Is it like that for you all the time?' Eldred asked. 'In every lesson?'

'Yes,' she said simply.

They stood in silent companionship.

'We could run away,' said Jilly hopefully.

'Where?'

Jilly looked around for inspiration. 'We could live in the sports shed?'

Eldred sighed. 'It wouldn't solve anything. What we want to escape from is not having any choice. They don't take any notice of your choices until you're grown up. When we leave school, then we'll be free to decide what to do with our own lives.'

'I don't think I will,' said Jilly. 'My mum couldn't cope without me. She says I'm her cross in life.'

'Is that good?' asked Eldred doubtfully.

'It's something,' said Jilly. 'Better than nothing for her, I suppose.'

Eldred mused on this. 'Do your mum and dad talk about you a lot?'

Jilly nodded silently.

'Mine too,' said Eldred. 'Do they complain about you and wonder why you are like you are?'

'Yes,' she said. Her expression was sad.

'I wonder,' said Eldred, 'what they would talk about if they didn't have us?'

'Maybe they'd complain about somebody else,' Jilly suggested.

'But somebody else wouldn't be theirs to change, so there'd be no point in that,' said Eldred. 'They can only try to change us, because they made us; we're their flesh and blood.'

'They didn't make us,' said Jilly sagely. 'God did.'

'Do you believe in God?' asked Eldred, surprised.

'Yes. Don't you?'

'I haven't seen much evidence of him so far,' Eldred said.

The bell rang. Automatically, they turned away from the gate and lined up with the other children, to return to thirty-five minutes of basic geometry shapes.

Chapter Thirteen

Keith's younger brother came in to see him after school. Keith watched him walk across the ward, looking from one bed to another in search of him. The admissions staff were never sure whether to put Keith in an adult ward or the children's ward; he was fourteen but the size of a child half his age. Most people thought he was seven or eight – nine at most – until they looked into his eyes, which were wise and old. This time they had put him in an adult orthopaedic ward, because the place he'd been allocated in the children's ward had been taken at the last minute by a baby.

Keith wondered what it did to Andrew to come in to see his brother, only one year older than himself, in a ward full of middle-aged and elderly people with broken bones. He thought it must be like walking past a breaker's yard and suddenly seeing your own car, dumped in the midst of a pile of rusted and twisted metal. Andrew had said once to Keith, 'I don't see you as any different from me – till I see you with other people.' When Andrew caught sight of him now, would it be with an outsider's appraising gaze, seeing the disabilities, or would he see straight through the disguise, to Keith?

'Oh, there you are!' Andrew's face registered nothing but relief. 'I thought I'd got the wrong ward.' He punched him on the shoulder, throwing the punch from a distance, like a boxer: a violent movement that landed on Keith's thin body as a feather-light touch. From an early age, Andrew had learnt to treat his brother with restraint. He settled himself on the bed. 'I got myself some crisps: want one?'

'What flavour?'

'Smoky bacon – what other flavour is there, man?'

Keith laughed. It was a long-standing joke. Andrew liked cheese and onion; Keith liked smoky bacon, but they would pretend it was the other way around. When their father took them to the pub and left Andrew keeping an eye on Keith in the garden while he went to the bar for their order, he'd say, 'What kind of crisps, boys?' and Andrew would say, 'Well, I would like smoky bacon, but just for Keith's sake I'll have a bag of those disgusting cheese and onion crisps that he likes, just so he can have one of mine and not throw up all over the place.' And Keith would say, 'Well, cheese and onion are my real favourite of all time, but I'm doing penance, so get me a pack of those horrible smoky bacon.' And their Dad would come back with the smoky bacon for Keith and the cheese and onion for Andrew and give them the packs the wrong way round and pretend to be surprised when they complained. 'Come on, lads; it's Saturday – no sacrifices! I got you both what you really like! Let me see you eat them up and enjoy them!'

The fact that Andrew had bought smoky bacon meant that he'd bought them for Keith, though he'd end up eating most of them himself, as he always did on Saturdays, because Keith could only eat very little, very slowly. It took him a long time to chew and a long time to swallow.

Andrew had taken two crisps out of the packet and was breaking them into morsels in the palm of his hand. He took Keith's hand off the control panel on the arm of his wheelchair, formed a grip between Keith's finger and thumb, and inserted a morsel of crisp between them.

Keith didn't like to be fed; he always wanted to feed himself, though the journey his hand had to make from armrest to mouth would take him a long time, and the effort would leave him short of breath. In the meantime, Andrew would pop bits of crisp into his brother's mouth. Keith allowed that, as long as he was also allowed to feed himself.

It was a compromise they had worked out one day when, after Keith's return home from his twenty-eighth hospital stay, they found his arm movements had weakened considerably but he was still insisting on feeding himself. Their mother, who had decorated the house with streamers and balloons and made a cake to celebrate his homecoming, as she always did, broke down and ran from the room in tears. When Andrew had run after her, she said, 'He won't get anything, at this rate! He'll starve to death!'

'He won't,' said Andrew.

He had come back to Keith, who was white as a sheet, not far from tears either, but stubbornly determined to do everything himself.

'This is the way we'll do it,' said Andrew. He was eleven at the time; Keith was twelve and a bit. That was when he'd devised the method of forming Keith's hand into a pincer-like grip round a piece of food. Keith accepted it. Then Andrew had tried to raise Keith's hand to his mouth. 'No,' said Keith. 'I can do it.' Andrew let him. It took ages. Andrew waited. Keith's face was rigid, daring him to make any comment. Andrew said nothing. Finally the small piece of celebration cake reached his mouth. Keith chewed. Andrew still waited.

When Keith had finished, he looked at Andrew. Andrew didn't move. Keith looked down at his finger and thumb and back at Andrew, waiting for his brother to repeat the manoeuvre.

'That mouthful was for you,' said Andrew. 'This one is for Mum.' He picked up another few crumbs of cake and held them to Keith's mouth. Keith kept his mouth closed. They stared at one another – a battle of wills.

Keith, wordlessly, looked down again at his finger and thumb. Andrew waited till he looked back at him. Then Andrew, wordlessly, looked around the room: the streamers, the balloons, the banners on which their mother had painted, 'Welcome Home, Keith', and, 'We love you!' Keith opened his mouth and Andrew put in the food. As Keith chewed, tears rolled out of his eyes and down his face. When they reached his chin, Andrew wiped them.

He had finished the slice of cake, small piece by small piece, chewing more and more slowly every time. Their mother stood in the doorway, watching them. When the plate was empty, Keith looked at her with eyes that were red and swollen and said, 'The cake was lovely. Thanks.' Then he looked up at Andrew and said, 'Thank you, Andrew.' His mother flew across the room and hugged him. Andrew walked out of the room with a thunderous expression on his face, shut himself in the garden shed and, throwing himself down on a bag of peat, cried.

That day, the relationship between the brothers had changed. It was as though Andrew took on the role of elder brother and Keith became the younger. Of all the things Keith had ever had to let go, that was the hardest. For both of them, it seemed to herald the day when Andrew would not be the younger brother any longer, nor the older brother, but the only child of a family that was heartbroken.

Chapter Fourteen

Eldred decided to talk to his parents about Mr Austin keeping the computer disk. They could not always be relied on to be parental, he reflected, but maybe in this case they would take his side.

His mother greeted his return from school with a broad smile and a big hug. She had also had her hair done and was wearing her best polyester two-piece.

'What's wrong?' asked Eldred.

'Nothing's wrong,' she whispered. 'There's a reporter in the living room. From the local newspaper.'

Eldred's hopes rose. Terry Smith had kept his promise.

'Does he want to talk to me about the reprocessing plant?' he asked.

'She. It's a young girl. She's been asking me questions about you half the afternoon.'

'But you don't know about the plant,' said Eldred unwisely.

Mildred flushed. 'I know about my own son, don't I? Who better to tell the paper about you? And it's difficult to interview children, so Susan said. Susan Bourne, she's called. Lovely girl. Only lived in this area two years; she's working her way up to a job on one of the nationals. Brush your hair before you go in and say hello, Eldred. I'm just making Susan another cup of tea.'

Eldred ran his fingers through his hair and went into the sitting room, trailing his school bag. Hope died as soon as he saw the girl. Every inch of her had been carefully clothed, in fishnet tights, short skirt, low-cut top, boots, make-up, earrings, hair dye, and a wide expanse of bright smile. This person was fully covered against being affected by others.

'Hi! Eldred, isn't it?' she greeted his arrival. 'Your mother's been explaining to me about your name: called after both your parents, Edgar and Mildred, because you're the only child and they didn't expect to have any more after you, isn't that right?'

Eldred sank into a chair and searched her face for some sign of life. The bright mask smiled more widely.

'Nothing to say for yourself? You can't be shy, a clever boy like you! Your mother's been showing me some of your work.'

'Where did she get it?' asked Eldred.

'Didn't you know? She's got folders of everything you ever did, the first picture you drew, all your school exercise books full of little sums, the birthday cards you made her with poems written by you...'

Eldred cringed. 'Those are baby things,' he said. 'The real work is all on hard disk on my computer.'

'I've phoned your father at work, Eldred,' said Mildred, coming in with a tray of tea, 'and he's going to try and come home a bit early, as it's a special occasion. One sugar, isn't it, Susan? See, Eldred, we've been getting to know one another this afternoon. Susan and I have been getting on famously.'

Eldred shot Susan a sharp glance. She met it and looked away. The woman's a fool, her eyes said, and I'm bored with this. Eldred's eyes threatened: make fun of my mum and I'll know about it.

'Mr Austin from your high school was on the phone to me this morning,' Mildred told Eldred. 'He rang to say he thought I'd like to know he had permission from the Head to bring you into his computer class. With fourteen and fifteen year olds,' she told Susan, 'and Eldred's only just nine!'

'You told me,' said Susan. 'Amazing.'

'Did he say anything to you about it, Eldred?' Mildred asked.

'Yes. Mum, he won't give back my disk. He says it's school property. He won't even let me copy it.'

'This is the famous compost machine, is it?' Susan asked.

'Farm waste reprocessing plant,' said Eldred, 'with a variation for an inorganic waste model, but I'm still working on that. It's a process for reducing bulk very quickly into a concentrated usable form. Organic waste can take up a lot of space on a farm, you see, and land values are at a premium.'

Susan and Mildred burst out laughing.

'He's like this all the time?' Susan exclaimed.

'All the time,' laughed Mildred.

Eldred went very still. 'What is your article about?' he asked Susan.

'Sorry, Eldred, I didn't mean to hurt your feelings. Take no notice of me,' she said, giggling. 'The article's about you, of course: all the clever things you've done, for a boy of your age.'

'Was it your own idea to write it, or did someone else tell you to?' Eldred asked.

'Well, there's a person called a features editor on a newspaper, Eldred,' Susan explained, 'and we all have a meeting once a week and pool our ideas on what would make a good story for next week's issue, and then the features editor decides who should write what. I usually get human interest stuff like this – children, animals, babies, family concerns. They're all sexist pigs in the newspaper world,' she added with a big smile.

'Isn't it the same everywhere?' sighed Mildred.

'Don't you like children?' asked Eldred.

'Of course I do, Eldred,' said Susan. 'They're just not the only thing women can write about, that's all. Now, let me finish my tea and then I'm going to ask you some questions about yourself, Eldred – all right?'

'How do you interview animals?' Eldred asked.

'Let Susan finish her tea in peace,' Mildred suggested. 'Have a chocolate biscuit, Eldred. They're his favourite,' she told Susan. 'They say the brain feeds on sugar, don't they? I don't know whether intelligence has something to do with good nourishment. Being an only child, he has more time devoted to his welfare, so it could be.'

'I just wondered,' Eldred explained, 'as you interview the parents when the article's about a child, whether you'd interview the child if the article was about an unusual pet animal owned by a child, or whether you'd still interview the parents who owned the child who owned the animal.'

'Goodness me!' said Susan. 'What a mouthful.'

'Yes, don't talk with your mouth full, Eldred,' said Mildred. 'Susan will think we've no manners in this house.'

Eldred craned his neck to read Susan's notebook and saw she had written lists of his school term results at different ages. Underneath the notebook was a sheaf of folded papers he recognized as half-page essays written at school, under strict guidance.

There was also a page of what looked like algebra, which was in fact a collection of unconnected doodlings Eldred had made to concentrate his mind while thinking of something to do with the structure and decomposition of matter. He thought he had thrown it away. He had thrown it away. It was crumpled. His mother must have taken it out of the bin.

'You're not going to print that, are you?' he asked, pointing to it. 'It doesn't mean anything. I was just working something out.'

Susan held up the sheet and studied it. 'Looks good, though, doesn't it?' she said. 'The photographer should be here any minute.

I thought we could have a shot of you at your home computer, Eldred, holding this up.'

'I'll give it a quick going over with iron first,' said Mildred. 'Can't have it looking all scrummed up.'

'But people might try to read it,' said Eldred, 'and realize that it's rubbish.'

'I hope you're not referring to my article!' Susan laughed. Mildred joined in. 'It will be brilliant, I assure you, Eldred!'

'What questions did you want to ask me?' asked Eldred.

'Oh, just about your hobbies and interests, what you watch on telly, which football team you support, that kind of thing.'

'I thought the article was about the work I've done,' said Eldred.

'Oh, your mum's told me all about that,' Susan said. 'I've covered that angle – unusual standards achieved by a nine-year-old boy. What I want you to give me now is the normal schoolboy side: you know, "Although he spends his free time reading reference books in the library and inventing machines and things, in other ways Eldred Jones is an ordinary little boy who rides his bike and supports Spurs" – that kind of thing.'

'Arsenal,' said Mildred. 'Always watches Arsenal with his dad, don't you, Eldred?'

'But you haven't seen my work,' Eldred said.

'We'll take some pictures of it,' Susan said. 'That's the best way. You go and fetch some more of your stuff, if you like, and we'll pick out a few things for Rod to photograph when he gets here. That's if he ever arrives,' she added, looking at her watch.

'It's all on disk,' said Eldred. 'Shall I print some pages off?'

'No, leave it till he comes, then,' said Susan. 'He can take some shots of you actually at the computer, with something complicated-looking on the screen.'

'It's only a small VDU,' Eldred said. 'You can't really see the whole picture at one time. That's why I had to use the school one for the design. Do you think a design should be the property of the person who designed it, Susan, or the person who owned the empty disk?'

'I really wouldn't know,' she said. 'Oh, look, here's Rod now.'

'Do you want Eldred to change into his nice new sweater and jeans?' asked Mildred.

'No, school uniform's fine,' Susan said. 'I'll just go and let Rod in – okay?'

Chapter Fifteen

'You were difficult, Eldred,' Mildred reproached him later. 'Why wouldn't you smile?'

'I tried,' he said, 'but I didn't feel like smiling.'

'And refusing to hold up that page of sums for the man to photograph,' said his father. 'That was rude of you.'

'They weren't proper sums,' said Eldred. 'It was rubbish.'

'After your mother ironed it so nicely and everything,' said Edgar.

'They wouldn't take any pictures of my real work,' Eldred protested.

'He explained why that was,' said Mildred. 'It's hard to photograph things on a computer screen.'

'I could have printed it off.'

'You should have done what you were told, without arguing,' said Edgar. 'I was ashamed of you. Those people know what's needed for a newspaper article, and we don't. You have to learn to recognize your limits, son. You may be a clever boy but you don't know about everything.'

'Well, never mind,' said Mildred. 'They got what they wanted in the end, didn't they, Dad? Eldred, run along and wash your hands and change out of your school uniform and I'll start the tea.'

'Can I go down to the library for five minutes first?' Eldred wanted to see Terry Smith before Terry heard from his friend on the paper how hopeless an interviewee Eldred had been. He couldn't stand it if Terry was ashamed of him too.

'You certainly can't, at this hour of the evening. By the time you've done your homework and watched a bit of telly, it'll be your bedtime.'

'I don't want to watch telly, Mum.'

'Don't whine, Eldred. I can't stand children whining. Of course you must watch a bit of telly in the evening; it does you good to relax and it's the only time your dad gets to see you.'

When the local newspaper appeared on Friday morning, the article was every bit as bad as Eldred had anticipated. Worse, the journalist had phoned the school and spoken to some of the teachers. Eldred's class teacher Mrs Garcia stated that Eldred Jones was 'above average' intelligence but nothing special. 'We have a lot of bright children in this school,' she said.

Mr Austin confirmed that Eldred 'showed promise' but added, 'It's important not to exaggerate his abilities. He's an ordinary child.'

There were few direct quotes from Eldred's parents. Mildred was aggrieved. 'All that tea I gave her and all the time I talked, and all she can write is, "Mrs Jones claims her son taught himself to read by the age of five." It sounds as if she's calling me a liar!'

There was only one quote from Eldred himself, at the bottom of the column: 'Eldred claims, "My schoolwork's not my proper work; my proper work's done at home."'

Eldred could not remember saying that. He thought it was unlikely to make him any more popular at school with Mrs Garcia.

There was also a photograph of Eldred, looking miserable, seated beside a blank-screened computer. A second photo showed the despised page of algebra, with a child's hand holding a pen poised over it.

'That's not me!' cried Eldred, enraged.

'They must have found another boy to be your hand in the picture,' said Mildred, 'because you were so difficult about it.'

'They've no right to print my stuff without permission,' said Eldred.

'You're getting above yourself,' said Edgar severely. 'Just because you've got into the paper doesn't mean you can act like a film star in your own home. Eat your breakfast and get ready for school.'

'I don't want breakfast,' said Eldred. 'I'm not hungry.' He left the room.

Mildred dabbed her eyes. 'It's terrible of me, I know,' she told Edgar, 'but at times I almost wish Eldred was back in that hospital. He was no trouble to anybody then.'

'Getting up at nights and reading all those textbooks, though,' Edgar reminded her. 'There was obviously a devious streak, if only we'd known.'

'Yes, but we didn't know, did we? As far as we knew, he was just a sick little boy. At least the sickness was only in his lungs. Now what's he turning into? A smart-alec no one will want to know. I only hope it's not bad blood.'

'He'll grow out of it,' said Edgar uneasily. 'All children get a bit full of themselves if they're not kept under control.'

'Why can't he be like little Darren down the road? Always out riding his bike and playing games with other children on the estate. A normal boy.'

Edgar grunted. 'And throwing stones at car windows. If you call that normal.'

'I wouldn't mind if he was a real genius, like Mr Austin said,' Mildred responded, 'but they seem to be saying he's ordinary now. If he's ordinary, why isn't he like the other kids? He can't have it both ways.'

Edgar poured himself another cup of tea. 'You never know,' he said. 'He might give us cause to be proud of him one day.'

'I hope so,' said Mildred, 'or this worry will drive us both to an early grave.'

On Saturday morning, Eldred was sitting at the desk in his bedroom feeding a new box of disks through his computer to check them.

'Get ready to go out, Eldred,' Mildred called up the stairs.

'Why, Mum?'

'I have to go to the shops, and your Dad's out.'

'Can't I stay here? I'm in the middle of something.'

'I can't leave you alone in the house, Eldred; come along.'

'I promise I won't get into trouble, Mum. I'm working.'

'Is that schoolwork you're doing?'

'Sort of.'

'Come on, Eldred; don't be a trial.'

Eldred emerged from his room. 'Do you need me to carry your shopping?'

'There's not much to carry,' she said. 'I did a big shop during the week.'

'You don't really need me then?' Eldred asked hopefully.

'I can't leave you here, Eldred. You're too young.'

'I was left alone in the hospital, Mum. For hours sometimes.'

'That was different! There were people all around you there.'

'There are neighbours all around here. Please let me stay. Please?'

'Really, Eldred, I don't know why you're so difficult! Why do you have to make all this fuss every time? Oh, all right; have your own way again. But next time you do as you're told, do you hear me?'

'Yes, Mum.'

So it was that Eldred was alone in the house when Louise Palmer phoned.

'Four-two-three-seven; this is Eldred Jones speaking,' said Eldred, pressing the receiver to his ear. He was rarely allowed to answer the phone; his mother usually got there first.

'Thank goodness for that; I've tried all the Joneses in the phone book,' said Louise.

'Who did you want to speak to?' asked Eldred. 'My parents are not available at the moment.'

'I wanted to speak to you. My name is Louise Palmer. I'm a freelance journalist supplying features to national newspapers and magazines, overseas press, TV, radio – you name it, I do it. I live in this area myself and I saw the piece on you in the local paper.'

'Oh, that,' said Eldred. It sounded like a groan.

'Terrible article,' said Louise cheerfully, 'but that's the local rag for you. Were you disappointed?'

'Yes.'

'I'm not surprised. Hardly one direct quote and only the vaguest reference to your achievements outside school.'

'I didn't even say that,' said Eldred. 'I didn't say I only did proper work outside school.'

'Journalists do that,' Louise told him. 'They think people are too thick to say what they actually mean, so they rewrite their quotes to make them say what the reporter thinks they ought to mean. But I won't do that, I promise. Word for word.'

'Are you going to interview me?' asked Eldred.

'If you'll agree to it, after that disaster,' said Louise. 'And your parents, of course.'

'Are you going to ask my parents what they think I ought to mean, or are you going to write what I say?' asked Eldred.

Louise laughed. 'No flies on you, are there? I'll write what you say. We won't let your parents answer for you, but I will want a few of their comments as well. Okay?'

'Will you interview me first, on my own, then?'

'If you want, Eldred, yes.'

'Are you going to speak to the teachers at my school?'

'Probably. Why?'

Eldred made no reply.

'Don't you get on with them?' Louise enquired.

'Mr Austin – the high school computer teacher – took my disk,' Eldred said. 'The one with my farm waste reprocessing plant design on it. He said I must have stolen the idea on the class trip to the farm because I couldn't have designed it myself, but I did. He says the disk is school property and I can't have it back to copy it and he's going to erase the information. Then he asked me to join his class, then he said he was disappointed in me and I had to go back to the primary school again.' Eldred drew breath.

'I see,' said Louise slowly. 'This is a better story than I thought.'

'It's not a story,' said Eldred. 'It's true.'

'Of course it is. That's just what we call an article or a feature, in the media. We call every item a story.'

'Is that because it's not really the truth?' Eldred asked. 'Because the quotes are made up by the reporters?'

Louise laughed again. 'I can't wait to meet you,' she said. 'Can you make it this weekend?'

'I'm free now,' said Eldred hospitably.

'Good. Tell me where you live.'

'43 Cottrill Court, Aylmers Road. It's on the Hopthorp Estate.'

'I know it. Give me five minutes.'

'Can I ask you something?'

'Sure,' said Louise.

'What made you want to interview me, if the article – the story – in the local paper was so terrible?'

'I thought there might be more to you than met the eye,' Louise said. 'The reporter made you sound like nothing special but I got the impression it could have been sour grapes – and the teachers' comments as well. You get a knack for reading between the lines, when you're in the business yourself. Never believe what you read in the papers, Eldred! It's all subjective. Besides, the photo was a real give-away.'

'You mean my face?' said Eldred, perplexed.

'No, the page of equations,' said Louise. 'I'm leaving right now, okay? See you soon.'

Eldred returned to his room and started slotting disks into the computer and printing documents. When he had a batch of copies, he stuffed them into a carrier bag, put his football on top, and went to stand by the front gate.

Mildred arrived before Louise. 'What's this?' she asked. 'A welcome home committee for me?'

'Can I go and play football in the park, Mum? As soon as a friend of mine turns up?'

'Yes, I don't see why not, love.'

'What time do I have to be back?'

'No rush,' Mildred said generously. 'Much better for you to be playing with your little mates than stuck in your room on that computer, and it's only a sandwich for lunch. Your dad and I can have ours and keep yours for when you come back.'

'You look a bit tired, Mum,' said Eldred. 'Why don't you sit down and have a cup of tea?'

Mildred kissed him on the top of the head. She needn't have worried about Eldred, she thought, as she went in the front door and he closed it promptly behind her. Her son was all right: a nice thoughtful, straightforward boy.

Chapter Sixteen

'Pull in here, Jake,' said Lulubelle. 'I have to go.'

'You know what Mr Mannfield's like about taking stops on the journey,' Lucinda warned her. 'Can't you wait?'

'I have to go,' said Lulubelle urgently.

Jake pulled in to the service station. 'Won't hurt to stop for a few seconds,' he said. 'Weren't you wanting fags, Luce? You've smoked all mine. You can get me a pack as well.'

'I'll give you some of mine,' she said, but he shook his head.

'Can't stand that brand you smoke.'

Lucinda sighed. It just showed it was no use being nice to people; they couldn't even spare you a few cigarettes without wanting a whole pack in return. Nothing was for nothing, these days.

It wasn't as if she was putting Jake to any trouble, making him tow her caravan, even though everyone went on at her and said in her line of business she should have learned to drive; after all, if he wasn't driving her, he'd have had much heavier work to do, driving one of the fairground trucks and then getting stuck with unloading all the equipment the other end. This way, he might avoid it. She knew why he wasn't too unhappy that Lulubelle had asked for a stop; she might make him late, late enough to miss some of the work, and he could say she was to blame.

'Okay,' she said with resignation. 'But I don't know if I've got enough on me for two packs. I might have to smoke some of yours.'

Lulubelle jumped out of the cab. 'Don't forget to get me some aspirin.'

'Made of money, am I?' Lucinda said.

'I've got gut-ache,' said Lulubelle. 'Really bad, Mum; I'm not joking.'

Lucinda followed her into the service station.

'Meet me back here?' Lulubelle said.

'You can find your way back to the van,' said Lucinda. 'It's big enough to stand out, isn't it?'

'No, wait for me here,' Lulubelle insisted. 'I feel really weird. Promise?'

'Oh, all right.'

When Lulubelle came out of the toilet, Lucinda was retouching her make-up in front of the mirror over the washbasins.

'I'm bleeding,' said Lulubelle.

'You're what?' said Lucinda, applying red lipstick carefully.

'You know,' Lulubelle hissed. 'It's started: my... you know.'

'What?' said Lucinda again.

'Mum! It was you that told me about it; you can't have forgotten!'

'Oh no!' Lucinda gave her daughter her full attention now. 'You haven't started already? I might have known. I started young. Just my luck that you're the same, I suppose.'

'I need some things,' said Lulubelle.

'I haven't got any money,' Lucinda said. 'It's all gone on fags and aspirin.'

'What am I meant to do, then?'

'You'll have to wait, I suppose. It probably won't get that heavy, just to start with. You'll be all right for a while. When we get to the site, I'll borrow you a few pads from Mabel or someone.'

'No!' said Lulubelle, revolted. 'I'm not walking out of here, Mum. It'll show! What if blood comes through on to my clothes? Everyone will know!'

'It's not the end of the world, for God's sake,' Lucinda said irritably. 'You seem to think I can get money whenever you want it. What d'you expect me to do – wave a magic wand? Flag down Max the magician's van on the motorway and say, "Oh, Maxie, you do magic: conjure me up some sanitary towels for my daughter, will you?"'

'I hate you,' said Lulubelle.

'Hate away,' said Lucinda. 'You can't just expect me to solve all your problems, Lulubelle. What am I meant to do about it?'

'Get upset,' said Lulubelle. 'Like I am.'

'I am upset,' said Lucinda. 'You hurt my feelings when you talk like that. You know I love you; no one can say I don't try to be a good mother to you, and all on my own; it isn't easy, you know.'

'Ask the toilet attendant,' Lulubelle begged. 'Say it's an emergency.'

'She won't give you the things for free; they're in a machine; you have to pay.'

'She might if you ask her. Just try. Please.'

'You ask her. She's more likely to help if she thinks you're a child on your own. I'll go outside.'

'Mum! Don't leave me!'

'I'm not leaving you,' said Lucinda, exasperated. 'I'll wait outside.'

Lulubelle came out after a couple of minutes.

'Well?'

'I couldn't,' she said. 'I went up to her and I just couldn't say it. You do it, Mum. Please.'

'Only if you stop calling me that word.'

'Lucy. Lucinda. Anything you like. Please try.'

Lucinda went back into the Ladies and came out a minute later. 'There's one in there,' she said, handing Lulubelle her bag. 'I had to give her five of Jake's fags; he won't be happy. Go and change quickly.'

'Only one?' said Lulubelle fearfully. 'How long will it last me, Mum... Lucy?'

'Long enough,' Lucinda said. 'Hurry up or Jake'll drive off without you.'

They walked back to the van, Lulubelle walking awkwardly.

'How long will I bleed?' she asked.

'Few days – four, five.'

'How many pads will I need for four or five days?'

'Stop worrying, will you? I'll borrow some for today and I'll get you a whole pack tomorrow when we get paid.'

'Don't say anything to Jake, will you?' Lulubelle said urgently, as they approached the truck.

'How else am I going to explain why I gave his fags away to the toilet lady?' Lucinda demanded.

'Tell him something else. Say someone asked you for some.'

'You put me in some awkward situations,' Lucinda grumbled.

'Promise you won't tell?'

'Okay, okay.'

Jake was standing by the cab smoking. Lucinda held out the packet of cigarettes to him. 'Here.'

'Right,' he said. 'Let's go.' He put the pack in his jacket pocket without opening it.

'There's a few taken out of it,' said Lucinda. 'I took pity on the toilet lady; poor old soul, she was telling me all her life story. Couldn't get away.'

He got into the cab. 'Watch me out,' he said. 'We should have gone in the lorry park; there's no space to reverse here.'

They waved him out of the parking space safely and climbed back into the cab, Lulubelle shifting about on the seat uncomfortably.

'How long before we arrive?' she asked.

'Three hours, two and a half if we're lucky,' said Jake.

Lulubelle looked anxious.

'Don't worry, kid,' he said. 'Might never happen.' He took a bar of chocolate out of his pocket. 'That'll keep you going,' he said.

'Thanks,' Lulubelle said. She broke off a couple of chunks and offered the bar to Lucinda and Jake. He shook his head.

'No, go on,' Lucinda said. 'You have it. Growing girl and all that.'

Lulubelle took it as an apology. She leaned against her mother and sucked on a square of chocolate.

'Growing faster than I thought,' Lucinda said. 'They start young these days,' she told Jake. 'Ten years of age. Still, might as well find out what life as a woman's all about, eh?'

Lulubelle sat up straight and dug her elbow furiously into her mother's ribs, betrayed.

'What?' said Lucinda. 'No use making a fuss about it, is it? Happens to everybody soon enough, don't it?'

Jake, glancing sideways, caught Lulubelle's flushed cheeks and hostile look at Lucinda. 'Right enough, kid,' he said pacifically.

'The show must go on, as they say,' Lucinda said. 'Did I tell you she might be going on TV again, Jake?'

'I'm not performing tonight,' said Lulubelle flatly.

'Tell that to Mr Mannfield,' Lucinda said with a sniff. 'It'd take more than the curse to get him to give you a night off. You'd have to be dead, at least. Isn't that right, Jake?'

Jake, overtaking a removal van, had stopped listening.

Lucinda turned the radio up.

'That's right,' she agreed with herself. 'Show must go on, at all costs. That's what showbiz is all about. You pays your money, folks, and you takes your choice.'

Lulubelle put the rest of the chocolate bar in her pocket. She might need it more later on than she did now.

Chapter Seventeen

When a car driven by a blonde young woman drew up, Eldred ran towards it.

'Are you Louise?'

'Yes. Hello, Eldred.'

Eldred opened the passenger door and jumped in. 'We can go to the park or the library,' he said. 'I've got some of my work with me.'

Louise looked at him. 'Does your mother know you're getting into a stranger's car and driving off?'

'No. She thinks I've gone to the park with a friend.'

'Then we'd better go the park,' Louise said. 'Easier to talk there than in the library anyway.'

'Those equations were rubbish,' said Eldred, as they drove away from the house. 'How could they have told you I was worth interviewing?'

'What were you working out, when you did them, Eldred?'

'Nothing,' said Eldred. 'I just write any old thing when I'm thinking.'

'But what were you thinking about, at the time?'

'Decomposition of matter,' said Eldred.

'So you've no idea what those equations mean?' Louise asked.

'They don't mean anything,' Eldred insisted. 'I was just doodling.'

Louise pursed her lips and whistled. 'Some doodles,' she said. 'I

wish my mind idled like that. My brother's a maths and science buff;
I got him to check those meaningless equations, Eldred, and he said
they were similar to the calculating processes used in quantum
physics and every one of those complicated calculations was correct.
What do you make of that?'

Eldred shook his head.

'Did you ever hear of quantum physics, Eldred?' Louise pursued.

'I might have read an article on it once,' said Eldred. 'There's a
parking space. Do you mind if I leave my football in the car?'

As they walked through the park gates, Louise said casually, 'You
retain whatever you read then, do you?'

'I suppose everybody does,' said Eldred. 'Otherwise there
wouldn't be any point in reading because you wouldn't learn
anything from it.'

She smiled. 'Our powers of learning are usually very selective,
Eldred. I can read something three times and only retain a fraction
of it, and my IQ is well above average. Why do you think that is?'

'I don't know,' said Eldred. 'Don't you find that rather frustrating?'

'Not until now,' said Louise. 'I never knew what I was missing.'

'Can you remember things that happened to you before you were
born?' Eldred asked her.

'I can't – or not consciously. Some people claim to. Can you?'

'Some things,' said Eldred dismissively. 'Shall I show you my work
now?'

For an hour, Eldred talked, pointed, turned pages and explained.
Louise listened, asked occasional questions, asked him to repeat
certain points, and wrote shorthand notes to record Eldred's exact
turn of phrase. Eldred had never been attended to so thoroughly.
He became excited, expounding theories, detailing plans for future
projects. Louise began to feel exhausted.

'You want to acquire all the knowledge in the universe all at once,'
she said, laughing. 'You do know you can't do that?'

'Not all at once, no,' Eldred conceded. 'But building on the
foundation of knowledge already acquired by mankind up to this
time, and given sufficient resources and motivation, future

generations must surely be able to acquire total knowledge eventually, don't you agree?'

'It's a plausible theory,' said Louise, 'but I wouldn't agree that it's possible, or even desirable really. There is such a thing as mystery, the unknowable... knowledge beyond the grasp of mortal beings.'

Eldred pondered this. 'Are you talking about the occult?'

'No. The occult has a perennial fascination for generations of human beings – the dark arts, hidden knowledge of good and evil, whatever it has been called in different centuries – but it's generally considered among responsible people to be misleading, if not downright damaging. No, I'm talking about the infinite. If it's true that we are created beings, then we have to accept that the uncreated can never fully be fathomed by mere creatures. We're limited beings with limited minds.'

'The uncreated?' said Eldred. He frowned. 'You mean other beings? Beings from other planets?'

Louise laughed. 'No! If there are any, I would assume they must be created as well, wouldn't you? I'm talking about the creator of everything, mortal and immortal.'

Eldred blinked. 'You don't mean God?'

She smiled at him. 'Why not?'

'I don't wish to offend you,' said Eldred carefully, 'but the only other person I've met who believed in God was mentally retarded.'

Louise let out a hoot of delighted laughter and scribbled on her notepad. 'I've got to get that quote in!' she said. 'Too good to miss!'

'I didn't intend to imply that your intelligence was impaired in any way,' said Eldred anxiously. 'I was just surprised, that's all.'

'But why?' said Louise. 'Surely you're taught about God at school? You must have met other people who believe.'

'The teachers tell you about the facts, or the theories,' said Eldred, 'but they don't present it as something they believe. If they did, they would live differently, but they live just the same way as everybody who doesn't believe. And from the books I've read, religious belief seems to be one hypothesis among others, and one with little or no established proof.'

'Ah, Eldred,' said Louise, 'you're mixing two quite different ways of acquiring knowledge here. Some things you can't learn about in books, and not everything is provable scientifically.'

'I know that not all knowledge can be taught,' said Eldred, 'but how can it not be scientifically proved or disproved? It wouldn't be knowledge if it couldn't be proved.'

Louise smiled again. 'I can't believe I'm having this conversation with a nine year old,' she said.

Eldred flushed. 'You're telling me I'm too young to understand.'

'Basically, yes,' said Louise, 'but that's no reflection on you. We will all be still too young to understand creation, let alone the creator, when we're on our deathbeds. That's what I'm saying, Eldred. Science is just a word meaning "knowing". Humans can only know and prove what is knowable to human beings and provable by existing human standards of knowledge. By definition, science has no power to examine what is beyond human powers of knowing.'

Eldred felt agitated and sad. 'But if there is a God and he's good, how can he allow human beings to go in search of knowledge which he knows they're not capable of attaining?'

Louise put her arm round him. 'I've worried you,' she said repentantly. 'I'm not a theologian, Eldred, and I'm probably not explaining very well. All I'm trying to say is, there are different ways of knowing and not all of them come as the result of human effort or even human intellect. They may come in response to genuine endeavour for truth, though. Some knowledge is given – vouchsafed. Did you ever hear that word before? Well, then, call it grace or faith or enlightenment, whatever you will, but knowledge that comes in that way isn't earned or worked for. I guess I'm only trying to tell you this because you worry me slightly, Eldred.'

'Why do I worry you?'

'Because your zeal to learn could burn you out,' said Louise seriously. 'Because I have never before met anyone – adult or child – with such a capacity for acquiring information, but information isn't everything. In this society we're living in, intellectual knowledge is almost worshipped, to the exclusion of the emotions, art, creativity, integrity, relationships, and especially that more-than-human relationship with God, the relationship between the limited created being with the infinite.'

Eldred rubbed his forehead. 'I'm tired,' he said.

'I'm not surprised,' she said. 'I'll take you home now. It's been wonderful meeting you, Eldred.'

Eldred studied her eyes and realized she meant it. She was tiring, this lady, but she was worth being tired for, he reckoned. He felt suddenly overwhelmed with love for this Louise Palmer. It was a new event for Eldred.

Chapter Eighteen

'That Miss Palmer's going to your school today,' said Mildred, returning to the breakfast table from answering the phone.

Eldred's heart leapt. 'What for?'

'For her article on you, I suppose,' Mildred said, 'though you'd think she had enough to write about now, wouldn't you, Daddy, with all those questions she asked us?'

Edgar chewing toast methodically, nodded.

'Be sure and answer politely if she asks you anything, Eldred,' his mother told him. 'You won't be difficult, will you, like you were with that other journalist?'

'I won't,' Eldred promised. 'Can I go now?'

'You'll be too early,' Mildred pointed out, but Eldred had already gone.

There was no sign of Louise at Eldred's school until breaktime, when Charlie Austin sent word for Eldred to come up to the high school complex. Last time Mr Austin had sent for him, Eldred had gone reluctantly. This time he ran all the way, arriving out of breath.

Louise, looking elegant and professional in a mushroom-coloured suit and high-heeled shoes, stood beside Charlie Austin in the computer room, looking at something on one of the display screens. Eldred recognized it. Mr Austin had not erased Eldred's design.

'Here is the man himself,' Charlie declared, turning to Eldred. Eldred was taken aback by his friendliness. 'Come here, Eldred,' said Charlie encouragingly. 'We've just been taking another look at your little machine.'

If Eldred thought this a patronising term for an industrial plant that converted bulky waste material into compact pellets, he gave no sign of it. He looked at Louise. Louise was looking at Charlie. Her face was expressionless.

'This very intelligent lady has made it clear to me,' Charlie said, 'that the design is quite obviously your own, Eldred, because although it's very good – very good indeed for a nine year old to dream up – there is of course a fatal flaw in it.'

Charlie looked at Louise and smirked. Louise gave him a dazzling smile. Eldred stood speechless, looking from one to the other. For a few moments the three of them stood in front of Eldred's cross-section graphics on the screen, without a word.

Eldred cleared his throat. 'A fatal flaw?' he said.

'Yes,' said Charlie, smirking even more. 'At first I didn't see it. I thought, in fact, that you must have copied this whole project from somewhere or other.'

'I didn't,' said Eldred.

'I know that now,' said Charlie patiently. 'Louise has shown me that couldn't have been the case.' He showed his teeth. Louise smiled on. Eldred felt bewildered. He examined their faces for clues. What was going on here?

'It couldn't work,' Charlie explained. 'The concept is very interesting, but there's a fault in the second chamber. There wouldn't be enough gases present for the necessary breakdown and conversion of the solid matter.'

Eldred opened his mouth. Louise, for the first time since Eldred had entered the room, looked him full in the face and winked. Eldred closed his mouth again.

'It was a very good effort,' said Charlie kindly. 'Quite impressive, in fact. For a nine year old. Well done, Eldred. I'm sure by the time you reach my class in the high school you'll be capable of some excellent work, if you keep up the pace. Run along back to Mrs Garcia now. We don't want you being late for class, do we?'

'No,' said Eldred. He paused by the door. 'Goodbye,' he said to Louise.

'I might as well walk down with you, Eldred,' she said. 'Mr Austin has given me all I need.'

'Charlie,' said Mr Austin, smiling fit to split.

'Charlie,' Louise conceded. She held out her hand as Charlie removed the disk from the machine. Charlie held out his hand to shake hers. Louise took the disk from it. 'May I?' she said. 'For my article?'

'Oh, please,' said Charlie, 'be my guest.'

Eldred followed Louise down the corridor. Mr Austin watched them depart. Round the corner, out of sight, Louise abandoned her dignity, scooped up Eldred and whizzed him round and round. 'We did it!' she exulted. She handed Eldred the disk. 'Guard it with your life,' she instructed, 'until we've got this sorted out with the Patents Office, signed and sealed in your name. Make at least two copies.'

'But what about the fatal flaw?' said Eldred, bemused. 'The deficiency of vital gases in the second chamber?'

'Are you kidding?' said Louise. 'The design is perfect. I checked it out with my brother. It'll work.'

Eldred began to laugh and found he couldn't stop.

'What are you thinking?' Louise asked.

'Thank you,' Eldred hiccuped. 'Thanks very much.'

'My pleasure,' said Louise. 'Your computer teacher is a pompous idiot, if you don't mind my saying so.' Eldred didn't. 'Are all your teachers like that?' Louise asked. 'Think they've nothing left to learn and everything to teach?'

'More or less,' Eldred admitted.

'Is this the right place for you?' Louise wondered. 'Isn't there some school for bright kids where you could find your own level without being penalized for not being average?'

The advertisement Eldred had memorized from the magazine found in his hands in the staffroom swam into his brain. Without pausing for thought, he recited, 'Verne House School, The Coppices, Shalford, Dorset.' He omitted the postcode, not considering it necessary in answer to a casual enquiry.

Louise blinked. 'Wow,' she said softly. 'Is that where you'd like to go?'

'I don't know,' said Eldred. 'I only just thought of it.'

'Well, think on,' she told him. 'You're wasted here. I'll be in touch, okay? Keep that disk somewhere safe.'

Eldred was sorry to see her go. But for the rest of the morning, as he laboured to keep his mind on reading aloud in turn with his classmates, agonizingly slowly, he kept experiencing little darts of hope. It seemed to him – though without any concrete evidence – that the worst might be over now and life might never be quite the same again.

Chapter Nineteen

Keith knew that all the family loved him. They told him so regularly, and showed it by being protective and loyal and taking care of him. But they loved him as a child who was disabled, and inside he felt like neither of those things.

Watching his grandfather coming into the ward now, his heart ached with love for him. His mother's father was the one who had spent a lot of time with him when he was young, when Andrew was born and their mother, still distraught over giving birth to a child as handicapped as Keith, now had another baby to care for.

Their grandfather had always tried to treat them equally. Sometimes he would take them both to the park, while their mother had a sleep or went out to have her hair done – the only luxury she allowed herself. At other times he would look after Andrew, while their mother took Keith for a hospital appointment. He would offer to babysit in the evenings so that both parents could go out, but Keith's mother never wanted to go out and leave him. She was afraid he might die if she left him, and if she wasn't with him, she'd never forgive herself.

But the times Grandad most enjoyed, as both Andrew and Keith realized, were the times he spent alone with Keith.

When Andrew was older, he and Grandad started to go on fishing trips – originally with Keith as well, then, after Keith had pneumonia, on their own. Andrew said that Grandad always enjoyed their day out, and cheered loudly whenever either of them caught a fish, excited as a young boy with his first catch. But the moment when his eyes would really light up and his face would shine was the moment when they walked back into the house and Grandad saw Keith. 'You are the light of his life,' Andrew told Keith solemnly.

He wasn't jealous; it was a fact of life which Andrew accepted. Keith was Grandad's favourite relative, as Uncle Dan had been Andrew's. Even after Uncle Dan went off, Andrew didn't mind about Grandad preferring Keith. 'I know he loves me as well,' he explained. 'It's just that you have more understanding of him. Like I understand Uncle Dan more than anyone else does.'

'Do you understand why he went away without telling anyone?' Keith asked him, but Andrew shrugged and heaved a deep sigh.

'I wish I could ask him,' he said.

'Perhaps he'll just turn up again one day, or phone you,' Keith suggested.

'I don't think so,' Andrew said sadly, though when Keith asked him he couldn't say why.

Uncle Dan had looked a bit like Grandad, though father and son were very different in character. According to Keith's mother, her brother Daniel was 'a live wire', and according to his father, 'a bit off the rails, if you ask my honest opinion'. Neither description could ever be applied to Daniel's father. Grandad was a man of routine and unshakeable beliefs, prone to odd fits of exuberance but generally calm, and safe as houses, with the same slow, sleepy smile and clear-eyed gaze as Keith.

'Hi, Grandad,' Keith greeted him.

Grandad dropped a kiss on top of Keith's head and rubbed his arm affectionately. 'How goes it?'

'Not bad.'

'Andrew gone home?'

'Yes, half an hour ago.'

'Read any new books recently?' Grandad asked, and Keith laughed obediently. It was another family joke. Keith had read avidly till the age of eleven, any title he could get hold of, on any subject, till the day when, having run out of reading material, he resorted to the old Bible gathering dust on a shelf in his father's study. Since then, he had been reading little else.

'What are you on now?' Grandad asked him. 'Still a big fan of Elijah?'

'Daniel,' Keith said reluctantly. He didn't like their names to be used in a joking tone, since they had become friends of his – sometimes the only ones, he felt, who could really understand him.

'Daniel in the lion's den, eh?' said Grandad musingly. 'What d'you see in all those old stories? Isn't the New Testament more use to people nowadays?'

'It's the same,' said Keith. 'None of it goes out of date, does it? People don't really change.'

'Well, you may have a point,' Grandad conceded. 'Though I wonder what Moses and Elijah, and Matthew, Mark, Luke and John for that matter, would make of all this technology. Look at you – electric wheelchair, complicated computer, special bed. They'd think you were an alien from outer space. No, they wouldn't: they wouldn't know about life on other planets either, would they? They'd think you were... I don't know.'

'An angel,' said Keith and chuckled.

'You are an angel,' said Grandad seriously. Tears came into his eyes and he turned his head aside and coughed discreetly into a large linen handkerchief. His ideal of manliness was traditional and did not allow for crying. He sometimes felt that when Keith died he would have to die too; his heart would not accommodate any more grief.

He always tried, though, to let Keith express his feelings. He was aware that the boy put on a brave face for his brother and his parents.

'How are you feeling,' he asked now, 'about this operation tomorrow?' Sharp-eyed, he saw Keith's face cloud over. 'It's all right to be afraid,' he added.

'I know,' Keith said. 'Jacob was afraid when he wrestled with the angel. He didn't know what he was fighting with or why.'

'Are you fighting it?' asked Grandad gently. 'Can't face going through with it all over again? Your fifteenth, isn't it?'

'Yes. If I decide to go ahead with it.'

Grandad pursed his lips sympathetically. 'Don't have much choice, old son, do you? If the doctors advise…'

'The last doctor thought I'd had enough operations now,' Keith pointed out. 'He said there comes a point when even extensive surgery can only effect a minor improvement, and it's not worth the risk of the anaesthetic and the deterioration in health.'

'But this new doctor's more optimistic,' Grandad said. 'He thinks if they straighten the leg bones there'll be less strain on the hip joint.'

'The kneebone's connected to the thigh bone, the thigh bone's connected to the hipbone!' Keith sang out suddenly, in a high wavery voice.

Grandad sat and watched him. His eyes were grave.

'So hear the word of the Lord,' sang Keith. He stopped singing. 'But what is the word of the Lord, in my case? Have any of the doctors asked him?'

'What's the problem, son?' asked Grandad. 'You can tell me, you know.'

Keith, like his grandfather had, turned his head aside. Grandad handed him a tissue from the box on the bedside locker, beside the Lucozade and the oranges Keith's mother had brought in earlier.

'I don't want to sound horrible,' Keith said.

'Won't sound horrible to me,' said Grandad staunchly.

'Well… what if whatever is done to the body affects your soul? I mean, the thigh bone's connected to the hip bone, and so on. I know the anatomy. But where do all these bones connect with me? I mean, who knows what it does to the person's soul, having all these adjustments made to the joints and bones?'

'I'm not sure I follow you,' said Grandad. His forehead was furrowed with the effort to understand.

'The last doctor that was here, the one that's left now, seemed like a good man to me,' Keith said. 'I mean, he mightn't have known everything but when he wasn't sure about something he said so, and he asked me. Like last time, he said it wasn't certain the operation on my knee would make that much difference to me. A bit more mobility, he expected. But then, the anaesthetic always affects my breathing, and sometimes it doesn't go back to being easy.'

'I know,' said Grandad. He'd noticed his grandson becoming shorter of breath after each operation.

'And he said any surgery is weakening, and whereas a relatively healthy body will recover from the weakness, mine might not. My arms never got back their strength, did they, after that operation on my neck?'

'No, but that might have happened anyway, Keith.'

'Bit of a coincidence, though,' Keith said. 'Anyway, Mr Gannet said it was up to me whether I had the operation or not. I told you that.'

'Yes, you told me at the time. And you decided to go ahead with it.'

'Only because Mum got upset, Grandad, really.'

His grandfather bowed his head. 'She wants to do what's best. She doesn't like you having all these operations, believe me.'

'But she keeps insisting on them,' Keith said. His voice was becoming strained, and he cleared his throat. 'Everybody does.'

'I suppose she believes the doctor knows best,' said Grandad simply. 'If a person's not going to take the experts' advice, what's the point of going to them?'

'But Mr Gannet didn't advise it,' Keith said. 'He said it was up to me.'

'Yes, but obviously he must have thought it worth trying,' said Grandad, 'or it would never have been suggested in the first place. It was kind of him to leave it to you to decide whether you felt you could go ahead with it, but in the end, these surgeons wouldn't operate unless they believed it was necessary.'

Keith's face reddened. 'He wasn't saying it was necessary but I could refuse if I couldn't face it. He was saying that things aren't that cut and dried, Grandad. There might be advantages, but there are also drawbacks and risks. He let me decide because it was something that couldn't be decided by him, because he wasn't the one who had to live with the results. And he was right.'

'I'm sure he was,' said Grandad soothingly, but Keith saw that he was becoming agitated, twisting his handkerchief around his hand and straightening it out again, like someone bandaging and unwrapping an invisible wound.

'But this man,' said Keith, 'is talking about the benefits to the family, in making it easier to lift me, and the contribution I'm making to medical research. And I don't think he's putting me first. He's thinking about his career. He's not being a man with me, Grandad, like Mr Gannet was; he's treating me like a successful specialist with a young patient who doesn't have the wisdom to understand his own case.'

Grandad looked bewildered. 'But he is the specialist, Keith, and you are a young lad who hasn't studied medicine like he has...'

'I don't trust him as a person,' said Keith flatly. 'I don't feel I want to put my soul into his hands. I did with Mr Gannet, not because he was perfect or knew everything about medicine, but because he was a good man. Even if he got it wrong and I came out of the operation with more disabilities than I had when I went in, I knew he wouldn't do my soul any harm.'

'How can a doctor affect your soul, Keith?' said Grandad, concerned. 'Your soul's in the hands of God. You just have to trust him.'

'I do trust him,' said Keith. 'And he trusts me to make up my own mind. He gave me free will. And as long as I'm a good man, I could make decisions that might not be God's first choice, but I won't come to any harm.'

'Of course you won't,' Grandad said, feeling more sure of his ground. 'Of course God won't let you come to any harm.'

'Unless,' said Keith sombrely, 'I go against my God-given instincts, and go along with what someone else wants – someone I believe is not really listening to God or to me and just wants to tinker about with the body as though it was a machine; someone who wants to justify his authority and must do something to every patient, even if it's not for the patient's lasting benefit.'

Grandad put his hand on Keith's arm. 'Don't be bitter, son,' he said. 'You won't come to any harm if you trust God and do what the doctor says.'

Keith moved his arm. 'What if trusting God, in this case, means not doing what the doctor wants or what Mum wants or what anyone wants, but what I feel is for my benefit, even if everyone thinks I'm stubborn and selfish?'

'No one thinks that,' said Grandad. He looked suddenly old. Keith had never shaken his hand off like that before. 'I don't know what to say,' he said.

A round lady in a pink overall appeared with a trolley. 'Steak and kidney pie for my favourite boy!' she announced. 'And caramel custard for afters. Are you going to feed him, Grandpa?' she asked.

'No,' said Keith. 'You'll be late for your tea at home,' he told his grandfather. 'You go, and I'll wait for the auxiliary nurse to come and help me eat.'

Grandad was about to protest but thought better of it. 'See you soon,' he said.

Keith didn't like to see him looking sad. 'Thanks for coming,' he said. 'I really appreciate your visits, Grandad.'

Polite with him now, Grandad thought; that was another first. He went to kiss Keith on the top of his head, then took his hand and shook it instead. Perhaps what the boy had been trying to say was that it was time they stopped treating him like a child. And Keith hadn't meant any offence; it would be over-sensitive to take it personally. It was natural for the child to be depressed. Once the ordeal of this operation was over, Keith would be back to his normal self – sunny-tempered with a smile for everyone.

'You're a brave lad,' he said.

Keith watched him walk away.

'That's right,' said the lady in the pink overall, fitting the detachable tray across the arms of the wheelchair ready for his meal. 'You certainly are the bravest boy of all time.'

Keith shook his head. 'Sometimes it's braver to stand up for what you think's right,' he said. 'And I'm not brave enough.'

The anaesthetist came to see him before the nurses settled him down for the night. 'All right about tomorrow?' he said. 'Any questions you want to ask me?'

'No,' said Keith. 'Everything's fine.'

He dreamt that night about Daniel in the lions' den, only Daniel, instead of standing proudly among the ravenous animals, armed with faith in the God who kept his chosen ones safe from being harmed, was clinging to the bars, pleading with the lions to stay away from him. Keith woke up sweating, with pain in his arms.

Chapter Twenty

Eldred's feeling that events might have taken a turn for the better was quite soon confirmed.

The Head of the First School announced that as there were spare places on the coach for the top class's visit to a nuclear power station, a limited number of children from the lower classes would be allowed to go. Any children wishing to go on the trip should give their names to their own class teacher and bring the money to school by Monday at the latest.

Eldred accosted Mrs Garcia immediately after assembly. 'Please,' he said, 'I'd like to go to visit the nuclear power station.'

'I might have known you would,' said his class teacher. 'The question is, should you be allowed to go, considering your behaviour after the last school trip you went on? Not to mention your behaviour during it, Eldred. You were disruptive and selfish.'

'Please,' Eldred begged. 'I won't be again. I'll be extremely good.'

'That's the trouble, Eldred,' Mrs Garcia sighed. 'You're extremely everything. Why do you have to be so extreme?'

Eldred bowed his head. 'I don't know.' He recalled Louise's words to him in the park. 'Maybe it's because I have a zeal to learn,' he suggested.

'Well,' said Mrs Garcia, 'that's not a bad thing in itself. I would be the last person to discourage that in a child. Bring your money to me by Monday – provided your parents give their permission, that is.'

Mildred and Edgar had a private discussion that evening about whether to give their permission.

'The teachers know about him now,' Edgar reasoned. 'They wouldn't let him go if they thought they couldn't keep him under control, would they?'

'I don't know,' said Mildred. 'They thought he was under control the last time, didn't they? What harm can a child come to from visiting a farm? But look what it did to his mind: all het up over that machine he thought he could design. What effect's a nuclear power station going to have on him? He won't sleep for nights after that.'

'We can't hold him back, Mother,' said Edgar. 'That journalist said it must be a strain for him, being so clever and not having enough to learn at school. If he has something he can get his teeth into, it might calm him down and then he'd be easier at home too.'

'It has the opposite effect, if you ask me,' Mildred said. 'This trip is likely to get him all worked up again. It's better when he is a bit bored; he's less trouble than when he's trying to know more than his elders. He only puts people's backs up, and what good will that do him?'

'It's not his fault exactly,' Edgar defended him. 'He can't help being one step ahead.'

'He doesn't have to show it all the time,' Mildred said irritably, 'as though he must be trying to prove he's better than the rest of us.'

Edgar stubbed out his cigarette as carefully as he did everything and handed the ashtray to Mildred to empty. 'Perhaps he is,' he said.

Eldred was sitting on the stairs trying to hear what they were deciding but failed to make out the words. After a while he went back to bed but he couldn't sleep. Experience warned him it was no use trying to rush his parents into letting him know their decision; he would have to wait till morning.

Lying in his bed, rigid with fear that they might not let him go, Eldred addressed his first-ever remarks to the Unknown.

'If there is a God,' he said aloud, 'who can't be known by the intellect alone, please make yourself known to me by whatever your usual method is – grace or faith or whatever else it's called. And if it wouldn't interfere with your wider plan, a good sign of your existence, for me, would be to arrange for me to go to the nuclear power station as this would be of great interest to me and, I would imagine, of benefit to my soul, though I expect you would know better than me whether this assumption is correct. Thank you and goodnight.'

Eldred slept.

In the morning, Mildred handed him the money in an envelope and said, 'You can go. On one condition.'

'All right,' said Eldred, who would have agreed to anything.

'You don't get all overexcited between now and then, you come straight home afterwards, and you don't give Dad or me any trouble over this.'

'Okay.' A bit unfair, Eldred thought; that was three conditions, not one. But he said nothing.

'And Eldred?'

'Yes.'

'I know you don't listen to me, but will you, on this one occasion?'

He was hurt. 'I do listen to you, Mum.'

'Well, just this once will you believe I might know better than you, Eldred?'

Eldred nodded his agreement.

'The people who work in these places – the people who'll show you round – they're experts in their job, right?'

'Right,' said Eldred. 'Well, they may not be expert scientists, of course; they may just be experts in showing people round and explaining...'

'Eldred,' Mildred said. 'Just listen.'

'Okay,' said Eldred.

'Whatever it is they do, they are trained to do it and paid to do it, all right? And they know enough about it to do their job, in the ordinary way of things. If someone like you comes along – a little boy, not trained to do their kind of job – and asks a lot of questions they don't know the answers to, they don't like it. Do you understand?'

'I understand they might not like the idea,' Eldred conceded, 'but the questions, which they might not have thought of asking themselves, might arouse in them a greater interest in their field of work and inspire them to go and find out the answers and so learn more about it and become even more expert, and they might find that rewarding, don't you think?'

'No,' said Mildred.

'Oh.'

'Not everyone wants to be inspired to know more,' Mildred explained. 'Some people are quite content with what they know already. Does that make sense to you, Eldred?'

Eldred thought about it. 'I suppose so,' he said.

'Good, because I want you to keep that in mind while you're on your school trip. All right?'

'All right,' Eldred said. He inserted a fingertip up one nostril thoughtfully. 'Maybe,' he said, 'not everybody has a zeal to learn.'

'Maybe not,' said Mildred, 'and maybe it's a good thing that we're not all alike. Don't pick your nose, Eldred.'

'I wasn't picking it,' Eldred explained. 'I was feeling what it was like on the inside.'

Mildred drew a deep breath. 'Go to school,' she said.

Chapter Twenty-one

Eldred thought Terry Smith had been a bit cool with him recently. He waited till Terry left his place behind the counter in the reference section of the library and followed him to the coffee machine.

'How are you, Terry?' he asked politely.

'Oh, nice to know you remember me,' Terry responded.

Eldred frowned. 'Is something wrong?'

'Just that I thought you might have said thank you to me for arranging that interview with the local paper,' Terry said.

'Oh.' Eldred tried to think of something tactful to say. 'I am grateful to you for arranging it,' he said, 'but I was disappointed in the result.'

'That's not my fault,' said Terry.

'No. But your purpose in kindly arranging for me to be interviewed,' said Eldred carefully, 'was to publicize my farm waste recycling machine because Mr Austin was saying it wasn't mine. And the article didn't mention it.'

Terry shrugged. 'The publicity won't do you any harm. No one's going to publicize my problems; I have to work them out all on my own. You can't complain.'

Eldred looked up at him. 'What problems would you want publicized? And why would it help?'

Terry pressed the button and watched coffee trickle into a plastic cup. 'Never mind,' he said. 'What are you in here for today, Eldred? Looking for information on something?'

Eldred hung his head. 'Don't say "never mind",' he said softly. 'I do mind. You're my friend.'

Terry hesitated, his cup halfway to his mouth. 'Do you mean that?'

'Of course.'

Terry stood looking at him intently. 'I could get off work now,' he said. 'Say I'm getting the flu; everyone's going down with it. You could come back to my place and we'll have a talk.'

'I can't,' said Eldred. 'I said I'd be back in time for tea.'

'You don't always do everything your parents tell you, do you?' Terry said.

'I have to at the moment,' Eldred explained, 'or I won't be allowed to go to the nuclear power station.'

'Oh, nuclear power is it now?' said Terry bitterly.

Eldred was troubled by him. He had never known Terry in this mood. 'What's wrong with you, Terry?' he asked.

'What's wrong with me?' Terry said. 'Nothing's wrong with me. I have no life of my own, so how could anything go wrong with it? I'll be stuck in this place till I retire, my mother is too sick to recognize who I am any more, I don't know if I can rely on my friends to stand by me...'

'Do you have to keep visiting your mother every evening?' Eldred asked. 'If she doesn't know you?'

'I don't know me either,' said Terry. 'Maybe there's no one to know any more. I've become a nobody, an attachment to someone else's life, and now she doesn't need me. And what is there left to show of Terry Smith's life?'

'You could make a fresh start,' Eldred suggested. 'Go back to university?'

'Too old and too lethargic,' said Terry. 'What's the point? If I did finally get a degree, I'd probably only end up in the same kind of job anyway – or worse.'

Eldred felt weighed down by Terry's sloth. 'What about outside interests?' he said. 'Leisure, learning, social activities?'

Terry started walking away from him. Eldred followed. 'Terry?' he said. It sounded like a plea.

'Who'd want to socialize with me?' said Terry. 'Even I don't want to. You're better off not knowing me either, Eldred. Go on – nuclear power, bottom shelf over there. See you around.'

Eldred watched Terry return to the counter and start leafing through a catalogue in response to someone's enquiry. He thought Terry seemed angry. He didn't know what to do to make him feel better. Eldred knelt down and began scanning a book on the history of nuclear energy, running his finger down the pages and stopping to read certain paragraphs, then moving on. He felt unbearably sad and didn't know why.

After a while, for no reason he could identify, he abandoned the account of early nuclear fission experiments and went to the dictionary to look up 'anguish'. 'Severe misery or mental suffering,' Eldred read. The word was derived from the Old French for 'choking', which in turn was derived from the Latin for 'tightness' or 'narrow'.

From his position, hunched on the floor in front of the open dictionary, Eldred stared across at Terry. He saw that Terry's eyes, squinting at the screen of the microfilm reader, were narrowed and his face looked pinched. In his throat, his Adam's apple stood out starkly, moving visibly as he gulped. Narrowed vision, choking. 'Anguish,' said Eldred softly.

Satisfied with his diagnosis, he turned to the medical dictionary to find the remedy, but anguish was not listed as either a symptom or a disease, and Eldred didn't know where else to look.

Over the tea table, watching his father's Adam's apple tackle the task of swallowing egg and chips, Eldred asked him, 'Do you ever suffer from anguish, Dad?'

His father snorted. 'No time for hysterics,' he said. 'I keep myself busy, my bowels regular and my conscience clear.'

'You mean,' said Eldred, 'that mental anguish is caused by leisure, constipation and guilt, then?'

'I didn't say that at all,' said Edgar. 'You're putting words into my mouth now.'

'Don't annoy your father, Eldred,' said Mildred automatically. 'Eat your tea.'

Eldred sighed.

Before going to bed that night, Eldred read four chapters of a library book on the history of the North American Indians, helped himself to a laxative tablet from the bathroom cabinet, and examined his conscience carefully for signs of guilt. The sense of anguish remained. His mother came in to put the light out and kiss him goodnight.

'Pleasant dreams,' she said.

'Okay,' Eldred said dutifully. He no longer told his parents when he had nightmares. Unpleasant dreams, according to psychologists, always came to an end just before the moment of crisis – before the world was destroyed or the dreamer was caught by the lion chasing him. In Eldred's dreams, he was chased, caught, savaged and consumed. He frequently dreamed he was dead or that he was the sole survivor of the virtually obliterated planet. There were no limits to desolation in his dreams.

Thinking of unlimited desolation led Eldred to think of the Unknown. There was something troubling his conscience after all. He had not remembered to thank the Most High for delivering his requested sign. He put this right now.

'This may of course have been coincidence,' he said aloud, 'but according to some theories there is no such thing, so I feel it's only right to thank you, Unknown Creator – if it was you – for listening to my request for a sign and arranging circumstances so that I'm allowed to visit the nuclear power station.

'I don't want to abuse this relationship by using you as a kind of vending machine, so I won't make any more requests for signs now, but if you wish to give me a faith implant, I would like this, to increase my understanding of your methods. I'm signing off now. Eldred Jones. Thank you and goodnight.'

He turned on his side, pulled his Intergalactic Trojans duvet cover over his head, and slept. Apart from three visits to the toilet, he had an undisturbed night. In the morning, the anguish seemed to have left him, at least for the time being. Eldred was relieved.

Chapter Twenty-two

Jake said it wasn't his fault they got lost; the sign was wrong. How could a sign be wrong, Lucinda argued? Anyone could tell it said Uxbridge, not Oxford. Anyone who could read, that was.

Lulubelle wasn't listening to the argument. She was watching a boy weaving his way along the pavement. If he hadn't been so young – a year or two less than herself, judging by his size, though perhaps he was small for his age – she would have sworn he was drunk. She leaned forward to study his crab-like progress and as he came nearer she saw he was reading a book. He came so close, as they pulled up at the crossroads, that Lulubelle was tempted to call out of the window and ask him what the title was; she had never seen anyone so engrossed in reading anything. His legs were moving as if by clockwork and he hardly looked up to see where he was going, but let passers-by buffet him from one side of the pavement to the other.

He reached the edge of the road just as the traffic lights changed from red to amber and Jake, incensed by Lucinda's remarks, tried to beat the oncoming traffic by lunging the truck into an unsignalled U-turn. The boy and the truck moved in unison. Lulubelle let out a piercing scream, echoed by the squeal of the air-brakes as Jake reacted sharply to the warning, catching a glimpse of the boy just before he disappeared from their view, high up in the cab.

Lulubelle flung open the door and hurled herself to the ground, with Jake and Lucinda seconds behind her. The boy, mildly surprised, stood in the road, inches away from the vehicle towering above him. Jake, his fear turning to rage, seized him by the shoulder and shouted incoherent obscenities. The boy didn't flinch. 'The lights weren't green yet,' he said. Cars hooted behind them. 'You're holding up the traffic,' the boy told Jake. 'Hadn't you better get going?'

Detaching himself from Jake's grasp, he continued on his way, pausing briefly at the island while the lights changed, then strolling across the other half of the road. The first in the line of cars turning right from the lefthand junction hooted and braked, but his attention was already claimed again by his book. Lulubelle had the impression he hadn't really seen any of them. 'Cool as a cucumber!' Lucinda marvelled. 'Someone up there must be looking out for that one.' Lulubelle hadn't managed to catch the title of the book, but she'd seen the boy's name on his schoolbag: a strange name to match a strange boy – Eldred Jones.

Despite the detour, they weren't the last to arrive. As always, Lulubelle's first action was to go and look round the site and see where everyone was.

'Don't get in people's way,' Lucinda warned. She was getting a lift into town with Sam and Molly. Her first action on arriving anywhere new was to get off the site and out of the way before anyone started arranging rehearsals or asking her to lend a hand at shifting something.

'Can you get me a packet of those things?' said Lulubelle, in a stage whisper.

'I told you, we don't get paid till tomorrow,' said Lucinda. 'I'm only going to town for a look around. Ask Belinda to lend you some; she's just started too.'

Of course, Lucinda would know that, thought Lulubelle, as everyone in the circus knew everything. 'There's no privacy,' she said bitterly, but Lucinda was already linking arms with Molly and walking towards the car.

Belinda's family hadn't arrived yet. Finula's van was packed solid with male cousins and uncles. Running out of other options, Lulubelle tried Arto's trailer.

Arto the Incredible and his wife Marisa were newcomers to Mannfield's, but Arto's reputation had preceded him: he was well-known on the European circuit, both East and West, had made numerous television appearances and was signed up with one of the most ruthless agents in the business. It was rumoured that the strongman was the highest-paid performer ever to join this circus, and he was already proving a sound investment: the crowds had increased significantly and he was working his way up to top billing, having already overtaken the trapezists, to Lucinda's scarcely concealed chagrin.

Lulubelle had never spoken to him, awed by his fame and daunted by his vastness. Marisa, his wife, she had talked to a few times. Marisa was shy and her English was unsteady, but she always had a smile for the children; she and Arto had none of their own. She presided over one of the hamburger stands in the fairground, and twice when Lulubelle had gone there, hungry after her act, and asked Marisa for credit till Lucinda got their pay, Marisa had given her a hot dog free of charge, with plenty of onions. When Lulubelle went back with the money later on, Marisa had waved it away.

Their trailer was the latest and most sophisticated model of mobile home, its solidity testifying both to the bulk of its owner and to his wealth. Lulubelle tapped on the open door cautiously.

'Yes, come, who it is?' It was Marisa's voice.

'Hello, Marisa. It's Lulubelle.'

'Come, child, come, come,' said Marisa encouragingly. 'Arto not here,' she added, seeing Lulubelle peering anxiously round the door. Laughter lurked behind her eyes. Her husband was too big to hide, even in a trailer the size of this one.

Lulubelle came in, and tried to suppress a gasp as she looked round. This home was the last word in luxury. I will live in a place like this when I'm famous, she vowed, if Mum doesn't get us fired first. Gold tassels hung from red plush upholstery on fitted two-seater settees – or maybe to someone the size of Arto the settees were chairs. A crystal chandelier was set in a recess in the ceiling. And the kitchen was a real kitchen, not a little foldaway cooker and sink like theirs.

'Wow,' said Lulubelle reverently.

Marisa laughed. She opened a full-sized fridge and took out a bottle of Pepsi. 'You like drink?'

'Oh, thank you,' said Lulubelle. She accepted the drink as though it were champagne, then remembered her reason for coming here. Marisa watched all the pleasure drain out of her face. It was a pretty face, she considered, but too thin and pinched; old before her time. A child shouldn't look so anxious.

'You... trouble?' she asked hesitantly. 'You sit and tell Marisa, okay?'

'I can't sit,' said Lulubelle. 'That's the trouble. I'm afraid... I need something for my... you know... I just started, you know... I've got one of those pads on but it's three hours now and time's up, isn't it? I mean, I have to change, and I don't have any new ones, and Mum – Lucinda – she hasn't got any money.'

Marisa's expression, which was deeply perplexed throughout this explanation, cleared. 'You need money?' she said, reaching for her bag.

'No,' said Lulubelle. 'I mean, thanks and everything. But Lucinda's gone into town already and I can't get there to buy anything.'

'You want go to town?' Marisa asked.

'No,' said Lulubelle. 'I mean, not unless you're going anyway, but in any case I don't know what to ask for in the shop. I'm sorry,' she said, noticing Marisa's incomprehension. 'I'll leave it, okay? Thanks for the Pepsi.'

'No,' said Marisa firmly. She pushed Lulubelle into a sitting position on the beautiful couch, and Lulubelle sprang up again. 'No!' she said, agitated. 'Blood!'

'Ah!' said Marisa. 'But you so young! You want... what is word?'

'Yes,' said Lulubelle.

'Wait now,' said Marisa. She opened an inner door and went through into the separate bedroom. Lulubelle caught a glimpse of a gold satin bedspread and a thick gold-coloured carpet. This is the way to live, she thought.

Marisa re-emerged with an object that looked like a large white cigar. 'This I use,' she said. 'You understand?'

Lulubelle looked blank.

Marisa unpeeled the wrapper and mimed using the tampon. The horror on Lulubelle's face stopped her. 'You no use this,' she said. 'You too young. I understand. Wait always again.'

This time she went into the en-suite bathroom. Lulubelle thought she saw gold taps, and the carpet was thick as the mane on Simba the lion.

'Here, now,' said Marisa triumphantly. She presented a pack of cotton wool. 'Thanks,' said Lulubelle, embarrassed and relieved equally. She opened the pack and began to tear off a length.

'No, take all,' Marisa said. 'You need change again later.'

'How much later?' Lulubelle asked. 'One hour, two hours?'

'This – one hour,' Marisa advised. She stroked Lulubelle's head, which Lulubelle didn't normally like, but she found she didn't mind it on this occasion. 'Poor child,' Marisa said. 'So young. First time – yes? First day today?'

'Yes,' said Lulubelle.

'Where your mother?'

'Gone to town,' Lulubelle said. She thought she'd explained that already. Misunderstanding Marisa's wondering shake of the head, she tried to explain further. 'She likes to see the shops, even if she hasn't the money to buy anything.'

'She not knows you begin periods?' said Marisa.

'Oh yes, she knows,' said Lulubelle. Feeling she was being disloyal, she added hastily, 'She'll buy me some things tomorrow, a whole packet, as soon as we get paid; she said she would.'

Marisa pressed four one-pound coins into Lulubelle's hand, catching it firmly as she tried to draw it away. 'You take,' she said, 'for yourself. From Marisa. Secret. We tell nobody; nobody angry. Okay?'

'Won't Arto be angry, if you give money away to people?' asked Lulubelle.

'Arto no angry,' said Marisa confidently. 'No never angry man.'

Lulubelle was impressed. 'I thought all men got angry.'

Marisa looked sad. 'Poor child,' she said again.

A bell was being sounded from the Big Top, a signal that all the equipment was installed and rehearsals would soon begin. Lulubelle moved towards the door.

'First change,' Marisa invited. 'In bathroom.'

'Oh no,' said Lulubelle, scandalized at the idea. Supposing she dripped blood on that beautiful carpet! 'I'll go home now.' She put out her hand to shake Marisa's. 'Thanks for everything.'

Marisa enveloped her warmly in a hug. 'Come again,' she said. 'All the time, yes?'

Lulubelle smiled at her, and found the smile was still on her face when she reached their own caravan, walking with her normal easy stride. She no longer felt uncomfortable or ashamed. She clutched Marisa's gift as though it were something valuable, something more than a whole new roll of clean white cotton wool that had come from the most beautiful caravan in the world.

Chapter Twenty-three

Eldred was terrified. The coach taking the children to the nuclear power station had stopped at the motorway services, and there was an adventure playground there. All the children were pleading to be allowed to spend time there. Eldred was silently, mentally pleading for the request to be refused so that not one minute would be wasted. He focused his attention on Mr Johnson, teacher of the top form, and willed him to recognize that half an hour spent playing would mean half an hour less to spend at the power station, learning about nuclear energy.

Mr Johnson looked at his watch. 'Ten minutes,' he conceded, 'then everybody back on the coach. And those who haven't been to the toilet yet, go now.'

Eldred trailed around while the other children played. Impatience gnawed away at his soul. He clenched and unclenched his hands, feverish with anxiety. What if there was a traffic jam on the motorway? What if they arrived at the nuclear power station and were turned away because they were too late?

He didn't want to be like this, and didn't understand why he was. He saw children several years older than himself happily hanging upside down from the climbing frame, scratching their armpits and making monkey noises, and wished he could be like them.

He was certain they didn't lie awake at nights worrying about what would happen if the presently available sources of power ran out, or if there were no more monkeys and no more jungles and no more leafy canopies to freshen the world's air. They thought about these things when they were taught about them in class, but they remained no more than interesting ideas. Other children, Eldred reflected, didn't seem to experience the terrible weight of responsibility that he felt about the world. It didn't occupy all their waking thoughts and their dreams and prevent them from playing and enjoying life. He wondered, not for the first time, if there was something wrong with him.

Back on the coach, with the other children alternately grumbling about having to leave the playground and boasting about the athletic feats they could have achieved if they had had only five more minutes on the top bar, Eldred felt relieved. His relief lasted twenty minutes, then questions started crowding into his mind, questions he would not be allowed to ask. Mrs Garcia was not supervising this trip, but she had threatened him that she would find out from Mr Johnson and Mr Singh if Eldred drew any attention to himself, and he would be banned from going on any more school trips... 'ever', she said.

While the older children threw hails of crisps at one another, fought to prise the personal stereo headphones from each other's ears, and stamped on each other's sandwiches, all unchecked, Eldred plotted his tactics.

Quietly, he rose from his seat and went to sit beside a child who was by himself. After a few minutes' casual exchange of words, he got up again and moved to an unoccupied seat beside another child. When he had done this several times, he returned to his own place and waited.

At the last stopping place before they reached the power station complex, Mr Singh called for everyone's attention. 'As we told you in the briefing session before this trip,' he said, 'there will be an opportunity for you to ask questions of the staff, but past experience has shown us that you children can waste the whole of a trip asking lots of rather foolish questions about things that have already been answered in the talk, if only you were listening. So, as we explained to you, I am going to make a list of the main points you want to know, so that the power station representative can include these in the talk and not be bombarded with individual questions from you which would take up the time needed on the tour.'

A boy put his hand up. 'How will we know what to ask about when we haven't seen anything yet?'

'You have been learning in class about nuclear power for four weeks now,' said Mr Singh, 'and I hope you've been thinking about it, Garth, enough to give you some idea of what you still need to know.'

One of Eldred's classmates raised her hand. 'We haven't been learning about it,' she said.

'I meant the top form pupils,' said Mr Singh. 'You little ones haven't, no. You will do, later on, so just observe for today. I can answer your more basic questions myself this evening, at the hostel, so don't waste time with them while we're at the power station.'

Eldred drew a deep breath. He scanned the faces and backs of heads of the top form children he had spoken to earlier. Had he been successful in implanting in their minds his own curiosity and the questions he so burningly wanted to ask? The children had not been able to answer them. Now they had heard them, would they want those questions answered? Would they present them as their own desire to learn?

One after another, the children raised their hands and asked their questions. Other children did the same. Some of the questions were foolish ('Will we see any nuclear bombs going off?' 'Are there any spaceships there?'), others were simple enough to be answered on the spot, and others got written down on the list. Eldred sat back and relaxed.

'Will we be issued with radiation suits while we're there?' asked a red-haired boy who had spent ten minutes in conversation with Eldred. 'And will we get to see the reprocessing plant?'

'There's no need for suits,' said Mr Singh, still scribbling down the last question designed by Eldred and delivered by a solemn girl in a skirt two sizes too big, to allow for growth. 'We won't be going into any of the actual areas where the work is going on.'

There were roars of disappointment. Eldred felt his heart sink to the very depths of his being. Tears filled his eyes. He dug his fingernails hard into the palms of his hands. He wanted to scream and yell, to beat his breast till it bled, to lie down and die. He sat, white-faced and mute, while the others protested.

'What are we going to see, then?' shouted a boy in the seat behind Eldred. 'We could have stayed at the adventure playground.'

Mr Singh grew flustered. Mr Johnson stood up beside him and flapped his hands and shushed, for moral support.

'We're going to visit the information centre,' shouted Mr Singh above the noise. 'We will have a talk which is very interesting and you can ask questions, and there will be a presentation and a fascinating exhibition for you to walk round, and then we will have a coach tour around the site. I assure you that it is very enjoyable and informative.'

The children quietened down, some mollified by these promises and some dissatisfied. 'What a con,' grumbled the boy behind Eldred. 'Better than being at school, though, eh?' said his friend, and the boy agreed. 'S'pose so.'

Only Eldred remained filled with black despair. He wished he had never come on this trip. He wished he had never been born into this world, where the promise of fresh experience and learning always, inevitably, turned into a sour denial of his deep need to know. He felt like one of the starving children he had seen on the News, dying for lack of nourishment that would take away the pain, waiting for a relief plane that was always reported to be arriving and never came.

At the same time, he felt ashamed. Wasn't he fortunate, compared with those wide-eyed, despairing waifs, to be healthy and well-fed, educated and cared for with average competence? He had no right to feel the way he did.

He turned his head to the window and wept.

Chapter Twenty-four

In spite of his disappointment, Eldred felt his spirits lift when the coach entered the power station complex. He had a sense of being on hallowed ground: the premises of technology and science, one of the power hubs of the universe. Even if he was not to be allowed near the holy of holies, surely he would derive some benefit just from sharing the same air with real scientists?

There was so much he wanted to know. If only he could swallow a capsule of knowledge! The processes of acquiring it seemed painfully slow.

Inside the Information Centre, the talk did nothing to encourage him. The presentations were sophisticated, the displays interesting, the computer simulations cleverly devised but, grieved Eldred, it was all fun. He wanted the real thing. As the group was herded out of the Centre again and on to a bus for a tour of the site, Eldred slipped to the end of the queue.

A group of fifteen year olds had assembled, waiting for a separate tour which would include a visit to areas of the plant and a talk on nuclear waste disposal. Eldred hovered. He held back from the queue. He would never be allowed to go on school trips again, he knew, if he joined this other group now and separated himself from his own school, but it might just be worth it. He was sorely tempted.

The fifteen year olds' queue moved forward. Eldred moved with it. Just as the last of his own group disappeared out of the door, the girl in front of him turned and saw him. 'Oh look!' she cried in a loud and carrying voice. 'One of those little kids has got lost!' Everyone turned round and stared at Eldred. Eldred hated her.

Mr Singh's hand grasped him firmly by the back of the neck. 'Come along,' he said. 'We can't have anybody getting lost.' The teenagers laughed as Eldred was led out.

There was only one ruse left to him, and he used it. 'I have to go to the toilet,' he told Mr Singh. 'Urgently.'

'All right,' said Mr Singh, resigned. 'But be quick. The driver is ready to leave.'

Eldred headed towards the toilets, then, checking that Mr Singh had gone outside, made for the main information desk. He hoped he wasn't trembling too visibly. 'Excuse me,' he said to the uniformed lady.

She gave him a professional 'I'm good with children' smile. 'Yes?'

'I have an elder brother who's sixteen,' Eldred gasped. 'Can I take some information home for him?'

She frowned. 'Sorry? Say that again?'

The words had come out jumbled; he knew it. He repeated his request. The woman looked at him. The child was white in the face with a line of sweat beading his upper lip, his hands clenched and his voice quavering. 'Are you feeling all right?' she asked.

Eldred looked over his shoulder. He grew desperate. 'Please,' he said, 'I need some information for sixteen year olds. My brother. Please give it to me.'

The woman paused for what seemed to Eldred like ages. Finally she said, 'You want an information pack for over-twelves?'

'Yes. Or older if you have it. Even one for scientists,' Eldred said. 'He's very bright. My brother, that is.'

'Sure,' the woman said. She drew out an information pack and began to take the documents out of it. 'Now, this is the basic summary here of what a power station does,' she began.

'I can't wait,' Eldred said. 'My bus is about to go. I'm sorry. Thanks. Thanks very much.' He snatched the folder and the documents from the desk. The woman raised her eyebrows. 'Sorry,' he said again, stuffing the papers under his coat. 'Sorry, sorry. Thanks.' He ran out of the door and jumped on the bus. Choosing a seat by himself, he folded the documents into small squares and put them into the various pockets in his clothes. Only then did he relax.

He was surprised to find he enjoyed the rest of the tour. Even the sight of the teenage group going into the plant itself failed to make him miserable. They probably wouldn't be allowed to see very much either, he consoled himself. They would probably only be humoured with a few basic facts and theories, only slightly more advanced than those offered to the under-twelves. But Eldred had some information now. It was a start. It would help him to know what questions to ask in order to know more. He could write to the authorities, using his computer so they would not know from his handwriting that he was a child, requesting reports. Surely if the authorities were so keen for people to understand nuclear power that they organized school tours, there would be no limit to the information they would provide to someone who was really interested?

Reassured of his chances of being treated like an adult, at least by post, Eldred relaxed and began to behave like a child. He enjoyed the tour, talked to the other children during and after it, happily boarded their own coach leaving the power station, cheerfully disembarked at their overnight accommodation and fought good-naturedly with his room-mates over the choice of beds, ate sausage and chips for tea, and cheered along with the rest when they were allowed to make a visit to a local shop to buy ice-creams and sweets.

That night, he slept well, better than he had slept for a long while. The boy in the bed next to him snored and snuffled and talked in his sleep. Eldred was consoled by the proximity of other children. There were times when it was good to be a child, he thought as he fell asleep.

Chapter Twenty-five

He always felt sick after operations, with a taste of burnt plastic in his mouth from the anaesthetic and a sore throat from the breathing tube they used. Turning his head slightly, he noticed he was on a drip. It seemed to take him longer to recover from each operation, and the period of depression afterwards seemed to get longer too, though he always tried hard not to let it show.

'What a brave boy!' everyone said. 'Always smiling; never lets it get him down.' He was, they agreed, an example to them all.

When people asked Keith's mother how she managed to keep going, looking after him, she said that if Keith could be so happy, with all that he had to go through, then surely she could cope too. If he'd been the depressive type, she'd probably have gone to pieces. But there: some people had a naturally happy personality and whatever troubles they had, life just didn't get on top of them.

Knowing that his mother could only cope with him because he seemed to be coping for her too was a heavy responsibility. He could see how hard she worked and how tired she often became. He was lightweight, but awkward to lift because his body was twisted and rigid and didn't yield, and because it caused him pain to be handled clumsily.

Several of the operations had been for the sake of his carriers, to make his stiff limbs bend so it was easier for them to take him to the toilet, or so that his wheelchair required fewer adaptations to accommodate his oddly shaped body.

Keith was angry about that, though he tried not to be. There seemed something wrong with a world that decided to redesign a human being to fit a bathroom or a wheelchair, or even another person's convenience. Always, he was told it was for his benefit. He had gone along with it, smiling, ever smiling, but now he could feel the anger he had suppressed over the years beginning to rouse itself, like a sleeping lion.

He tried to reach the bedside locker to pick up his Bible, but couldn't manage it. He needed something to distract his mind. Lately, he'd been reading the book of Daniel, over and over again. He liked all the prophets: Elijah and Elisha, Ezekiel, Judith, Jonah, Isaiah and Jeremiah – probably Isaiah most of all, with his brilliant portraits of the archetypal human being, the suffering servant whom everyone rejected and overlooked but who, in silent love, shouldered everyone's troubles without them realizing and took on himself all the consequences of their sins, their compromises and hypocrisies and refusals to listen.

But just recently he'd felt he had most in common with Daniel, who had survived not only being thrown into the blazing furnace and the lions' den – not uncommon punishments in those days for the dangerous offence of speaking truths no one wanted to hear – but who had also stood up for a woman who was wrongly accused, and used his gift for interpreting dreams and supernatural phenomena with meticulous truthfulness, even to the extent of telling the king that God was warning him to change from greed to humility.

A night in a pit full of hungry lions was only one incident in the life of this particular 'suffering servant', this man of courage that Keith so much wanted to be. And God knows, he tried.

But now he needed Daniel with him, Daniel who understood lions, for there was this lion within him and however hard he struggled with it, like Jacob wrestling with the angel all night, the lion was getting stronger all the time and one day soon, Keith felt, it was going to get out. Then, with a ferocious roar, the lion – whose name was Anger – would throw itself on all the good, loving, anxious people who surrounded him and whose whole lives revolved around doing what was good for him, and would devour them.

Daniel had known the lions didn't want to eat him, because lions too were creatures of God. But lions who had been tormented, used for sport and trained to be vicious with criminals of all sorts, and who had been starved for days and nights, could be driven to override their divine command not to harm the innocent and could perceive any creature as food. That they didn't turn on each other was only because – as Daniel knew – each animal had a strong sense of who it was, and the King of the Jungle does not comply with even another lion's demand to become its food supply.

Daniel had known, more strongly than the lions, who he was, and his faith in himself as a 'son of man', made in the image and likeness of God, had convinced those hungry beasts of prey not to regard him as food.

And Keith only had to ask now and Daniel would come and give him a hand to remember who he was – the brave and loving child of a caring and well-meaning family – and not let the beast of Anger attack their frail hopes and their fond delusions, leaving them hurt and confused and unable to cope.

His only prayer nowadays was that he would die before the lion caught up with him and destroyed all their lives.

He must have slept, because he opened his eyes to find his mother leaning over him, bearing a large bunch of flowers and a handful of envelopes.

'How are you, my darling? Does the leg hurt?'

'It's not bad. How are you, Mum?'

'Oh, bless you, my love, always thinking of others. I'm all right; you're the one we've all been worrying about. Look, all your schoolfriends have written and sent you cards.'

'That's nice.'

She would have been to the school, Keith thought, and asked his class tutor to give the class time to sign and scribble messages on the pile of cards she had brought in for them. Each envelope bore his name in a different handwriting. He could tell without opening them which of his classmates had addressed which one. The messages would be unvarying: 'We miss you'; 'Get well soon'. But they were used to missing him by now, and when he got back to school his place would be taken by an ordinary desk, which would have to be moved. There had been no point in keeping vacant a prime position – near the door, with an easy view of the board – for a boy who was hardly ever there.

By the time he came back, he would have missed so much work that he would hardly be part of the class, at any rate. The teacher would come and lean over him, explaining in whispers what he would need to read, while the class was set some work. And he would try to concentrate on reading up on the subject, while the teacher was leading the class in a noisy discussion, with everyone waving their hands and shouting out answers to questions, and he could take no part in the debate because he hadn't yet found out about what they were debating.

'Want me to prop you up so you can open them?' Keith's mother offered.

'No, thanks.' If he moved, he would be sick. Seeing her face drop, he said, 'I can look at them later on. I'd rather talk to you now.'

It wasn't too hard to make her smile. How could he refuse her anything, when she was so transparently eager to do things for him and so easily transformed from sadness to contentment?

She sat on the edge of his bed now, ready to chat. He wished he felt more alert, less nauseous.

'How's everyone at home?' he said.

'Oh, fine. Andrew's out with his girlfriend again.' She laughed.

'Jessica?'

'Yes. They live in each other's pockets now. It's so sweet. We mustn't tease him, though. He's very solemn about it.'

Keith tried to move his neck, which had cricked.

'Are you uncomfy, love?'

'No. Go on. Is he seeing her often, then?'

'Every evening after school. He doesn't come home any more; he goes straight to her place.'

Keith must have somehow missed this. After school, he either had physiotherapy or was put to bed to rest at home. He hadn't heard Andrew around the house recently, it was true, but then he rarely did. His mother didn't let anyone make a noise during Keith's rest times.

'Don't her parents mind Andrew being there every day?' he asked.

'Parent. Her mother died last year. Her father's usually out at work. She cooks the tea for him when he comes home. Andrew's been helping her.'

'Helping her cook?'

'And with the housework apparently. Her father got talking to Grandad in the newsagent's last week; they were both in there early one morning when Andrew brought back his bag from the paper round.'

'He's been doing a lot,' said Keith. And coming in to see me, he thought, and remembering to stop off and buy me the crisps I like. His little brother was growing into a responsible and capable man. He would need to be, to support his parents through their bereavement. Keith didn't envy him that responsibility. But maybe Andrew had more courage than Keith. Keith hadn't even been able to speak up for himself about this operation, for fear of unpopularity.

He breathed deeply, but that set off a fit of coughing. His mother was immediately anxious, reaching for the bell to summon a nurse.

'I'm all right,' he said, wheezing.

'Is your chest bad, Keith?'

'It's only the anaesthetic. It's always like that,' he reassured her.

'It was never that bad before.' She was hunched up, her hands gripped together between her knees, white across the knuckles. She had been like this all his life, listening to every breath, watching every move. He wondered if she'd relax once he'd gone, if in some respects she'd find it a relief not to have to worry about him, or if the worry had become a habit and even a security and she'd look for other things to be terrified of once there was no longer any risk of his death.

'Mum,' he said, 'there's something I want to say to you.'

'Of course, sweetie-pie. What is it? Do you want some more Lucozade brought in?'

'No. No, thanks.'

'Oh look,' she said, 'here's Grandad.'

'Just before he comes,' said Keith urgently. 'Please, listen to me.'

'I'm listening. What is it?'

He had to be quick; it had to be said, and it had to be said by him because she would only accept it from him; whenever the family doctor had suggested it, over the years, she wouldn't listen to any hint of it. And it had to be now, or else he would lose his nerve.

There was no time for tact. 'Mum,' he said earnestly, fixing his eyes on hers, 'this operation is my last one. There aren't going to be any more.'

Too late, he realized the interpretation she would put on it – not that he'd made a decision for himself, but that he had some premonition he would die before the next stage of surgery could be arranged.

Tears filled her eyes and overflowed. Grandad, arriving with sweets and comics, shot a concerned glance from her face to Keith's.

'Something wrong?'

'No, no!' she said, springing up and giving him a brief hug, then pushing him away from her in Keith's direction. 'Everything's fine. Doesn't he look well after his operation, Grandad?'

Keith had tried his best to hold it in. But now, turning his head, he was very sick.

Chapter Twenty-six

'Can I go to the library?' Eldred asked, coming in through the kitchen door and dropping his overnight case on the floor.

'Hello Mum, how are you, I had a nice school trip, thank you,' Mildred prompted him.

'Yes, yes,' Eldred agreed. 'Can I?'

Mildred sighed. 'I suppose so. Don't be late for tea.'

Eldred found Terry Smith using the microfiche reader in the reference library. He waved the package of information on nuclear power under Terry's nose. 'I need to know where I can get hold of the actual reports on these topics,' he said. 'I've got a list here I made on the coach.'

Terry took the list. 'Fuel reprocessing,' he said. 'There's no shortage of reports on that at the moment; it's a political minefield. That's what you're getting into here, Eldred: politics. Science doesn't operate in isolation, you know.'

'I only want the facts,' said Eldred anxiously.

'The facts?' said Terry. 'Or the truth?'

'Aren't they the same thing?' said Eldred.

Terry pushed his chair back and stood up. 'Let me show you something. I've taken a bit of an interest in this myself.'

Eldred followed him to the main enquiry desk, where Terry retrieved a folder, then followed him to the computer terminal in the back office. 'Am I allowed in here?' he asked.

'No,' Terry said. 'Come and look at this.' He selected the scroll bar and ran through documents on the screen. 'Official report on the value of nuclear fuel reprocessing, with particular emphasis on re-using uranium – right?'

'Can I read that?' asked Eldred, as Terry banished it from the screen.

'In a minute,' said Terry. Eldred could tell he was enjoying himself. 'Now look at this: official report by a leading environmentalists' group on the dangers of reprocessing nuclear fuel, including a claim that reprocessed uranium is of minimal value and that recycling actually generates more toxic waste than if the material was simply disposed of – okay?'

Eldred nodded. He wanted to read the documents for himself but he could see that, as was so often the case with adults, Terry wanted

Eldred to receive his personal opinion before being given the facts to judge for himself.

'And here,' said Terry, rolling the screen again, 'are newspaper reports on the fierce debate between major industrial organizations – see? European and Japanese companies, mainly. Some say they are being forced to accept useless recycled fuel in return for using British reprocessing facilities; others say they welcome the arrangement and the fuel is valuable.'

'So who is right?' asked Eldred.

'Oh, *right*,' said Terry. 'Everyone is right. It all depends on their point of view and their criteria. The same product can be useful to one group and rubbish to another. Or perhaps it's useful because of political reasons, rather than industrial ones. Perhaps the receiving country needs its population to believe its industrialists are being ecologically responsible by taking part in recycling rather than dumping – even if, in practice, recycling results in more waste being dumped and a worse hazard to public health.'

'But the brochures I have here,' Eldred said, 'say there are stringent checks to ensure that nuclear fuel doesn't pose any risk to health.'

'So they say,' Terry agreed. 'And some medical experts have said the same thing. Others have said just the opposite: that there are significantly higher rates of serious disease among people living in the vicinity of nuclear power stations or in coastal regions affected by the power stations' outflow, and that it can't be sheer coincidence.'

'But if they keep within the prescribed safe levels, how can it be harmful?' Eldred enquired.

'Whose prescribed safe levels?' Terry countered. 'There are people who say that any level of radiation, over and above what's found naturally in the environment, is unsafe. Others say you could safely double the present rates of liquid and gaseous discharge, without causing any damage to people's health or to the planet. Take your pick.'

'If you only asked the real experts...' Eldred began.

'They're all experts,' Terry said. 'In their own opinions, anyway.

You can have as many theories as you have experts, Eldred. And even when a theory is proved to be true and backed up with genuine scientific evidence, there's nothing to prevent other scientists – or even the same ones, a few years later – from proving the exact opposite and backing up their findings with impeccable evidence.'

'So how does anyone arrive at the truth?' Eldred asked.

Terry shrugged. 'Lucky dip,' he said. 'Whichever theory you like the sound of, you can always find some professional to prove it for you.'

'And some other professional to disprove it?' Eldred said.

'Exactly,' Terry said.

'Does that mean all the theories are true, then?' said Eldred. 'Or are there different kinds of truth?'

'I suppose there can only be one truth,' Terry said. 'Maybe just a million ways of looking at it.'

'But are all the ways of looking at it true, or can only one of them be true?' Eldred pursued.

'Now that,' Terry said, 'is a question that has kept philosophers busy since Moses was a boy, and I doubt you're going to be the one to solve it, Eldred. Mind you,' he added, ruffling Eldred's hair, 'I could be wrong about that.'

'I have to go home now,' Eldred said. 'Can I read those reports first?'

'Sure,' Terry said. 'Give me a shout when you've finished.'

Eldred rolled the documents across the screen, reading quickly. Within a few minutes, he was back at the enquiry desk.

'Can't find something?' said Terry.

'No,' said Eldred. 'I've finished. Thanks for your help, Terry. See you.'

Terry pursed his lips into a silent whistle. As Eldred reached the door of the reference section, Terry called him back. 'Eldred,' he said.

'Yes?'

Terry beckoned him close and said in a near-whisper, 'You won't forget what I said about the truth being more than mere facts, will you?'

'No,' said Eldred. 'Why?'

'The truth about a person, for instance,' said Terry, still in the same low voice. 'I mean, you could know facts about them but even if those facts are true, the person is sure to be more than the sum total of those facts, if you know what I mean?'

'I don't think I do,' Eldred admitted.

'Keep it in mind,' said Terry. 'It might make more sense to you later on, okay?'

'Okay,' Eldred agreed. He would have to run home now. If he was late for tea, his mother would be annoyed and might curtail his solitary trips to the library.

As he left the building, two uniformed police officers were walking up the steps. Eldred wondered briefly what they wanted. A library seemed the last place anyone would expect to find disturbances of the peace.

Chapter Twenty-seven

Louise Palmer was at the house when Eldred returned. Mildred was annoyed with her, Eldred could tell, for arriving at teatime. Eldred was delighted to see Louise.

'Good news, Eldred,' she said immediately.

'What?' Eldred asked.

'Don't say "what", Eldred,' said his mother. 'You say "pardon".'

'I meant, "What's the good news?"' said Eldred patiently.

'Wash your hands,' said Mildred. 'Before your tea,' she added pointedly, looking at Louise.

'I won't keep you long,' Louise promised.

Eldred seethed. What did it matter what time they had tea? Who would want to eat mince and mash when they could talk to Louise?

'I'll have my tea later,' he told Mildred, rinsing his hands perfunctorily at the kitchen sink. 'You and Dad have yours, and I'll talk to Louise.'

Mildred's lips tightened. 'You'll do as you're told,' she said. 'Tea won't be ready yet for ten minutes anyhow.'

Eldred knew she was lying. Tea was always ready at six o'clock on the dot. If the plates were put on the table at five past six, his father would say, 'Running late today, Mother?' and if it was five to six Edgar would say, 'Early tea, Mother? What's the rush?'

The News was always on at teatime, but nobody was supposed to let on that they were watching it, because Mildred insisted that eating meals in front of the telly caused the destruction of family life and values. So although the television was left on, Mildred and Edgar only gave it surreptitious sideways glances when the news item changed, and Eldred, whose chair faced the window, was scolded every time he turned round to look at the screen. 'Concentrate on your meal,' Mildred would say, though a second later, when Eldred had something to say, she would make faces at him to keep quiet because Edgar was listening to something the newscaster was saying.

So Eldred knew that Louise Palmer had walked into a minefield by calling on the Joneses at teatime and that the tension would build until the moment she left. Louise, presumably coming from a family where the mealtime routine was not so fixed, seemed unaware that she only had ten minutes in which to say all the important things, and was making small talk to Mildred. Eldred's hands clenched and unclenched.

As soon as Louise paused for breath, Eldred said, 'What's the good news?' and she smiled.

'Two lots of good news,' she said. 'First, the *Telegraph* bought my article about you, Eldred, and second, I've brought the registration forms from the Patents Office. I'll give you a hand filling them in.'

'Eldred's father can do that for him,' said Mildred quickly. Edgar cleared his throat and looked out of the window.

'Oh,' said Louise, 'I'm sure, but there is a specific procedure for applying for a patent and it helps to know what they're looking for. For example, you must be able to detail exactly what advantages this piece of equipment has over others already on the market.'

'We can sort all that out,' Edgar said.

Eldred was watching Louise's face. 'What do you think I ought to put?' he asked.

'Well, as far as I've been able to ascertain,' Louise said, 'the most remarkable aspect of your machine, Eldred, is the speed at which it converts the waste matter to usable material. The current models are much slower.'

'But I can't say for sure how long it takes,' said Eldred anxiously. 'I haven't talked to Bruce Mackeson about making the prototype. Don't you have to have a working model or something, to get the patent?'

'No, just a detailed description and diagrams,' Louise reassured him. 'Don't worry, Eldred. Just an estimate of the time will do fine. You know roughly how long the process takes, don't you?'

'Between thirty-six and forty-eight hours for the domestic model,' said Eldred, 'but longer for the industrial one, of course. As long as a week perhaps.'

'That's still quick,' Louise said. She smiled at Edgar and Mildred, who were looking bemused. 'You must be very proud of him,' she said.

Edgar cleared his throat again. 'What exactly does this machine do, Eldred?'

Eldred was reading the forms and didn't hear him. Louise, sensing the tension in the room now, handed Edgar a few sheets of typescript. 'A copy of my article on Eldred,' she said. 'I thought you might like to read it before it's published.'

'I'll read it after tea,' Edgar said. 'The time's getting on a bit.'

'Would you like me to leave all this with you and come back another time?' Louise suggested.

'That would be best,' said Mildred. 'We're about to have tea, you see.'

'What does it matter,' said Eldred, without raising his head from the Patents Office application, 'what time we have tea? You and Dad can have yours while Louise and I do this.'

Edgar grew red in the face. He shot a furious glance at Mildred, who said, 'Eldred, go to your room. I'm not going to tell you off in front of visitors, but you know well enough not to speak to your dad like that.'

Eldred looked up in alarm. 'What did I say?' he asked.

'That's enough, Eldred,' said Mildred. 'Just go.'

Eldred gathered up the forms and prepared to leave the room.

'You can leave that stuff here,' said Edgar. 'I'll deal with it later on for you.'

Eldred's eyes were full of tears.

'I can see I've inconvenienced you, Mr Jones,' said Louise. 'I didn't mean to intrude. May I call back for the forms another day? Tomorrow, at whatever time suits you?'

'The weekend is best,' said Edgar gruffly. 'Weekday evenings are inconvenient for us. We're working people.'

Eldred had so much to say that he couldn't say anything, not even "goodbye" to Louise. In his room later on that evening, Mildred found him sitting at his desk staring at the blank computer screen.

'There's no need for sulking,' she said. 'It's all forgiven and forgotten now, Eldred. I've kept your tea for you. Come and have it in the kitchen.'

Chapter Twenty-eight

Lulubelle hadn't intended to end up in the lions' den.

The day had seemed to get better, after she'd seen Marisa. The sky, which had been overcast all day, threatening rain, cleared. And the rehearsal had gone quite well.

She was a bit worried, when she started. They rehearsed in the order of the performance, and as she was so young and was always billed for the first half of the show, she was always called for the early shift of rehearsals. Lulubelle usually had no trouble arriving on time, but she had been trying to find herself another costume; she was afraid to wear white, in case Marisa's cotton wool provided inadequate protection.

So the first thing that went wrong was that she arrived slightly late, and out of breath, and the second was that Mr Mannfield remarked on her wearing a plain black leotard under her white tutu skirt, instead of her usual spangled white one. She could have said the white one was in the wash, but that would have landed either her mother or Emma, the wardrobe lady, in trouble.

Artistes were responsible for their own costumes, but Emma was in charge of making sure they were all assembled in the changing booth on time, and in practice she often helped out with washing and ironing or organizing dry cleaning, especially for performers like Lucinda who were liable to turn up in grubby costumes and laddered tights. When that happened, it was Emma who got into trouble with Mr Mannfield, as well as Lucinda, so it was in her interests to do Lucinda's laundry herself, and required less strain on her patience, in the long run, than chasing her with reminders to check in her clean costume before the performance.

Lulubelle thought it was safer to say it was torn, and luckily Mr Mannfield didn't pursue the issue. It didn't save her worrying about next time, because surely no one could tear a white costume once a month, regularly as clockwork, and take four or five days to repair it. She would have to ask Lucinda to explain that Lulubelle had changed her image and would appear in black or red from now on. Mr Mannfield wouldn't be keen; he had said before that he liked white on his young girl performers because it looked 'both glamorous and virginal', though in fact, Lulubelle reflected, she hadn't been entitled to look virginal, technically, since she was nine.

But still, the rehearsal went well. Her fears that this new burden of womanhood might impede her skill were unfounded. She was slightly distracted at first, worried in case the cotton wool might slip during her more ambitious routines, but once she got past the warm-up exercises and the simpler part of her act, she regained her normal total concentration. Even her new routine, walking up a plank on her hands, with her knees bent outwards over her ears and her toes tucked under her chin, went better than ever and drew a spontaneous cheer from the site build-up men who were fixing the last of the tiers of seats.

She thought she saw someone she recognized among them, and froze for an instant, but she was upside down at the time and couldn't be sure, and when she flipped upright and looked again in that direction, whoever it was had gone.

So it couldn't really have been that that unsettled her; it was more likely to have been the moment when Lulubelle, back in her normal leggings and sweatshirt top, returned to the Big Top to watch Lucinda rehearsing and found only Juan and Pedro on the trapezes.

'Where is she?' they shouted, as soon as Lulubelle came in.

Lulubelle's heart stopped.

'I'll get her,' she promised. In her haste to run to the caravan, she tripped over a guy-rope, fell, and cursed herself. Starting to run again almost before she was up, she nearly bumped into Molly.

'Where is she?' Lulubelle gasped. 'She's late for rehearsals.'

'I don't know, and I couldn't care less,' said Molly.

Lulubelle stared at her. 'Didn't she come back from town with you?'

'She came back with Sam,' said Molly, 'and I was there too but I may as well not have been, for all either of them noticed.'

Lulubelle kept running. Taking the steps in one leap, she pushed open the door of the caravan and found Lucinda on the pulled-down bunk bed, with Sam, half-dressed.

'You'll get us sacked again!' Lulubelle yelled. 'They're all waiting for you! Where's your costume?'

'Get the fuck out of here,' growled Sam.

Lucinda pushed him aside, laughing. 'It's only my minder; you mustn't mind!'

Lulubelle stood in front of her. 'You're drunk,' she said, 'aren't you?' Her voice was flat. This was it, she thought, or if not this evening then another evening soon. And she didn't want to have to leave Mannfield's. 'Please,' she said. 'Please, Mum... Lucinda,' she amended, seeing Lucinda pouting. 'Please get up.'

'She's staying here,' said Sam. 'In the warm. She's got a bit of a cold, haven't you, Luce?'

'You don't have to rehearse!' Lulubelle flared at him. 'If you don't get your rides started on time, it's only your own money you lose out on. We could lose our jobs.'

Sam got up, pulling his clothing together, and advanced towards her. Lucinda, behind him, held him back. 'Leave her alone. All right, Lulubelle, go on and get my costume. I'll follow you. I promise,' she affirmed, as Lulubelle still hesitated, though Sam was towering over her threateningly.

So she ran ahead to the costume tent where Emma, too, was annoyed, because Lucinda had upset her schedule of changing times for the artistes – not that Lucinda demanded one of the tiny booths; she had no objection to changing in full view of anyone who walked in or out, but she got in Emma's way when she did that, and it was unprofessional.

Emma, before her little problem developed into a more significant one, had been a wardrobe lady in Covent Garden, and never liked anyone to forget it. She knew how things should be done, she said, and even when she'd just been paid and had sniffed too much of the powder Lulubelle used to think was a different type of resin for the acrobats' shoes, she expected her own part in the evening's schedule to run like clockwork – and it usually did.

Lulubelle managed to pacify her till Lucinda arrived.

'Drunk,' said Emma, after one expert glance.

'Stoned,' Lucinda retaliated. Lulubelle pushed her into a booth and pulled Lucinda's dress up over her head. Emma, offended but ever-professional, helped her into her spangled tights and feathered, bejewelled costume while Lulubelle held her steady.

'You doing tightrope tonight?' Emma asked her.

'No, she isn't,' said Lulubelle firmly. 'You're not,' she told Lucinda. 'I'm telling Mr Mannfield you're not up to it. Just do the trapeze, all right?'

'One of my migraines, is it?' Lucinda's smile was unpleasant.

'Whatever you like,' Lulubelle said.

'Just not that I've had a few gins and been bonking the owner of the Waltzers, huh?' said Lucinda, with a tinkling laugh.

Lulubelle gritted her teeth. 'Don't talk, then no one will know you're pissed,' she advised.

'Until she flies off her trapeze,' Emma sniffed. 'I wouldn't be risking my job if I was in your place, Lucinda. There's not much call for trapezists nowadays.'

'What would you know about it?' challenged Lucinda.

Lulubelle pushed her towards the tarpaulin tunnel leading into the artistes' entrance to the Big Top. 'Shut up,' she said. 'Concentrate.' There wasn't time for Lucinda to get into an argument, especially with someone who knew how to hit her sore spot about how employable she'd be in the future. Drunk or sober, Lucinda wasn't getting any younger, and it was true that trapeze and high wire acts, though as popular as ever, were not easy to stage in the smaller arenas many circuses had resorted to now that circus audiences were smaller, and were often excluded from the repertoire.

Lulubelle had heard every trapeze joke in the book and hated them all; they were too near the truth for her liking.

'Trapeze work is a dying art,' was the worst.

'There's many a slip between grip and... aaargh!' closely followed it.

And, 'Trapeze artists do it with a swing,' made her squirm as well.

She seemed to give in to tears easily these days; she must learn to be less sensitive, Lucinda said. 'It's a tough world out there, honey, and only the tough guys survive it. But we are the tough guys, aren't we?'

Perhaps it was to give herself time to recover her calm, and perhaps it was to avoid having to watch Lucinda brave Mr Mannfield's reprimand first and then face the shaky climb to the high platform to start her rehearsal, that Lulubelle looked around for a quiet dark corner to hide in for a while, and had the bright idea of squeezing through the half-open outer door, made of reinforced steel mesh, and then through the wide bars of the vacant lion cage.

The lion act was part of the second shift of rehearsals, with half of the act before Lucinda's trapeze work and half later on. In between, and for the duration of the circus's stay, the lions were kept in a secure compound adjoining the Big Top. This cage was only their travelling quarters, so from now until a week on Monday it would be unoccupied.

Except that it wasn't. As Lulubelle settled herself on a pile of clean straw in the near corner of the cage, there was a rustling response from the far end. In the gloom she could just see the shadowy bulk of Savage, the youngest lioness, rising slowly from her haunches. She growled under her breath as she stood on the bandaged septic paw that was the cause of her unaccustomed isolation in the travelling cage.

Chapter Twenty-nine

Eldred's class was peacefully huddled on the floor of the video room watching a schools programme on road construction when Eldred started crying and couldn't stop. All Mrs Garcia's questions, commands, threats and, finally, cajoling, could not elicit the reason for his uncharacteristic behaviour.

'For the last time of asking, Eldred, what is wrong?' she said, but Eldred could only sob, 'Everything! Everything's wrong!'

'I'm taking you to the Head,' she decided.

The Head, a kindly if unimaginative man, was concerned. Eldred emitted only muffled sobs while Mrs Garcia explained, but as soon as she left the room he broke down and howled. The Head had never heard a nine year old cry like that; it was the cry of a heartbroken adult who had lost his reason for living. He was shocked. He phoned Mrs Jones and suggested she take Eldred home for the rest of the day.

Mildred was shaken by the request. She arrived at the school looking white and worried.

'Does he usually cry like this?' Mr Vaughan asked her.

'Never,' Mildred said. 'He never cries at all. Did something happen?'

'No,' said Mr Vaughan. 'Not that we know of. The class was watching television.'

On the bus, Mildred sat Eldred in a vacant section and kept her arm round him, shielding him from inquisitive stares. Eldred found it comforting. Neither of his parents normally cuddled him. He had noticed that other parents hugged their children quite often and thought that the fact that his did not might be his own fault. If he had not been in hospital all those years, perhaps they would have learned. It must have been difficult for them, having an infant who lived in an oxygen tent for most of the time, and it was probably too late for them to learn new habits when he went home at the age of five.

At home, Mildred made them both a cup of tea and gave Eldred a chocolate biscuit. Only when he had eaten it, crumb by crumb, between sobs, did she say, 'That's better. Now, tell me what's wrong.'

Eldred's eyes brimmed over again. 'Everything,' he said.

'Was it something you were watching on the television programme?' Mildred asked. She was upset to see Eldred like this. He was always so self-possessed. At the same time, she found him easier now he was crying. She had occasionally wondered if her child was really a child at all, and if he was hers. He seemed so far away from her at times.

'They were digging up all the countryside for roads,' Eldred said. 'Tearing up great chunks of fields and woods. They do it all the time. It's so ugly. There's going to be nothing beautiful left.'

'I know, it's a shame when that happens,' Mildred said, thankful that he was talking about something she could understand. 'But you can't take it all to heart, Eldred, everything that happens in the world. They think it's progress, and that's all there is to it.'

'Everything gets destroyed,' Eldred sobbed. 'Everything good gets mucked about with and wasted, till there's nothing left.'

Mildred wrinkled her brow. 'Is this just about roads, Eldred, or is there something else?'

Eldred put his head down on the table and howled. Mildred moved her chair next to his and took him in her arms, rocking him as she had never rocked him when he was a baby. Finally he lifted his head, blew his nose on the tissue she held out for him, and said, 'Dad's going to put all the wrong things on that form. He doesn't know what he's doing. He won't let Louise tell him.'

'Of course your dad knows what he's doing,' Mildred began, but this caused such a storm of renewed crying from Eldred that she stopped. 'Come and sit over here,' she said. She led Eldred to the sofa and they sat in silence broken only by Eldred's subsiding sobs.

'All right,' she said, when he grew quieter. 'I'm going to talk straight to you now, Eldred – all right? Like a grown up.'

Eldred nodded.

'It's not easy for your dad,' she said, 'having a clever son. You seem to know more and more every day, and we can't keep up. It's not that we're trying to hold you back, love, or that we're not proud of you or anything, but sometimes we don't know what to do for the best, and the school doesn't seem to help much. We know you're bored and there's things you want to learn, but we don't have the knowledge to teach you ourselves and sometimes we can't understand what you're talking about when you try to explain things. I know we must seem very slow to you, Eldred, but that's the way it is.'

'I don't mean to be like that,' Eldred sniffed.

Mildred tightened her arm around him. 'Nobody's blaming you,' she said. 'I'm just worried about you. The world isn't a very kind place, Eldred, and not many people are going to understand you. If you let it be seen that you're too different from the rest, your life isn't going to be easy. On the other hand, it's no good pretending you're average when you're not, is it?'

'No,' Eldred said. 'But there are other children like me, aren't there?'

'There must be,' said Mildred. 'There was that boy who got into university at the age of twelve, wasn't there? But would you like that?'

'No,' said Eldred. 'I don't want to leave school and not have any friends.'

'One thing Louise said,' said Mildred carefully, 'was that you might be better at a different kind of school. Your dad wasn't keen on the idea, but if you want that we can give it a bit more thought. What d'you think?'

Eldred wriggled round to study her face. 'It would be a boarding school,' he said. 'Probably. Wouldn't it?'

'It probably would,' Mildred said.

'Would you mind?' said Eldred anxiously. 'I mean, you haven't had me with you very much, with me being in hospital all that time. And you and Dad tried so long to have a baby, didn't you?'

Tears came into Mildred's eyes. 'Is that what's stopping you?' she said.

'It's one reason,' Eldred said. 'Also, I'd be scared.'

'But would you be happier at a school for clever children?' Mildred asked. 'I mean, you'd be normal there, and there'd be people who could teach you at your own level.'

Eldred stretched out his toes and heaved a deep sigh. 'We'd never be able to afford it,' he said.

'But if we could find the money somehow,' Mildred pursued, 'would you like to go to a place like that?'

'I think I would,' Eldred admitted. 'You'll think I'm being silly, but I don't think I can go on like this.'

Mildred looked at his tear-blotched face. 'No,' she said, 'I don't think you can.'

Chapter Thirty

Mrs Garcia was using Eldred's junior information pack from the power station to give the class a lesson on nuclear energy. The children were half paying attention, more interested in a wasp that had found its way into the classroom.

Mrs Garcia passed one of the booklets round for the children to look at in groups of four. It depicted a little uranium atom with a smiley face which turned anxious at the approach of a whizzing neutron. The neutron split the atom's world apart and created a lot of heat in the process, leaving two hot and sweaty little atoms instead of one complacent one.

Eldred was studying the curves of the wasp's flight path and mentally plotting it in digital form. He would have liked to have his computer to help him do this, but he found that sometimes by imagining himself tapping in the information and pressing the relevant keys, he could visualize the results appearing on the screen. Then when he went home he would repeat the process on the computer to see if the answer he had arrived at was accurate. So far, it always had been.

When he grew tired of this occupation, Eldred mused over what Jilly Martin had told him at breaktime.

'I'm leaving this school, Eldred,' she said. 'I'm being sent to a special one where you can go at your own pace.'

Eldred was interested. 'Do you have to pay to go there?' he asked. 'No,' she said.

He was even more interested. 'Can anyone go? Anyone who needs to go at a different pace from the one in a normal class?'

'I suppose so,' Jilly said, wrinkling her brow. 'But somebody else has to decide for you to go there. A teacher, or your mum and dad. You don't choose it yourself.'

When the last bell rang and the children hurtled towards the cloakrooms, Eldred waited behind for Mrs Garcia.

'Yes, Eldred?' she said, seeing him hovering by the doorway.

'Jilly Martin is leaving to go to a special school,' he said.

'Yes, I know. It's the kindest thing,' said Mrs Garcia. 'She can't cope with the work here. We've all been very understanding, but there are limits after all.'

'I was just wondering,' said Eldred, 'whether I could go there as well?'

She turned and looked at him incredulously. 'What?'

'It's a school where children can learn at their own pace,' Eldred said. 'And there aren't any fees to pay.'

'It's a school for special needs children,' said Mrs Garcia. 'Children who cannot learn at average speed.'

'But I don't learn at average speed,' said Eldred. 'That's why I want to go. Mightn't it be the kindest thing for me too?'

Mrs Garcia put her hand to her mouth and started laughing. Eldred was bewildered.

'Jilly Martin,' said Mrs Garcia, 'is educationally subnormal. Do you know what that means?'

'Slow to learn the kind of things that are taught in school,' Eldred said.

'Slow to learn anything at all,' said Mrs Garcia. 'You are not slow to learn, Eldred, though you do lack common sense.'

Eldred bit his lip.

'Run along home,' Mrs Garcia said, 'before I have to be admitted to a home for teachers who need to be confined to a padded cell.'

Mildred was waiting for Eldred to arrive home. 'I've got some good news for you,' she said, as soon as he came in through the back door.

'That's good,' said Eldred bleakly.

'Don't you want to know what it is?'

'Yes, please.'

'I phoned that Louise Palmer,' said Mildred proudly, 'and I've asked her to come on Sunday while your father's gone out for his drink before lunch.'

'Is she staying for lunch with us?' asked Eldred.

'I didn't ask her,' Mildred said. 'I don't think your dad would be too keen. But she can fill in that patents form with you while your dad's not here. It'll be less trouble all round if we do it that way. All right?'

Eldred looked more cheerful. 'Okay. Will she stay for a while, though?'

'I don't want her staying all day,' Mildred said. 'She'll have to understand that lunch will be on the table as soon as your dad gets back.'

Eldred sighed. 'All right. Can I go down the library, Mum?'

'Half an hour only,' she warned.

'Okay.'

'What are you studying now?' she asked.

'Still nuclear power,' he said. 'Waste reprocessing.'

His mother looked concerned. 'You're not going to start designing machines for recycling nuclear waste now, Eldred, are you?'

'No,' Eldred said.

'Are you sure? We don't want that kind of stuff near the house; it isn't safe, Eldred, and don't let anyone tell you otherwise. Children are dying from it.'

'I couldn't build a machine in the garden for reprocessing nuclear waste,' Eldred said.

'Well, thank goodness for that,' said Mildred. 'I suppose that's one weight off my mind.'

On his way to the library, Eldred amused himself by working out equations at the pace of his footsteps. When he worked out the answer too quickly, he speeded up; when he needed more time he slowed down or took bigger steps, altering the rhythm of his feet to match the rhythm of his brain. His progress down the street looked rather eccentric. Several children pointed at him and laughed, but he didn't notice.

In the Reference section, Eldred approached the assistant. 'Is Terry Smith here?' he asked.

'No, he isn't.'

Eldred was surprised. 'Has he taken a day off?'

The assistant, a lady in her sixties, peered at him closely. 'Are you a friend of his?'

Eldred considered the question. 'Yes,' he said.

'But do you only see him here, in the library?' the woman continued. 'You don't go to his house, do you?'

'No. Why?'

The woman let out a sigh. 'No reason,' she said. 'But he's not here now, I'm afraid.'

'Will he be here tomorrow?'

'I don't think so.' She seemed uncomfortable. 'Can I help you instead?'

Eldred put his head on one side. 'You might be able to,' he said, 'but I don't know. I don't know if Terry was really allowed, or if I was really allowed, you see. I don't want to get him into trouble.'

She looked alarmed. 'What are you talking about? Allowed to do what?'

'Go into the back office,' Eldred said.

Her eyes grew wider. 'To do what?'

'To look at articles on the computer. There were some others on there I'd like to have a look at. If it's not against the rules,' Eldred added.

'Oh, right,' she said, exhaling again. Eldred thought she seemed to be rather a tense individual. 'Well, I don't see any harm in that. Do you know how to call up the articles you want?'

'Yes, thanks. Thank you very much,' he said politely. 'I hope I haven't got Terry into trouble or anything.'

She looked at him with sad eyes and shook her head. 'No,' she said. 'It would take more than that, I'm afraid.'

Eldred tapped keys and rolled pages on the screen, speeding past the articles he had scanned last time; he had no need to re-read them. He just wanted to see if Terry had filed any other documents on the subject that might be of interest to him. He hadn't, but in the process Eldred flicked through articles on fossil classification and different palaeontologists' methods of identifying fragments of bone, and as he read he memorized them. It wasn't something he needed to know about at the present time but, he reflected, you never knew when information might come in handy in the future.

When he had read all he wanted to, he went home. He had spent less than the half-hour Mildred had allowed him in the library, but it wasn't worth starting new research now. Anyway, it was his favourite tea tonight, he remembered happily: sausage, beans and chips.

He walked home at an even, steady pace.

Chapter Thirty-one

Keith was in the lions' den, talking to Daniel. As far as the nurse who had taken him there knew, he was in the toilet, which was the only place Keith found he got any privacy, but mentally he was with Daniel.

'Ring the bell when you need me,' the nurse told him. 'Sure you don't want me to wait?' She had wanted to bring him a bedpan in the ward, or at least a commode, but he had insisted on being taken to the toilet, even though the plaster on his leg made it hard to balance and he had to be put in a harness so he didn't fall off. He refused to let someone stay and hold him.

He needed to be alone, just Daniel and himself and a few hungry lions. They came out of the shadows now. Keith could feel the roar starting in his throat.

'What would you do?' he asked Daniel. 'I don't want to be angry. All my life I've been told God made me like this and I'm special. But all my life they've been trying to improve me. And if I just want some part of me left as it is, they tell me not to do or say anything to upset my mother. I can tell you this, Daniel, and I can't tell anyone else. I'm starting to hate my family.'

He closed his eyes and focused on his friend, standing upright and watchful in the centre of the lions' den. Interesting, that he chose to stand there, Keith mused: not in the corner or clinging to the bars for security. Right in the middle. In charge, like the ringmaster of a circus.

Daniel's eyes were cool, unshockable.

Keith was encouraged to continue. 'Everyone says how wonderful my mother is, Daniel. And at other times, how wonderful I am – how brave, putting up with my disabilities. But it's just life, isn't it? This is my life, and I might as well make the best of it. And this is her life. She could put me in a home or send me away to a special school. But she doesn't. Why doesn't she?'

Daniel shifted his weight slightly. The lions around him were immediately alert. Their eyes were huge, like spotlights trained on this human being whose body language refused to spell 'victim'. He was not afraid of their jaws. Even Keith's claim to hate his family didn't make him flinch. His eyes were steady.

'I'll tell you why I think she keeps me at home,' Keith said. 'Partly, it's guilt. She feels guilty for having given birth to a child who's such a mess. She'd feel even more guilty for sending me away, even though sometimes it would be a relief for her not to have to look every day at the mess she made. But it'd make her feel like a bad parent, not looking after her child herself, and then she'd see herself as being a worse mess than me. So it's better for her if I stay. Then I'm the cripple, not her.'

Daniel continued to gaze, as if thinking over what Keith was saying, suspending judgment until he'd heard the full complaint.

The nurse pushed the door open. 'Have you finished?'

A couple walking past with a bunch of flowers looked in, then looked away. Keith was embarrassed.

'Shut the door!' he said.

'All right, but have you finished? I'm due to go on my break.'

'No,' he said.

'Okay,' she said. 'Call me when you're ready.'

She was tired, he could see, and looking forward to ten minutes with a cup of coffee. He was being selfish again. How was it that someone had to suffer if he put his own needs first? Staying in here was his only way of being left alone to think. But asking for this concession meant a nurse had to wait for her break.

'Everything's my fault,' he told Daniel bitterly. 'It's great that Mum puts up with me, because of course it wasn't her fault I was born like this and yet she's accepted that this is how her child is. So it must have been my fault, for being so tactless as to expect any family to want me. Perhaps they think I should have quietly aborted myself – not with their help, of course, but spontaneously, so no one could blame themselves for it. What made me, as an unborn child, be so arrogant as to expect a family welcome?

'What kind of visitor arrives in this state, needing everything, with nothing to give? We're expected to be helpless when we're babies, and then grow out of it. Because I still need help, I get seen as the baby who didn't have the decency to move out and let the grown-up take its place. I'm the baby who outstayed his welcome. That's how everyone sees me. I'm told all these operations are meant to increase my chance of a normal life and normal activity, but really what they're designed to do is make me more grown-up and self-sufficient and less of a burden on the family and a drain on society.'

Daniel, among the lions, looked tiny. He was not tall, and of slight build. He would only give the lions a couple of mouthfuls. Hardly worth eating, except that they were hungry and would have eaten anything. How had he convinced them not to devour him? How could he resist their accusing gaze? We're not asking much of you, their expressions said; just let us feed on you, just a little bit. You haven't got much to offer us, but what you have we're entitled to, surely? Otherwise, why would you be here, in our territory? How can you refuse our modest request, when we ask so nicely and wait so politely for the consent you're bound to give?

But Daniel knew he wasn't there to feed their desires. Their need was genuine and he was sympathetic but it would have to be met by somebody else.

'God put you in that lion pit,' Keith told him, 'to be his representative. A great prophet, to be a sign to everyone of what a real man is: a man who listens to God.'

A wisp of a smile, an almost imperceptible shake of the head – his hair long, like the lions' manes. A lion of a man himself, but a small-scale one. Not a great prophet, the smile seemed to say. Not a great anything. A child who remained a child, a child of God, always helpless, dependent on his Dad for safety.

Keith seemed to see people around him, crowding in – people who glowed with light, with huge featherlight folded wings. The lions, after all, were nowhere near Daniel, even though he could feel their breath on his bare skin. They were centuries away from devouring him. He was shielded from them more effectively than by any electric fence, by the sheer depth, tier upon tier, of spiritual beings who took up no space in the pit but surrounded this one human being with a wall of eternity. Keith was overawed by the sight. He had never suspected that angels had been in the lions' den with Daniel – much less in the hospital toilet with him.

'Come on now, Keith,' said the nurse, coming in without knocking, and leaving the door open again. 'You must be finished by now.'

He shook his head mutely.

'You all right?' she said. 'You look funny. You're not going to have a fit?' She shifted him towards her and peered into the toilet. 'Oh, you have finished,' she said. 'Good boy. I was thinking we'd have to give you an enema.' Her tone was indulgent; she wiped him without thinking. Her coffee break was in sight.

She wheeled him back to bed in a hospital wheelchair, not his own electric one, and lifted him in. 'I'm putting you back to bed for a while,' she said, 'because you look a bit white. You'll be having your lunch in half an hour, but I can make you a slice of toast now if you like?'

He looked at her in amazement, seeing a rim of white light around her head. She had looked normal a minute before.

'Thanks,' he said, 'but I'll be all right. You have your coffee break now. Have a sweet,' he added, nodding towards the bag that Grandad had left on the bedside cabinet.

She smiled, unwrapped a sweet and popped it into his mouth. 'You have it for me,' she said. 'I'm on a diet.'

She looked perfect to him. Though, when she walked out of the ward, he couldn't see any wings.

Chapter Thirty-two

'This is what we'll do,' said Louise, 'if you're really sure about trying a special school, Eldred.'

Eldred was watching her face. She had filled in the Patents Office application with admirable speed and conciseness. This woman was obviously intelligent. Eldred trusted intelligence. People who were confident in their own intelligence would feel no need to denigrate his. He could be himself.

'Yes,' he said. 'I'd like to go.'

'Then the first thing is to go and look at one or two,' Louise said, 'and the second is to appeal for some funds.'

'Appeal to who?' asked Mildred. 'Is there a grant he can get?'

Louise sighed. 'Slim chance, though it's worth trying. Some schools do have funds for children who are exceptionally able but can't manage the fees, but the kind of school we're thinking about for Eldred is likely to have a long waiting list of pupils in that category. There are so few schools for gifted children. If he was way *below* average, you'd have far less of a problem: everyone's aware now that children with learning difficulties can't be expected to struggle along in schools designed for the average. But above-average children in average schools achieve average results, so they're not considered a problem, except to themselves. Unhappiness doesn't count as a problem requiring the use of government funds.'

'We've got a bit in the building society,' Mildred said, 'but not enough.'

'What we do is this,' said Louise. 'We go public, attract a lot of publicity for Eldred. It won't be hard to arouse media interest if the story is presented in the right way.'

Mildred looked worried. 'You mean – your article in the *Telegraph*?'

'Tip of the iceberg,' said Louise cheerfully. 'I hate to give work away to other journalists, but I've got a couple of friends in TV who will let me work with them and have a say in how we present this. You can make much more impact on television. I know what you're going to say,' she added quickly, seeing Mildred open her mouth. 'You're afraid Mr Jones won't approve, yes?'

'He wouldn't want us begging for money,' said Mildred. 'Not publicly like that. Eldred's our son. It's up to us to provide for him, not strangers sending in cash.'

'I appreciate your feelings,' said Louise, 'but Eldred's situation is unusual, isn't it? You provide for all the needs that a child would normally have, but in an abnormal situation we have to face the fact that Eldred needs more than parents can provide, in the ordinary way of things.'

'Well,' said Mildred, 'you may be right but I doubt his father will see it like that.'

Louise sat further forward on her chair. 'Suppose Eldred was handicapped,' she said. 'Would you prevent someone for appealing for funds for him to have an electric wheelchair?'

'No,' said Mildred, but her tone was doubtful.

'Talk to your husband about it,' Louise suggested. 'We've got till Thursday anyway.'

'What do you mean, we've got till Thursday?' said Mildred sharply.

'The researchers for the programme I have in mind will need to know the candidates by Friday,' said Louise.

Mildred held her hand over her heart. Eldred found the gesture a bit dramatic. 'You mean, you've got something planned?' she said. 'Without consulting us until now?'

'It was just an idea I was vaguely involved in,' said Louise. 'An informal discussion with these few people I happen to know. It was only when you said Eldred had decided he wanted to go to another school that I thought this could be the next step to try. I think we should go for it, personally. It could be a while before a similar opportunity arises.'

'How do we know you're not just using our son to make a name for yourself?' said Mildred.

'Mum!' Eldred protested. 'She's not!'

'I'm not stupid,' said Mildred. 'We know what journalists are like.'

Louise, who had drawn in her lips, relaxed them into a smile. 'I don't blame you for being suspicious,' she said. 'But we're not all tabloid foot-in-the-door guys.'

'You're young and you're ambitious,' said Mildred steadily. 'And television has more clout than newspapers – you said that yourself. I don't want to be unfair to you, but how do we know this would be in Eldred's interests and you're not just doing it for your career?'

'Okay,' said Louise. 'I'm not saying I'm being entirely altruistic – without self-interest,' she added quickly, seeing Mildred look blank. 'I'm good at my job and that includes having a nose for a good story, and Eldred is one. But someone else could come along, do a mediocre job on this – like that patronizing article in your local rag – and get nothing out of it for Eldred himself. Now I'd like a chance to be in on this because I'd like to see it done well. I think Eldred is more unusual than just another bright child: he's original; he's got something to say for himself. Naturally, I'm not going to hand him over to some presenter as a free gift and let them get all the glory. I'm going to bargain fairly hard before I give names and phone numbers. All right. But I'll also do my best to make sure that Eldred, and you as his parents, get what you need out of this. What do you say?'

It was Eldred's turn to have doubts. He had thought Louise was doing this for his sake. She sounded tough when she talked like that. Mildred, however, seemed relieved.

'Well, now you're being frank with us,' she said. 'That sounds more like it. I'll talk to my husband; that's all I can say. But I can't see anything against it myself – that's as long as they're not going to laugh at Eldred or make a fool of him.'

'Trust me,' said Louise. 'These people are good at their job. It won't be a freak show.' She held out her hand to Mildred.

Mildred held it a moment before she shook it. 'It had better not be,' she said. There was a warning look in her eyes that Eldred knew meant business.

After Louise had left, Eldred followed his mother into the kitchen, where she had immediately gone to start peeling carrots, and gave her a hug.

'What's that for?' she asked.

'I don't know as much about people's motives as you do,' he said sadly.

Mildred wiped her hands on the apron she had just put on. 'Some things you learn with age,' she said. 'The world's a hard place, Eldred. Most people are in things for their own gain.'

'Do you think the new school will be the same, then?' asked Eldred. 'Will the teachers be like Mrs Garcia only with different names?'

'We'll have to see,' Mildred said. 'I expect they won't take such exception to clever children, though. They must be used to them in those places.'

'Does everyone learn the same things there, only at a higher level than normal schools, or are people allowed to learn what they're interested in?' Eldred asked.

Mildred patted his shoulder and pushed him away in one movement. 'I don't know,' she said. 'You can ask all these questions yourself when we go to see the place. That's if the money can be found, Eldred. Don't get your hopes up too soon. Go and lay the table for me, there's a good boy. Your dad'll be home in twenty minutes.'

Chapter Thirty-three

Edgar came home in a bad mood. Mildred, hearing him open the front gate, said warningly to Eldred, 'Your father's out of sorts. Leave the talking to me.'

'How do you know?' Eldred asked. 'Before he even comes in the door?'

'Believe me,' said Mildred.

Eldred reflected that his mother seemed to be changing, becoming more self-assured, maybe even more intelligent. This was a new thought. Children, obviously, grew in knowledge because they were continually being taught new things. Even if they failed to retain a lot of the information, a certain percentage of it was bound to stick. But, growing in information, did they grow in intelligence?

As for adults – without spending their days sitting at a desk being fed information, did they go on growing in knowledge or did they live their adult lives according to the information they had gathered as children? And even if they did continue to accumulate information, did they actually become more intelligent as a result of this? Or was intelligence a given factor over which the recipient had no personal control? Did only the intelligent adults continue to inform themselves while the less intelligent refused new information?

Eldred judged this a topic worth pursuing. His father came in and slammed the local newspaper down on the kitchen table. His mother edged past him with a pan of brussels sprouts. 'Dinner in five minutes,' she said.

'Do you think,' said Eldred, 'that adults get more intelligent?'

Mildred caught him by the collar and wheeled him round. 'Go and wash your hands,' she said.

'I just wondered...'

'Wonder after lunch,' she said.

'That boy is out of control,' Edgar said. 'We've no idea what he gets up to, half the time. Are we his parents or aren't we? He makes fools of us.'

Eldred, halfway up the stairs, paused. What was his father talking about? He watched Mildred follow Edgar into the living room.

'What's troubling you, dear?' she said.

'We don't know what he gets up to,' Edgar shouted. 'We've no idea what goes on in his head, or who he meets when he's out, or anything.'

'Who he meets when he's out?' Mildred repeated. 'He doesn't go out. Only with me to the launderette or to the park to play football with his friends.'

'Stupid woman!' Edgar shouted. 'How can you keep track of him with that devious brain of his when you're so stupid!'

Eldred was shocked. His father had never called his mother stupid before.

Mildred sat down and put her hand on her husband's knee. Eldred wondered why she didn't shout back at him, complain about being insulted.

'What's happened to upset you?' she said quietly.

Edgar leaned forward and shook out the newspaper. 'Read that and you'll see!' he said, stabbing his forefinger on the open page.

Eldred tiptoed up the stairs, ran the tips of his fingers under the cold tap, wiped them dry on his jeans, and went down again. His mother was reading. His father glared at him.

'What's wrong?' asked Eldred.

'Nothing, dear,' said Mildred, folding the paper quickly.

'Let him read it,' said Edgar grimly. 'Then I've some questions to ask him.'

Mildred stared at him. 'Surely you don't think that Eldred...?'

'What is it?' said Eldred impatiently. He held out his hand for the paper, but his mother was twisting and squeezing it in her hands as though trying to wring its neck.

'Terence Arthur Smith,' said Edgar. 'Do you know him?'

'Terence Arthur Smith?' said Eldred, bewildered. 'I don't think so. He's not in my class, anyway.'

'I'm not talking about school!' his father shouted. 'Don't play silly buggers with me!'

'Edgar!' Mildred protested. 'Don't talk to the child like that!'

'Child!' Edgar roared. 'Is he a child, Mildred? Is he? Or have we reared some monster?'

Mildred put an arm round Eldred's shoulders protectively. 'Of course he's a child,' she said reprovingly. 'You're getting carried away, Edgar.'

'Getting carried away, am I?' Edgar said bitterly. 'And what if our son has got carried away, under our very noses, and his own parents have neglected to notice that he is in moral danger?'

Eldred was interested. 'Why am I in mortal danger, Dad?'

'Not mortal,' his father snorted. 'Moral danger, I said. This Terence Arthur Smith. Do you mean to deny that you know him?'

'I don't know him!' Eldred protested. 'Why d'you keep saying I do?'

'Eldred, your father means Terry,' said Mildred gently. 'That man you talk to, who works in the library.'

'What's happened to him?' asked Eldred. A terrible sense of foreboding came over him.

'When did you last see him?' said Mildred.

'Friday,' said Eldred. 'No, not Friday, no.'

'You see?' said Edgar. 'He's lying.'

'I'm not lying!' Eldred shouted.

'He's not,' Mildred said.

'So how come his brilliant memory fails him on this point?' said Edgar acidly.

'Edgar,' said Mildred. 'Give him time to think. You've got him confused, with all your accusations.'

'I went to the library on Friday,' said Eldred with dignity, 'but he wasn't there. I talked to a woman; I don't know her. She said he was having some time off or something.'

'He'll be having a lot more time off,' said Edgar. 'Go on Mildred, give it to him to read.'

With reluctance, Mildred handed the paper to Eldred. Scanning it quickly, he read that Terence Arthur Smith, aged twenty-three, had been arrested at his home, following allegations by several pre-teenage boys that Terence Arthur Smith had molested them. Eldred put the paper down on the table and turned away.

'Read it,' his father insisted.

'I've read it,' he said.

'All of it,' Edgar pursued.

'I've read it,' said Eldred.

'And what have you to say?'

'I'll have to think about this,' Eldred said.

'You will not think!' his father shouted. 'You will give me a direct answer straight away!'

'What answer?' said Eldred.

'What answer do you think? The truth! I want the truth, boy!'

'I meant,' said Eldred, 'what is the question?'

'What d'you suppose the question is? What did he do to you, this Terence, this pervert, eh?'

'Edgar!' Mildred protested again.

'I'm not going to apologize,' Edgar said. 'Call a spade a spade, that's my way.'

'He didn't do anything,' Eldred said.

'What do you mean, he didn't do anything? He was your *friend*, wasn't he?' Edgar gave the word a sinister emphasis. 'You're always talking about Terry, aren't you? Terry this, Terry that, Terry the clever man who knows so much more than your parents about just about everything, except how a decent man should behave!'

Eldred swallowed.

'Answer me!' his father shouted.

'I will answer you,' said Eldred, though his voice, Mildred noticed, was shaky. 'He was my friend. I suppose he still is. He didn't do anything – that is, he talked to me and found me books and helped me to look things up, and sometimes he talked about himself or he gave me advice about things I didn't know how to do...'

'What kind of advice?' Edgar demanded.

'Edgar, let him finish,' said Mildred. 'Please.'

'Son,' said Edgar more gently, 'I'm not going to punish you. It's not you I'm angry with. I just want you to tell me straight.'

'I am,' said Eldred. 'You're not listening to me. I'm afraid you're not going to believe me, even if I do tell you straight.'

'I'll believe you,' his father said, 'as long as you tell me the truth.'

'Okay,' Eldred said. 'I don't know if these... these allegations are true, by these other boys. They might be. Something makes me feel they might be true. He did ask me back to his flat once, but I said I had to get home for tea.'

Mildred, imperceptibly, let out a small sigh of breath and her hands, which had been twisting her apron into a knot, relaxed.

'He is not a bad man,' Eldred said, 'whatever anyone says, and whatever he did.' Edgar moved to interrupt, but a look from his wife silenced him. Eldred continued. 'I think he was very lonely. Isolated. His mother was sick. She didn't recognize him any more. He'd given up his chance of university to stay home and look after her, and then she didn't need him any more and he had nobody. No friends his own age or anything.'

'That doesn't excuse…' Edgar began.

Eldred raised his voice slightly. 'It's not our business,' he said. 'Those other boys' parents can say what they like about him. But he didn't… he didn't expose himself indecently to me, or in any way interfere with me genitally, or commit sodomy with me.'

Edgar gasped.

'He reads,' said Mildred quickly. 'It doesn't mean he's talking from personal experience. He knows all these terms because he reads, that's all. Isn't that right, Eldred?'

'I'm telling you the truth, Dad,' said Eldred. 'Really.'

His father's forehead was covered with sweat. Eldred felt sorry for him.

'I don't think he would have tried to do those things to me,' Eldred reassured him. 'I mean, I wouldn't have let him, but anyway I don't think he would have done that to me. I was his friend.'

'That's what worries me,' Edgar said. 'What kind of friends are you making? What's wrong with your schoolfriends?'

'It's different,' said Eldred. 'They're people I play with. They can't teach me things.'

Mildred smoothed her apron as though she meant business. 'Dinner,' she said firmly. 'It's nearly two o'clock. What is the world coming to?'

'I don't want any,' Eldred said. 'Can I go to my room?'

'You'll sit with us and have something, at least,' said Mildred. Seeing Eldred's hesitation, she said, 'The subject is closed now. It won't be discussed all dinnertime. Will it, Dad?'

'It isn't finished yet, by a long chalk,' Edgar said.

'Eldred,' Mildred said, 'go into the kitchen and fetch me the mustard, will you? There's a good boy. Top cupboard, bottom left shelf.' When he had gone, she said quietly. 'It is finished, Edgar. Let it go. He's upset enough.'

'He's standing up for the fellow,' Edgar said. 'He calls him his friend.'

'No, it'll be all right,' Mildred said.

'How do you know?'

'Because,' Mildred said, 'he'll think about all this when he's on his own and he'll work it out for himself. That's what he always does. We mustn't interfere with it. Well done, Eldred, you found the mustard. Put it by your father's plate, and we'll eat.'

Chapter Thirty-four

From watching wildlife programmes Lulubelle knew the only safe thing to do in the presence of a lion was to keep still and stay quiet. She found she had no other option anyway, because the shock of finding Savage in the cage took her breath away and froze her bones.

She was sitting cross-legged, her usual position for thinking, with her hands round her ankles. Now she found she was gripping them, and forced herself to stop. The last thing she needed was to get pins and needles in her legs.

If the lioness pounced, she stood no chance. One stride forward and one swipe of that huge armoured paw would be all it would take. But if the lioness, who might have been given some drug for her infected paw, was lethargic or just lost interest in this small distraction, Lulubelle might have a chance – one chance and no more – to move very swiftly and get herself out of the cage the same way she had got in, through the wide bars.

Savage was motionless, still standing, looking in Lulubelle's direction. She was alert; Lulubelle could tell that by the smell of her. She had loved lions when she was small; their pungent smell had never put her off, as it had some of the other fairground and circus children, and she had never found them frightening. Many times, the trainers had warned Lucinda to watch her small daughter more carefully. Once before, she had been found in their compound, snuggled up against a yearling lion cub. Thankfully, the lions had seemed to regard her as another cub and hadn't reacted, and the trainer had rescued her before the cub woke up and stretched out its claws for a rough and tumble with this unexpected new playmate.

But that had been when she was two and a half. Now she was ten, nearly eleven, she knew more about lions than she had then, and knew it was no mere fussing by grown-ups when they insisted even the most passive and placid beast must be treated with extreme caution. She had seen a keeper mauled.

She tried not to remember it now – the man, experienced with lions, having followed the same careful routine with them that he had for years, staggering and collapsing on the ground outside the cage, blood pouring from his face, and his arm almost hanging off.

Lulubelle forced herself to stop thinking of the possibility. Savage would smell panic on her, just as Lulubelle could smell the animal's warning mechanism. Girl and lioness were both still, apparently passive but totally alert. Neither was fooled by the other's stillness.

Think of something relaxing, Lulubelle told herself. Her mind went to Lucinda, rehearsing now. She liked to watch her, never tired of the hypnotic swinging to and fro of the trapezists, knew to a millisecond when they were ready to throw themselves from the comparative safety of the handbar into mid-air. She imagined the perfect curve of Lucinda's body, every muscle tensed, flying high above the tiers of seats which would later be filled by a rapt and petrified audience, craning their necks to see Lucinda, her hands outstretched, apparently miss making contact with Pedro, hanging by his feet from the other trapeze.

The audience would gasp as she seemed to mistime her arrival and spin out of control into a half-somersault. Only Lulubelle never doubted, never blinked, till she saw Pedro's hands firmly gripped round Lucinda's ankles and Lucinda, upside down, waving and smiling triumphantly.

Savage extended her neck slightly, sniffing Lulubelle's scent. There must be no trace of fear in it. Thinking of Lucinda's act, and of her fellow trapezists, both so professional, so experienced, was safe. Lulubelle had never seen either Pedro or Juan miss a catch. She had seen Lucinda, a few times, drop into the safety net, but only from the high wire, never during the trapeze act.

Sometimes, when they were rehearsing a new move on the trapezes and she hadn't quite perfected it, Lucinda would mistime a catch and land awkwardly in her catcher's grasp, spraining an ankle or a wrist, but she had never had any serious injury, and it was never the fault of Pedro or Juan. They were tense, dour men, homosexual partners who kept themselves to themselves and didn't socialize much with the others. But their intense, introspective characters were part of Lucinda's safety net. They never relaxed.

Lucinda herself was reckless, the one who enthusiastically embraced all the new ideas and wanted to emulate every other trapezist's latest feats of skill. No one seeing her launch herself off the high platform, held only by her neck between Juan's feet as he swung out into the air with both muscled hands gripped like steel round the bar of the trapeze, would suspect Lucinda capable of feeling fear.

No one, that is, who hadn't seen her sobbing into her pillow because some ringmaster had reprimanded her for being late or had threatened her with the sack for some affair that had disrupted relationships among her colleagues, or because some man had left her, or hit her, or failed to use contraceptives and the circled date on the calendar had been and gone with no reassuring event. It was men who caused Lucinda to fear, not heights or physical risks or the ever-present possibility of a slip, a clumsy landing, or a rebound over the edge of the safety net.

Lulubelle never worried about her safety, or not consciously, though she did have nightmares. And Lucinda had been drinking more recently. Tonight, for example. Lulubelle had been so concerned about her mother being late for rehearsal that she hadn't really stopped to consider whether Lucinda was too drunk to work. And would she remember to tell Mr Mannfield she wouldn't be doing the high wire act tonight? He always accepted that, never pushed her, but would Lucinda, more reckless than ever when drunk, insist on going ahead with it?

There was a sudden shout from the Big Top. Lulubelle, instinctively, moved her head sharply. Had Lucinda had an accident?

Savage, about to settle down again in the corner, lifted her head and snarled, moving forward a pace. Lulubelle, turning back quickly, found the lioness's head two metres away from her face and panicked. Forgetting what she'd learned, she let out a scream, jumped to her feet and tried to force herself through the bars.

The manoeuvre, so easy when she was relaxed and believed the cage empty, was not easy now. Twisting her slim frame sideways, she still couldn't make it fit, and her head seemed huge. She had one leg through and one arm; she wriggled and twisted. Screams escaped from her throat, beyond her control. Savage, her jaws open, tensed her huge shoulders and waited, watching her victim squirm and squeal.

There were footsteps outside, people running, looking for the source of the noise. At least they weren't all in the Big Top, responding to the other crisis – but would they find Lulubelle?

The trailer shook slightly as a man ran up the ramp. She was beyond noticing who it was. He was shouting instructions to her. Then there was another man, also shouting, shouting at the lioness, trying to distract her. Another voice was accusing the first of having left the door of the outer cage open. Everyone was talking to her, shouting at her, pulling at her, then trying to push her back into the cage, forcing her to move round towards the locked door.

She was paralysed with fear. She had almost forgotten the lion. It felt as though every fear during the whole of her life gathered force and bore down on her, like a giant snowball gathering weight and speed as it hurtled downhill towards the point of her life where she was now poised, between the freedom beyond the bars and the one swift bite of the lion's jaws.

Screaming uncontrollably, her eyes tightly closed and her hands tightly gripped round the bars, she was impossible to help. Savage was becoming agitated, pacing between the man who was trying to distract her and the more interesting distraction of the young girl screaming. Someone ran to fetch meat, another in search of supplies of a tranquillizer drug.

Suddenly the trailer shook heavily. Savage snarled, and swiped a lethal paw through the bars towards one of the men, who backed hastily against the mesh of the outer cage.

Lulubelle hadn't noticed the trailer shaking. Her first indication of Arto's arrival was a roar that made Savage cower. Then the bar she was clinging to suddenly bent away from her hand; a strong grip gently but irresistibly detached her fingers from the bar and she felt herself pulled through the widened space, to safety.

Still screaming and gasping, she was slung effortlessly over one massive shoulder, the width of a normal athlete's entire shoulder span, and carried from the cage. Crossing the fairground, now coming alive with music and trial runs of the mechanisms driving the different rides, Arto strode towards his own caravan and deposited Lulubelle on to the cushioned lap of Marisa his wife.

Chapter Thirty-five

'I'll have to stay in bed this morning,' said Eldred when his mother came to call him on Monday.

Mildred placed a hand on his forehead. 'Are you ill?'

'I'm tired,' he said.

'You don't feel like you've got a temperature,' Mildred said.

'I'm not ill,' said Eldred. 'I'm tired.'

'You've had all weekend to be tired,' said Mildred. 'If you're not ill, you have to go to school.'

'Why?' said Eldred. 'I don't learn anything.'

'Come on, Eldred,' said his mother. 'Don't be difficult. You know children have to go to school.'

'I just want one day off, that's all,' said Eldred. 'I'll go back again tomorrow.'

'I'll call your father,' Mildred threatened.

Eldred sighed and turned to face the wall.

He heard his father come into the room and felt his weight as he sat on the end of the bed. There was silence. It was unusual for Edgar to have nothing to say. Eldred was surprised. It reminded him of the day his father had come to see him in the hospital, out of breath after tackling the stairs – the day Eldred first talked. Well, he wasn't going to talk today.

Edgar took a deep breath. 'This Terry fellow,' he said. 'Is that what's bothering you?'

More silence.

'You're not afraid I'll be angry with you, son?' Edgar said. 'Look, I know I can be a bit hasty. We worry about you, your mother and I. It's only natural. And perhaps we don't understand you as well as we would if you were more... well, more like other children.'

Eldred pulled the duvet over his head.

Edgar, quite gently, tugged it back. 'You don't have to say anything if you don't want to,' he said. 'But I want you to listen to me. We love you. All right? Now, I don't find that easy to say, Eldred. You know me. I'm not one to wear my feelings on my sleeve. But we care about you. We're your parents.'

Eldred made a muffled response.

'What?' said Edgar, but Eldred didn't repeat it. After a pause, his father continued, 'Everyone has problems, son. But there's nothing so bad that it doesn't get better if you talk to someone. Can't you talk to your dad?'

He laid a hand on the top of Eldred's head, tentatively, as if expecting to be shaken off. This unprecedented act melted Eldred's defences, where the words had not. He sat up and caught hold of his father's hand.

'I would talk to you,' he said, 'only you don't seem to listen. I only say one thing, then you come in with all the answers and then the subject is closed.' He waited for Edgar's rebuke.

Edgar bowed his head. 'I'm sorry,' he said.

Eldred's eyes widened. He hunched up his knees, gripped his father's hand in both his own and began to talk with urgency, looking into Edgar's eyes anxiously to gauge his response. Edgar looked back at him. Mildred, peeping round the door, withdrew quickly and left them to it.

When Edgar came downstairs, Mildred had his toast and tea ready on the table, but her husband went straight to the phone. She heard him phone the office and say he'd be late, and then phone the school and leave a message that his son was indisposed and would not be in today.

When he sat down at the table, she sat opposite him, and waited. She reflected that Eldred, alien though he seemed to both of them at times, was like Edgar in one way, at least. You got more information out of either father or son by waiting till they were ready to tell things in their own way than by asking questions.

'I've been talking to Eldred,' said Edgar finally.

Mildred, who knew this already, nodded.

'He hasn't been having an easy time,' Edgar said. He looked at Mildred for confirmation.

'No,' she agreed.

'We've always been careful not to treat him as any different from other children,' Edgar continued. 'We could have ended up as doting older parents, thinking their only child was something special. And then, with what happened before he was born...'

Mildred nodded again. Tears were in her eyes, but she kept her gaze on her husband.

'Tell me, Mildred,' said Edgar, 'do you think we've done the wrong thing by him? Tried to make him too normal?'

'You've always done what you thought best for him, dear,' said Mildred, 'so how could that do the child any harm?'

'But maybe it's not enough to be well-meaning,' said Edgar earnestly, lowering his glasses to peer at her. 'You can want the best for a child and cause him suffering. It's terribly easy to make a child suffer, Mildred.'

Mildred reached across the table and took his hand. 'And it's easy to make a child happy,' she said. 'All he needs to know is that we're on his side. Then he'll cope with everything. He's stronger than us in some ways.'

'In most ways,' said Edgar ruefully. 'I've been so afraid he'd get laughed at. I've thought, if we take him seriously he'll think it's all right to be himself with everyone outside this house, and then he'll get crucified. Best to make him toe the line early on in life, and then he'll survive.'

Mildred said nothing.

'I was wrong,' he said, 'wasn't I?'

Mildred poured a cup of tea, sugared and stirred it for him and pushed it towards him.

'After all,' said Edgar, 'if we, as his parents, aren't proud of our own child, all we're teaching him is that the world is right to make him ashamed of being himself. And what kind of lesson is that, to prepare him for life?'

Mildred got up, walked round the table, and kissed him.

'Did he tell you what Louise Palmer had to say?' she asked.

'Yes,' Edgar said. 'He told me everything. I hope it was everything. I was listening.'

'I know you were, love,' Mildred said.

'What do you think of the idea of Eldred appearing on television?' Edgar asked.

'I've got a few doubts,' Mildred admitted. 'But if it's the only way for him to get to a private school where they'll help him be who he is...'

'Did you know,' Edgar interrupted, 'that his class teacher fiddled the end-of-term marks so he wouldn't come first every time?'

'Yes,' said Mildred.

'It's wrong,' Edgar said. 'That's all wrong, that attitude. It's playing God.'

'I suppose she thought the other kids would get discouraged, if Eldred was always ahead of them,' said Mildred. 'And the other parents aren't happy, if their child has no chance of coming first.'

'What about Eldred getting discouraged?' said Edgar. 'He's bored stiff there, day after day. He finishes his work in five minutes and he's given nothing to do while the other kids work – just has to sit there and stare into space for hours. He's told off if he asks too many questions, he's told off if he calls out all the answers, he's told off if he daydreams and doesn't listen – what is he to do?'

'I know,' said Mildred.

'It's not good enough, Mildred,' Edgar said. 'We're not going to stand for this. If he was subnormal, or dyslexic, or blind, he'd get special education to suit his needs. It's insulting to make a child sit all day pretending to learn what an atom is when he spends his free time inventing industrial machines.'

'Yes, dear,' said Mildred.

'Mildred,' said Edgar, 'I've been blind. I've been a coward and I've been a fool. But now the worm has turned. We're going to fight.'

'Right, dear,' said Mildred. She smiled.

'We're going to help Eldred to do what he wants to do, and we're going to be proud of our son,' Edgar said fiercely. 'Am I right now?'

'You're right,' said Mildred. 'And Edgar – you may be blind and a fool, if you say so, dear, but I'm proud of you too.'

Edgar picked up his cup and sipped it hastily. Mildred couldn't be sure, but she thought it wasn't just the heat of the tea that made him blush.

Chapter Thirty-six

When Edgar left for work, Mildred found Eldred still huddled under the bedclothes.

'Are you getting up for breakfast?' she asked.

Eldred eyed her warily.

'You don't have to go to school,' she assured him. 'Your father's told them you won't be in today. You can stay in bed a bit longer if you're tired.'

'I'll get up,' Eldred decided. He sat up, flung back the duvet and jumped out of bed. 'I don't feel quite so tired now.'

Over cornflakes, he said, 'What are you going to do today?'

'Nothing out of the ordinary,' said Mildred. 'What do you want to do?'

Eldred considered. 'Are you going out to the launderette?'

'I would do, normally,' said Mildred, 'but it can wait till tomorrow. You can't be seen out at the shops with me, Eldred, if you're meant to be too ill to be at school.'

'No, I meant I'd be all right here,' said Eldred, 'if you want to go out.'

'I can't leave you at home on your own,' said Mildred. 'People get prosecuted, going out and leaving nine year olds.'

'I don't see why,' Eldred said. 'You've done it before.'

'I know,' said Mildred. 'No, the launderette can wait. Your father's got enough shirts to last him till Thursday.'

'I don't mind,' Eldred repeated. 'If you want to go out.'

'Well, there's no need, so that's all right,' said Mildred. 'Is there something you'd like to do, or are you going to work on your computer programming?'

'I wondered,' Eldred said, 'if we could play a game.'

'Oh Eldred, you know I'm no good at the games you play,' said Mildred. 'I never could get the hang of chess, or all those strategy games you like.'

'No, I mean an ordinary game,' said Eldred. 'Don't we have any of those? Ludo or snakes and ladders or something?'

Mildred stared at him. 'Ludo?'

'Don't we have it?' Eldred asked. 'I thought we used to play that. Did we give it away?'

'It's under the stairs,' said Mildred, 'with all your other toys.'

'Have I got toys?' Eldred asked.

'You've got loads of toys,' said Mildred. 'Toys, games, puzzles that we bought you that you never played with.'

Eldred's eyes were bright. 'Can we get them out?' he said.

Edgar phoned at lunchtime. 'Is he all right?' he asked.

'Fine,' said his wife.

'How has he been, since our talk this morning?'

'Like a child,' said Mildred.

'What?'

'A real one,' she said. 'He's been playing board games, without making up new rules to make it complicated. And doing jigsaw puzzles.'

'What do you mean?' said Edgar, after a pause. 'Jigsaw puzzles?'

Mildred lowered her voice. 'He's asked me to go out,' she said, 'and get him a colouring book.'

'Why?' said Edgar blankly. 'What does he want to do with it?'

'He found a set of felt-tip pens that we got him when he was four,' Mildred said. 'He wants a colouring book. To colour the pictures in.'

'Is he ill?' Edgar asked anxiously.

'Not at all. He seems very happy.'

'Mildred,' said Edgar. 'Do you think I should come home? What's happening?'

'I don't know,' she said. 'Did you tell him he could go to that school, if we could find the money?'

'Yes,' he said. 'I did. Do you think that was the wrong thing?'

'No,' she said. 'Perhaps he's just decided, before he goes, to have a childhood.'

She returned to Eldred, who was busily making paper planes and colouring in the logos of different airlines on the wings.

'Did Dad say it was okay?' he asked, without looking up.

'Say what was okay?'

'If I have a colouring book,' said Eldred.

'Well, of course you can have a colouring book. Why not?'

'I thought he might be worried,' said Eldred, 'and think I needed psychiatric treatment because I was regressing to infancy or something.'

'I don't think he's that worried,' said Mildred.

'People do that, you know,' said Eldred conversationally. 'They can suddenly go right back to being children. Out of the blue, no warning. I read about it.'

'I'm sure they do,' said Mildred. 'But not usually at the age of nine.'

She put on her coat. 'Anything else you'd like, while I'm out? Apart from a colouring book?'

Eldred hesitated. 'If you don't think it's detrimental to my character to get spoilt when I'm skyving off school,' he said, 'would it be possible to have chocolate cupcakes?'

'I expect it would,' said Mildred. She kissed him on the top of his head. 'I won't be long. Don't answer the doorbell if it rings.'

'Okay,' said Eldred absently. He watched through the window as she went out of the gate and turned right, towards the shops.

Then he picked up the phone and dialled the operator. 'I'm afraid I don't know the number I want,' he said, 'but I believe it's a freephone call. Do I have to go through directory enquiries?'

'Who did you want to call?' asked the operator.

'The child abuse helpline,' said Eldred.

Chapter Thirty-seven

Breathless with sobbing, Lulubelle was trying to ask if Lucinda was all right but the words made her choke and Marisa silenced her. Arto, his bulky form half-filling the large van, lowered himself onto a stool which creaked under his weight, and left it to his wife to calm the child. His furrowed brow expressed concern but no anxiety about the outcome. The crisis had passed. He had done his part. Before too long now the cause of the problem would be sorted out.

His confidence and Marisa's sympathy had the desired effect on Lulubelle. She snuffled into the tissue Marisa held out, stopped sobbing and started to breathe again.

'Is Lucinda all right?' she asked.

'Lucinda?' Arto was surprised.

'I heard a shout from the Big Top.'

'An intruder,' said Arto. His English was noticeably more versatile than his wife's. 'Tripped over a wire, fused some lights. Mr Mannfield had him thrown out.'

Lulubelle stared. 'Was it a man with dark hair, wearing an anorak hood with a puffa jacket?'

'I don't know; I didn't see him. You thought the shout was for Lucinda – that she fell?'

Lulubelle, again, felt disloyal. It was hard to talk about her mother to anyone. But Arto's face was calm, non-judgmental, and Marisa she'd never seen gossiping with the other women. Were they safe or not? She took a deep breath.

'You worry for her when she works?' Marisa enquired.

'No,' said Lulubelle.

When they seemed to be waiting for a further answer, she said reluctantly, 'She'd had a few drinks this evening. Normally, she'd never fall, of course. I mean, she is good, you know. The best really. Very professional. Better than any other trapezist I've ever seen in any other circus.'

She was gabbling, trying to make up for the disloyalty of mentioning Lucinda's drinking.

Arto was nodding his great bull-head slowly. 'She drinks often?'

'Oh no, hardly ever. Not when she's working.'

Those large placid eyes set in the huge face were hard to lie to, somehow. Lulubelle was reminded of a poster she'd seen in some town, advertising an art exhibition or something: The Ancient of Days, the picture was called. It showed a huge white-bearded man bending down with a measuring instrument poised above a formless world. Arto's face was like that man's face, whoever he was.

'At least,' she corrected herself, 'she used not to drink when she was working; only after the show, late at night. But lately she has been. And she keeps being late for rehearsals. And people don't like her because... well, not everybody does. They get upset sometimes, you know. And if we lose this job,' she finished in a rush, 'there's nowhere else to go, and I'd really hate to go back to the place we were before, even if they'd have us. And if Lucinda can't work any more, I can't earn enough for both of us.'

Marisa and Arto were exchanging glances over her head. Lulubelle had the impression that none of this was news to them. Maybe they weren't as detached from the circus and fairground grapevine as she had thought.

'I shouldn't be saying all this,' she said. She slid off Marisa's lap. 'You mustn't tell anybody I said that.'

Arto stopped her progress to the door by extending a hand the size of Lulubelle's head and gently holding it in front of her.

'You don't worry,' he said. 'We don't talk about it with others. But we talk about it together, okay? Marisa, hot chocolate and some cakes.'

Marisa, all smiles, moved towards the beautiful kitchenette. Lulubelle, unable to resist looking again at the gleaming hob, the white enamel-lined sink and the full-sized fridge, followed her.

'We won't be late for the show, will we?' she said anxiously. She glanced automatically at her left wrist, forgetting that Lucinda had sold her watch, two towns ago now, when the money ran short.

'Plenty of time,' said Arto easily.

'I'm not meant to eat before a performance,' she said wistfully, watching Marisa open a tin full of little cakes. 'Are those home-made cakes?'

'Of course,' said Marisa. 'Arto only eat my cakes. Much too many,' she chided, and Arto laughed. These two seemed to like each other, Lulubelle thought. They were different from the other husbands and wives she knew.

'Very light, Marisa's cakes,' Arto said. 'Very good before a performance. Don't worry, they don't make you become like me, not in one night!'

Lulubelle giggled. She couldn't imagine being Arto's size.

Arto and Marisa were delighted. 'So, laughing!' Marisa applauded. 'Better already, yes? And better still after hot chocolate.'

She poured the hot milk (all milk, thought Lulubelle, awed) into three large mugs and Arto, balancing them on the palm of one hand, led the way back to the plush tasselled settees.

'Your van is lovely,' Lulubelle sighed. 'You must be really famous, Arto, to have all this.'

'I work very hard, all my life,' said Arto seriously. 'When I was young, I was thin and weak.'

'You're kidding me!'

'No, truly, Lulubelle. I was not a small boy, you understand. All my family are, what's the word – thick?'

Lulubelle grinned. 'Not thick – that means stupid! Big-built?'

'Big-built, yes. Stocky. But no muscles, and no fat – not enough food, always, at home. Poor family. You know?'

'Yes,' Lulubelle said.

'But I work,' said Arto. 'I lift weights – not real weights at first, but sacks of coal, heavy bricks. More each day. I train myself. And as soon as I earn some money, I eat. My family say, "Arto, you are selfish. You eat what you earn. What about us?" And I say, "I am not selfish. I am eating for all of us. I am an investment for the family. When I am rich, you will all be rich as well. Trust me."'

'Where is your family?' Lulubelle asked.

'All over the world.'

'Don't you see them now?'

'Of course I see them. Every year we meet. In winter, I go to work in pantomime, and everyone comes to see me – all my family, all Marisa's, from all over the world. We celebrate Christmas. How we celebrate it!'

Marisa was smiling agreement.

'Are they all in showbusiness?' Lulubelle asked.

'Nobody. Only Marisa and me. Some have their own family business, some work for other firms, some have no work. But everyone is rich. I keep my promise.'

'You mean,' said Lulubelle, 'you give money to your family, as well as having all this?'

They were both laughing.

'As well a house in south of France,' said Marisa. 'As well a smaller house in Greece.'

Lulubelle sighed. 'It's better being a strongman than a trapezist, or an acrobat, then. I'll never be that rich. But I will be famous.'

Arto was suddenly serious. 'I think you could be,' he said. 'But it's no good waiting to be noticed. You must have an agent. You must work in different places – theatre, variety, pantomimes, television – not just circus. Even in circus, you must have a career plan. You move from one to another, across the world. You work everywhere; you play to different audiences; you don't waste your time. You get known.'

'I have to work where Mum works,' Lulubelle said. 'She's the one who gets us the jobs. I'm extra.'

'But you are more talented,' Arto said.

Lulubelle looked shocked.

'It's true,' Arto said. He looked at Marisa but she was frowning slightly. 'I know these things,' he said. 'Your mother is good, yes, but for how many more years? Trapeze work is not for ever. It's very... exacting. And high wire, even worse. At high wire, she is not excellent, Lucinda, even now. At trapeze, she is very good, but not exceptional. There are many others just as good – and younger, prettier, more reliable, who come to rehearsal on time, do not drink, do not chase the married men and anger their wives...'

Marisa was shaking her head at him in open disapproval now. 'Arto, you don't say these things! It's not right.'

'It's all right,' said Lulubelle. She felt relieved. 'It's only the things people say behind our backs. I know it really. That's what worries me – what will happen when Lucinda runs out of ringmasters to sleep with and can't persuade them to take on our acts? We don't get paid much as it is.'

Marisa's eyes were sorrowful. 'So terrible to know these things, so young a child she is!'

Arto shrugged his mighty shoulders. 'It's life. It's circus. You must look further than this, Lulubelle. You have talent, but you must start using it to the greatest advantage. Your own career, not following your mother's only.'

'I've been on TV a few times,' said Lulubelle defensively. 'And I might be getting an interview for a documentary on special children; we have to phone someone back this week.'

'How did it come about, this TV?'

'It started when someone came to the circus – the last one we were with – who worked in TV research for children's programmes and asked me...'

'Children's TV!' said Arto dismissively. 'No. No good to promote you as a child star, no. You grow out of it too quickly. You must be promoted as an artiste.'

'How?'

'I speak to my agent tomorrow,' said Arto. 'I tell him all about you. He will listen to me.'

'He listen always to Arto,' Marisa confirmed.

Lulubelle could believe it. 'If I was as big as Arto, I expect people would listen to me,' she said. 'Even Savage did, didn't she?'

Chapter Thirty-eight

'I've finished,' said Eldred, putting down the felt-tip pen and closing the box of coloured pencils.

'That was quick,' said Mildred. 'Which picture did you choose? The one of the children on the beach?'

'No,' said Eldred. 'I mean I've finished the book.'

'You can't have coloured them all in, in that time,' said Mildred. 'Let me have a look.'

Eldred handed her the colouring book. 'Can I have a cupcake?'

'Yes. They're on the worktop.'

'Do you want one, Mum?'

'Pardon?' she said, looking through the pages. 'I mean, no thank you, Eldred.'

She was bemused. Trust Eldred to make something odd, she thought, even of a child's colouring book. She rebuked herself. She must stop comparing him with other children. Hadn't she warned that Louise woman against putting Eldred in a freak show? She shouldn't, in her own mind, keep thinking of her son as different from 'normal children'. What was normal, after all? All children had their funny little ways. She was surely exaggerating things, because her child was an only child; if he had a whole horde of brothers and sisters he wouldn't stand out at all, Mildred told herself.

She stopped at a picture of families at the zoo. A zebra gazed over the edge of a fenced-in pen. Eldred had coloured the fence panels alternately black and white. 'Did you do that to match the zebra?' Mildred asked.

Eldred, hanging over her shoulder and dropping chocolate cake crumbs on the page, nodded, his mouth full. 'Mm.'

'And the people,' Mildred said. 'They're all dressed in black and white.'

'It's the way the zebra sees them,' Eldred explained, through the cake. 'He's colour-blind.'

'Oh,' said Mildred. 'And that's why the seal is black as well, is it?'

'No,' said Eldred. 'Seals are black.'

'Oh,' said Mildred. 'Of course. And you've given the man here a ponytail. And his children are black, though he is white.'

'Yes,' said Eldred. 'I thought the person who drew the picture was a bit out of date. I expect that's because the book was designed quite a few years ago. All the people in all the pictures have old-fashioned hairstyles and clothes, and they're all white people. It isn't really representative of today's society, is it? I mean, I'm not being politically correct or anything, but that isn't the way a crowd of people at the zoo would look, is it? The chances of them all being white and having short hair and fringes must be statistically quite low.'

'Why is the fish that the seal is balancing on its nose gold, when everything else in the picture is black and white?' asked Mildred. 'Isn't the seal colour-blind?'

'I don't know,' said Eldred. 'I just thought, if the seal has been there for a number of years – which it could have been, because it looks quite big and therefore might be quite old – it would have been looking at the zebra for a long time. So it might think all the other creatures around – like the people in the crowd, for instance – were zebras, since it can tell they aren't seals. So it sees all the people in black and white.'

'But not the fish?' said Mildred.

'No, not the fish,' said Eldred. 'The fish is the high spot in its life. The light of its life, see? The excitement.'

'I see,' said Mildred. 'So it sees it in gold?'

'Glorious Technicolor,' said Eldred.

'What about this one?' said Mildred, turning to a picture of children building sandcastles on the beach. 'I can see why you finished quickly. You didn't take much trouble over this one.'

'I did!' said Eldred indignantly. 'It doesn't mean you don't take trouble, just because something is quick.'

'Well, all you've done is a blue scribble for the sky, another blue scribble on the sea, a yellow scribble on the sand and the sandcastles, and everything else is in yellow and blue. All blond-haired children in blue swimsuits with blue buckets and spades and blue flags on the sandcastles.'

'That's because they're all the same family,' said Eldred patiently, 'and the parents are unimaginative. They like blue, and they like all their children to be alike so that everyone can tell who they belong to. So they've given all the children the same colour swimsuits and toys, just as they gave them the same colour hair and eyes and the same kind of faces.'

Mildred laughed. 'That's not the parents' choice, what kind of looks their children have. That's fate.'

'But human beings are free creatures with power of choice,' said Eldred, 'even when they exercise that power over their fate from their deep unconscious and don't recognize it with their conscious mind.'

'Is that right?' said Mildred, still laughing.

'Yes,' he said.

'So your father and I chose for you to have brown eyes like him and mousy hair like me?' said Mildred teasingly.

'Well, you chose for me to have a name that was half of both your names, didn't you?' said Eldred. 'So perhaps you agreed I would have half of each of your physical characteristics.'

Mildred turned to look at him. 'Then tell me the answer to a mystery,' she said. 'Who chose for you to have a brain like yours?'

'It is a mystery,' said Eldred earnestly. 'I came from both of you but I'm just me.'

'But I'm not brainy,' said Mildred, 'and your father is no more than average.'

'Why aren't you brainy?' said Eldred. 'Why do you say that?'

'Oh, Eldred,' said Mildred. 'You know me. Brain like a sieve. I'm always forgetting things. And I can't answer any of those general knowledge questions on the game shows on TV.'

'That's not intelligence, that's acquired knowledge,' said Eldred. 'It's not the same thing. The brain selects which information to retain because it can't keep everything on the front page. The rest goes into a pending file somewhere.'

'So I've got the answers somewhere in the background of my brain?' said Mildred. 'Then why can't I find them anywhere?'

'You may not give the appropriate instruction for their retrieval,' said Eldred. 'Like on my computer. I can open a file, then use the windows facility to open another file on top of it, so you can't see the one behind. If I want to go back to the one behind it, I have to do the right procedure to close the one in the foreground. Otherwise the currently displayed information obscures the previously viewed document.'

'Ah, right,' said Mildred.

'Do you understand that?' asked Eldred kindly, 'Or shall I show you on my computer screen?'

'No, don't bother,' said Mildred. 'You see – I'm not brainy enough even to understand the explanation.'

'No,' said Eldred, 'you're making a choice. You're deciding, on past evidence, that being shown or told something more will make you feel tired and discouraged, probably. And you've convinced yourself that even if I showed you the procedure for retrieving information, you'd forget how to do it.'

'Very likely!' said Mildred.

'That's because part of the software which drives your computer – your brain – includes an instruction to block out certain kinds of information,' said Eldred. 'It doesn't mean you don't have a powerful and fully functioning brain. It means that to call up all the information, you must adapt your usual program.'

'Uh-huh,' said Mildred. 'Have a brain transplant, you mean?'

'No, no,' said Eldred, distressed. He rubbed her head protectively. 'There's no fault in the hardware, you see. Only, the program you're running it on isn't adequate to access the growing quantity of information you've been taking in, over the years. The memory is sufficient, but you need more commands to retrieve it. And that may involve cancelling previous commands.'

'What previous commands need cancelling?' said Mildred, becoming intrigued.

'Say, the one to regard yourself as a brainless person incapable of handling new information,' said Eldred.

'I never told myself to be brainless,' said Mildred. 'I worked terribly hard at school. I just never got any results from it.'

'You may have had a stronger counter-command,' said Eldred seriously, 'overriding the conscious command to achieve. Suppose your conscious command was to work hard and achieve your potential. But your counter-command was to believe that however hard you worked you'd achieve only very little. Then your potential would actually reduce itself in proportion to your work, in order to keep the same input/output ratio.'

'What?' said Mildred.

'You would always achieve about the same level of success,' said Eldred, 'regardless of how hard you worked.'

'That sounds like me,' said Mildred ruefully. 'But why would I tell myself not to succeed? I mean, why would my unconscious do that to me?'

'I don't know,' said Eldred. 'But you must know, at some level. Knowing you, Mum, I would think it must have been quite a good reason.'

'Oh, you do?' said Mildred. 'Thank you.'

'Not that there is a good reason for failing to achieve your potential really,' said Eldred, considering. 'But there could be a reason that seemed relatively good to you in your schooldays, and then, even when that reason became superfluous, you continued to make the same pattern of choices, from habit.'

'Now you're losing me,' Mildred admitted. 'I don't really know what you're talking about.'

Eldred screwed up his face thoughtfully. 'Well... suppose your mother didn't have much self-confidence and felt she hadn't achieved very much with her life, at least not intellectually.'

'Mm,' Mildred said. 'Well, she brought up four children, which is an achievement in itself, but she never did anything you might call academic.'

'Right,' said Eldred. 'So maybe she thought of herself as the unintelligent one of the family. And you, out of sympathy with her, produced evidence of low intelligence, so that she wouldn't feel isolated. That would be a choice, wouldn't it? Because you would also have the choice of producing evidence of high intelligence. But you chose not to.'

'It's not that simple,' said Mildred, becoming ruffled. 'It's a nice theory, for those who succeed, to believe that we poor duffers had a choice. But, conscious or unconscious, Eldred, I can tell you, no one would choose to be bottom of the class. It's not nice.'

'No,' Eldred conceded. 'But then few would choose to come top. There's a price to pay for success as well.'

'That's life,' said Mildred. 'Nothing's for free, as they say.' She flipped a page in the colouring book. 'I thought you said you'd finished, Eldred,' she protested. 'This one's only half filled in.'

'Which one?' said Eldred. He was lying on the floor on his stomach, reading the newspaper editorial upside down.

'The one with the family at the supermarket. You've coloured in the people but only one of the tins on the shelves. You've left the rest blank.'

'The other tins aren't theirs,' Eldred explained. 'That one stands out for them, because it's what they're going to choose to eat this week. The other ones are going to stay on the shelves, so they won't take on any reality till someone else comes along. Hence the absence of substance and colour, you see?'

'Seems like a waste of a colouring book to me,' Mildred grumbled. 'Only filling in little bits of a picture like that. And what about this one? The boy and his little sister? A few little details in red, and that's it. I suppose they're colour blind as well, are they?'

'No,' Eldred said. 'It's seen through the little girl's eyes. The best thing in her world is her brother, and because he's wearing a red sweater she notices the other things that are red. The rest isn't meaningful to her.'

'What about this one?' Mildred said. 'The children in the park. A few little blobs of colour. You haven't even kept inside the lines, Eldred. A five year old could do better.' His comment about her choosing to be unintelligent was rankling. 'And it's not that you can't do it if you want to. Look, this child is perfectly coloured in. And the park-keeper you haven't bothered with at all. Just a messy black scribble around his head.'

'It's depression,' Eldred said. He swivelled the newspaper round and studied a word. 'I can't find an anagram for "platonic",' he said plaintively. 'Claption isn't a word, is it?'

'Depression?' said Mildred, alarmed. 'Are you depressed?'

'Not me,' Eldred said. 'The park-keeper. Surrounded by a black cloud, seeing all the children out of focus, except for one. That's the one he sees as alive, and because he feels dead inside he's going to drain the colour out of that child's life. He's a paedophile.'

Chapter Thirty-nine

Edgar came home late. 'I went for a drink,' he said, 'with Mr Elliot.'

Mildred was astonished. 'The boss? What did he want with you?'

'It's not what he wanted with me,' said Edgar with dignity, 'but what he could do for me. I asked him if he could recommend a public school that might suit Eldred. He was only too pleased to talk about how he and his wife had chosen the one they did for their sons. He was in a more junior post then himself, and they had to do without a dishwasher or a video or a loft conversion, to afford the fees.'

'Edgar, it's not a question of giving up luxuries, for us,' said Mildred nervously. 'If Eldred doesn't get some kind of a grant...'

'Getting the information costs nothing,' Edgar said. 'And Elliot mentioned there's going to be some restructuring in the firm; there'll be a job vacancy at head office if I'm interested.'

'Aren't you too...? I mean, haven't you been turned down for promotion in favour of younger people before, love?' said Mildred tentatively.

'They want someone in this post who won't rock the boat,' Edgar said. 'It's administrative, with responsibility for keeping an eye on the young staff. Elliot said he hadn't thought of me before: I was part of the fixtures and fittings at the Uxbridge branch. But since I had ideas about advancement for my son, he wondered if I was as unambitious as I'd seemed.'

'Oh Edgar,' Mildred said, 'do you really want to start commuting to the City again every day, at your time of life?'

'I'm fifty-two, not seventy-five,' said Edgar. 'And if our son needs a better education, it's his father's responsibility to do what he can to provide it for him,' he said. 'It's not only the well-off who can make sacrifices, Mildred.'

'Of course not,' said Mildred. She picked up the local paper and opened it. Several entries on the Local Jobs page had been ringed. 'I've been thinking,' she said shyly, 'that I've got a bit of time on my hands now. Of course, I'm not qualified for anything and I don't suppose anyone would want me...'

'I don't want you both overworking for me!' said Eldred, horrified. His father raised a hand and stopped him.

'You leave this to us, son,' he said. 'This is a matter for your parents to sort out. You go and read your books.'

Eldred gave him a strange look and backed out of the room. Looking over his shoulder as he went up the stairs, he saw Edgar take the paper from Mildred and sit down with her on the sofa, saying, 'You value yourself too low, you know. You can do better than maildrops and cleaning jobs. How about this one? Mature receptionist?'

Eldred went to his room and picked up his current library book, but even Professor Stephen Hawking's theories on space and time failed to enthral him. He felt strange. Something was happening to his parents that seemed to Eldred as unpredictable as any shift in galaxies. He couldn't quite put his finger on what it was.

Tea was late. Even more extraordinary was that when the phone rang during tea Edgar, instead of saying, 'Let them ring back, Mother: don't decent people know it's teatime?' got up to answer it and, on hearing that it was Louise Palmer, talked to her for at least four minutes without a trace of hostility.

'We're to go up to town on Friday for the initial interview,' he told his wife and son, sitting down at the table again.

'What interview?' asked Eldred.

'For this television programme,' said his father, as though it was a settled thing that they had all discussed and agreed on. 'I shall take the day off work. People do take days off, you know,' he said, seeing Eldred and Mildred staring at him. 'I'm as entitled as anyone else.'

Later, when Eldred was in bed, preparing for sleep by mentally redrawing the diagrams from *A Brief History of Time*, Mildred waited for the commercial break, turned the television's sound down, and said timidly, 'Are you set on the idea of public schools, then, dear? You've always said they're for people with more money than sense.'

'I've said a lot of things,' Edgar said. 'But when you get a child who doesn't seem to fit the mould, you've got to throw away the theories and let the child show you what he needs, haven't you?'

Mildred hesitated. 'Does it have to be a public school? You hear such dreadful things.'

'What kind of things?'

'You know. Boys.'

The adverts came to an end, the tail-lights of the last Peugeot disappearing into an orange sunset. Edgar automatically reached for the remote control to turn the sound up again, then sat back and looked at his wife.

'You mean,' he said, '...homosexuality?'

'Well,' said Mildred, 'you know. These things happen.'

They were both embarrassed.

'You make it sound like it's part of the curriculum,' said Edgar jovially.

'All very well you saying that, Edgar,' Mildred said, 'but they don't do a good job of preventing it happening, and if everyone knows it goes on and nobody says anything, then the child just accepts it as normal. Then, by the time he leaves school and can decide for himself, it's too late; he's affected for life.'

'You are worried about Terry Smith,' Edgar accused. 'You told me you believed Eldred when he said nothing had happened.'

'I said we had to leave him time to think,' Mildred said, 'and not go leaning on him, asking questions. It won't work like that with Eldred.'

'He talked to me this morning quite freely, about everything else,' Edgar said. 'Surely, if there was something, he would have mentioned it.'

'Not if he hadn't worked it out for himself first,' said Mildred. 'He didn't talk at all to either of us for five years, and goodness knows how long he'd been understanding everything.'

Edgar sighed. 'Is it wrong,' he said, 'to wish we had a normal child?'

'Not wrong, I don't suppose,' said Mildred. 'But we have to be thankful he's well now, don't we? He's not in an oxygen tent in a hospital ward.'

'No, that's right,' Edgar said. He put one arm round his wife and reached with the other hand for the remote control. 'By the way, what kind of a day did you have?' he said, turning up the sound. A row between two police constables blurred his last words.

'Quite good, dear, thank you,' said Mildred. 'Educational.'

Chapter Forty

'Good news!' said Andrew. 'They said I could be the one to tell you.'

'What?' said Keith. His leg hurt and the drug trolley was late. He felt light-headed and his perceptions were heightened: the light coming through the window seemed dazzling, and looking at each person he could see the emotions they were feeling, more clearly than he could see the features on their faces. He mistrusted this lucid state. He hoped it didn't mean he was going to have a fit.

'Dad's getting you a modem for your computer,' Andrew said. 'You can send e-mail. And get hooked up to the Internet.'

'That's great.'

Looking at his brother, Keith saw billows of distress pouring out of him, like smoke from the windows of a burning house.

'Is there any other news?' he asked.

'Yes. This is even better. Some TV people rang up. They're doing a programme on special children and they might want you to be on it. They're interviewing people this week.'

'I won't be out of hospital till next week. Mr Abdul came round this morning and said.'

'Mum told them that. They said someone could come to the hospital. It's only the first interview. You mightn't be selected.'

'Is it disabled children, or what?' Keith didn't feel enthusiastic. Was this one of those 'reward for being a brave little chap' shows? If so, he was sick of it. He would have said something cynical, but Andrew worried him. If he was about to have a fit, Keith wanted a chance to ask Andrew what was the matter with him first.

'No, all kinds of special kids, special talents and so on. Kids with unusual lives, you know.' He was shifting about, rearranging the position of the water jug and Lucozade bottle and box of tissues and sweets on Keith's bedside table. 'Do you want to go on it, if you get the chance?'

'I don't mind. Would you?'

'Go on telly? Sure. If I had a special life.'

'Everyone's life is special,' Keith said. 'How's yours going at the moment?'

Andrew shrugged. 'All right.'

'Something upsetting you?'

'No.'

'Oh,' said Keith. 'I thought there was.'

Andrew shot him a quick glance, then lowered his head. Keith studied his own left hand. The fingers were opening and then gripping shut of their own accord. It might not be long before his head started shaking. Then Andrew would have to call the nurse and the curtains would be drawn around the bed so the other patients and visitors wouldn't be disturbed by the sight of a poor deformed boy, red-faced, frothing at the mouth, gasping and shaking, tossed to and fro like a rabbit in the mouth of a frenzied dog.

Andrew sat down on the edge of the bed. 'You don't miss much, do you? I can never hide anything from you, even if I want to. Which I don't really, Keith; it's just that I don't know how to say it. It's embarrassing.'

He would have to be quick and use his instincts. He would prefer to wait and let Andrew find the words in his own time, but time was running short.

A young woman in a white towelling dressing gown walked down the ward. 'Anyone got a light?' She had an unlit cigarette in her hand. She looked at Keith, did a double-take, then looked away quickly.

A nurse, drawing back the curtains from the bed in the corner and carrying away a bedpan, stopped her. 'You shouldn't be smoking before your operation.'

'She doesn't look very ill, does she?' Andrew whispered. 'D'you know what she's in for?'

'I haven't seen her before,' said Keith. 'She must have just come in today.' Looking at her, he saw, as if on an X-ray, an embryo curled up in a corner of her body, its tiny unformed fists clenching and unclenching as his own hands were, flexing its infant muscles as it slept. Sensitive to every vibration, every sensation and sound, it received all the information in the world through the filter of its mother's protective body. But not for long.

Keith didn't so much hear the scream as the baby was torn away from its lifeline as feel the agony within himself, as if it were his own life being rejected. Sucked out of its home with the force of a passenger sucked out of the shattered window of a sky-borne jumbo jet, the baby shot into a blaze of light and a deafening cacophony of sound, unable to breathe, with the delicate cells of its body wrenched apart. The defencelessly thin flesh was grabbed up in rough hands and deposited into a cold metal kidney dish, ready for disposal.

Keith flinched and writhed on the bed. Andrew was instantly alert. 'What's wrong? Shall I call the nurse?'

'No, I'm all right. Sit down.' He forced his mind back to the present. 'Tell me what's wrong. Is it something to do with Jessica?'

Andrew stared at him. 'How did you know?'

Keith turned his eyes away from the young woman who was about to have an abortion, who was protesting to the nurse about her right to have a cigarette. He looked at Andrew, seeing him enmeshed with a girl of about his age, the veins in his arms connecting with her arteries, his blood supply draining into hers.

'You're very involved with her, aren't you?'

'Yes.' Andrew looked away. 'Everyone thinks I'm silly. Or that it's *sweet*,' he said venomously. 'I know I'm only thirteen. But I'm in love with her, Keith. I think about her night and day. I can't think about anything else.'

Keith felt a pang, even while realizing it couldn't be literally true. Andrew had thought about him, had come visiting him, come to tell him good news. Jessica hadn't replaced Keith in Andrew's life, just occupied a lot of space that had previously been taken up with other things. Or perhaps she had filled a large gap in Andrew's life. Maybe that was more like it.

'How does she feel?'

'The same as me,' Andrew said. Keith, watching him, saw the girl clinging on to him, desperate with need.

'She lost her mother, didn't she?' Keith said.

'Last year, yes.'

'She must feel very alone and afraid.'

Andrew looked suspicious. 'You're saying it's not really love; she just needs security, and I'm handy?'

'Is that what you think, yourself?'

'No!' he said vehemently.

'She must be feeling quite lost, though,' said Keith. 'And you're a really kind person to people who need help. I ought to know,' he added, seeing Andrew grow angry.

Andrew softened. 'It's more than that. I don't think about you night and day, do I? Why do people think someone my age can't be in love? Do you think that?'

'I haven't had the experience,' said Keith sadly, 'and I'm probably not likely to have. I don't know the dividing line between love and need. All the people I love, I need in some way, so I can't really be objective.'

'We need you as well,' Andrew said. He fought back tears. 'You look after all of us as well. It's just not so obvious.'

'Maybe,' said Keith cautiously, 'you're both quite vulnerable, for other reasons, and you're being a bit of a lifeline to one another.' He mustn't let his mind dwell on that baby whose lifeline was about to be ripped away; push the thoughts away and concentrate on Andrew. His feet were beginning to clench now, along with his hands, and his head was starting to throb and feel very hot. He tried to think clearly; his speech would soon become slurred. His voice already sounded to him as though it was coming from a long way away.

'Jessica's on her own,' he said, 'with her mother gone and her father at work all day. You're all she has. And you may soon lose me, and we've got on pretty well. I can't be rescued. Maybe it seems to you that she can, so you're giving her all the strength you have. But keep some for yourself, Andrew. Your life is important too. And don't become Mum and Dad's life-support when I've gone. You have a right to a life of your own.'

He couldn't distance the baby any more now; he could feel her distress, right inside his bones; he was the embryo, with no life of her own, torn away from her moorings, ejected into a cruel, cold world, exposed and alone, facing death ill-equipped and unprotected.

Dimly, he heard Andrew say, 'Are you all right? Keith!' then, a little while later, in a higher pitch, 'Keith, don't die on me! Don't leave me!'

But by then the waves were breaking over his head and he was in the grip of the merciless force that suctioned out his breath and closed his lungs and destroyed the only freedom Keith ever had, the freedom to think his own thoughts and be himself.

Now he was just a pawn, held down by the hands of the same young nurse who would assist this afternoon at her first abortion. She was looking forward to the experience, proud to be used to help save a poor young girl from the fate of giving birth to a creature who – like this boy here – was too poorly formed to be considered fully human or to have a real life to live.

Chapter Forty-one

Friday couldn't come soon enough for Eldred. He phoned Louise three times, once to ask what kind of questions he'd have to answer, once to enquire whether the other children would be like him, and once on Mildred's behalf, to ask what the Jones family should wear.

Louise was amused by his excitement and didn't seem to mind phoning him back when he left a message on her answerphone, though Mildred had feared she would resent it. They could wear what they liked, she said; it wasn't going to be televised yet as it was only a preliminary chat with one of the programme's researchers. Eleven children were to be interviewed but only three or four would be selected. It was possible that Eldred would not appear at all on the final programme, which had not been scheduled and might not be seen until next year.

He should come prepared to answer questions about himself, his life and his interests, as well as giving a concise and simple explanation of the workings of his inventions, and yes, it would be helpful if he brought diagrams. He shouldn't be disappointed, however, if half an hour's explaining got finally condensed into one sentence. Television was like that, she said: all impact and no depth, so be warned by one who knew and had suffered from it!

Eldred promised solemnly to expect nothing at all, then dreamed all night of fame and fortune, of terrible errors and disgraceful failure, of being forcibly ejected from television studios, and of public schools at which Stephen Hawking lectured about black holes in space, in a computer-voice that only spoke ancient Greek, which all the pupils except Eldred understood perfectly. Friday came at the end of a sleepless week.

Edgar, meanwhile, had brought home a prospectus for the school his boss's sons attended. Eldred studied it carefully, though there was little to be gleaned about the school's approach to children who learned too quickly for their age group. The brochure's main claims were about sports achievements, university admissions and caring staff. What the staff cared about was not made clear: presumably sports achievements and university places gained by their pupils, Eldred deduced.

From the whispered conversations between his parents, he also gathered that the fees were beyond their reach, even if Edgar did get promotion and Mildred took what she described as 'a little job'. Elation, when Edgar first brought the prospectus home, had given way to despair when he had discovered that the fee stated was not for the year, as he had thought, but per term.

'Even if this television thing does come off,' said Edgar, 'no one's going to see it till next year, are they? And I can't imagine anything coming of it. Who's going to pay for a child to go to a posh school, just because he's bored? And what public school would take him for free, when they could have a fee-paying, normally bright child who's good at sport as well and who fits in? Who wants a little eccentric who invents machines at home but doesn't do what he's told in his computing class because it's too easy?'

So it was only Eldred who was excited when Friday came. His parents, neatly dressed and nervous, had low expectations. Their only hope was that they wouldn't be asked any difficult questions themselves.

The studio building, at first sight, was daunting – large, modern, busy and with an air of uncompromising efficiency. Here people were siphoned in off the streets, scanned for their story-worthy value, purged of their irrelevancies, dosed with instructions on what to tell the presenter and how to face the cameras, and packaged into two- or five- or ten-minute slots, before being discharged and returned, shaken and disorientated, to pick up the threads of their everyday lives.

'It's like a hospital, isn't it?' said Eldred, in the lift.

The secretary who had come to collect them from the foyer smiled. 'I don't think the architect and designers would like that, but you're probably right!'

'I didn't mean the building,' Eldred explained. 'I meant the process of coming to be interviewed. It's like being X-rayed and waiting to hear if the experts say you're all right.'

The lift doors opened. 'Down here, follow me,' said the girl.

She walked into an office – without knocking, Eldred noticed – and announced, 'Elbert Jones and his parents.'

'Eldred,' Edgar corrected.

A woman who looked slightly older than the secretary stood up from behind her desk and came forward to shake Edgar's hand. 'Good to see you, Eldred,' she said. 'And?' She raised her eyebrows enquiringly at Mildred.

'My wife Mildred,' said Edgar.

'Eldred and Mildred!' the woman exclaimed. 'Well, that's an unusual partnership of names! And you're Elbert?' she said to Eldred. There was a laugh in her voice that Eldred suspected would be used in her coffee break, telling her colleagues.

'No,' he said firmly. 'My father is Edgar, my mother is Mildred, and I'm Eldred. My name is a mixture of their names, which is logical because I am a mixture of their genes.'

'Oh,' she said. He had succeeded in stopping the laugh. He was only surprised, on looking at his parents, to see them both blushing.

Maybe genes were embarrassing. His parents seemed uncomfortable with biology, Eldred had noticed.

'Well,' the woman said. 'My name is Rachel Hicks. I'm a researcher here, and I've invited you along to get to know you a little bit, especially you, Eldred, with a view to including you on a programme we're planning about unusual children.'

Edgar and Mildred nodded. Eldred stared at Rachel Hicks, memorizing her face and style. Rather hard, he thought, spends a lot of money on her clothes, impatient with her make-up, long nails, greedy fingers.

'Before I start asking you questions,' she said, 'are there any questions you'd like to ask yourselves?'

'Yes please,' said Eldred. Edgar gave him a warning glance, which Rachel, sharp-eyed, noticed.

'Go ahead,' she said.

Eldred decided to heed his father's glance and be concise. This woman had already consulted the clock on her desk twice since they walked in.

'Is the programme definitely going to take place or is it just an idea?' he asked. 'And if it's definite, when will it be scheduled? And if only three or four of the eleven children at the interviews will be selected, how much time will be allocated to each? And what criteria are being used to select whether a child is unusual, and is it all the same kind of unusual – I mean, are they all unusually intelligent, or are they all unusual in different ways?'

Rachel, who had opened her mouth to answer Eldred's first question, closed it halfway through his speech. 'That's not a question, that's a questionnaire!' she said now.

'It's generally a mistake to let Eldred ask questions,' said Edgar dryly.

'Let me try to answer them in one sentence,' said Rachel. 'The programme is definitely scheduled to be made but won't be scheduled for screening until after it's completed. The eleven children being interviewed this week are all unusual for different reasons; some are like you, Eldred; some are very talented musically or at sports; some have shown great bravery... that kind of thing.

We'll probably pick one child from each category, depending on personality as well as their achievements, and the programme will last forty minutes, probably divided equally between the different stories. Okay?'

'Thank you,' said Eldred.

'Now, if you don't object, I have a questionnaire for you, Eldred,' Rachel said. She reached into her desk drawer and pulled out a sheaf of papers. 'I'd like you, if you will, to fill in the answers to these questions as best you can in ten minutes, while Sonia here, who brought you in, will take your parents to see round the studios.'

Edgar and Mildred looked at Eldred, disconcerted. Eldred shrugged.

'Okay, I don't mind,' he said.

'Oh, we'll just stay here,' Mildred said. 'We're not really concerned to see the studios, are we, dear?'

'If you wouldn't mind,' said Rachel, her smile setting. 'I'm sure you'll find it interesting.'

Mildred hesitated.

'You go,' said Eldred encouragingly. 'I expect this is a test to see if I'm really intelligent, and they want to make sure you don't tell me the answers or anything. Is that it?' he asked Rachel.

'No, not at all,' she said quickly. 'It's just easier to concentrate if you're on your own.'

'Will you be going too then?' Eldred said.

'No,' she said. 'I'll be here but I won't distract you. I'll be getting on with my own work.'

Sonia lifted Mildred by the elbow. 'This way,' she said.

Eldred pulled the questionnaire towards him. It was not so much questions to be answered, he saw, as a series of puzzles. He sat back in the chair and looked through them.

Rachel, watching him, was struck by his concentration. The child was completely still, focusing on the page before him. After a few seconds, he turned the page, immediately after that movement resuming his stillness. Then he turned to the next page, dwelling on this one for hardly any time, then the final one.

'Yes,' he said, under his breath. 'I see how it works.' He turned back to page one and laid the questionnaire face downwards on the desk. He sat back and looked round the office, craning his neck to read the titles of books on the shelves.

'Can I have a look at your thesaurus?' he asked Rachel. 'I have one at home but it's much more concise. I'm compiling my own on the computer, but I need some more words.'

'Yes, you certainly can later,' she said. 'But just for now I'd like you to fill in the questionnaire – all right?'

Eldred looked surprised. 'Oh, sorry,' he said. 'I thought you said I had ten minutes. Ten minutes aren't up yet, are they?'

'No,' she said, 'but you haven't started.'

'Oh, that's all right,' he said. 'It doesn't take long to write, once you've done it in your head.' He sat down at the desk, picked up a pen and filled in the answers swiftly, without pausing to look at each question again. He did not fill them in consecutively, Rachel noticed, but picked the questions that required an answer in words first, then flicked back to the ones which asked for a diagram, and finally picked out the multiple choice questions which needed one of a list of possible solutions to be ringed.

He returned the sheets to their original order and handed them back to her. 'Can I look at the thesaurus now?' he said.

'Yes.' She looked at the clock on her desk. Four minutes had elapsed. There were sixty-five questions on the sheets. Even before she started checking them, she had a feeling the answers were all correct.

Chapter Forty-two

'How do you think it went?' Mildred asked on the way home.

'Not bad,' said her husband judiciously. 'Where was that Miss Palmer, though? I thought she was going to be there?'

'I asked that,' Eldred said, 'while I was waiting for you to come back from the tour. Rachel said Louise didn't work there; her role had been to supply one of the subjects for interview, in a freelance capacity, and she wouldn't be involved in the project any further.'

'I don't suppose she'll like that,' said Mildred.

'Oh dear.' Eldred hoped Louise wouldn't be too disappointed.

'How did you get on, Eldred?' Mildred asked, 'while we were out of the room? Did you have any problems with that test?'

'Not really,' Eldred said.

'Well, that's good. A bit of a cheek, springing that on you, I thought. I must say, Eldred, you explained it very well when she asked you about your machine. I almost understood it myself.'

'Thank you,' Eldred said.

'And you answered all the questions nice and clearly,' Mildred continued. 'Didn't you think so, Dad?'

'Yes, certainly,' Edgar said. 'He did very well. Perhaps a little celebration is called for – what do you think?'

They smiled at one another above Eldred's head.

'What do you say we get a take-away on our way home from the station, Eldred?' his father said. 'You choose – fish and chips, Chinese or Indian?'

'Can we have Indian?'

'We can have anything you like, son. It's your day.'

Eldred felt happy. Things were changing. Whether he was able to go to a new school or not, the process of trying to do so was having a new effect on his parents, it seemed to him. They were listening to him and talking to each other more, and it might be his imagination but they didn't seem so ashamed of him nowadays or so worried about what he might say or do in public. He might almost be sorry to leave now and go to a boarding school, even if he was accepted at one. Acceptance at home seemed worth almost more than attending a school where he was allowed to learn.

Over chicken korma and rice eaten at home, sitting not at the table but in front of the TV – an almost unprecedented event in the Jones house – Mildred showed Edgar the pictures in Eldred's colouring book.

Edgar studied them.

'He says,' Mildred said, 'that certain people only see certain things; that's why only some of the picture is coloured in. Is that what you said, Eldred, or am I getting it wrong?'

'No, that's it,' said Eldred. 'Everyone sees things differently, according to what's important to them.'

Edgar thought about this. 'I see things differently from you?'

'Yes.'

'And differently from your mother, or do she and I see things the same, but differently from you?'

'No – different from each other too,' said Eldred. He was reading the words on the take-away menu backwards. Korma was Amrok, which sounded tasty and still quite Indian, he thought, and Bhaji was Ijahb, which was not too easy to pronounce and sounded more Middle Eastern than Far Eastern. Popadom was Modapop – more like a fizzy drink. And Naan was Naan whichever way you read it, and that was interesting, Eldred thought – a bread that couldn't be anything but itself, a bread with an unchanging identity. 'A bread of integrity,' he murmured to himself.

'What's that?' said Edgar.

Eldred, unaware that he had spoken aloud, answered Edgar's earlier question. 'Well, you see things through one kind of filter, and Mum sees them through another kind.'

'What filter?' Edgar asked. 'I would have thought everyone sees what's in front of their nose to be seen.'

'No,' said Eldred. 'They have different noses, so they see past them differently.'

'I don't get it,' said Edgar.

'Eldred, don't annoy your father; eat your curry,' said Mildred automatically.

'He's not annoying me,' said Edgar. 'I just want to be told why he thinks I can't see past the end of my own nose.'

'Oh dear,' said Mildred. The day had gone so well, she thought sadly, and now it was about to be spoiled.

Eldred wriggled off the sofa and sat on the floor, facing his father.

'You see like this,' he explained. He held the menu at arm's length in front of him, closed one eye and squinted down his nose. 'Can't make this damn thing out,' he muttered. It was a fair impression of Edgar trying to read without his reading glasses on. Mildred reminded herself sternly not to giggle.

'And Mum sees like this,' Eldred continued. He placed his hands on his temples, facing outwards, like a horse's blinkers – or like his mother with a migraine, shielding her eyes from the light. 'Oh dear,' he said, in Mildred's most plaintive voice, 'I'm not going to be able to understand this; it's too bright.'

Edgar threw back his head and laughed. 'Oh, that's you all over, Mildred,' he said.

'Yes dear,' said Mildred, relieved at the remission of his annoyance.

'And Mrs Garcia at school sees like this,' Eldred said, enjoying the attention. He placed both hands firmly over his eyes and said with severity, 'It's pitch dark and no one can see anything, so don't you go telling me that dark is light, Eldred Jones, or I'll lop twenty per cent off your end-of-term marks.'

'Now, that's going far enough, Eldred,' said his father. 'A joke's a joke but you don't go making fun of your elders and betters. A teacher is superior to a little boy. Have some respect.'

Mildred sniffed, though quietly. 'I'll go and wash up,' she said. 'Hand me your plates.'

Chapter Forty-three

Lulubelle stood in the wings, clenching and unclenching her hands, taking deep breaths. It was only recently, since joining Mannfields' Circus, that she'd been allowed her own solo spot in the show; it didn't last very long, but it was a spectacular entrance, a high-speed routine that demanded precision and total concentration on her part.

The second part of her act was more familiar, as part of the troupe of acrobats, but she hadn't been working with them very long and the timing of the finale had to be accurate. This troupe was good, probably the best she had worked with, and their pyramid work was superb; she never ceased to be impressed by it. The secret to getting her own timing right was to watch them out of the corner of her eye, even while she was still cartwheeling round the ring, so that she knew the precise moment Carmel and Lucia launched themselves from the trampoline and landed on the shoulders of the line of three acrobats at the top of the pyramid.

Then it was time to pivot herself on one hand and throw herself into the air in a series of backward flips and hurtle towards the tower of human beings, all precariously balanced on one another. She wasn't experienced enough yet for the trampoline – not to get up to that height and land perfectly poised above Carmel and Lucia, without wobbling.

So, to add to the excitement of the act's finale, they had devised this risk: the little blonde acrobat, circling the ring apparently regardless of the others forming their pyramid, carelessly doing her own thing… then the shout from everyone in the pyramid, warning her of the risk. One or two of them on the outside of the formation waved their arms. The men on the bottom layer – the foundation – would appear to be the most frightened, would shake and wobble their knees, and the girls on the top – Carmel and Lucia – would shriek.

The audience would be divided in its response. Some, especially the smaller children, would scream. The older ones would laugh. But nobody took their eyes off the scene in the ring.

Then just as Lulubelle, at dangerous speed, hurled herself right up to Ian, standing foursquare and solid in the centre of the foundation row, Manuel above him would grab her by her feet as she performed her final – and apparently lethal – flying handstand, and throw her up to Carlo, who threw her to Sabina and Elsa, who apparently threw her – but in fact passed her quite gently – the right way up, to Carmel and Lucia, who placed her on their shoulders. That was her moment of glory, high above the crowds, waving and acknowledging the applause, shiny-eyed and brilliant-smiled in her jewelled white tutu and sparkling tights.

The other young performers could be a bit jealous. She had to be careful, out of performance hours and at rehearsals, to include everyone in her circle of friends. Feuds arose so easily, with everyone living and working on top of one another. Lulubelle had seen only too clearly, from Lucinda's example, what happened when a star performer favoured one person and alienated another. She couldn't afford to have 'best friends'. She had to be best friends with everyone, for the sake of their future in the circus.

Even so, there were a few who would have been only too pleased to tell Mr Mannfield this evening that Lulubelle Lacosto had got into the lions' cage and had to be rescued. But there were only a few who knew, and although the circus grapevine was hard to evade, the different groups of workers could form a closed circuit when it suited them.

None of the men who had come to her rescue would breathe a word of the incident to anyone else, because most of them were connected to one another by family ties – so distant and complicated no one could quite specify what relation he was to the next one – but still, tied by blood and bound to silence in cases such as this, where the man who had left the door of the outer cage ajar for a few minutes could lose both his job and his chance of employment anywhere else.

So Lulubelle wouldn't be reprimanded or risk being sacked herself by Mr Mannfield, who would never get to know about her escapade, but that meant that neither was there any chance of being let off tonight's performance. All the tumultuous events in Lulubelle's life in the past twenty-four hours had to be relentlessly banished from her mind now, as her hands clenched and unclenched and she awaited her cue to enter the ring with a rush of energy and a dazzling smile.

Even Arto's promise of contacting his agent on her behalf, and his affirmation of her talent and her potential; even the possibility of being picked for the TV documentary, she mustn't think about now. Nothing must be allowed to distract her attention.

It was only at the successful conclusion of the acrobats' routine that she felt her concentration waver. That was when, standing tall and proud at the top of the pyramid, her arms outstretched in triumph, she scanned the crowd and, as earlier this afternoon, thought she saw someone she recognized. For a second, she lost her balance and thought she would fall.

Lucia automatically tightened her grip round Lulubelle's ankle, and she and Carmel, who had been chatting casually out of the corners of their mouths, caught their breath and went rigid for an instant, till she steadied herself.

A little more promptly than usual, they reached up and grasped her hands and started her on her descent from the pyramid, catching the performers lower down unawares. But they were trained to react, and their smiles never faltered as they responded to the early cue to send Lulubelle tumbling from hand to hand, followed by Lucia and Carmel, till they all lined up on the ground and gave a final wave to the cheering audience before tumbling and somersaulting their way to the exit.

'Nearly give us a heart attack there, Lu!' Carmel complained. 'What came over you?'

'My mind wandered,' Lulubelle admitted.

'Well, don't let it wander again. I've had one fractured bone in my wrist this year already and I'm not planning on another one.'

'Sorry.'

Lucinda passed her on her way back from the changing tent to the caravan. She was never on till after the interval, when the audience were becoming blasé about performing seals and wacky clowns and needed a real thrill of fear to get them sitting upright in their seats again. Trapeze acts, high wire, and lions: that was the dessert course on the menu.

'Everything go all right?' she asked, ruffling Lulubelle's hair. She looked refreshed and smiling; she seemed to have forgotten the incident in the caravan when Lulubelle had disturbed her liaison with Sam, and she obviously hadn't heard about the lion episode.

'Fine,' said Lulubelle. 'You okay?' She couldn't smell drink on her now, and Lucinda's eyes looked almost clear.

'Never better, sweetie.'

'Is there anything to eat at home, Mum... I mean, Lucinda?'

'Don't know, love. Have a look. Shouldn't think there's much of anything. We'll go shopping when we get paid tomorrow. How's your... you know what?'

'Okay. Marisa gave me some cotton wool.'

'Oh, that's all right then. Why don't you go and help Bernard's children on the rifle range? You might get a hamburger out of him if he's treating his own.'

'Okay.' She wouldn't, though; she didn't feel like company this evening. She would probably just go to bed; it had been a long day. She wasn't really that hungry anyway. 'Oh – listen,' she said, as her mother turned away. 'You didn't see anyone that looked like that bloke who was at Bepponi's, did you? I thought I saw him around here at rehearsals, and then just now. But it might have been somebody else.'

'You mean that guy who...? Would you recognize him, Lulubelle?'

'I don't know,' she said. 'I know he had dark hair and dark eyes and wasn't all that tall. But all I really remember about him was that he was wearing an anorak hood that was separate from his jacket, and a different colour. I couldn't even tell what colour, because it was dark.'

'That isn't much help, is it?' Lucinda agreed. 'Well, look, darling, have a nice evening and stay close to Fee and Tom and Samantha, okay? Don't go back to the caravan on your own. If there's people around that you know, you can always ask for help, can't you?'

'What time will you be home?'

'Oh, I don't know.' Lucinda's expression became vague. 'I might go for a nightcap with some of the others.'

'Whose van will you be in?'

'Oh, Lulubelle, how do I know? It depends who's inviting, doesn't it? I won't be that late. Tell you what, I'll pop back home sometime during the evening, just to check you're sound asleep and safe. Okay? Can't say fairer than that now, can I?'

She seemed to have forgotten she'd told Lulubelle not to go back to the caravan on her own. She waved, blew a kiss unthinkingly, and was gone.

Lulubelle thought she might as well go back to the caravan now, before it was late and while the man – whoever it was – was still with the rest of the audience in the Big Top, before they all started milling around in the interval, fetching drinks and ice-creams and candyfloss and sweets.

She would go in and get straight into her pull-out shelf of a bed, pulling the curtains across the windows and leaving no lights on. The door never locked properly and anyway had to be left open for Lucinda, who would come home without a key more often than not, but if she pulled the covers right over her head, even if someone came in they would think the caravan was empty. She was so thin, her form hardly made any hummock under the bedclothes.

She was probably worrying for nothing, in any case. The chances were it wasn't him at all.

Chapter Forty-four

Eldred was listening to Mrs Garcia talk about the life cycle of the honey bee, and thinking about something else.

In his mind he was back in the television studio, recapturing a moment of his visit that at the time he had hardly noticed. It interested him that the mind chose to replay certain snatches of experience at certain times. He believed there must be a reason, but his reasoning did not supply him with one.

When the interview was finished and Sonia was escorting the family back to the lift, Eldred had needed to go to the toilet, so Sonia had directed him towards the door labelled Men. Mildred went into the Women's and Edgar took the lift downstairs, saying he would meet them in the foyer. Mildred told Eldred to wait for her here in the corridor if he came out before her.

As he came out of the Men's, a girl of about his own age ran down the corridor – no, not ran, Eldred thought; bounded, or pranced, might be a better way of describing the way she moved. She seemed, Eldred reflected, almost weightless. She was more or less his own height, of very slight build, with fair hair caught back in a careless plait with escaping strands, and was dressed in a hooded tracksuit top and cropped leggings in brightly clashing colours.

It was not only the way she dressed, though, Eldred thought. She seemed colourful, in herself. As she pushed open the Women's door she gave him a swift glance and smiled. The glance was direct and shrewd, through clear blue eyes that didn't waver when they met his, but the smile was warm. Then she disappeared through the door.

Mildred came out a few seconds later. 'All right to go?' she said.

'Yes,' Eldred said. 'Did you see a girl go in there after you?'

'I certainly did,' said Mildred. 'Wearing make-up too! She can't have been more than ten years old. I don't know what kids are coming to.'

'Eldred Jones,' said Mrs Garcia, appearing at his side and tweaking his ear suddenly and painfully, 'this may be news to you but you are not in this class to daydream but to work. What have I just been saying?'

'About drones,' said Eldred, 'letting the worker bees do all the work.'

'Exactly,' said Mrs Garcia. 'And who is the drone in this class, children? Who can tell me the answer to this?' She stepped back and pointed at Eldred theatrically. The children laughed.

Eldred was used to this. The teacher would frequently turn the class against one child she wished to rebuke. For some reason, today he felt a sense of injustice and didn't immediately fight it down as usual. Perhaps it was the memory of the girl's smile. He could see her now as though she was in the class, standing behind Mrs Garcia, and the smile seemed to hold a certain sympathy. I know how you feel, it said.

This sense of being understood made Eldred bold.

'That's not true,' he said. 'I do work.'

'Oh,' said Mrs Garcia, 'you work, do you? You don't simply sit here gazing into space and taking in none of the things that you're here to learn?'

'No,' Eldred said. 'I was listening too.'

'Too?' said Mrs Garcia. 'You're not meant to be listening *too*. You are meant to be listening and doing nothing else. What else were you doing?'

'Thinking,' Eldred said simply.

'Well, I have more news for you,' Mrs Garcia said. 'You can't listen and think at the same time, even if you think you can. So concentrate on listening, please... dronc.' She turned to her audience again and the children laughed obediently.

Eldred lowered his head and let hatred and rage sweep over him. From the depths of his heart, without any conscious decision by his mind, he heard himself say silently, 'Please, please, get me out of here and send me to a school where this doesn't happen.'

He accepted that it was illogical to address the Most High when God was a theory that Eldred still wasn't sure he subscribed to. Perhaps the heart didn't always respond to the beliefs of the mind. That in itself was interesting. He pondered the possibility; the discipline of thought calmed him. Rage and hurt began to subside and didn't even return when Mrs Garcia handed out sheets of coarse blue paper – stolen from the infants' class since her own supply of proper drawing paper had run out – and instructed her eleven year olds to draw a beehive.

'And the child who draws the best one just might deserve a prize,' she said. Her eyes settled on Ryan Andrews who was never any trouble and her hand jingled the collection of badges in her pocket to gauge how many were left. The badges were silver or gold and they all said, 'I did well in school today.'

Eldred considered that the only unknown factor in this beehive-drawing competition was whether Ryan would go home wearing a gold or a silver badge today. He picked up the nearest biro and scrawled a dome shape on the page, with a few dots around it for bees, then lost interest and used the rest of the paper for jotting down a jumble of equations that came into his head just then for no apparent reason. Reason wasn't everything, he thought.

Chapter Forty-five

Louise phoned. 'Good news, Eldred!'

'Have I been selected?' Eldred asked eagerly.

'For what?'

'For the documentary on unusual children,' he said.

'Oh, that. I haven't heard from my contact on the team yet,' said Louise. 'They'll let you know direct. No, there's something else I've been able to arrange.'

Eldred was pleased. He had been afraid that Louise would be upset at not being involved in the TV programme after all. He hoped they might still pay her something for finding him, even if her name wasn't even in small print in the credits.

'What is it?' he said.

'You're going to be on the local television news,' Louise told him.

'Have you asked my dad?' said Eldred cautiously.

'Is there likely to be a problem? He agreed to the other programme, didn't he?'

'Yes. But now he's saying there's no point,' Eldred said, 'because it won't be shown till next year, maybe, and he doesn't think anyone will contribute anything to a strange child's education as a result of it. And he's got a prospectus for a small public school and it's much too expensive for us to even think of.'

'All the more reason to try everything,' said Louise. 'You get your mum to talk to him, all right? Shall I talk to her now?'

'She's gone out,' said Eldred, 'after a job.'

'Oh, right. Well, you talk to her then.'

'Why the local news?' asked Eldred. 'Nothing's happened to me.'

'The waste recycling machine,' said Louise. 'I've got hold of a few people to say it's a viable product.'

'Who?' said Eldred.

'Someone from the Patents Office and Bruce Mackeson and the project manager from a German chemical company.'

'Bruce Mackeson?' said Eldred.

'The farm manager,' said Louise, 'from your school trip, remember?'

'I remember,' said Eldred slowly, 'but how did you know where to find him?'

'You told me his name and the area the farm was in,' said Louise. 'It wasn't too hard to track him down. The only thing I didn't know was the farm name.'

'Oh,' said Eldred. He felt betrayed. 'I suppose that's the way journalists find out about things,' he said.

'No problem,' said Louise. 'And he's quite a convincing speaker. You might be on the way to getting a buyer out of this publicity, Eldred.'

'Would it pay for my school fees?' asked Eldred.

'No, don't bank on it. It'd be years before you saw much return from this, probably. What we're looking for is publicity. We'll do this, then go for a follow-up if it generates some interest. The public like stories with a happy ending.'

Eldred noted the 'we'. 'Will you get paid for this?'

She laughed. 'I certainly hope so!'

'And will I?'

'No,' she said. 'You get publicity. I'm the journalist who gets paid for doing the research and selling them the story to use.'

'Will your name get mentioned on the local news?'

'No,' she said.

'So you won't get any credit for yourself, either on the TV documentary or on local TV?'

'My name won't go on the credits,' said Louise, 'but the producer will get to know me, and I'll get an acknowledgment of my contribution which will go in my file and may be useful in helping me get other commissions.'

'Oh,' said Eldred, 'so there is something in it for you?'

'Right,' she said. She was sounding rather annoyed, Eldred thought. 'Why are you asking?' Louise added. She hoped to God the child wasn't trying to blackmail her into giving him some of her fees.

'I just thought it wasn't fair of them to take all the credit when you were the one who gave them the idea,' said Eldred, 'but if you're getting paid and getting some help in your career out of it then it's probably worth it, isn't it?'

'Yes, it's all right,' she said. 'Don't you worry about me. Now, what will happen, Eldred, is that someone from the TV network will contact your parents and ask if they can send a team round to the house. So get your parents' agreement as soon as possible, will you?'

'Yes,' said Eldred.

'You think they'll agree?'

'Yes,' he said firmly. 'We'll do it.'

Edgar came home looking tired. 'Where's your mother?'

'Gone to see about a job. She phoned up this afternoon and they told her to come in right away.'

'Leaving you alone in the house?' said Edgar.

'I'm very sensible,' said Eldred modestly.

Edgar sat down and shook out the newspaper roughly. 'What kind of job is it?'

'At the supermarket. Filling shelves.'

'She won't be able to do that,' Edgar said. 'I've seen people doing that, pushing those great multi-storey trolleys stacked with tins. She couldn't do it, even if they were foolish enough to give her the job in the first place.'

'Would you like me to make you a cup of tea?' offered Eldred.

'Your mother should be here to do that,' Edgar grumbled. 'I wouldn't mind if there was a cat in hell's chance of paying those school fees but as there isn't, what's the point in her taking a job?'

'I've got some news that might help,' said Eldred cautiously, 'though maybe not directly.'

'What news?' said Edgar from behind the sports page.

'I'll make the tea first, shall I?' Eldred suggested. He hoped his father would be in a better mood by the time Mildred came in all disappointed from being too old and weak for the job.

'Cooee!' called Mildred, closing the front door behind her. 'Put the kettle on, Eldred, I've bought us a cake for tea. I got the job!'

Chapter Forty-six

It was a false alarm. No doubt there would be a few more of them.

Keith opened his eyes to find a ring of white, stricken faces around him. They were all there: Mum, Dad, Grandad, Andrew – and a young girl Keith had never seen before. Andrew must have phoned Jessica. She was crying more than any of them.

Hazily, he said, 'I'm all right. I'm okay.' His voice sounded hollow. His mouth was dry and his tongue stuck to the roof of his mouth. He would have liked to ask for a drink but he couldn't remember the word for it right now. Perhaps one of them would think of it. They were all staring at him.

'Hello, darling,' said his mother, coming forward. Her voice was bright. She always felt it was best for him if everyone pretended nothing was wrong. He wasn't sure why that was: whether she really believed that he wouldn't realize there was a risk he would die, or whether she was asking him to pretend he was fine and not to display any difficult emotions that she might not be able to soothe away.

She smoothed his pillow now, stroked his hair away from his face and kissed him, then rearranged his hands on the hospital counterpane. Finally she repositioned the bottle of Lucozade on the bedside locker. He tried to turn his head to look at it, to give her a hint he was thirsty, but she didn't notice. She was looking at Jessica, who was sobbing uncontrollably. It was not a look of sympathy but a look that said, louder than words, *Behave yourself.*

Andrew was trying to comfort her, uncomfortably. The look he received from his mother was equally clear: *You shouldn't have brought her.*

Keith summoned all his energy and lifted his hand. 'Here,' he said to Andrew.

Andrew left Jessica and moved to his side.

'No,' said Keith. He moved his hand again, in Jessica's direction. 'Come here.'

Andrew stood back and drew Jessica by the arm, gently, to stand by his brother's bed.

'Hi,' said Keith. His fingers twitched, in the semblance of a wave. He smiled.

'Hi,' she said. Tears streaked her face. She looked younger than her thirteen years. She took the hand he held out.

'I heard a lot about you,' said Keith. 'Nice to meet you, Jessica.' His breath ran out before the end of her name, which came out as Jessi...

The girl broke into a fresh burst of crying. 'Sorry,' she sobbed. She looked unseeingly round at the whole family, addressing her apology to all of them. 'Sorry. My mum used to call me Jessie...'

She was pulling away from Keith's hand, about to run out of the curtained cubicle and out of the hospital ward, away from this family where she didn't belong. Keith tightened the grip of his hand, as much as he could, and widened his eyes at Andrew, who understood. He moved forward and put his arm round her shoulders, awkwardly, aware of his mother's eyes boring into him: *Get her out of here; she's upsetting Keith.*

Grandad pulled up a chair and gently pushed the girl into it. 'Here,' he said.

Keith smiled at him. The girl slumped forward, her head on her arms on the bed, and sobbed more loudly. There was a note of fear in her crying, Keith heard. She had been trying to stop herself doing this for so long, trying not to upset people – her dad probably, and now Andrew's family – and she was afraid of their reaction, afraid to be seen as causing more grief to those who were already grieved, yet she'd reached the point where her own grief couldn't be held in any longer, and now she was frightened it would overwhelm her and all of them and she would have started a flood she couldn't stop.

'Sorry,' she kept saying, in between sobs.

With immense effort Keith lifted his hand and laid it on her head. 'I'm sorry,' he said. 'I'm sorry your mother died. You've had a rough time.'

Grandad stood behind her still, between Andrew and his mother. His father held back.

Keith looked across at his mother. She knew him well enough to know what he was saying to her; she wasn't the only one who could give 'speaking looks' – instructions she would never acknowledge but expected the receiver to obey.

Keith held her gaze for a minute, looked back at the girl and then back at his mother. *You do it. She needs a mother.*

His mother looked away. When she looked up again, reluctantly, Keith was still staring at her. She turned back to the bedside locker, rearranged the box of tissues and the Lucozade.

'Want a drink, darling? It was a long fit; your throat must be sore, isn't it?'

When he didn't answer, she was forced to meet his eyes again. The look was more insistent – across to the girl, back to her. She resisted. *Haven't I got enough on my plate?*

She poured a drink and held it to his lips. He pursed them shut. She tried again, pretending she hadn't understood his message. His father, growing uneasy at this silent battle of wills, looked at his watch. The girl's sobs were more painful now; despair was creeping in.

It seemed to Keith she was crying for all of them. Only Andrew was joining in, quietly. Grandad was clearing his throat; Dad was taking directionless steps forward and back in the confined space; Mum was trying to be busy; Keith was getting angry. His family was not good at expressing grief; they were using this poor girl to do it for them. The least they could do in return was comfort her.

He gave up hinting, turned to his mother and said clearly, 'Look after her.'

Slowly, she put down the glass and moved to the other side of the bed. Grandad moved aside to let her pass. Standing behind Jessica, she put a hand awkwardly on her head, on top of Keith's hand. Keith pulled his hand away. His mother's stayed there. He could see her struggling to choke back her emotions, and he knew what the gesture spoke to her: *Take care of her. Let go of me.* His look at her now held sympathy: *I know.*

His mother helped Jessica to her feet and hugged her. The girl's sobs subsided the moment his mother's started, and it was Jessica who composed herself first and led the way out of the cubicle, saying to Andrew, 'I'll take her to the cafeteria and get her a coffee.'

Andrew went to follow her but his father said, 'I'd leave them to it, son.'

They pulled up chairs and sat down, the men of the family together.

'Andrew said you got me a modem for the computer,' Keith told his dad. 'Thank you.'

His father was embarrassed. 'Thought it might make it easier for you to stay in touch with those friends from the disabled group you're always writing to.'

'It will. Quite a few of them are on e-mail; people kept asking if I was.'

'Well, now you're one of the technocrats!' His father leaned forward, serious suddenly. 'Your mother said you feel you're at the end of the road. Do you?'

'No. Not yet. Just at the end of having operations. They won't do me any more good, Dad. I've had all the improvements my body can take.'

'I've been talking to Mr Abdul. He thinks something more could be done to ease the pressure on your hip.'

'That's what he's just done this operation for,' said Keith.

'No, he thinks if they operated on the femur...'

'No,' said Keith.

'I told him it was too soon to think about it. Give you time to get over this one before any talk about the next stage.'

'There is no next stage,' said Keith.

'Isn't that a bit defeatist? You're usually keen to try anything.'

'Anything that will help,' Keith corrected him.

'There was something else he suggested,' his father said diffidently. 'He thought he might be able to ease the strain on your breathing.'

'How?'

'Because your ribs are indented, he says there must be pressure on the lung. So...' His father hesitated.

'So, he wants to remove my ribs,' Keith supplied. 'Turn me into a jellyfish.'

'No. Just remove one. And reset the one below it.'

'Reset it?' Keith craned his neck to get a better look at him. 'You mean break it, then reset it.'

'Yes.'

'Dad,' said Keith. 'I've never asked you this. Will you give me an honest answer?'

'Sure. What is it?'

'How do you feel about all this? I mean, for fourteen years you've been with me before, during and after fifteen operations. How does it make you feel when someone says, "Mr Harper, what we'd like to do next with your son is break his ribs?"'

His father lowered his head. His hands were gripped together in his lap.

Andrew and Grandad were silent. Andrew was white as a sheet. Keith knew they were both feeling for his dad. It was a terrible question to ask him. But then, thought Keith, it was a terrible situation. If no one ever allowed him to voice those questions openly, each one of them would have to face them in his or her own mind, privately and alone, after he died. He wanted to spare them that if he could.

His father's shoulders were shaking. Jessica's open grief had unsettled all of them. It was a family rule not to show each other their real feelings. Keith felt it was high time the rule was broken.

'Your dad's always done what he thinks best for you, Keith,' said Grandad. His tone was reproachful but gentle.

'I know that,' said Keith. 'It's been a heavy responsibility for him. And now I want to take it for myself. I want to make the decisions.'

'I've never forced you,' said his father. 'We'd never have done anything unless you agreed.'

'And I did agree,' said Keith. 'But now I've decided to live out what's left of my life without any more operations. And I want you, and Mr Abdul, to agree, even if you don't really think I'm right.'

Grandad cleared his throat. 'When you say, "what's left of my life…" what are you thinking of, Keith?'

They had discussed this among themselves, he could tell. How long does he think he's got? How much has he been told? Does he have some instinctive knowledge of when he's going to die, or is this just depression, being morbid?

'What prognosis have you been given for me?' he asked. 'How long have the doctors told you to expect me to live? You've never told me.'

'They all say different things,' said his father. 'Most of them say it's impossible to estimate. So much depends on the person, how much of a fighter he is, the individual spirit. We've always just taken it one day at a time, son. When you were a baby, no one really expected you to live, and we've had fourteen years of you now.'

'Give me a rough estimate,' said Keith.

His father shrugged but didn't meet his eyes. 'How can anyone tell?' he said.

'I'd find it much easier,' said Keith, 'if people were honest with me. I'm not a child.'

'Are you angry?' said his father.

'Yes,' said Keith.

'Son, believe me, we've tried to do what's best for you, always. Don't be angry with us.'

'Why shouldn't he be bloody angry?' said Andrew. 'I would be.'

'Andrew.' His father put a hand on his arm. Andrew shook it off.

'Answer his bloody questions,' he said. 'Don't give him all this bullshit. Tell him what you told me.'

'Andrew, will you please let your mother and I deal with this in the way…'

'He doesn't want to be dealt with!' Andrew shouted. 'He wants the bloody truth.'

'There's no need to swear at me. Why don't you go down and join…?'

'You tell me,' said Keith. 'Tell me what they told you, Andrew.'

His brother hesitated. His father's expression warned him to silence.

'Please,' said Keith.

'Mr Gannet, who's left now, said it was only due to your spirit you'd survived this long,' said Andrew, almost inaudibly. 'He said you could go at any time. Particularly if you keep having fits.'

'Thank you,' said Keith. 'And thank you for bringing Jessica to see me. She's a very nice girl. And Dad, thanks for getting me the modem. I appreciate it. Could someone please give me a drink now?'

Chapter Forty-seven

The man in the blue padded jacket was impressed with the young girl. Even hiding behind the pillar, he had a clear view of her.

It was a spectacular routine. He wondered if she had invented it herself, or whether it was that stuffy ringmaster who seemed to think so much of himself. Dirty old man, probably. He knew the sort. Never took his eyes off her.

She moved with such grace and ease. So thin you could almost see through her. Probably anorexic. A lot of young girls were nowadays. He didn't mind. Some men only liked women with a bit of flesh on them, but he wasn't fussy. She had been scared of him last time, but that was only because she was young. This time, she'd know who he was, that he wasn't frightening.

The fire was a great idea. Fire was exciting. Maybe she'd thought of that idea herself? It was brilliant, that entrance of hers – spinning herself over and over like that, towards the fire in the centre of the ring, just missing it every time, then finally... ooooh! Right over the flames! He giggled and rubbed his hands, then clapped a hand over his mouth. No noise! What have I told you before? Been thrown out of here once already, silly boy.

He could watch her forever, he thought. That would be his dream: just her and him. There shouldn't be all these people watching her perform. That great ugly hulk of a man in the front seat, with the little woman beside him, and the man in the suit with the briefcase and the mobile phone – who did he think he was? No, none of them should be allowed near her. She needed protecting from their ugliness. He wasn't ugly, never had been. Women found him attractive, even though they pretended to be frightened of him. That was what women did, wasn't it?

As a young lad he'd been told off for frightening his sister, but she wasn't really frightened. They never were really, only pretending to be. Really, they found his games as thrilling as he did. He was imaginative. No one could call him boring.

If he had his way now, he'd get rid of the ugly, boring people in the front row, and all those dirty workmen standing around watching his girl, with their shirt-sleeves rolled up over their dirty, hairy arms. He shuddered. It was unspeakable: Beauty and all those beasts.

This girl's skin was so smooth and white, her neck so slender. Once she got to know him and trust him, she would be bound to him and him alone. Then she would dance for him whenever he wanted, round and round the leaping flames of their undying passion.

Lulubelle was nervous, performing in front of Arto's agent. He looked out of place in a circus, she thought, with a briefcase and all. He must be important.

Her timing was crucial, with this new entrance routine. She could feel the heat of the flames as she hurtled towards it, counting the turns, pacing the length of the backward flips; it had to be perfect. She'd done it enough times to get it right, but would she lose her nerve now?

Applause from Arto and his wife. Was the agent clapping as well? She thought he was. She landed upright, the other side of the fire, and faced them – arms out, palms upwards, eyes laughing, mouth smiling – the picture of confidence. No hint of the question in her mind: Was I all right?

She was. Arto and his agent were walking towards her, all smiles. He was impressed, she could tell. It was going to be all right.

She had heard from him on the same day as the initial interview and try-out for that TV programme about special children. He said he would like to see her perform – just on Arto's say-so. And now he had seen.

'Well done!' he said. He shook her by the hand. 'I think we can say we're in partnership!' He shook hands with Mr Mannfield.

'I hope you're not going to steal her away from us,' said Mr Mannfield jovially, but there was an edge to his tone.

'No way,' said the agent smoothly. 'She's doing good work where she is, and the other bookings will only create publicity for her act here – and for your circus.'

Mr Mannfield stroked his moustache. 'We have quite a reputation already,' he said. 'We know how to nurture young talent here.'

'I'm sure, I'm sure,' said the agent. 'Now Arto, where can we go for a little talk with this talented young friend of yours? Your caravan? Splendid. Of course, Mr Mannfield, of course – come and check the contract for yourself. I assure you, it in no way contravenes your own rights over the artiste in question...'

The artiste in question was sweating.

'I'll go and have a wash first,' she whispered to Marisa.

'Come take a shower,' Marisa offered. 'We go ahead now, Arto, okay? You follow. These men,' she confided in Lulubelle, 'they take their time; they talk! You have time for shower in our caravan.'

'Okay, thanks.' She was a star now, with an agent of her own. It was only fitting that she should take a shower in Marisa and Arto's glamorous bathroom, instead of having a quick wash at the little sink in their own caravan. 'But I'll just run home and tell Lucinda where I am,' she said. Lucinda would want to be in on signing the contract.

There might be a little celebration drink if everything went well, she had said this morning.

'Yes, child, go tell your mother. Invite her come, yes?'

'Yes, right.' You try stopping her, Lulubelle thought; she'll be there, invite or no invite!

She skipped over a guy rope and ran for the caravan. A group of children shouted her name, and she waved. 'See you later! Can't come now!'

Looking over her shoulder at them, she had turned the corner before she saw him ahead of her. Count Dracula. That's what he'd called himself, last time. She'd been wrong to imagine it must have been somebody else in the Big Top that day. She'd recognize him anywhere – even, as now, with his face in profile, looking the other way. He hadn't seen her.

She ran, behind the Waltzers, past the shooting range, across the helter-skelter compound, through the rows of caravans and trailers. What if he was following her? She wanted Lucinda, but she didn't want him to know where they lived. Would he remember the caravan? It was the same one they'd had at Bepponi's. But it had been dark then. Would he recognize which caravan belonged to them?

Turning sharply, she ran in the opposite direction, away from their home, towards Arto's. Arto's van represented safety.

She could hear laughing. Was it coming from behind her? Was it him?

Careering into Arto, laughing at something the agent was saying, she let out a scream.

'Hey!' he said. 'What's wrong?'

'Someone's following me!'

'Where?'

Clinging to him, she turned and pointed in the direction from which she'd come. There was no one there.

'Who was it?' said Arto. 'Someone you know?'

'He's gone now.'

'I go find him.'

'No, it's okay. Let's go in.' She didn't want to make a fuss in front of the agent. He might think she was a hysterical girl. And after all, what harm could come to her while she was with Arto the Incredible?

Chapter Forty-eight

Things were definitely changing, Eldred thought.

Edgar, though thoroughly negative about Mildred's job, was excited about appearing on local TV. He instructed Mildred to get his good suit dry-cleaned and had to be talked out of the idea of wearing a bow tie with it.

'They'll want us to look like we normally do at home,' said Mildred. 'You wouldn't normally wear a suit and bow tie around the house, would you? I wonder if I'll have time to get my hair permed? And those curtains will have to go in the wash.'

Mildred, to Eldred's surprise, took no notice at all of Edgar's remarks about the pointlessness of her taking the new job. Even when Edgar said, 'They're only paying you peanuts anyway. If you think that's going to pay fees at a private school, you need your head seeing to, woman,' Mildred only replied soothingly, 'We'll see what happens. Sometimes if you take the first step, something else comes along.'

'Louise went and found out what farm we went to on the school trip,' Eldred said, 'and talked to that man who asked me to phone him when my design was complete. He's going to go on the news and say it's a useful invention.'

'That's good, isn't it?' said Mildred.

'But I didn't phone him,' said Eldred. 'She didn't ask me if I wanted to involve him. I might have decided not to.'

'Well, I'm sure it'll turn out fine,' Mildred said. 'Don't worry about it. He won't say anything bad about you, will he? Not like Mrs Garcia?'

'No,' said Eldred. 'It's not that.'

'What is it, then?'

Eldred heaved a deep sigh. 'It's hard to know who to trust,' he said. 'You never know whether someone is trying to be kind, or whether they think you can be of some use to them in their career.'

Edgar and Mildred exchanged glances.

'You leave it to us,' Edgar said. 'If anyone tries to make use of you for their own ends they'll have your father to deal with. At least you know your parents can be trusted to want what's best for you, Eldred, even if we can't always find the way to go about it. We're not trying to make use of you, are we?'

'No,' said Eldred, but he thought, privately, that these changes in his life were turning out to be quite useful to them all. He had never known his parents talk to each other so much.

The news team came on a Wednesday afternoon and filmed Eldred coming in through the gate on his way home from school – only, by the time they had arranged it, it was five o'clock and Edgar was also coming through the gate, having left work an hour early. So the film crew had to ask Edgar to wait out of sight while they filmed Eldred coming home alone first, then filmed Edgar coming through the front door (in his best suit and a new haircut, with a briefcase positively bulging with work) at a supposedly later hour.

Eldred had to go into the kitchen and be shown eating biscuits, though in fact he had only taken one bite when the man said, 'Cut!' and they moved him on to the next shot: sitting in his bedroom working on the computer, with a large hot light shining behind him, out of sight of the camera, and a microphone inside his shirt. He hoped for more biscuit-eating shots, but all the crew wanted after that was talk. Eldred talked about school, the farm outing, the reprocessing plant he had designed, and his hopes for the future. His parents talked about Eldred. Eldred took little notice of what they said, and gave very little thought to what he himself said. He answered the questions and hoped they would not stay long. He was hungry.

When they finally left, Edgar and Mildred talked excitedly about what had been said and done, and speculated on the neighbours' reactions. 'I saw that Mrs Bone twitching the front nets,' said Mildred with satisfaction. 'She'll be on the doorstep in five minutes, what do you bet, asking to borrow something. She always has to know the gossip before anyone else.'

The phone rang. 'That'll be her!' Mildred said triumphantly, but it was Louise to ask whether everything had gone well. Mildred and Edgar both talked to her, in unnecessary detail, Eldred thought. He disliked spending too much time on any one thing. A thing was exciting when it hadn't happened yet, but once it was over it was gone, and surely it was better to move on to the next thing than dwell on the last one? 'Can we get fish and chips?' he asked, when his parents came off the phone.

'Why not?' said Edgar jovially.

'Because there's salad in the fridge, all prepared, that's why not,' Mildred said.

'Save it for tomorrow,' Edgar said. 'If we can't push the boat out when we go on telly, when can we?'

'We don't get paid for all this telly stuff,' Mildred reminded him. 'It doesn't put any more money in our pockets, does it?'

'Well, now that you've got this new job,' Edgar said, 'we can maybe afford a few little treats.'

'That money's for Eldred's schooling, every penny of it,' said Mildred firmly. 'It's going straight into my account and it's not going to come out.'

Edgar stared. 'You haven't got a bank account,' he said. 'I handle all the finances in this house.'

'I have now,' said Mildred. 'I opened one today.'

Yes, thought Eldred, things were definitely changing. Personally, he thought the change was for the better. He had never seen his mother in this light.

'Just chips, with the salad, then?' he hazarded. 'Out of my pocket money, if you like.'

Mildred smiled suddenly. 'Oh, go on then,' she said. 'I'm no match for both of you ganging up on me. Fish and chips it is, all round.'

Chapter Forty-nine

Eldred was very worried about his machine.

The local news caused a big stir at school. All the children wanted to talk to Eldred. Even the older ones from the high school came down to the playground at lunchtime to tell him, 'We saw you on telly.' The headmaster announced at assembly that the school was proud of Eldred. Mrs Garcia was strangely subdued.

The evening before, as soon as the programme was finished, the Jones' doorbell had started ringing. Neighbours who had never spoken to Eldred except to warn him not to kick his football into their garden suddenly treated him like a member of their family. After the first couple of visits, when the doorbell rang again, Eldred took the stairs two at a time and refused to come down.

'He's doing his homework,' Mildred said.

Eldred heard the Simmonds from number eleven and the Bells from the next street outside the Jones' front gate discussing his parents after this. Poor little boy, they said, no wonder he does so much brainwork; his parents push him so hard they won't let him come downstairs and take five minutes off his homework, even to celebrate when he's been on the telly.

Eldred felt guilty, but he continued to hide. When Mildred called him to come to the phone, he said, 'Can you tell them I'm not in?'

'It's one of your schoolfriends. Matthew Evans.'

'Matthew?' Eldred was surprised. Why would Matthew Evans, streetwise bold man of the class, phone him, Eldred Jones, who couldn't do wheelies on his bike without wobbling ferociously? He went to the phone.

'Hi.'

'Hi, Eldred. I seen you on the telly this evening.'

'Oh, right.'

There was a pause. 'Seems you invented some machine?'

'Yes,' said Eldred.

'How come you didn't tell us?'

'I didn't think anyone would be interested,' said Eldred. 'It's just for industry, that kind of thing.'

'You're kidding,' said Matthew. 'You must be an effing genius!'

Eldred was at a loss to know what to reply to this so he stayed silent.

'Anyway,' said Matthew, 'see you at school tomorrow, okay?'

'Okay,' said Eldred.

'You can be in my gang at breaktime if you like,' Matthew added.

Eldred hesitated. Matthew's gang's chief activities ranged from climbing drainpipes to pulling little girls' knickers down. 'I'll think about it,' he said cautiously. 'Thanks, anyway.'

'No bother,' said Matthew cheerily. 'See ya, then.'

'Yeah,' said Eldred. 'See ya, Matthew.'

Being famous had its compensations, Eldred thought. But now he was worried about his machine. He had hoped to sell it to some company that might develop it, but his fantasy had been to achieve this anonymously, as a Mr E. Jones on the end of a telephone line, driving a hard bargain. Now he had been seen on television as a nine year old riding his bike, coming home from school in his uniform and eating biscuits in the kitchen.

The next night for Eldred was a series of dreams in which he demonstrated his processing plant to a team of engineers who turned into wolves or fed him into the machine or snatched his patent form from him and sent it whirling away on the breeze, out of reach of his anxiously grasping hand. Eldred had missed so many catches at games, and now that everyone knew that Mr E. Jones was no more than an uncoordinated little boy, surely his invention would be taken away from him, along with his credibility as an inventor?

He wished he had had enough confidence in his invention to phone a couple of companies and ask for their product development manager, or whoever it was, and ask them directly if they'd be interested. It was out of his hands now. Louise had involved Bruce Mackeson and this German guy. No doubt they would arrange something between themselves and tell Eldred they'd done him a favour. He was confused. He wanted to be able to decide for himself, but he was a child and a child was someone that no one listened to, and also someone, Eldred knew, who lacked experience of human adults and their wiles. He disliked being forced to trust people, yet he knew it was no good relying on himself and his own discernment. Nor did he really trust his father to know who was acting in Eldred's best interests, because Edgar was not free of his own self-interest at times.

Eldred suffered the frustration of knowing he was not perfect and having to live with others' imperfections as well. He knew in his heart the only answer was to take one step at a time, remaining calm, taking advice, and then making his own decision.

Only if he stayed calm and listened to everyone could he assess the situation carefully. Only if he insisted on being the one to make the final decision could he be sure the invention would only pass out of his hands when he was ready to relinquish the next stage of its development to a person of his own choice. And only if he took his time and refused to be swept along by others' opinions would he develop the discernment about people's motives that he lacked now and needed to acquire for the future.

His head ached and his eyeballs felt pressurized, trying to see for himself all the ins and outs of the present situation and knowing that they were beyond his line of vision. Who to trust? He would have preferred to have to trust no one but he knew that this wasn't human. He wanted to talk to Terry. Terry could always be relied on to find him the information he needed. Eldred longed for the peace of the reference library, to take refuge there after school, throwing down his bag of easy homework exercises on the floor and sitting at a table with people writing notes, waiting for Terry to bring him a pile of psychology books and articles on lie-detector techniques and the revelations of body language.

Thinking of Terry, though, reminded Eldred that in this respect as well he had been spectacularly lacking in shrewdness. Terry, so unfailingly reliable in providing the right books to suit Eldred's current need, had not been reliable in other ways at all and had used his adult authority to overrule a child's need for respect and privacy. How could someone so sensitive in some ways be so ruthless in others? Eldred sat at his desk in his room and stared at the blank computer screen which stared back at him, awaiting his instructions. He didn't know how to tell himself what to do next. He felt if he let his first major invention slip out of his hands he would lose control of his whole future.

He called up on the screen the finely drawn diagrams of his processing plant and studied the detailed equations set out in boxes beside each stage of the process.

He felt deeply depressed. There was so much he didn't know.

Chapter Fifty

Mildred came home from her first day at work white-faced and shaking with tiredness. 'I'm not as young as I was,' she said. 'Where's Eldred?'

'He left a note on the table saying he'd gone to the park to play football,' Edgar said. 'It's not right. There should be someone here when he comes home, Mildred. He's only nine.'

Mildred sat down and eased the shoes off her feet, wincing. 'We can't have it both ways,' she said. 'He'll get plenty of supervision if he goes to boarding school.'

'You can give up that idea,' Edgar said irritably. 'You're wearing yourself out for nothing. Look at the state you're in after one shift.'

'I'll get used to it,' said Mildred. 'The first week's always the worst, so they say.'

'The first week!' Edgar scoffed. 'You won't last another day in that place, by the look of you.'

'I'm going to get the tea ready,' said Mildred with dignity.

Edgar relented. 'Sit there for five minutes first. I'll make you a cuppa.'

He returned with two cups of tea and found her sitting back on the sofa with her eyes closed. He nudged her gently and handed her the cup. 'I put a sugar in it. Good for energy.'

'Thanks, love.'

'I don't mean to be discouraging,' he apologized. 'I feel we should be able to provide for him. We only have one son and we can't give him what he needs.'

'Maybe he just needs us to try,' said Mildred.

'If he was slow at his schooling the State would provide,' Edgar fumed. 'Special needs. But Eldred has special needs and they don't give a damn. All that head teacher says is that he'll do well anyway and he'd probably learn even without any teaching.'

'He has a point,' said Mildred. 'He does teach himself things, doesn't he?'

'Not at school,' said Edgar. 'Why send him to school at all, if it's the only place where he doesn't learn anything?'

'I expect he learns something,' Mildred said, 'even if it's only how to get on with other children.'

'That school's not fulfilling its responsibility,' said Edgar wretchedly. 'Why can't they at least give him extra work, if they won't put him up another class?'

'I know,' said Mildred. 'Perhaps the programme will shake them up a bit, make them think.' She yawned. 'Eldred's late.'

'I'll go down the park and fetch him,' Edgar said. 'You get the tea on.'

He caught Eldred coming out of a public phone box. 'What are you doing?' he asked, seizing his arm.

'Nothing,' said Eldred. 'I was on my way home.'

'Who were you phoning?'

'Nobody,' Eldred said. 'I mean, a friend.'

'Why can't you phone him from home?' Edgar demanded. Frustration at his inability to earn money to help Eldred turned to rage at Eldred's ingratitude. 'You don't appreciate the sacrifices your parents make for you,' he told him. 'Your mother's been slaving all day at that job of hers and you can't even be home on time.'

'I forgot it was her first day,' Eldred said. 'How did she get on?'

'You forgot because you're selfish,' Edgar said, 'and you think the whole world should revolve around you and your clever ideas of yourself.'

They finished the walk home in silence. Eldred went straight to the kitchen to find Mildred. 'Sorry I'm late,' he said. 'How was your first day at work?'

'Fine, love; I enjoyed it,' Mildred said. 'Come here,' she added, on a note of concern. She turned Eldred towards her. 'You're crying.'

'I'm not,' he denied. 'I'll go and wash my hands.' He ran upstairs.

'What have you said to him, Edgar?' said Mildred.

'Told him to show a little concern for others, that's all,' said Edgar gruffly.

'He's only nine,' Mildred reproached him.

'He has to learn he can't just think about himself,' Edgar said.

'Eldred thinks a lot about others,' said Mildred. 'He worries too much at times. Let him play with his friends and be late home occasionally.'

'He was in a phone box, by himself,' Edgar said.

'Phoning who?'

'He wouldn't say. A friend, he said.'

As if on cue, their own phone started ringing.

'Shall I get it?' said Eldred, jumping down the last three stairs.

'No, leave it to me,' his father said. 'Someone else about that damned television programme, I expect.'

'Come and taste this cheese for me, Eldred,' Mildred said. 'I got a new kind. It was going cheap. One good thing about working at that supermarket is you get discounts on your own shopping.'

Eldred took the wedge of cheese she held out to him. 'Quite nice,' he said politely. 'Was it hard work today, Mum? You look a bit tired.'

She hugged him. 'I expect it's because I'm hungry. Nothing a good tea won't put right.'

They both heard the change in Edgar's voice.

'Yes,' he said in his most formal tone, 'I am almost certain that will be suitable but of course I will have to check with my wife to ensure she has no prior engagements.'

Mildred and Eldred moved to the doorway of the living-room and stared at him.

'Yes,' said Edgar, 'I shall telephone your secretary at approximately that time tomorrow morning. Not at all. Thank you. Thank you. Goodbye. Yes, of course. Thank you. Goodbye. Goodbye.' He put down the phone and mopped his forehead with his hand.

'Who was that?' said Eldred.

'That was Mr Clinford,' Edgar said impressively, 'headmaster of Abingdale School – that big private place on the way to the crematorium.'

Eldred giggled. 'Does he get his pupils cremated if they don't behave?'

'This is no time for a joke, Eldred,' Edgar said. 'He's offered us an interview. I'm to ring his secretary tomorrow to confirm that we can go. He suggested Wednesday at 6 p.m. You'll be home by then, Mildred.'

'An interview for what?' said Mildred, bemused.

'For the school,' Edgar said. 'One of his teachers told him about the local news on the television; he didn't see it himself, he said, but they would be very interested to meet Eldred, with a view to offering him a place at the school.'

'I hope you told him we couldn't afford the fees yet,' said Mildred. 'Not for a year or two.'

'Do I have to go?' asked Eldred.

'Well!' Edgar exploded. 'Listen to the two of you! The headmaster – the headmaster himself, in person, not a secretary, mind – phones our house to say he's interested in offering a place to Eldred, and who knows what *offering* means until we meet him and talk to him, eh? And all you can do is raise objections. Eldred, this is for your benefit, you know. Where's your gratitude?'

'All they'll want is to say I'm a pupil at their school,' said Eldred, 'and that I invent things, and then they'll take all the credit for themselves. And when I'm not good at the things they want me to do, they'll drop me like a hot brick. I'd rather wait and see what Louise comes up with.'

Edgar clenched his fists and opened his mouth to speak.

'Tea first,' said Mildred hastily. 'We'll discuss everything afterwards. Lay the table, Eldred, will you?'

Chapter Fifty-one

Keith was being interviewed by a television researcher. So far, his mother had done nearly all the talking. He could feel the anger rising inside him again.

'Thank you,' said the woman, who was called Rachel. 'So that's the whole list of Keith's operations and hospital admissions. Now, Keith...'

'I may have missed one,' said his mother. 'I wish you could have spoken to Mr Abdul. It's such a shame he's not here.'

'Mr Abdul only met me this week,' said Keith. 'I can speak for myself.'

'Yes, but this lady wants the medical history, Keith.'

'I know my own medical history,' Keith pointed out. 'I've lived it.'

'Yes,' said Rachel. 'And what I'd like you to talk a bit about, Keith, is what it's been like to live through all...'

'He's been terribly brave,' said Keith's mother. 'He never complains, never. Always a smile for everybody.'

He'd thought he'd defeated it, this anger. He'd thought it would have been enough, speaking up for himself as he had, first with Mum and then with Dad. But they still weren't listening. The lions were growling again, hungry for blood. He closed his eyes and prayed.

'Are you all right, Keith?' said his mother. 'I don't think he's up to this,' she told Rachel. 'It's not a good day.'

Keith opened his eyes. 'I'm fine,' he said. 'Please go on with what you were saying, Rachel.'

'But, darling, you will say, won't you, when you've had enough or if you feel you're going to have a...'

'Mum, why don't you go back to Grandad now and I'll see you tomorrow?'

'Go back? Darling, the interview isn't nearly finished – is it, Miss... sorry, I've forgotten your name?'

'Rachel.'

'I can't just leave Rachel here with you. She wouldn't know what to do if you weren't well. It isn't fair on her to give her that responsibility.'

She was offended and hurt, he could tell. He nearly relented and said she could stay. But if he gave way on this occasion, she wouldn't take any notice next time he objected to her answering for him, and his earlier bids for independence would have been wasted.

'I'm in a hospital, Mum,' he said gently. 'If I need anything, I'll call a nurse. I can phone this evening and tell you how the interview went. But I'd like to do it on my own.'

'What d'you mean, you'll phone, Keith? I'd be coming in this evening anyway. I always come in twice, don't I?'

'Okay. I'll see you this evening, then.'

She gathered up her handbag and scarf, taking her time. Her mouth was tense and there were patches of angry red colour on her cheekbones.

'I'll leave you to it, then,' she said. She went out without a backward glance, a goodbye to Rachel or a kiss for Keith.

'I'm sorry,' Keith told Rachel.

'Families of disabled children can get a bit overprotective,' she said. 'Is that a problem with yours?'

Her pen was poised over the notepad. He didn't want to say that.

'It may be as much to do with becoming adult as with having certain physical disabilities,' he said. 'I'm the eldest, and I suppose all parents find it difficult to let their children grow up and be more independent.'

'Right,' said Rachel. 'Well, on the subject of independence, Keith, if you don't mind my asking you, how independent can you be in your circumstances? I mean, I don't want to be offensive, so do tell me if...'

'No,' he said. 'Go ahead and ask anything you like. People tend to handle me with kid gloves and it can get a bit wearing. So can having to be the boy who never gets depressed and always has a sunny smile. I hope that's not what you're looking for on your programme, because it isn't me. I can get quite cynical.'

Rachel laughed, and relaxed, stretching out her legs. 'Good. That'll be much more refreshing than the boy with the sunny smile. Tell me what you get cynical about, will you?'

'I get cynical about the attempts to redesign me physically, supposedly for my benefit, and about the attitude that no one must mention my disabilities, let alone talk about death, and that I mustn't have any feelings that might upset other people, and about people's attempts to treat me as normal.'

'What's wrong with being treated as normal, Keith? Isn't that what disabled people want? Or should I say "differently abled" people?'

'I'm not normal,' he said simply. 'I don't look normal or function normally, physically, and I can't do normal things. Pretending I'm not disabled, or calling it something that sounds more positive, isn't the answer. Most people, seeing me for the first time, are shocked and upset. I expect it. I respect their embarrassment with me and I try and help them with it. I do know I'm disabled; I don't need people to pretend they haven't noticed or that the disabilities don't exist. Or that I don't know my condition is terminal. I do prefer people to be honest and blunt, rather than tactful or evasive.'

'Oh.' She hadn't been warned about this.

'So if you'd been led to expect Little Mister Nice Guy, I'll quite understand if you'd rather pick some other disabled young person to interview,' said Keith. 'I have been well-behaved and smiling in the past, but recently I've been feeling really pissed off.'

'Mmm. Your grandfather mentioned on the phone that you had a strong faith and he thought that helped you. It's not sustaining you at the moment, then?'

Keith's eyes flashed. 'It is, in the sense that I feel God is prompting me to speak up for myself, not just to sit back and accept everything.'

'Ah.' Rachel was interested. 'You think God's will means that you fight your condition, not give in to it?'

'Not fight my condition, no. I'm not talking about willpower, or mind over matter.' Keith paused, trying to get his thoughts clear. He couldn't have talked like this with his mother here; by now she would have rushed in to fill the gap in the conversation. Rachel seemed prepared to wait for the answers.

'My condition is me,' said Keith slowly. 'I was born like this; it's the way I am. I can't imagine a non-disabled version of me. Fighting my condition would be fighting myself. I accept that this is the way God designed me, and I believe he must have a good reason.'

She was scribbling notes on her pad. 'But...?' she prompted.

'But I'm fighting the view that I'm not the best person to decide on my own treatment and that doctors always know more than the patient. And I want to be allowed to say I believe that all these operations to alter bits of me are not always motivated by the aim to ease my discomfort. I'm suspicious of some of the other motives there may be.'

'Which are...?'

'To make life easier for the carers – in my case, my family – by making me an easier shape to lift. For instance, my tendons were cut, to make my legs bend; the knees used to be straight, which made it difficult for people to dress me or sit me on the toilet. That put paid to my dream that I might someday walk, because you've more chance of walking with legs that won't bend than with floppy legs that won't stay straight when you want them to. In my case it was just a dream, that I might walk. But the same operation was done to a boy I know – for the same reason, the convenience of the carers – when it might have been possible for him to walk eventually.'

'You're saying he would have been able to walk if he hadn't had the operation?'

'It was a possibility for him,' said Keith. 'He'd managed a couple of steps, on a few occasions. But the doctor didn't think it was significant.'

'And it was done without the patient's consent, this operation?'

'He had some degree of damage to his brain. The doctor didn't consult him. He didn't consider him capable of making a decision. Neither did the family.'

'And was he capable of making the decision, in your opinion?'

'He was capable of being upset about the decision that was made for him, and he made his distress very obvious,' said Keith. 'Only nobody listened.'

'Keep talking,' said Rachel. 'What other motives are there for carrying out operations, even if the patient doesn't want them?'

'Medical research. If you're an interesting case, with multiple disabilities, there's more to be learned from trying out new treatments and different types of surgery on you than from leaving you as you are, obviously. Sometimes you're asked if you'll have a couple of extra tests done, or try out an untested drug, in the interests of research.

'On other occasions, I suspect it's done without asking; it's presented as being necessary, beneficial to the patient, when it actually isn't. It all goes to create a fuller case history, of more use to future generations of medical students and research scientists. And carrying out experimental treatments and innovative operations doesn't do any harm to the surgeon's reputation either.'

'You believe some of the operations you've had may not have been necessary?' asked Rachel.

'None of them were actually necessary,' Keith said. 'Some of them have benefited me. The early ones did. My hands were made more movable, more use to me. And it's easier for me too to have knees that bend. Later on, though, I did wonder why some of the operations made so little difference to me and why the doctors still seemed satisfied with them and keen to get on with the next one. And the more recent operations have actually weakened me. I lost a lot of the use of my arms after the one before this.'

'And are more operations proposed?' asked Rachel.

'Two, as far as I've heard – that is, as far as the consultant has suggested to my father. He hasn't discussed them with me.'

'What are they for?'

'To break and reset my left femur, and to break and reset one of my ribs and remove another one completely.'

'Would that be for your benefit, Keith, do you think?'

'Would it benefit you?' he retorted.

She looked serious. 'It sounds barbaric to me.'

'That may be because it is,' said Keith.

'Whew!' Rachel flicked back through her notes. 'Look,' she said. 'I'll level with you. This isn't the interview I expected. What you're saying is quite challenging – quite controversial. I'm not sure if the programme's presenters will go for it, to be honest; they might well tell me to forget it.

'But I'm interested in what you're saying. You could make a lot of people think twice about only admiring disabled people who accept their fate with a smile and don't make the rest of us feel uncomfortable. And I'm particularly intrigued by your view of faith as a... what did you say? A prompting to speak up for yourself and fight this way of being treated, rather than sitting back and accepting it as God's will?'

'I accept my condition as God's will,' Keith confirmed. 'But I don't accept that the doctors' decisions about my treatment are necessarily in accordance with the way God wants me to be treated. I've never met a doctor who asked God how he wanted him or her to treat a particular patient. In fact, some doctors appear to believe that medical science is the highest authority. That's dangerous, in my opinion.'

'Why dangerous?'

'Dangerously limited. Treatment is only as deep as the practitioner. Some doctors have no love or respect for people, as human beings with all the authority and dignity God gives his creation. Their medical practice starts and ends with an interest in disease and remedies and science. God doesn't come into it, so neither, really, does the patient.'

'So your faith means, to you, that you fight the doctors?'

'No,' said Keith. 'I'm not fighting any doctor. They have a job to do, in the way they think best.'

'Then who or what is it you are fighting? Let me be sure I understand what you're saying here.'

'I'm fighting for the right to decide for myself what treatment to have, without pressure being put on me to conform to the doctor's advice. I want to take the ultimate responsibility myself, not delegate it to the doctor or to my family. *I* decide.'

'Right. I've got that. What about the right to live or die, Keith? You don't mind if I ask you about that? Okay. Well then, would you claim you had the right to end your own life if it became unbearable?'

'No,' Keith said. 'I don't have that right.'

'Why not?' asked Rachel. 'Isn't that the logical extension of your right to decide your own treatment?'

'No, it's the opposite,' said Keith. 'I'm claiming the right to decide what's best for my health and my quality of life. I don't have the right to destroy it. No one has that right.' He thought of the unborn child he had visualized being aborted, again seeing it writhe.

Rachel, still writing, said, 'But doctors take an oath to preserve and enhance life, not to destroy it. So if that's your priority as well, how can you be in conflict with their policies?'

When he didn't answer, she looked up, surprised to find him crying.

'That used to be their priority,' he said. 'But these are changing times.'

She put down the notebook. 'Let's leave it there,' she said. 'I can see you've had enough for one day. Thanks very much, Keith. I'll be in touch, okay?'

'Yes,' he said, so quietly he could hardly be heard. 'Yes, I have had enough.'

Chapter Fifty-two

Eldred jumped off the bus and ran all the way home. Flinging down his schoolbag in the hall, he went into the kitchen, grabbed a biscuit and ate it, then took the hoover out of the cupboard under the stairs and hoovered the living-room, moving the chairs. He laid the table for tea, filled the kettle and placed one tea-bag into a cup ready for Mildred's homecoming.

Unable to think of any more he could do to help, he went up to his room and did his homework. Part of it involved measuring the perimeter of his room, writing down the measurements and working out the area. Eldred borrowed Mildred's tape measure from her sewing basket and crawled around the floor.

As soon as he had the measurements, he worked out the area in his head. To make it more interesting, he deducted the areas of floor space occupied by the wardrobe, the desk and the bed and calculated the area of uncovered carpet. Then, to make it more interesting again, he measured the height of the room and calculated the total air space.

Then he deducted the volume of space occupied by the furniture, the light bulb and lampshade, and the computer, and calculated the unoccupied air space. He worked out the difference in free air space when the room was empty and when he was in it. By the time Mildred came home, he felt he had saturated the subject and was bored with it; glad of the diversion, he ran downstairs. He forgot he hadn't written down the answer to the original question of his room's measurements and area. Mrs Garcia would scold him the next day for not doing his homework.

'How did you get on at work today, Mum?' Eldred asked, hugging her.

'Not bad,' she said. 'You laid the table for me, you good boy.'

'The kettle's boiled,' he said. 'I'll make you a cup of tea.'

She was leaning on the back of a chair when he returned.

'What's wrong?'

'Nothing, love. My back aches a bit.'

Edgar came home. 'Mildred?'

'In here, dear.'

'Mum's got backache,' Eldred told him.

'I'm not surprised,' Edgar said. 'Doing the work of a packhorse. It's your body telling you you're not up to it.'

'It's you who keeps telling me I'm not up to it,' snapped Mildred.

Edgar was taken aback. This was not Mildred's voice.

'I'm sorry,' she said, 'but it would help if you gave me some support instead of saying I can't do it. You used to get tired when you first had your new job. I didn't tell you to go back to your old one, did I?'

'I have to go to work whether I'm tired or not,' Edgar said. 'Your job is your choice. I didn't make you do it.'

'And you're not going to make me stop,' said Mildred firmly. 'But if you want to help get the tea, I won't say no.'

'You know I can't cook,' Edgar said.

'Anyone can fry sausages and peel and mash potatoes,' said Mildred. 'It doesn't take any great skill.'

'Shall I do it?' offered Eldred.

'Yes, go and give your mother a hand,' Edgar said, relieved.

'No,' said Mildred. 'You go and do your homework.'

Eldred looked from one to the other. His mother never countermanded his father's instructions. He didn't know which one to obey.

Edgar gave a deep sigh. 'Do as your mother says, Eldred,' he said. 'How many potatoes do you want me to peel?'

'As many as you want to eat, and two more,' Mildred said. 'I'll be in to give you a hand, dear, when I've finished my cup of tea.'

Eldred was looking anxious. Edgar, rolling up his shirtsleeves in the kitchen, winked at him. '"The old order changeth,"' he said, '"making way for the new." That's a quote.'

'From where?' Eldred wanted to know.

'From Mrs Mildred Jones, from now on,' said his father. They both smiled.

'Enough of your cheek, you two,' said Mildred, from the sofa. Her cup of tea was lukewarm. Eldred must have boiled the kettle some time ago. She sipped appreciatively. Her backache was beginning to ease.

Edgar brought the plates to the table, as nervous as a young bride. 'I burnt the sausages slightly.'

'I like them burnt,' said Eldred.

'And the mash might have a few lumps.'

'Good for the teeth to have something to chew on,' said Mildred cheerfully.

Eldred wondered what was happening to the family. Mildred made an art-form of cooking perfectly and having a spotless house, and had no time for anyone who was less than perfect. 'Sloppy housewives', she called those women who didn't clean their windows every week or left their Monday washing till Thursday to be ironed.

'Somebody hoovered this carpet,' she said now, looking at the track marks where Eldred had manoeuvred the machine.

'I scuffed it up a bit,' he noticed.

'It looks lovely and clean,' Mildred said.

'This interview at the school tomorrow,' Edgar said. 'Six o'clock's a funny time, isn't it? When everyone's wanting their tea?'

'Some people have it late,' Mildred reminded him. 'Is it a posh place? I don't know anyone who sends their children to it. That's not where Sheila Suffolk's daughter went, is it?'

'It's only for boys, isn't it?' Edgar said.

'I'd rather go to a school that's mixed,' said Eldred.

'Most private schools are for just girls or boys,' Edgar told him. 'If you went to boarding school, it would be just boys.'

'No, I'm sure I heard that Abingdale had gone mixed now,' said Mildred. 'Or perhaps it was another place.'

Edgar grew agitated. 'We should find out something about the place. What will it look like if we turn up there knowing nothing?'

'How can we find out, by tomorrow,' Mildred asked, 'if we don't know anybody who goes there?'

'Would it have a prospectus, or is that just for boarding schools?' Eldred asked. 'Could we get it from the library?'

'They probably have one,' said Edgar, 'but I shouldn't think the library would have it. How could we get hold of one?'

'From the school office?' said Eldred.

'Mildred, you could go in on your way to work tomorrow and ask the secretary for a prospectus,' Edgar said.

She was horrified. 'Not me. I wouldn't know where to go.'

'There'd be people around you could ask,' said her husband.

'Oh, I couldn't,' she said. 'Not just walk in. You'd have to do it, Edgar.'

'I'm at work! And if I went in at lunchtime the headmaster might be around and he'd know it was us who had come in to ask for it. It might seem like a cheek.'

It struck Eldred for the first time how nervous his parents were when it came to dealing with people. He wondered how they were at work, whether Edgar put on his formal tone all the time when he was with senior managers, whether Mildred stood timidly at the back of the queue for her cup of tea at tea-break and whether she talked to anyone.

'Have you made any friends at work, Mum?' he asked her.

'I haven't had time for that,' she said. 'I'm run off my feet.'

'But do you think you will, when you've been there a longer time?'

'I'll probably get to know one or two. Why?'

He shrugged. 'Just wondering.'

Mildred stood up. 'Hand me your plates.'

'I'll do the washing up in a minute,' said Edgar humbly.

She smiled at him. 'You watch the telly. The old order doesn't have to change all at once.'

Chapter Fifty-three

Lulubelle had been accepted for the TV show on special children. The researchers had been unanimous about the choice, the letter said, and she was the first to be selected, so they were unable to tell her yet about the other children who would share the programme. A date and time were given for her to attend the recording of the show, which would be televised in a few months.

She was excited. Things were moving. When the letter came, her first impulse was to run and show Arto and Marisa and tell them the good news. It was only when she opened the door of the caravan that she remembered the bad news, and closed the door again. Lucinda was sleeping.

She sat on the floor cross-legged, her thinking position. There would probably be a few people in the Big Top; there were always a dedicated few, rehearsing and refining their acts, early in the morning. And there would be signs of life in a number of caravans: breakfast cooking, people leaving the site to fetch newspapers or cigarettes, arguments starting. From dawn till late at night, there was always some activity around the circus camp; that was what Lulubelle was used to and what she liked.

But it didn't mean there was always someone around to keep an eye on the children. Sometimes it meant there were so many people milling around, so much noise and activity, that any stranger could pass unnoticed and any sound could be taken for granted – even screaming. People expected to hear screaming, in a fairground. Even after the rides stopped and the lights went down, it wasn't an unusual sound.

She would have to go out this morning; there were classes to go to, and she had bunked off yesterday, for her audition. Lulubelle felt that lessons, on the whole, were a waste of time. Even with a tutor coming to the site, there seemed little continuity between what the children learned one week and what they studied the next, and attending local schools was even worse. Lulubelle could only read and write because the second daughter of the ringmaster at the circus Lucinda had worked for before Bepponi's and Mannfield's had taught her.

But there you were; it was the law that children had to go through the motions, at least, of being educated in something or other, she thought, so she didn't have any choice. All the important things, like performing, doing publicity parades, rehearsing, and trying out new routines, had to be fitted in around non-essentials like kings and queens and wars and maps and calculating the areas of things. Maybe when she was older she'd see the point of it all, but none of the adults around her seemed to have found it relevant to them.

She stood up and parted the curtains slightly and peered out. There was no one around she didn't recognize. She sat down again. There was no need to go out just yet. If she left it another half-hour, one of the other kids might call for her. It was not that she was scared, she told herself; just that sometimes a girl had to look out for herself.

She had felt protected before, when they worked for Bepponi's. It never occurred to her to look outside the door before she went tumbling out, running to join the other kids the moment she woke up. It was only after that night that she had become cautious; the night when everything went wrong.

She told herself she must think about it now. Only by facing up to it squarely, examining what had gone wrong, how and where, could she make sure it never happened again. She must plan a strategy, work out where her sources of safety were.

Lucinda was not a source of protection. Lulubelle didn't want to admit that, even to herself. It was frightening, and it hurt. But there was no point in pretending, because Lucinda had been there, asleep inside the caravan, all the time, and she hadn't woken up and come running, not even when Lulubelle had screamed with all her voice.

It had only happened because of Lucinda anyway – or that was how Lulubelle saw it. Lucinda disagreed. It had been nothing to do with her, she said. Lulubelle had jumped to conclusions; that's what had caused it.

She had simply had a bad headache, said Lucinda: one of her migraines. And she'd happened to mention to Lulubelle, just casually, with no intention for her to do anything, that if Gilby came round this evening she couldn't cope with him and that Gilby wasn't one to take no for an answer.

It was not her fault, said Lucinda, that Lulubelle had taken it on herself to sit on the caravan steps all evening waiting to tell Gilby her mother wasn't well and he wasn't to go bothering her. She hadn't asked Lulubelle to do it. Nor was it her fault that Lulubelle didn't know who Gilby was. That was to Lucinda's credit, if anything. She knew how to be discreet, with a young daughter.

She knew when to send Lulubelle to share a friend's bunk in another caravan and not come home that night, or when to wait till Lulubelle was asleep, tucked safely under the bedclothes, before she brought someone back with her for the evening. And often as not, the someone was gone before Lulubelle got up in the morning. No one could accuse her of being an uncaring mother, she said.

So it wasn't her fault, when the stranger had come along and stopped to talk to the little blonde nine year old sitting all alone on the caravan steps and asked where her mother was, that Lulubelle had told him her mother was fast asleep, out for the count, and couldn't be woken up for any reason.

She even had the right to feel offended that her small daughter had assumed this strange character was one of her mother's friends. By all accounts, he was very far from being her type. A nylon padded jacket, worn with a different coloured anorak hood? Torn trainers? Do me a favour! It was just plain insulting to think that this could have been Gilby, just because he asked where her mother was. And what was to stop Lulubelle coming in to ask Lucinda who he was? She wouldn't have bitten her head off, and even if she had, it was preferable to staying out there, wasn't it? Better than getting dragged into the bushes and...

Lucinda never let the conversation go further than this. It was over, she told Lulubelle. It was horrible; she was sorry it had happened, but there was no point going over and over it. Put it behind you, she told her. It won't ruin your life if you don't let it. Lots of bad things have happened to me, said Lucinda, but I don't dwell on the past, me; I get on with my life. What's done is done.

That was all very well, Lulubelle thought, if the past would stay in the past, nice and neat and obedient. But it had a habit of intruding on the present, either in waking thoughts and sudden fears, or in horrendous nightmares, or even – as seemed to be happening now – by repeating itself in reality.

The man who had held her down with his foot while he swirled his jacket around his head and claimed to be Count Dracula had not stayed in the past where he belonged – among the memories of another circus, another time of Lulubelle's life – but had trespassed into her life at Mannfield's now and was threatening her present peace of mind and possibly her chances of a real future.

Did he know she was here, or was it coincidence that he had

turned up? Was he a follower of circuses, as some people were, or a predator of young girls, or was he obsessed with her, Lulubelle, personally, and determined to find her wherever she was, at any time in her life?

Chapter Fifty-four

Before Eldred left for school, a letter arrived from the television company.

'That was quick!' said Mildred. 'I always thought these big companies worked very slowly.'

'Open it,' said Eldred.

'I can't. It's addressed to your father.'

'It says "Mr and Mrs" on the envelope,' Eldred pointed out. 'So either of you can open it.'

'We'd better leave it till Dad gets home,' Mildred demurred.

'It is about me,' Eldred said. 'If I wasn't nine, it's me they would have sent it to, isn't it?'

Mildred hesitated.

'Please,' said Eldred. 'I don't ask for much.'

'Not half you don't!' said Mildred. But she fetched the sharp kitchen knife she used for slicing potatoes and slit the envelope. 'But when your father comes home, let him read it for himself,' she said. 'No meeting him at the door and telling him what's in it.'

Eldred was craning to see the page, pulling down Mildred's elbow. 'They're going to feature me in the documentary,' he said, 'with two other children: a ten-year-old girl who's an acrobat and a fourteen-year-old boy who's had fifteen operations. What's clever about that?'

'Eldred!' said Mildred, shocked. 'Think what it must have been like for the poor child. How would you like it?'

'I didn't say it wasn't sad,' said Eldred. 'I said why is it clever?'

'The programme's about special children,' said Mildred, 'not just clever.'

Eldred wrinkled his nose. 'I still don't get it. I mean, he didn't have much choice, presumably. People just said to him, "You have to have another operation," and he had it. It's something that happened to him, not something he did himself.'

'Oh, Eldred,' said his mother.

'What?' he said.

She sighed. 'I don't know. Put your coat on. Where's your school bag?'

'Why did you say, "Oh, Eldred", though?' Eldred was not easy to sidetrack.

'I don't know. The way you look at things,' said Mildred helplessly.

'Tell me,' he insisted. 'I want to know how you look at it.'

'Well, this boy didn't ask to be handicapped,' said Mildred, 'and here he is, only fourteen years old, and half his life must have been pain and not being able to do things and recovering from nasty operations and feeling nervous about the next one. And you say he hasn't done anything because he isn't clever.'

'Oh,' said Eldred. 'You mean he didn't choose to be disabled but he's got on with it because it's the life he has?'

'Something like that.'

Eldred thought for a moment. 'Can you be successful at being disabled or a failure at it, then?'

'Life isn't just a question of success, Eldred,' said Mildred. 'Not everyone's in a position to be a success.'

'But surely...' Eldred began.

'You'll be late for school,' said Mildred.

'Just one more question,' he pleaded. 'Very short.'

'Very short is what your teacher will be with you if you're late for class,' said Mildred, managing to kiss him and push him out of the door in one movement.

When Eldred had gone, she read the letter again. Another appointment, for next week. It could take all day, this filming. These people gave no thought to parents who worked. She sat down at the table and read the second paragraph very slowly, word by word. Something troubled her about it. A poor deformed boy and an acrobat girl. And her Eldred.

She wished she was better at putting things into words, or even at putting her thoughts into some coherent shape. She didn't know what was wrong but she didn't like it, whatever it was. One thing she knew for certain: she wasn't going to give up this job. Hard work it might be, but at the moment that supermarket was the only place where Mildred felt she knew where she was and what she was supposed to be doing.

When Edgar came home from work, Eldred refrained from telling him about the letter. Instead, he gave him the prospectus for Abingdale School.

'Where did you get this?' said Edgar.

'I went down there at lunch break,' said Eldred, 'and asked someone where the school secretary's office was. She was really nice.'

'You did what?' Edgar said. 'You walked out of your school at lunch break and went all the way to Abingdale by yourself?'

'I got the bus,' Eldred explained. 'There wouldn't have been time to walk. I used my pocket money,' he said hastily, seeing Edgar's face turn purple.

'You are missing the point,' Edgar said. 'One, you are not allowed to leave school during the day; two, I will not have my nine-year-old child wandering the streets…'

Mildred came in. 'What's going on?' she said, scanning Edgar's face.

Edgar waved the prospectus in her face. 'Eldred went and got this, by himself,' he said.

'Oh good,' said Mildred. 'Don't give it to me now, dear; I have to go and get changed quickly. I'll read it later. Eldred, that shirt's all creased: go and take a fresh one out of your wardrobe. Edgar dear, the blue tie might look better. It's up to you.' She ran up the stairs.

Edgar looked after her in disbelief. 'Women!' he exclaimed. He looked round for Eldred, but Eldred had seized his opportunity for escape and had flown upstairs in the wake of Mildred.

All the way there on the bus, Edgar alternated between telling Mildred that Eldred was getting out of control and was being given too much pocket money, and wondering anxiously how they would know where to go when they reached the school. Eldred stayed quiet, deciding it was better not to remind him that he knew his way to the headmaster's office.

In the event, Mr Clinford met them at the gate. 'Delighted to meet you,' he said, addressing himself first to Mr Jones. Edgar relaxed slightly.

Mr Clinford shook hands with Mildred, and then with Eldred. 'Shall I lead the way?' he said. The family followed him mutely, not knowing where he was leading them. He seemed to know, Eldred thought. He felt relieved that somebody was showing confidence. It made him anxious when people were nervous, as though they might expect him to cope with whatever it was they couldn't cope with themselves. He often felt like that with his parents.

They found themselves on a tour of the whole school: First, Middle and Upper. Edgar and Mildred were overawed.

'All this expensive equipment,' Edgar murmured.

'Did you look at the fees?' Mildred whispered.

Edgar nodded and grimaced. 'Well out of our league!'

'What do you think of our facilities?' asked Mr Clinford.

'Marvellous,' said Mildred politely.

'Very impressive,' said Edgar, with deep gloom.

'There is just one thing,' said Eldred. Edgar and Mildred tensed.

'What's that?' said Mr Clinford.

'One thing that seems the same in every school,' Eldred said, 'is that all the interesting equipment is in the High School. The First School only has baby stuff, doesn't it?'

'Eldred,' his father admonished, 'you can't say that here. Computers for the five year olds!'

'Only for really easy programs, like learning to read,' said Eldred.

Mr Clinford put a hand on his shoulder. 'That is what I want to discuss with you,' he said. 'In this school, we try to give all the children the opportunity to fulfil their potential and go at their own pace. We start you off on the easy programs, certainly, but if you can cope with the work, you can move on as soon as you're ready to. There's no sitting around gazing out of the window here, Eldred.'

He steered them into his office and pointed them towards chairs. They sat.

'What I'd like to do,' said Mr Clinford, positioning himself on the big swivel chair behind the desk, 'is give you a run-down of what I believe Abingdale could do for your son.'

Edgar and Mildred exchanged agonized glances. Eldred understood.

'First, do you have any questions you'd like to ask me?' said Mr Clinford.

Edgar cleared his throat. 'No, no,' he said. 'You go ahead. Hmm.' Mildred looked at him. He turned his head away.

'I'd like to ask one,' said Eldred.

'Not you,' said Edgar firmly. 'Listen to what the headmaster has to say.'

'No, please,' said Mr Clinford. 'Ask away.'

'Can I say it in private?' Eldred asked. 'By myself.'

'Eldred!' Mildred hissed.

Edgar's lips were tightly compressed. 'Say what you have to say,' he said, 'here and now.'

Mr Clinford's eyes were shrewd, moving from one face to the next. 'Actually,' he said, 'now you mention privacy, I would appreciate a few words in private with you, Mr Jones, you and your wife, while Eldred occupies himself with a more detailed look at our library. Would that be all right with you?'

Edgar nodded gravely. 'Certainly.'

'Thank you,' he said. 'Eldred, come with me.'

'He can find it himself,' said Edgar. 'We just passed it.'

'No trouble at all,' said Mr Clinford, smiling and holding open the door. He ushered Eldred through it and closed it promptly behind them both. A smooth operator, thought Eldred. He wasn't sure whether he'd like this man to be his headmaster or not.

'What's your question?' asked Mr Clinford, walking briskly.

Eldred decided not to beat about the bush. 'My father works in insurance,' he said, 'and my mother has just started work as a shelf-filler at the supermarket. She's doing it so they can send me to a private school. But she's really tired when she comes home every evening. And they're not going to make enough. They think they will in a year or two, but I've worked it out. They won't.'

Mr Clinford stopped and faced him. He nodded.

'I'm probably being disloyal,' said Eldred, flinching slightly before his direct gaze, 'because they wouldn't want me to say this to you. I can tell they think this school is very nice but they'll probably tell you they'll think about it and then they'll say it isn't quite right for me. But really it's because we couldn't afford the fees.' He stopped.

'Thank you, Eldred,' said Mr Clinford. 'You've been very honest with me, and not at all disloyal; quite the opposite. Now let me ask you one question. Do you think this school would suit you?'

Eldred considered. 'I could probably only tell that after I'd tried it for a while,' he said.

A smile crossed the headmaster's lips and was swiftly banished. 'And would you be willing to give us a try?' he asked.

'You mean, like a free sample?' asked Eldred.

Another fleeting smile. 'Yes.'

'Okay,' said Eldred. He hesitated.

'But?' prompted Mr Clinford.

'If it didn't work out, I might not be allowed back to my old school,' said Eldred.

'Would you mind leaving your present school?'

'Oh no,' said Eldred, in heartfelt tones. 'Not at all. But it might leave me with nowhere to go.'

'Will you do something for me, Eldred?' Mr Clinford asked.

'Okay.'

'Will you leave it to your parents and me to make the arrangements for you and to worry about the money? Let us, between us, take the responsibility? And you just take the decision that, if it works out that you come here as a pupil, you will give us your very best work and let me know personally if you are unhappy for any reason?'

Eldred thought again. It sounded good. It even felt like something of a relief. They would be the adults and he would be the child. He let out a deep sigh.

'All right,' he said.

Chapter Fifty-five

They found Eldred hunched on the floor with open books spread out around him. He was so absorbed that he jumped when Mr Clinford's voice sounded from just behind him.

'What have you found to read, Eldred?'

'I was trying to find out the dividing line between philosophy and psychology,' Eldred said, 'because I wasn't sure which to start reading first.'

'Did you find where the division is?' Mr Clinford asked.

'I'm not sure,' said Eldred, 'but I think philosophy might be about different ways to live and psychology might be about why people act the way they do. I'm not convinced that there are all those different ways to live, though. I mean, not little differences like some families having tea at six and some having supper at seven, but different ways of being a person and experiencing life.'

'It's an interesting subject,' Mr Clinford said, 'and you seem to have dived into it at the deep end.'

'You see,' said Edgar, 'this is what he does. He has to find out for himself. He won't learn from people who know better than him. Eldred, you could ask Mr Clinford what philosophy and that stuff is. He's a headmaster; he knows about these things.'

'It's much better,' said Mr Clinford, 'for a child to ask questions and be guided to search for the answers than to be given all the answers on a plate. I would much rather have a child with an enquiring mind than a child who passively accepts what his teacher tells him.'

'A zeal to learn,' said Eldred.

Mr Clinford smiled. 'Quite.'

'It's not that I don't want to learn from people,' Eldred told him. 'It's just that most times there isn't anyone to ask – not anyone who knows.'

Edgar emitted a faint spluttering noise.

Mr Clinford bent down and picked up a couple of the books. 'No one can give you all the answers on any subject,' he said. 'What we can give you here is help to know where to look. These books you've picked, Eldred, are quite advanced. You'd do better to start with this.' He selected from the shelf a volume entitled *Introduction to Philosophy*.

'I read that,' said Eldred.

'Oh, you've read this book?' said Mr Clinford. 'Where did you find it before? In the public library?'

'No, here,' said Eldred. 'It was the first one I read when I came in here.'

'He doesn't read properly,' Edgar apologized. 'He learnt some speed-reading method from a book when he was four or five. I don't know how much he takes in.'

'Didn't you find what you were looking for, in this book?' Mr Clinford asked. 'Did you skim through it and find nothing to interest you – was that it?'

'No,' said Eldred. 'I wanted a general idea of what philosophy was, but then I didn't know how long I'd be in here for; I thought the time might be quite short, so when I got an overview of different branches of philosophy then I picked one or two to look at separately. I do know,' he said with dignity, 'that I can't learn all about it in one hour.'

'And the topics you selected,' said Mr Clinford, reading the titles of Eldred's choice of books, 'were phenomenology, ontology and existentialism. How far did you get with understanding them, Eldred?'

'Not very far, really,' said Eldred. 'It seems complicated.'

'That's a fair assessment,' said Mr Clinford. 'It's not an easy subject at all.'

'It made me wonder,' said Eldred, 'if this is the best way of looking at it. I mean, it's interesting and all that, but how useful is it in showing people how to live? Do you believe there are different ways of being?'

'Different ways of perceiving reality, perhaps,' Mr Clinford suggested, 'rather than different ways of being a human being. That is to say, human beings share more or less the same range of experiences and reactions and even the same kinds of thoughts and feelings, but we don't all perceive life in the same way. We all come at it from different angles, if you like, and give priority to different things. We choose to react differently from one another and we vary in the ways we express our feelings and form our thoughts.'

'Why?' asked Eldred. Edgar looked at Mildred and raised his eyebrows. Mildred shifted her weight from one aching foot to the other and clutched her handbag. They were both feeling the strain.

'Now that would bring you into the sphere of psychology,' said Mr Clinford, apparently enjoying the conversation. 'Factors defining individual personality – nature versus nurture: a person's inherent disposition, assuming there is such a thing, which some philosophers question, versus their social conditioning, their personal experiences, the circumstances of their life, the people who influence them.'

Eldred was thinking. 'Would that mean that a theory in philosophy, like whether you can prove if there is a God, is true for some people and not for other people?' he enquired. 'Could some personalities perceive some things as proofs that God exists while other persons see the same things as proof that he doesn't?'

Mr Clinford opened his mouth to answer.

'Or,' said Eldred, continuing, 'could it be that psychological factors actually make it impossible for a certain person to perceive God in any way, whatever the evidence? Or, could it be that social conditioning, for example, might predispose a person only to be able to perceive a distorted notion of God – like a tyrant or a big computer-mind – and then if that person also had a truthful disposition they would be obliged to reject this image, and then they would believe they were rejecting the real God and that God didn't exist, when in fact they were only proving that this tyrant-bloke or this genius figure couldn't really be true? Or might it happen that someone perceived themselves as totally religious and convinced about God's existence when in fact they were believing in an image they'd created in their own mind? And in that case, would...'

He stopped. Mr Clinford was laughing. Edgar was glaring at him. Mildred was looking at the floor. Eldred perceived his mother was tired, uncomfortable and embarrassed, that Edgar was out of his element and angry and probably wanted his tea, which was now an hour overdue, and that Mr Clinford... he wasn't sure what Mr Clinford thought and he didn't want to make assumptions.

'Sorry,' he said humbly. 'We probably should go home now.' He bent down and picked up the two remaining books, *Beginning Psychology* and *A Guide to Transactional Analysis* and replaced them on the shelves.

'It's been very interesting talking to you, Eldred,' said Mr Clinford seriously. He took Eldred's hand and shook it, man to man. 'I'm delighted to hear you ask so many questions and to see the interest you take in such a range of subjects. May I suggest something?'

'Yes,' said Eldred. He was embarrassed now. He had been carried away again. He had shown up his parents and overstepped the mark with this important man. His father would tell him he lacked respect for his elders and betters, as he had told him so many times before. Eldred wished he didn't forget things like that so easily, when other facts stayed in his memory with no trouble at all.

'Your thirst for knowledge is a valuable asset,' Mr Clinford told him. 'But if you try to learn everything you come across, chasing all these topics, you'll scatter your mind in so many directions at once that you'll become – yes, scattered is the word. Restless, always worrying about what you don't know yet and what there is still to learn.'

'That's how he is,' said Edgar. 'Isn't it, Eldred?'

'Maybe,' Eldred confessed. He felt ashamed.

Mr Clinford put an arm round his shoulders and steered him past the bookshelves. 'All these subjects,' he said, pointing at the signs on the shelves, 'all this history, philosophy, science, biography, literature... are the product of years of work by thousands of minds, each one an expert in some little area of a vast field of knowledge. And that's what you are, Eldred, a contributor to the world's great store of knowledge. Everyone has their own contribution to make to the world, just by being in it and being themselves. But you can't know everything or be everyone or learn all that all the other people know.'

'I know that,' said Eldred. He sounded despairing.

'You're not meant to,' said Mr Clinford reassuringly. 'You don't need to know everything, do you? You only need to learn the information you will require to be Eldred Jones and to make the contribution to the world that Eldred Jones is designed to make. All other knowledge apart from that can be acquired by other people who need it to fulfil their own particular function in the world.'

Eldred wrinkled his nose. 'I hadn't thought of it like that,' he admitted. 'But... how will I know what I need to know to be Eldred Jones in the world?'

'You'll be guided by circumstances,' said Mr Clinford firmly. 'You don't have to work it all out for yourself. Now what I've proposed to your parents and they will talk over with you at home, is that you allow this school to become one of those circumstances. You can either come here as a pupil – which is what I would personally prefer – or, as your father has certain reservations about you leaving your present school, you could stay there and come here for after-school-hours activities such as the chess club or information technology workshops or science clubs and so on.'

Eldred looked at his father. Edgar had never expressed any reservations at all about Eldred leaving his present school. Was this about fees and money? Was he meant to take the hint and leave

Edgar a let-out by saying that he, Eldred, would prefer not to leave his friends and become a pupil here?

Mr Clinford took Eldred by the hand and led him out of the library to the top of the flight of stairs leading down to the entrance hall. Once again, Eldred had the impression of being a child led by an adult. The sensation was unfamiliar.

'This is something you will discuss with your parents, as a family,' Mr Clinford said, 'and your father will let me know the outcome when you have reached your decision. I realize it's something you need time to think about and to consider together.' He smiled at Edgar and Edgar, Eldred was surprised to notice, smiled back. Mildred, white with tiredness and the effort to look interested and alert, put out her hand mutely to return Mr Clinford's handshake.

'I'll look forward to hearing from you, Mr Jones,' the headmaster said, waving them down the stairs, 'in your own time. And Eldred...' he added as an afterthought, as Eldred turned to follow his parents. 'Don't worry!'

'All right,' said Eldred automatically. But in his heart he knew this was a skill he hadn't yet learned.

Outside the front gate, Eldred took his mother's hand. 'We'll go home and have tea now, shall we?' he said comfortingly.

'Which way is the bus-stop for going back?' Edgar asked. 'Did you notice when we got here? I forgot to look.'

'Left,' said Eldred. 'Opposite the bank.'

Things were back to normal. He was the adult.

Chapter Fifty-six

Three days later, Mildred heard voices downstairs at six-thirty in the morning and found Eldred watching television in the living-room.

'What are you doing?'

He turned the volume down. 'Open University,' he said. 'Molecular structure.'

Mildred wasn't convinced. 'Why can't you sleep? Are you worrying?'

Eldred shrugged. 'Not really.'

'You'll have to let your father do this in his own time,' said Mildred. 'If he won't discuss this school yet, he won't, and that's all there is to it. He'll have to eventually.'

'Is he waiting to see if we get any money from people who see the television programme?'

'No,' said Mildred. 'He doesn't believe that will happen. Anyway, we don't have to pay the fees.'

Eldred was amazed. 'Can I go there for free? Is that what Mr Clinford said?'

'He said a school like that has hidden expenses like uniforms and sports kits and charges for some of the after-school clubs that use expensive equipment, and if we could meet those he would waive the fees. I think waive is the word he said,' Mildred said doubtfully. 'Anyway, your father looked it up in your big dictionary and it means we don't have to pay them.'

'So what's the problem?' Eldred asked. 'Why won't Dad let us mention the subject?'

'He keeps saying Mr Clinford told him to get back to him in his own time,' Mildred said, 'and that that's what he's doing – considering it in his own time.'

'We're meant to be considering it all together,' said Eldred.

Mildred sighed. 'Maybe he feels it's the only thing he has control over still,' she said. 'Everything else seems to be out of his hands.'

Eldred was disappointed. 'I thought he'd changed,' he said.

'He's changing,' said Mildred. 'Give it time.'

'How much time?' asked Eldred, but Mildred just shook her head.

'Want a cup of tea, love?' she said.

'You don't have to stay up,' Eldred said. 'You have to go to work later on.'

'I don't mind,' said Mildred. 'I was thinking of changing to the night shift; they asked for volunteers yesterday.'

'Work nights?' asked Eldred. 'You wouldn't get any sleep at all then.'

'I could sleep while you're at school and be here when you come home,' said Mildred, 'and go off to work at about the time you're going to bed. I'd be here for breakfast and seeing you off to school. You'd hardly know I was gone.'

Eldred frowned. 'What about all the other things you do, Mum? Shopping and cleaning the house and going to the launderette. Who'd do that for you?'

'Oh, I'd fit it in,' she said. 'Lots of people do.'

He was worried. 'Why do you have to work? If we don't have to pay school fees...'

'It's not that,' said Mildred. 'There'll be lots of extra things, now you're growing up. Uniform, for starters, if you do go to that school, and school trips, and then you're interested in so many things and it takes money to do anything nowadays.'

'Can't we get the uniform second-hand?' Eldred asked.

Mildred pursed her lips. 'We could, but we're not going to. Not when you're starting new; later on perhaps. You don't want people looking down their noses at you.'

'I don't want you dropping dead with exhaustion,' said Eldred.

She smiled. 'No fear of that. I'm as strong as a horse.' She stood up, tightening her dressing-gown belt around her as if girding herself for battle.

'Mum,' said Eldred, 'did something happen to you?'

'Pardon?'

He swivelled round to face her, cross-legged on the carpet. 'You say other people do all this work and you can do it too,' he said, 'but I don't know if you can. You seem to have had a lot happen to you.'

'What's ever happened to me?' asked Mildred. 'I haven't done anything with my life, except leave school with no qualifications to speak of, work for a time in a grocer's and then an optician's, marry your father, run the house and have you.'

'But what happened in between times?' Eldred asked. 'I mean, to you?'

Mildred grew flustered. 'I don't know what you're talking about.'

'When I was in your womb,' said Eldred, 'something happened to you. I don't know whether it was at the time or whether it had happened before I came along and I kind of picked up the memory of it on you. But what was it? I thought I'd erased the memory once, but it sometimes comes back again. I know what it felt like from my point of view, but how did it affect you?'

Mildred looked frightened. 'This is all nonsense,' she said. 'Stop it, Eldred. No one can remember before they were actually born. It's your imagination working overtime.'

'Pre-birth memories are very common,' said Eldred. 'It's well-known for people to suffer trauma in later life from experiences in the womb or even at the moment of conception. And as the body retains its own record of stressful experiences, it's natural for an unborn baby, who is totally vulnerable, to absorb these messages from the mother when it's in the womb.'

'You shouldn't even be thinking about these things,' said Mildred. 'It's not nice, Eldred. Let alone talking about them at quarter to seven in the morning. I can't cope with it. I'm going to get dressed.'

Eldred was remorseful. 'I'm sorry, Mum,' he said. 'I only wondered...'

'That's just it,' said Mildred with bitterness. 'You never do mean to upset people, but you do. All your wondering – where does it get you? Delving into things that are none of your business.'

Eldred picked up the remote control and turned up the sound on the television to a barely audible level. He crouched in front of the screen and listened intently, his arms wrapped round his chest, legs bent up to his chin, head down and shoulders hunched. From this foetal position he tried to concentrate on the information he was receiving from the screen about the movement of molecular particles. Relationships between atoms were easier than relationships between people. They followed immutable scientific laws and no one got hurt in the process.

Chapter Fifty-seven

Keith was coming home. Dad, Grandad and Andrew came to the hospital to fetch him.

'Mum's getting the lunch ready,' Andrew told him. 'Jessica's helping.'

Keith smiled.

As usual, the hall was decked with bunting and unseasonal paper chains. A helium balloon with WELCOME HOME, KEITH printed on it hovered near the ceiling, the string hanging from it just out of reach of the tormented tabby cat, who kept making frantic leaps for it.

'Darling!' His mother came out of the kitchen and hugged him. 'Is it good to be back?'

'Very good,' said Keith.

'We're having an early lunch, because I know you – once you get near your computer again we won't see you!'

'Is it hooked up yet?' He could only turn his head slightly, but his father was used to knowing when a question was aimed at him.

'It is. We had a bit of trouble with it; had to get your I.T. teacher over to show us what to do. But now you're ready to cruise the Internet, man!'

'My teacher? Came out here to help?'

'Saturday morning. Nice of him, wasn't it?'

'It certainly was. I'll have to thank him.'

'A lot of people care about you, son. He was only too pleased to help, and glad to hear you were coming home. You'll get a good welcome when you go back to school.'

They went into the dining-room. Paper napkins were folded into flower-shapes by every plate and a table decoration of leaves and silver twigs was the centrepiece.

'What's all this elegant living?' said Keith.

'Jessica did it,' said his mother. 'Isn't she clever?'

'It looks terrific,' said Keith. He hoped there wouldn't be too much to eat. He always felt a bit emotional, coming home, enveloped in everyone's relief that, once again, he'd made it through the operation and had come back to them.

'Did you tell him the news?' Jessica asked Andrew.

'Not yet. He and Dad wouldn't stop talking modems and software.'

'What news?' Keith asked.

'You tell him,' said Andrew generously.

'No, it's okay; you can,' Jessica responded.

'Why not wait for Christmas, while you argue about it,' Grandad joked, 'and let Santa Claus tell him? Oh no, of course, then it would be too late because the date for the TV show would be past by then... ooops! Nearly let it slip!'

'Oh, Grandad,' Andrew protested. 'You told him!'

'Am I going to be on it, then?' asked Keith.

'Yes,' Andrew said. 'The letter came this morning.'

'It's going to be you and two children,' Jessica said. 'A boy genius and a girl acrobat.'

She looked much happier, Keith thought; her eyes were shining, her hair was newly washed, and she was wearing what was probably her best dress. He was glad he had insisted that his mother should invite her to this family occasion. Family was what she needed. And Andrew's sense of responsibility for her would be shared. He looked more relaxed as well. Keith was happy.

'Well!' he said. 'An acrobat! I'll have to practise my handstands, to compete with that. What kind of genius is the boy?'

'Don't know yet,' Andrew said. 'Mum was going to phone them up to ask for details of how to get to the studios but Dad said to wait until you were home, in case there were any questions you wanted to ask as well.'

'Like whether to wear a flowery hat,' said Grandad. 'That's really what your mother's ringing to ask them. She wants to be sure she's wearing the same kind of outfit as every other woman in the audience, so she won't feel out of place.'

'Ooh no, not the same one,' Dad retorted. 'That would be a

disaster. She'd have to come all the way home again and change! She wants to be sure she's wearing something unique, but similar enough to the others not to stand out. Isn't that it?'

'Take no notice of them,' Mum told Jessica. 'What do they understand? They're only men.'

Jessica giggled. 'So what are you going to wear?'

'I haven't decided yet.'

'There you are!' said Grandad. 'She has to consult the powers-that-be before she can make such a major decision. I mean, they might not let her in if she was wearing last year's fashion, might they?'

'What are you going to wear for it, Keith?' Jessica asked.

'I haven't thought about it,' Keith said.

'You can wear that bow tie,' said Mum, 'with your suit.'

'No way,' said Keith. 'NO WAY is anyone putting a bow tie on me! That is my last word on the subject,' he added, seeing his mother open her mouth.

She laughed. 'I can't say anything to you these days! He's got such a mind of his own,' she complained to Grandad.

'I should hope so, a grandson of mine. Are we ever going to eat, or are we all going to stand round gassing all day? And talking of gas – where's that champagne?'

They had only finished the soup when the police came.

When the doorbell rang, Dad was in the kitchen carving the chicken, Mum was chopping up Keith's portion into small pieces, and Jessica and Andrew were carrying out the soup bowls and bringing in the gravy and roast potatoes. So it was Grandad who, getting to his feet with a groan of, 'Now who can that be?' went to answer the door. And it was Grandad who returned, like a very old man.

Grey in the face and shaking, he took his place at the table, clutching the edge of it. Everyone was alarmed.

'What's happened?'

'Who was it, Grandad?'

'The police,' he said. 'Wanting to know if we'd heard from Dan.

They're coming back later this afternoon. They want us to give them some photos of him.'

'Uncle Dan? Has something happened to him?' Andrew was alarmed.

Grandad hung his head.

'They've already got that photo we gave the police when we reported that Dan had gone missing,' said Mum. 'Why do they want more now? Oh no – Dad, he's not been found...?'

'He's not dead,' Grandad said. 'We might live to wish that he was.'

'Dad! How can you say such a thing? Your own son!'

Keith's father went round the table and laid a hand on his father-in-law's shoulder. 'Has there been some report of him? Has he done something?'

'They have some clues as to his whereabouts,' said Grandad heavily. 'They haven't got him. They need more evidence.'

'Evidence of what?'

Grandad shook his head. 'Not now,' he said. 'This is a family celebration. God damn Daniel, he's not going to spoil it for us. Serve the meal.'

They ate obediently. Keith's mother failed to keep up the usual stream of cheerful remarks. Andrew hardly ate anything, Keith noticed. Uncle Dan and he had always been close, till Dan disappeared one night, with no word to anyone. Jessica was nervous. Whatever the trouble was, Keith thought, it would be better spoken out loud than pondered in this heavy silence. This family was full of taboo subjects. Keith had broken the one about his death. But the taboo about Uncle Dan wasn't his to break. He supposed it was Grandad's. Even his mother hardly mentioned her brother Dan in front of him.

No one knew what Grandad had felt when Dan left. He had gone back to his own house and shut himself away for days. When he came back, he hadn't wanted to talk about his son, and by tacit agreement his name wasn't mentioned again in front of Grandad. Till now, by two uniformed police officers calling to the door in the middle of Keith's homecoming meal.

Chapter Fifty-eight

Eldred's headmaster gave him the day off to attend the television studios for filming, but grudgingly.

'I hope he isn't going to make a habit of this,' he told Mildred.

'I nearly told him we were only letting Eldred do it in the hope of getting him out of that school,' Mildred said at breakfast. She and Eldred looked hopefully at Edgar, but Edgar didn't take the opportunity.

'We'll discuss that later,' he said, not looking up from his newspaper. 'One thing at a time. You'll have enough to do to keep your wits about you today, with those telly people.'

Mildred sighed. 'I wish you were coming as well.'

'Can't keep taking time off work,' said Edgar importantly. 'Somebody has to put the bread on the table.'

'They weren't too keen on giving me a day off work,' Mildred said. 'I've hardly started there, after all.'

Eldred felt depressed. 'I could go on my own, if you don't want to go.'

'Don't be silly, dear,' his mother said. 'How could you go on your own? If you've finished that toast, don't play around with it, Eldred. Go and clean your teeth now.'

Travelling on the tube, Eldred felt happier. He liked the automatic gates that opened when you put your ticket in the slot, and the signboards that lit up with the destination of the trains and their time of arrival, and the smooth hum of the trains as they glided by the platform.

'Come away from the edge, Eldred,' said his mother, as he leaned over to study the design of the rails.

He even liked the black, sooty loops of thick flex coiled against the walls.

'What are they for?' he asked. 'What do they do?' He was talking to himself. He didn't expect an answer from Mildred and she didn't give one.

Changing to the second train, he picked a seat facing one way, memorized all the adverts, then changed sides and read the others.

'What's hydromassage, electrolysis and leg waxing?' he called out to Mildred.

Mildred fumbled in her handbag and drew out a tissue. 'Come over here,' she said. 'Your nose is running.'

Eldred knew she was annoyed. 'What's wrong?' he asked, going to sit beside her.

She wrenched his nose with the tissue.

'Ow! Mum!'

'Sit still,' she hissed, 'and stop changing seats all the time.'

'There was nothing to read,' he complained.

'Read the tube map on the back of the A to Z,' she said. 'Tell me how many more stops we've got to go.'

'Three,' he said. He closed his eyes and began to recite the stations on the Central Line: 'Notting Hill Gate intersects with the District and Circle lines,' he murmured. 'Bond Street connects with the Jubilee line, Oxford Circus with the Bakerloo line... Why is it called Bakerloo, Mum?'

'I don't know.'

'Does Bakerloo mean anything, as a word? Like District or Circle or Central or Metropolitan?'

'I don't know.'

'Don't think it does,' he said. 'Oh! Baker Street to Waterloo, is it? Baker-loo?'

'Probably,' said Mildred. 'Yes.'

'But it doesn't start at Baker Street and end at Waterloo,' Eldred pointed out. 'It starts in Harrow and Wealdstone and ends in Elephant and Castle. It should be called the Harrow Castle line, shouldn't it?'

'Yes, dear,' said Mildred.

'Or Elephant and Wealdstone. Mum?'

'Yes, Eldred.'

'Why Elephant and Castle?'

'I don't know.'

'Is it two different places, like Harrow and Wealdstone, or is it one?'

'It's just one place. Elephant and Castle.'

'Why, though?'

'It's a name. It's always been called that. There are some funny names in London.'

'There must have been a reason,' said Eldred, 'at the time when someone first made it up. I mean, it wouldn't be a name you'd just think of, would it? You wouldn't say, "Let's call this place Harrow and let's call this place... um, let me see, Elephant and Castle." Would you, Mum?'

'No.'

'Do you think there could have been a castle there once? With an elephant to pull open the drawbridge, instead of an ordinary winch?'

'Eldred,' said his mother.

'Yes?'

'When these people ask you questions today, just answer them,' said Mildred. 'Don't get into clever discussions or wondering about things or asking them loads of questions yourself, will you? They're busy people; they won't have that much patience.'

'I know what it is,' said Eldred.

'Know what what is?'

'The Bakerloo line,' he said. 'When they first built the Underground it was just for central London and it did start at Baker Street and end at Waterloo. Then later, when people knew what a good idea it was and started to use the tube and make the owners lots of money, the owners decided to extend it. Are all the lines owned by the same company, Mum? Or do different people own the Bakerloo from the ones who own the Jubilee?'

'Eldred,' she said, 'did you hear what I said to you?'

'Of course.' He was surprised. 'TV people aren't patient; just answer the questions.'

'Right.'

'Are they impatient because they work in TV and everything has to be done within tight deadlines? Or does the type of work you do in television attract people with personalities that aren't very patient?'

'I get the feeling this is going to be long day,' said Mildred.
Eldred looked at her sideways and went silent.

Chapter Fifty-nine

She was ready.

Lucinda, inspecting Lulubelle's eye make-up critically, was satisfied that she had done her utmost for her daughter.

'Perfect,' she said, 'if I say so myself. We'll put the final glitz on just before you go on. But don't smudge the base coats in the meantime, all right?'

'Okay.'

Sam was driving them to the studio, against Molly's wishes. This evening, they would get a taxi home from the station, because everyone would be busy, either performing or manning the fairground rides and stalls. Lulubelle had the taxi fare in her bag. 'Don't leave it in mine,' Lucinda said. 'I'll only forget and spend it on something else.'

Marisa was standing ready to wave them off. Lulubelle ran to see Arto in the Big Top, where he was practising. He put down a pile of steel girders to talk to her.

'You will be a great success,' he told her. 'I know it.' He laid a hefty hand on her shoulder. 'The show will not be the same without you this afternoon or this evening.'

'Thanks for getting Mr Mannfield to give me the day off. And Lucinda as well.'

He raised his eyebrows. 'I only asked for you. Lucinda, she told him herself how necessary it was, how you couldn't perform before strangers without the protection of your mother.'

Lulubelle laughed.

He was suddenly serious. 'The man who was following you: you saw him again?'

'No.'

'Tell me once more, so I will know him.'

'Quite thin, dark hair, dark blue quilted jacket. He might wear an anorak hood that doesn't match. What will you do if you see him?'

Arto flexed a huge bicep. 'Talk to him.'

'You'd better not hurt him or anything, Arto. It might get you into trouble with the police.'

'I don't hurt no one,' said Arto. 'I simply show him a little example of how accidents can happen – so easy in a circus, yes?' He seized a girder in one hand, pretended to slip, and dropped it. The ground beneath their feet rocked. 'You go and perform,' he said, 'and don't worry about nothing.'

So now they were here, being greeted by the cool, non-committal team who had stood and watched Lulubelle during her studio audition – only now they were warm and smiling, confident in her ability to make their show an event.

'Where are the others?' she asked. 'I'd like to meet them.'

'You will, but they're not here yet. Your agent told us you'd need a practice room for your warm-up, so we're going to put you in here, down this corridor – all right?'

Your agent, Lulubelle thought. It sounded great. She looked at Lucinda, who winked. She had been a bit afraid that Mum would be jealous, but Lucinda had been delighted. A day off work and the celebrity-mother treatment suited her nicely.

And with any luck the publicity might bring Lulubelle some more lucrative work, and Lucinda a nice bit of pocket money for nothing more than escorting her to and from her engagements. It had to beat hanging off trapezes and balancing on a high wire for a living.

Sonia showed them into a room with a mirrored wall. 'Will this be all right for you?'

'Lovely,' Lucinda approved.

'I'll call back for you in half an hour, if that suits you.'

'It's a bit early for her warm-up yet,' Lucinda said. 'She'd only have to do it all over again just before.'

'Oh, I see. Well, perhaps I'll show you your places in the studio first, and someone will call you to the hospitality room in a little while, then you can let me know when you're ready to come and practise.'

'That sounds more like it,' Lucinda said. 'You haven't got a cigarette you could spare me, have you, love?'

'No, I don't smoke, I'm afraid, but I'll see what I can get you.'

'Thanks, love. Don't mind me asking, do you?'

Lulubelle didn't know what to do with her kitbag. Sonia noticed her confusion.

'I'd bring it with you, if I were you. It would probably be safe here, but you don't want to take any chances, do you?'

Lulubelle hadn't expected to feel so nervous. She wished there wasn't such a long time to wait before she had to perform. She knew the nerves would go once the spotlight was on and she was heading towards it.

For a moment, she regretted getting involved in this and wished she was in the Big Top, rehearsing the pyramid with the adult acrobats, or even sitting in class with the children, doing a maths test.

Following Sonia and her mother down the corridor to the studio, she shook her head decisively. This was her big chance. This was where fame was born, in television studios, ready to have her brilliant act transmitted to an appreciative nationwide audience.

She had a practice room allocated to her alone. And an agent, prestigious enough to represent Arto the strongman and a host of other names that she hadn't personally heard of, but everyone obviously knew.

It was coming true, her dream. She was on her way. Look out, world, it's Lulubelle Lacosto – on TV!

Chapter Sixty

This time, they were received like celebrities. There was no confusion over their names; everyone they met seemed to know who they were. Mildred was bemused by it all, and by the fact that Eldred seemed to know everybody as well.

'Hi Sonia,' he said in the lift. 'It's Sonia,' he reminded Mildred. 'Rachel's secretary, who showed us in the last time.'

'Oh yes, of course,' said Mildred. They had been met this time by a young man with plaited hair. Eldred had seemed to know who he was too, as soon as he introduced himself.

'You've got the office two rooms down from Rachel Hicks,' said Eldred. 'I saw your name on the door last time we were here.'

Last time we were here, thought Mildred! He talked as though he was in and out of television studios all the time. She felt intensely uncomfortable.

The young man, whose name she hadn't caught, smiled at her. 'I expect it's a bit overwhelming, having your son become a star. Come and meet the other mothers. You'll be sitting together in the front row of the studio.'

Seeing Mildred look even more confused, he added, 'You did know it's being filmed in front of a studio audience, didn't you?'

'We weren't told anything,' said Mildred belligerently. 'Do the mothers have to be interviewed as well?'

'Not really,' he said. 'You might be asked the odd question, but just where you are. You won't have to go out in front of the cameras in the main studio area: that'll just be Janice and Peter and the three children.'

'Who are Janice and Peter?' Mildred demanded.

Eldred wished she didn't sound hostile when she was nervous. It was all right for her to tell him to behave and not embarrass her, but he wasn't allowed to ask the same of her, he thought.

The young man looked surprised. 'The presenters,' he said. 'Marrin and Sutfield. Haven't you watched the show before?'

Mildred's fists were tight around her handbag. Eldred answered for her. 'We thought it was a one-off documentary,' he said, 'about unusual children.'

'Oh right,' he said. 'It's a one-off on that subject, not a series, but it's part of the second series of weekly chat shows. There was a pilot on most of the local TV stations early last year and then this network bought the first series. It was quite a success. It's modelled on some of the studio shows from the States – Oprah Winfrey and such. You've seen the Oprah Winfrey show?'

'Yes,' said Eldred. 'She's a good interviewer, isn't she?'

Mildred was quiet. She wished she was a thousand miles away, among people who had never heard of Oprah Winfrey either. She wished Edgar was beside her. She wished she had never had a child. This whole business was beyond her. Why couldn't Eldred be normal, so they could all live in happy obscurity? Louise Palmer had fooled them. All this publicity would do no good. Eldred didn't even need money now for public school. They were just being used by the media. It would break up the family, sure as sure.

They were at the door of the studio. A computer-printed notice stuck on the door said 'Marrin and Sutfield – Unusual Kids – 10.30 a.m.' It was too late to flee, even if Mildred could have persuaded Eldred to leave. He ducked under the young man's arm as he opened the door, and bounded in ahead of them both, eager to begin. Mildred followed, her heart as heavy as lead.

'Mildred Jones, Lucinda Lacosto,' the young man said rapidly, holding Mildred's arm and pushing her towards a woman with dyed blonde hair and tired eyes. 'Excuse me, I'll just round up your children and take them to see the presenters. You stay here for now,' he said, as Mildred moved towards Eldred. 'Someone will call you for coffee soon.'

'Are you the mother of the disabled boy?' asked Lucinda.

'No,' said Mildred faintly. 'That's my son there.' She pointed to Eldred as he disappeared into a crowd of people who were standing round talking loudly, some with complicated-looking cameras and what she presumed was sound equipment.

'The brainy child who invents things?' said Lucinda.

'I suppose so,' Mildred said. 'I'm not used to this,' she said, in sudden despair.

'Don't worry,' said Lucinda kindly. 'Have a fag to calm your nerves. These were on the house, so help yourself.'

'I don't smoke,' said Mildred. 'I gave up when Eldred was a baby.'

'Do you knit?'

'I beg your pardon?'

'You need to do something,' Lucinda explained, 'to take your mind off all the waiting around. I don't knit, myself; could never learn. It'd be useful on these occasions.'

'Are you involved in this kind of thing very often, then?' asked Mildred. 'Mrs... I'm sorry, I didn't catch your name.'

'Lucinda. Lucinda Lacosto.'

'Oh. Is that... what nationality is your name?' Mildred said tentatively. Was there something foreign about the woman? She certainly didn't look like the kind of woman Mildred normally met; there was something different about her, though Mildred couldn't quite put her finger on what it was.

'No idea,' said Lucinda. 'It's my stage name. My employer-before-last thought it up. Lucy Hobbs doesn't sound showbizzy enough, does it?'

'You're in showbusiness?' said Mildred, shifting away from her slightly.

'Don't look so horrified,' said Lucinda, lighting a cigarette and drawing on it heavily. Mildred coughed. 'Sorry,' Lucinda apologized. 'I chainsmoke. My boss says he should have taken me on as a fire-eater! I work for Mannfield's Circus at the moment – you heard of them? No, I thought not. They're only a smallish outfit but they've got some good acts. I work the trapezes and do a bit of high-wire. My daughter's an acrobat.'

'Oh,' said Mildred. 'Where is she?'

'Around somewhere,' said Lucinda casually. 'She's used to this set-up. Been on local TV and children's telly. She has her own agent now. How about your boy?'

'He's been in the newspapers and on the local TV news,' said Mildred. She felt ashamed of it now. What was she letting poor Eldred get into? Mothers who walked the high-wire in a tutu and boasted that their daughters were acrobats. What had the

Jones family, respectable people, to do with such folk? 'They told me this wasn't going to be a freak show,' she murmured faintly.

'Nothing of the kind,' said Lucinda robustly. 'Don't you worry. It's a very professional programme, this. Do your boy's publicity the world of good.'

'We don't want publicity,' said Mildred desperately. 'I don't know how we got into this.'

'Funny old world, isn't it?' Lucinda nodded. 'I don't know where my girl got her talent from: I'm not a bad performer, if I say it myself, but she's above and beyond what I can do. Amazing to watch. It's like her bones are made of elastic. I never get tired of watching her do her act. There you go, though: doting mothers. You're the same, I expect.'

'Oh no,' said Mildred, from the heart. 'I wish he was normal. I'd give anything for a quiet life, myself.'

'Like to come and have coffee in the hospitality room, ladies?' said a colourfully attired young man appearing in front of them.

'No, thank you,' said Mildred hastily. This place was like a circus in itself, she thought. How could these freakish people promise her they wouldn't present her son as a freak? They probably thought they were normal themselves.

'Come on, do come,' Lucinda urged her. 'I never have time for breakfast and they usually ply you with food. Come and keep me company.'

Mildred stood up and followed her. Keeping this odd woman company was preferable to being left alone in a studio full of people who looked as though they had come from another planet. What had Eldred got her into? She swore a silent vow to herself that this was the last time she would agree to his appearing in public. And what on earth were they going to make him seem like to those people watching TV in their living-rooms, her sweet, strange, bewildering, irritating, abnormal little boy? Mildred shuddered to think about it.

Chapter Sixty-one

'I hoped it would be you,' said Eldred joyfully. The girl he had seen going into the Ladies on his first visit to the studios smiled at him.

'I'm Eldred,' he told her.

She considered this. Where had she heard that name? Eldred thought she looked cute when she wrinkled her nose like that. 'Is that a real name,' asked Lulubelle, 'or a made-up one just for you?'

'It's made up from my parents' names, Edgar and Mildred,' Eldred explained. 'I think they expected me to be half like each of them.'

'But you turned out to be just yourself,' the girl said.

Eldred was surprised. 'How did you know that?'

She shrugged her shoulders, a wide expansive gesture. 'Parents,' she said concisely. 'My name's Lulubelle.'

'I never heard that name before,' said Eldred. 'Is it from your parents' as well?'

'My mum's name's Lucy, or Lucinda when she's performing. I don't know what my father's name is.'

'Is he dead?'

'Not as far as I know,' she said casually. 'My mum just doesn't know who he was.'

Eldred pondered this. 'How can she not know?' He had learned the facts of reproduction early on in his life and could not imagine how anyone could go through that process and not know it was happening.

'It's like that in showbusiness,' Lulubelle explained. 'The women have to sleep with the bosses who give out the work, otherwise the job goes to someone else. It's a cut-throat business.'

'How old are you?' asked Eldred.

'Eleven next month.' She was wearing lipstick, rouge, mascara, eyeliner and three shades of eye-shadow, Eldred noticed: pink, purple and brown. He thought she looked wonderfully glamorous.

'But you don't have to sleep with the bosses to get work,' Eldred said.

'No,' she said. 'Mum does it for both of us. Only one bloke had a go at me, but that was because I thought he was after my mum and she was ill. But I made sure we moved to another circus after that.'

Eldred was horrified. 'That's child abuse.'

'It goes on,' said Lulubelle sagely. 'It happens to some kids all the time, and at home, which is worse because they can't get away from it. I wasn't sure about going on TV at first in case this guy saw me and found out which circus we're with now, but that might have happened anyway. But he's not going to ruin my chances.'

'Did he hurt you?' asked Eldred.

She shrugged again, but the movement was more constricted this time. 'Don't make a big deal of it,' she said.

Eldred looked her in the eyes. 'You must have been very frightened,' he said quietly.

Her face crumpled. She turned away from him quickly. 'Now look what you've done,' she said. 'My eyes will get smudged and my mum will be annoyed if she has to do them all over again.'

'Sorry,' said Eldred.

'It's all right,' she said, giving an enormous sniff into a very small handkerchief. 'It's nice of you to mind. No one else does.'

Eldred took a biro out of his pocket, took her handkerchief from her and wrote two sets of numbers on it. He handed it back to her.

'Phone numbers, are they?' she asked.

'The first one's Childline,' said Eldred, 'and the second one's mine. You can phone either of those any time.'

'How d'you know the number of Childline?' she asked. 'Have you been done over as well, then?'

'No,' he said. 'A friend of mine got into trouble and I phoned them to see if they could help him. But they told me to leave it to the police.'

'If they wouldn't help him, they wouldn't help me, would they?' she said. 'Especially as we're never in one place for long.'

'No,' said Eldred, 'they would. My friend wasn't being abused; he abused some kids.'

'Nice friends you have,' said Lulubelle, with another sniff.

'He wasn't a bad man,' said Eldred earnestly. 'I know what he did was bad, but the person himself was good. I don't understand how good people can do something bad, out of the blue, but they do sometimes.'

Lulubelle shook her head. 'No,' she said decisively. 'If someone does something bad, they are bad. They might not have thought they were before, but it just shows that they are. Bad people do bad stuff, good people do good stuff – simple as that, Eldred. Don't you be fooled.'

'Finished your Coke and crisps?' said Bob with the ponytail, reappearing beside them. 'Right, then. Lulu, you go with this lady here and run through your routine, and Eldred, you come and talk to Janice.'

'See you later, Lulubelle,' said Eldred as he was ushered away.

'Nice meeting you,' she said, over her shoulder. 'Have you met Keith?'

Eldred stopped. 'Who's Keith?' But Lulubelle was swallowed up in the crowd.

'Keith's the other child on the show,' said Bob. 'You'll see him in a minute. He's in a wheelchair. He's fourteen but he's tiny, so he looks about your age. Here, Janice, here's Eldred to talk to you.'

'Eldred, lovely to meet you,' Janice said. She was tall and thin with sharp cheeks and protruding collarbones. Eldred wondered if she ate her meals. Perhaps she worked too hard and couldn't be bothered to cook when she went home in the evenings. He hoped Mildred wouldn't get like that; he liked her comfortable and round.

'Pete will be along in a minute to meet you too,' Janice continued, 'but I'll be the one asking you most of the questions. Let me just show you the set and where you'll be. We're going to talk first to Keith, because he hasn't been very well recently and he might have to go off early, though if possible we're going to keep all three of you on set all the time, and hopefully get some interaction between you.

'Then Lulubelle will come on and do her acrobatic routine before we sit her down and have a talk, and we'll have a quick comment from her mum in the front row – over there – of the studio audience. Then it'll be your turn. Most of the questions are going to be flashed up there on that screen; you'll answer some of them into this little microphone we'll clip to your shirt and some others on a computer terminal, and others will be sums and so on shouted out by the audience.'

Eldred froze. 'I thought I was going to be interviewed,' he said. 'Is it a test or something, then?'

Janice smiled. 'Nothing to worry about,' she said. 'From what I heard about you at the preliminary interview, you'll do all this standing on your head.'

'But what kind of questions?' asked Eldred. 'What about?'

She patted his shoulder. 'We don't want to give away too much,' she said. 'Spoil the fun. They won't be any more difficult than the questionnaire Rachel gave you before. Very similar.'

'But that was in private,' Eldred said. 'This is like a performance, isn't it?' He looked around for Lulubelle or his mum.

'You'll be fine,' said Janice with finality. 'Now, Maurice the cameraman is going to have a quick word with you about which light you look at and which you don't, and Sylvie will check you for sound, and one of the girls in make-up will just adjust you for shine – I know it's not very macho, but it's just for the lights, Eldred, so bear with us, will you? Okay, Jeff, I'm coming.'

Eldred was bewildered. He forgot even to be interested in the workings of the cameras and lights. His father wasn't going to like this. He wanted to go home. He saw Mildred sitting next to a blonde lady in the front row and tried to catch her eye, but Mildred was staring into space while the lady talked and smoked. She looked petrified. Eldred knew how she felt.

'Hello,' said a voice. It sounded very calm. Eldred turned round in relief and found himself looking down at a small freckled face with huge eyes and a wide smile. The body attached to the face was small, very thin, very twisted, and arranged apparently haphazardly in a wheelchair with a headrest positioned to one side to support the tilted head. Eldred gulped. He had never before come close to someone deformed.

'I'm Keith,' said the boy. 'You must be Eldred the wonder-brain.' He grinned wickedly.

'Yes,' said Eldred.

'I heard them talking,' Keith said. 'Sounds like they're going to make you jump through hoops.'

'Yes,' Eldred said. 'I didn't know they were going to set me tests.'

'Make the answers up if you don't know them all,' the boy advised. 'If you come across really confident, people will be impressed.' One tiny bent finger pressed a switch on a panel set into the arm of the wheelchair, and the chair hummed and swivelled round so that its occupant was face to face with Eldred. 'At least,' Keith said, 'they can't make me jump through hoops.'

Eldred was overcome by the sight of him. 'What happened to you?' he said.

'I was born like this,' said Keith simply. 'Worse, really. I've had a lot of operations to get to this point.'

'How could it be worse?' said Eldred. He felt despair.

'I used not to be able to bend my legs,' Keith said. 'My knees were straight. And I couldn't use my hands or turn my head at all. And my speech is clearer now, though it's not always as good as it is today. I have good days and bad days.'

Eldred could not see how any day could be good for someone in the state Keith was in. 'Can't you be cured?' he said.

'Cured of being myself?' said Keith. 'This is the way I am. There are worse things to be than disabled.' He saw Eldred's face and laughed. 'Think about it,' he said. 'Only my body is crippled. Some people are crippled inside.'

Eldred leaned forward to look at Keith on his own level. 'How?' he asked.

'Resentment, hatred, greed, power.' He smiled, watching Eldred struggle with his thoughts. His eyes were the clearest eyes Eldred had ever seen in his life.

'Is that being crippled inside?' Eldred asked.

'Sure. Think about it. How can people be free if they're all twisted up inside with some grudge against somebody or some burning desire to make a lot of money? Whereas me, I'm free; I can think what I like when I like.'

'But what kind of life...' Eldred stopped himself.

'Go on,' Keith encouraged. 'You won't upset me.'

'I mean, what are you going to be?' Eldred asked. 'What will you do when you're grown up?'

'I am grown up,' said Keith, 'and it's a full-time job being me. I was never expected to make it as far as this. Me being fourteen is like you being eighty-five.'

'You mean you're going to die?' Eldred's hands rose to his heart.

'Sooner or later, like everybody,' said Keith. 'Only probably sooner. It doesn't bother me. It's this life that's hard. It suits some people, Eldred, but I'm out of my element here, like this. The next stage will be better for me.'

'Next stage?' said Eldred. He had never heard anyone talk this way before.

'Next life,' said Keith. 'Heaven.'

'Reincarnation?' said Eldred. He had read about that in a magazine.

Keith laughed. 'No way,' he said. 'I'm not going to be recycled. Once is enough. We live once, we die once, and we move on; we don't go round and round indefinitely.'

'How can you know?' said Eldred. 'Who told you that?'

'Jesus Christ,' said Keith. 'In his teaching.'

Eldred was aghast. 'You believe that stuff? In an age of science, the third millennium?'

'Truth doesn't change,' said Keith tranquilly. 'Read it for yourself. Haven't you read the gospels or the Acts of the Apostles, or the letters of Paul and the rest?'

'I've heard extracts,' said Eldred dismissively.

Keith shook his head, a slow, painstaking process, but his eyes were full of amusement. 'Very unscientific,' he said, 'relying on hearsay and second-hand judgments. Read them yourself.'

'Okay, okay,' said Eldred, stung, 'I accept that Jesus existed and was an actual figure in history, but I can't be expected to believe in miracles and things reported by a group of uneducated fishermen, and I don't believe he was God's son, though I expect he was a good man who impressed people and taught everyone the right way to behave.'

'Can't have been, can he?' said Keith. 'If he said he was the son of God when he wasn't, then he was lying so he wasn't a good man at all but a lunatic or an evil conman. But if he was telling the truth he was much more than someone who preached. And even uneducated fishermen, who were probably quite streetwise in their way, could cook up a better story than they did. They don't even agree on the details, which is exactly what you get from witnesses at a road accident or something. They all know what they saw, but they all saw it differently. If someone's making up a myth, they take the trouble to get their accounts to tally.'

He stopped and wheezed, out of breath from this long speech.

'Are you all right?' asked Eldred anxiously. Keith nodded. A woman shot out of the crowd and seized the wheelchair.

'You're tiring yourself out,' she scolded Keith, but her eyes accused Eldred. 'He would insist on coming on this programme,' she said. 'I was dead against it. It's far too much for him.'

Keith smiled his wide, sleepy smile. 'My mum,' he told Eldred.

The woman softened slightly. 'Come and have your snack,' she said. She wheeled him away. As he left, he lifted one bony finger in farewell. Eldred raised his hand and waved.

Chapter Sixty-two

Eldred was running for the exit when a woman came out of a room ahead of him saying, 'I'll be back in ten minutes, Lulubelle; you carry on.'

He stopped, and moved into the open doorway. Lulubelle, in a silver leotard and tights, was upside down in a corner of the room, standing on her hands. She flung herself backwards and towards the door in a series of very fast backward flips. Eldred jumped out of the way, but she threw herself sideways on to one hand and changed direction without losing a second's speed.

When she had travelled round the perimeter of the room in this way, she stood facing him.

'That's my entrance,' she said. 'Like it?'

'Wow,' said Eldred.

'My trademark,' she said, 'that change of direction. When I come on in the circus ring they have a fire in the middle of the ring and I head straight towards it, and just at the very last minute I go on to this hand and go round it. You can hear the audience gasp.'

'Are you going to do that in the studio?' Eldred asked.

'Yes. Not with the fire, though. They'll use a big vase of flowers.'

'Oh,' said Eldred. He thought it was just as well he had decided to go home. The audience would be bored watching him do maths problems, after seeing Lulubelle. In fact, he thought, anything would seem boring after Lulubelle.

'Shall I show you something else?' she asked. Without waiting for an answer, she went over to a kitbag in the corner, took out a pair of enormous loop earrings which held a row of small bells and clipped them on. Another set of bells went round her ankles. Sitting down demurely cross-legged, she then raised her feet to her ears and rang the earring bells with her toes. Eldred giggled.

Lulubelle lowered her feet again and, taking her weight on her hands, slid her body into a prone position, lying on her stomach, then raised her feet over her back, bending her knees outwards, and rang the bells again with her big toes.

'That's amazing!' said Eldred. 'How do you bend like that?'

Lulubelle put on a deep, raspy voice and intoned: 'She's the Incredi-belle, the Sensation-elle, the Flexi-belle... Lulubelle!' In one smooth movement, she took her weight on her hands again, straightened her legs and moved into a perfect handstand. After remaining absolutely motionless for a few seconds, she changed to a frenzy of movement, shaking her head and her ankles so that all the bells rang violently together. Eldred burst out laughing.

'Got to have an element of comedy,' said Lulubelle seriously, standing upright to face him again. She stood on her left leg and, raising the right foot to her left ear, unclipped the earring with her toes, then did the same with the other foot. 'How are you getting on?' she said. 'You don't look too happy.'

'I'm going home,' said Eldred, but as he said it he felt ashamed. He couldn't imagine Lulubelle running away from anything.

'Oh,' she said. 'Why's that?'

He was grateful for the absence of condemnation. 'I can't do all this performing, like you can,' he said. 'I'm not used to it, and I don't think the audience will be interested anyway. I thought I was going to be interviewed. I can do that.'

'And what are you going to do?'

'Jump through hoops,' he said grimly, quoting Keith. 'They're going to get the audience to call out maths problems, and I have to do something on the computer. I don't know if it's against the clock, or what. Janice wouldn't tell me too much. She said it would spoil the fun.'

'See what you mean,' said Lulubelle. She raised her hands slowly in front of her and leaned over backwards till the back of her head was level with her bottom. She looked comfortable. 'If they're trying to show you off as this genius brainbox boy,' she said, 'I don't suppose they want you to get things wrong.'

'That's just it,' said Eldred, agitated. 'What if I mess it all up?'

'No, I mean that's up to them,' said Lulubelle. 'It's their problem. So they'll probably be careful not to give you things that are too hard.'

'But how would that show me off, if that's what they want?' asked Eldred.

Lulubelle bent still further, placed her hands on the floor behind her and shifted her balance so that her head hung down and her back was a perfect arch. Eldred, watching her, thought that she moved her body as he moved his thoughts, sliding from one stance to another without using the normal sequence of movements. No wonder it unnerved people when he changed from one line of reasoning to another.

'You're equally graceful,' he commented, forgetting himself for a moment, 'whether you're moving slowly or very fast. None of the movements are sudden; it all flows.'

She flipped backwards and stood upright. 'Thanks,' she said, going pink. 'No, what I meant about you was... like you're a trapeze artist, right, and the television crew are the ringmaster? You're a new act, and the ringmaster isn't sure yet what you can do because he's only seen you audition. Right?'

'Right,' Eldred agreed.

'He knows a bit of what you can do and he puts you through your paces in front of his own audience for the first time. So what does he do? He starts you off on the easy stuff then he lets you work up to the real core of your act: things that you can do that other trapeze artists can't, things the audience may never have seen before. Okay?'

'Okay.'

'Then – only then, if you've performed without any faults, he'll signal to you to go on and do your really spectacular things. You finish on a high point, the audience clap themselves crazy, you go off, he takes a bow and gets some of the glory. You get me?'

'Yes,' said Eldred.

'Now – if you start doing your moderately impressive stuff and you don't quite pull it all off, or if you're okay but you've let him know beforehand you're having an off-day, he plays it differently. He tells you to spin out the easy stuff, vary it a bit, speed it up a bit maybe. Throw in a few of your tricks on the trapeze but space it out, take a few more swings back and forth, make things look more tricky than they need to look. After a while, when you've had a few rounds of applause, he'll signal to you to come off. You won't be the most stunning act in the show that night, but you've done all right, the audience is happy enough, you haven't looked clumsy or broken any bones. No one gets hurt.'

'I see,' said Eldred doubtfully.

'Point I'm making,' said Lulubelle, sliding down to prop her whole weight on her elbows and forearms flat on the floor, and raising her legs slowly above her head, 'is that making your act a success is their responsibility, not yours, and as they don't know what you can do until you get going, they'll play it by ear – take it gently to start with then if you deliver the goods they'll hot up the challenge. Of course,' she added, tipping her legs forward, placing her feet apart on the floor by her fingertips and popping her head through her legs to grin at him, 'I could be talking through my backside!'

They both started giggling and found they couldn't stop. Rachel Hicks found them sitting on the floor, doubled up and gasping with laughter.

'There you are,' she said. 'Eldred, I want to run through a few points we want you to talk about in the interview. Lulubelle, have you finished your warm-up?'

'Yes thanks,' said Lulubelle, suddenly demure. Rachel led the way out of the room. If Eldred had any more thoughts of running for the door, he gave no sign of it as he followed Rachel down the corridor, with Lulubelle behind him.

Chapter Sixty-three

Each of the children was taken through the notes made by the researchers at their preliminary interviews and was reminded of anything relevant they had said at the time. The presenters would prompt them, but it was up to them to pick up the cue and repeat a particular anecdote or comment.

After this, the three children and the presenters assembled on the set for a run-through. Some of the studio audience had already begun to arrive; they were welcomed by junior staff and diverted to a waiting room.

The two presenters made their preliminary speech about unusually gifted children, mentioning gifts of art, sport and music and skimming over them to focus attention on the kind of gifts exemplified by their guests. They whisked through the influence of genetics and inheritance, good luck or bad luck in being born gifted or handicapped, and came to rest on the power of a child's individual character to develop those gifts or overcome the disabilities with which nature or destiny had equipped them.

This introduction was delivered with smiles, earnest expressions, confidence and, Eldred considered, a total lack of conviction, but Simon, who stood in the corner wearing headphones almost bigger than his neat little head and who appeared to be in charge of the whole operation, smiled and raised his thumb and seemed satisfied with Janice and Peter's performance. Eldred dared to hope that the standard they would require of him would be equally undemanding.

Keith was wheeled on to the set by his mother, who then took her seat in the front row. A few rows behind her were occupied by studio staff, who were instructed by Simon to look, in turn, absorbed, curious, sympathetic and amused, and finally to give a round of applause, while the cameras turned on them.

'I thought this was just a run-through,' Eldred said to Lulubelle, as they waited where they had been put, in the wings of the little set. 'Why are they filming it?'

'Rachel said they'd film all the bits with Keith in,' said Lulubelle, 'in case he gets taken ill and can't finish it. Then they'll use the run-through as the actual thing, with those people sitting behind his mum as though there's a whole studio audience. And if he's too tired to stay on the set while we do our thing, they'll take the cameras off him and wheel him off. They're going to tell the audience not to applaud him if he goes off while we're doing something.'

Eldred was concerned. 'Is he likely to get ill?'

'He might. His mother told my mum he could die at any time,' Lulubelle said.

'Not here!' said Eldred, terrified. 'Why don't they just take him home?'

'He wanted to do it,' said Lulubelle. 'Let him have a bit of excitement.'

'If it kills him?'

'Better to die doing something you enjoy,' she said philosophically. 'I'd rather fall off a high wire without a safety net than lie for months in hospital with tubes up my nose or something.'

'Would you?' Eldred had never thought about it.

The mock studio audience gave a round of applause as Keith answered his first question.

'Ssh,' said Lulubelle. 'I didn't hear what he said then.'

'He said he'd had fifteen operations, eight on his body and seven on his legs,' said Eldred.

Her eyes filled with tears suddenly. 'Poor kid,' she said. Eldred took her hand and she squeezed his fingers painfully. Eldred didn't resent it, remembering that her mother would be annoyed with her if she cried and smudged her eyeliner.

The crew went silent while Keith talked about his life, the things he enjoyed, the highlights – family visits, television programmes, trips to the pantomime, receiving letters and cards in answer to letters he drafted on his modified computer – and the sufferings. With no change in his voice, he talked about operations that hadn't worked, scars that took months to heal, eagerly awaited holidays missed, the sadness of watching other children play football, go on the swings in the park or dress up for the disco.

Lulubelle, listening, wept, regardless of her make-up. Eldred stood very still, focusing on Keith. He felt that if he listened very hard, he might begin to understand what it was like to be Keith and then he might, in some way, be Keith, so that Keith would no longer have to bear the whole burden of being himself on his own. He took deep breaths, breathing in Keith, trying to absorb the essence of him. His self-preserving instinct impelled him to take the opposite way, to shut Keith out of his consciousness and close his heart to the painful recognition of how it felt to be Keith, but Eldred resisted it and felt his heart expand, contract, ache and flinch as Keith spoke.

When the boy stopped talking and Peter thanked him, there was a moment's stillness before everyone recollected themselves and clapped. The crew, Eldred could sense, were no longer pretending to be a studio audience applauding but were being themselves, applauding Keith. Several of them were discreetly applying handkerchiefs to their noses and eyes, including, Eldred noticed, Mildred.

'Ouf!' said Lulubelle softly. 'How do you follow that?'

'You're on in a second,' said the girl with the clipboard who had showed them where to stand while they waited their turn. 'As soon as Peter finishes this bit of talk.'

Lulubelle panicked. 'I can't go on and do cartwheels after that!'

'Now!' said the girl, giving her shoulder a slight shove.

'No,' said Lulubelle. 'I can't.'

'Hold it!' the girl shouted.

'Okay, cut,' said Simon, removing his headphones. 'That part was fine, thanks. What's the problem over here?'

'Stage fright,' said the girl.

Lulubelle stamped her foot. 'I do not get stage fright!' she said furiously.

'What's up?' Simon asked.

'You heard him,' said Lulubelle, wiping her nose on the back of her hand. 'Could you go on and leap about all over the place, after him saying he got upset watching kids play football when he can't?'

'Oh, right,' said Simon soothingly. 'Right. I take your point. You relax and take a break, love. Go and have a chat with your mum. I'll have a quick word with Peter and Janice.' He went.

'He's going to make them talk me into it,' said Lulubelle.

'Yes,' said Eldred. 'I think so.'

'What would you do?' she asked.

Eldred thought. He closed his eyes and tried to feel like Keith again. 'Go on and do it,' he said. 'Keith wants to see what you do.'

'How do you know?' Lulubelle asked.

'He's come on this programme because he wanted to,' Eldred pointed out. 'He knew about me and you. You said yourself, "Let him have a bit of excitement." Well, there's nothing much more exciting than watching you.'

Her eyes widened. 'Is that true?'

'True as true,' Eldred assured her.

'I've got an idea,' she said. 'Is my make-up smudged?'

He inspected her face. 'Not much. One corner of that eye.'

'I'll get Mum to fix it,' she said. 'Then watch this space, Eldred. This is going to be spec-tac-ular!' She did a quick somersault in the air for emphasis, and sprang off in the direction of her mother, leaving Eldred breathless at her sudden change of mood.

He watched and waited. Lulubelle, looking confident, suffered repair by her mother, spoke to Simon, Janice and Pete and then to Keith. Everyone stood back. The set cleared.

'We're not rolling the cameras,' Simon said, 'but treat this as if it was for real. Okay, go.'

Lulubelle appeared at Eldred's side. Holding both hands against her diaphragm, she drew in her breath and then let it out very slowly, very controlled. Eldred dared not move in case he distracted her.

She moved out of the wings into view, walking on her hands with exaggerated lifts, raising her head at each step so the audience could see her face. Peter, Eldred noticed, had wheeled Keith into the middle of the studio space. He wondered why he had done that.

Lulubelle pivoted round on one hand and flashed into the routine she had shown Eldred, the series of backward flips. Even though he had seen it before, he gasped at the speed. Keith, folded in his wheelchair with his head tilted sideways on his fragile neck, was open-mouthed. As Lulubelle shot towards him, apparently set for a fatal collision, he let out a delighted, high-pitched laugh. His mother half-rose from her seat, her hands over her mouth.

At the very last minute, Lulubelle threw her weight on to her left hand and still going backwards, flipped round him in his wheelchair. The timing was perfectly judged, without a second's loss of speed. The whole studio erupted in applause.

When it faded, Keith's laugh, infectious and exhilarated, still rang out. Eldred found, without knowing why, that his eyes were full of tears.

Simon took Lulubelle aside. 'We should have filmed it,' he said. 'Can you do it again?'

'Sure,' she said.

'Would you rather we filmed it first,' he said, 'without the audience here? To be on the safe side?'

'No,' she said. 'I'm better with an audience.'

'Honey,' he said sincerely, 'it would be hard to better that. You're something else!'

That, Eldred thought, was the turning point. After that, he didn't feel nervous at all. His own run-through went as Lulubelle had predicted: the visual tests they set for him, projected on to a screen the audience could see above his head, were easy enough to begin with. When he coped with them with no difficulty, Simon made signs to the operator to speed the problems up, then to cut the next few sequences and move straight to the ones that were more difficult.

What a very strange little boy, thought Keith. Jumpy and fidgety all the time, his expression ever-changing, his eyes constantly roaming, registering everything around him, then suddenly still, as if turned to stone, the moment someone asked him a question. Not only his quicksilver mind but even his body appeared to be thinking, suspending all activity till the answer arrived.

And 'arriving' did seem to be what the answers did. Eldred didn't appear to be working them out; there wouldn't have been time for it. No, he was frozen in time and space, totally concentrating, listening – then the answer came out of his mouth, while his normally mobile face was expressionless. Keith was mesmerized by him.

Eldred, conscious of Lulubelle and Keith behind him, willing him to be brilliant, forgot about the presence of everyone else and concentrated on the screen. They gave him a buzzer to hold in his hand and click when he found the right answer. The clicks got closer and closer together, the answers came faster and faster, till he was hardly aware of thinking at all, nor of the mounting excitement in the observers. He jumped when, after a final sequence of jumbled shapes in various patterns had been correctly selected to match their assembled forms, some of the crew shouted, 'Yeah!' and ran forward to slap him on the back, while the others applauded.

He looked towards Lulubelle and Keith. Lulubelle raised her fists in the air in a victory salute and Keith grinned and nodded as fast as he could.

'Terrific!' said Janice, kissing him on the top of his head. 'Do you need a break, Eldred? Before you do the random maths test? We can do the interview in the middle if you like, then go on to the other tests, or we can do them all now in one block.'

'Do them now,' he said. He was high on adrenalin. He could see why Lulubelle thrived on applause, how it could bring her to life when she had been crying a moment before. She was glowing now, smiling and giving him the thumbs-up sign, as thrilled by his success as by her own. Keith's eyes were bright and he smiled his wide smile without tiring.

They practised the maths test. Pete stood with Eldred, facing the make-believe audience, a few of the crew primed to shout out numbers and mathematical signs. Seated behind Peter, Janice sat at a computer ready to tap in what was called out. The computer would do the sum and flash the results on the overhead screen, while Eldred did the calculation in his head and spoke the answer into the little microphone clipped to his shirt.

'Start with low numbers and plus or minus signs,' Pete instructed.

Eldred was tense, his fists clenched by his sides. Pete patted his shoulder reassuringly. It was all right for him, Eldred thought; he didn't have to do anything.

'Thirteen!' came the first shout.

'Forty-five!'

'Plus!' shouted the person who had volunteered to call the signs.

Eldred took a deep breath, as he had seen Lulubelle doing, and let it out slowly, in his own time. He answered clearly and politely, a few seconds after the computer had flashed the solution on screen.

They moved on to division and multiplying.

'Sixteen!'

'Thirty-five!'

'Multiply!'

Eldred's attention wandered. 'Five hundred and sixty,' he said absently. You weren't meant to look the camera in the eye, but was it permissible to look around it, to try to see how it worked and how it was manoeuvred, or would that come out as Eldred staring straight out of the television screen into someone's living room?

The contest was not going as well as expected. He sensed disappointment around him.

Rachel Hicks came forward. 'Can I have a word?' she asked Simon.

'Go ahead.'

She murmured something in his ear. 'Sure,' he said.

'Eldred,' said Rachel. 'You've really slowed down on this one. Are you enjoying this test or are you bored?'

'It's all right,' said Eldred, glancing in Mildred's direction. She had told him to be polite.

'Can you think of a way to make it more fun?' she asked him.

Eldred considered this. 'Keith was part of Lulubelle's act,' he said. 'Couldn't they be part of mine?'

Chapter Sixty-four

Afterwards, the presenters and crew disagreed about whether that was the point at which a perfect TV show had started to go wrong.

Janice thought so; she blamed Rachel Hicks. All right, so the boy genius looked slightly bored and, according to Rachel's preliminary researches, had been performing below par, but it was hardly the end of the world. If Rachel had left well alone and not tried to get Eldred more interested, then Eldred would not have suggested involving the other kids and she, Janice, would not have been put in the embarrassing situation of having to point out that letting the little disabled guy ask some of the questions was slowing the whole process down and he would have to be left out.

It wasn't her fault that the other two damn kids had then gone on strike, or that Simon had had to step in and say that neither Lulubelle nor Keith would take part in calling out the numbers and signs but that the computer would flash them up on the screen. This had been accepted by everyone, so no one could say that the show had really begun to go downhill at this point, but there was a slight damper on the atmosphere. We lost the dramatic tension, Janice thought.

The show must go on, Lulubelle had said pacifically, settling back in her seat and taking Keith's hand; after all, it was Eldred's act. She and Keith would stay in the background and give moral support. Eldred had accepted this. The run-through had reached its conclusion smoothly.

The studio audience had filed in. Keith had another snack. Eldred was escorted to the toilet by Mildred, even though he didn't need it, 'in case he wanted to go at the wrong time'. Lulubelle was subjected to further adjustments to her make-up by Lucinda, and emerged with sparkling wings to each eye, which caused Mildred to click her tongue disapprovingly and Eldred to tell Lulubelle she looked wonderful.

The studio audience warm-up had gone well. Keith was in form to do his whole interview again in front of the audience, and they responded to him as wholeheartedly as the crew had.

Lulubelle's performance had been faultless. Agreed, there was a slight hitch when Keith, after his involvement in her spectacular entrance, couldn't stop laughing. It had been funny at first, his mirth infecting the audience, who renewed their laughter each time Lulubelle threw herself into a new contortion or rang the bells on her ears with her toes. Keith had been a real godsend, they thought at first; no need for a prompt to the audience, with Keith acting as cheerleader, always the first to start the laughter and the last to stop.

But he couldn't stop. At intervals during Lulubelle's chat with the presenters, and answering questions from the audience – all of which she handled very professionally, the crew agreed – Keith's chuckle would ring out and it would set Lulubelle off, so she forgot the question and started giggling at Keith instead. They had to cut the filming several times, which was never good news with a studio audience; they got restive if asked to make too many allowances.

Pete thought the show was okay up till then, even with the previous hitches. None of it was serious, he said. His heart only started to miss beats when Eldred came on from the wings while Lulubelle was talking about her circus career and said, loudly and unannounced, 'I've been thinking about this and I don't think she should say which circus she's with.'

The boy had no sense of professionalism at all, which was understandable, since he was unused to public performance in the way that Lulubelle was, but the worst thing seemed to be the way that the two amateurs, Eldred and Keith, unsettled the real star of the show. It was a mistake, some of the crew said, to attempt to have three children on at once. They should have kept them separate.

Janice was blamed for this. She was the one who had talked about interaction between the children. Lulubelle would never have giggled like that if Keith hadn't set her off. And she wouldn't have gone into that long, uninterruptable discussion with Eldred and Keith, in front of a live audience, about whether it was wise for her to risk letting some unspecified person (described by Eldred in a whisper in Keith's ear) find out her whereabouts.

That wasn't the end of it, even when Lulubelle finally gave way to Keith and Eldred's united pressure and asked Simon to cut the part out where she mentioned the name of the circus which currently employed her and her mother. The question was re-worded, Lulubelle gave a more general answer about her field of work, the interview resumed and the audience's attention was regained.

No, the worst part – definitely the worst – began when Eldred, having shone in all his computer tests, and impressed the audience by answering a whole range of maths problems and general knowledge questions thrown at him at random, was asked in his interview to talk about his experience of being a bright child in an average school.

When Janice – and again, it wasn't my fault, thought Janice

resentfully; it was one of the questions proposed by that Rachel Hicks – prompted Eldred to tell the audience what happened at school when he came top of the class too often, and Eldred, after a moment's uncertain silence, said his teacher altered the marks or marked his correct answers as mistakes, Keith had a fit.

Chapter Sixty-five

It could have happened at any time, said Keith's mother. And no, she told a white-faced, shaking Eldred, it was nothing to do with his answer to the question. Keith was not upset by anything Eldred had said. He was simply tired. When he got overtired he sometimes had fits.

For a woman who had been on pins all day, waiting for something to happen, when the crisis occurred she stayed remarkably calm.

It was she who got hold of Simon and told him firmly to make everyone stand back when they rushed forward to help. It was she who held Keith's convulsive little face steady while his eyes rolled and his throat emitted frightening constricted noises. And while Pete sent the sound man running to phone the ambulance, it was Keith's mum who assured Lulubelle that this was only a precaution and Keith would probably come round any second now and be fine.

He did, in fact, come round before the ambulance arrived, and looked round at them all with dazed eyes before they wheeled him off the set and took him to hospital, 'just for a check-up, though we know he's really okay,' as his mother told Lulubelle reassuringly.

At least they had completed the main part of the show, agreed Janice and Peter and Simon. They supposed it could have been worse, after all. But it was a day that nobody would want to go through again.

Eldred and Lulubelle, after persuasion and cups of hot chocolate, were ushered back to the set to complete Eldred's interview, at which both were well-behaved and very subdued. The studio audience were sympathetic, stayed the extra time without complaint, and were generous in their applause at the end of the show.

To anyone who hadn't actually been present, said Janice and Peter, it would look like a smooth-running, smoothly presented show. And it was to their credit as presenters, Simon told them, that it did appear like that. It would make good telly, no doubt about that. The children were real stars, each in their own way. But what a price to pay, they all laughed!

'We should have listened to the old adage,' Pete joked. 'Never work with children or animals!' He poured them all another generous gin and tonic.

The day was not over for the troublesome stars of the show. When Mildred and Lucinda came forward thankfully to collect their children, at the end of a long and nerve-racking day for both mothers, the children refused to go. They insisted on being taken to the hospital to see for themselves whether Keith was really okay.

'Rachel has phoned the hospital,' said Mildred, almost in tears from exhaustion and the stress of surviving most of a day in the studio. 'They're keeping him in for a night but the ward sister says he's fine now, just a bit tired. Now come on, Eldred, we'll get stuck in the rush hour if we don't go home now.'

'Stop crying, for God's sake,' said Lucinda irritably to Lulubelle. 'Anyone would think he had died.'

'He could have done,' sobbed Lulubelle. She was clutching Eldred's hand again and wouldn't let go of him, even when Mildred took his other hand and tried with all her strength to pull him away.

'You've only known him five minutes!' Lucinda exclaimed. 'It's not as though he was a friend of yours, either of you!'

At this, both children protested. 'He is a friend,' they said in unison.

Mildred and Lucinda looked at each other and heaved a deep sigh.

'A very, very short visit,' said Mildred finally. 'And if the Sister won't let you in because you're not relatives, or because he's too tired to see visitors, it's straight home without arguing. All right?'

It was all right. When the ward sister asked them to wait while she went into the little side room of the children's ward to check with Keith's mother, they heard Keith himself urging her to let them come in. 'Five minutes,' she told Mildred and Lucinda. 'Then I'll come in and turf them out.' But she smiled.

Keith's mother came out to see Mildred and Lucinda. The Sister, who had heard the story of their day, left them together in her office and sent a young auxiliary to bring them cups of tea. Eldred and Lulubelle went in to see Keith alone.

He was propped up in bed with extra pillows instead of his headrest, his face looking even paler and smaller against the white pillowcase.

Lulubelle sprang towards him and gave him a kiss. Eldred moved up beside her and patted his arm awkwardly. 'How are you feeling now?'

'Not too bad,' said Keith. His speech sounded much more slurred. 'Tired.'

'Was it too much for you?' asked Lulubelle. He shook his head slowly, almost imperceptibly.

'Were you upset,' asked Eldred, 'by the questions they asked me?'

Keith looked at him directly. Even when very tired, his eyes were piercingly clear. They could pierce your soul, thought Eldred. The thought unnerved him.

'You had a tough time,' Keith said, 'at school. I didn't realize. Not easy to be clever.'

'Don't talk,' said Lulubelle, 'if it wears you out.'

He turned his head and looked at her. His eyes lit up and his face was swept by a sudden wide, sweet smile.

'It was fun today, wasn't it?' he said.

Lulubelle smiled back at him. 'Yes,' she said, 'it was.'

'We were good,' he said, turning the smile now on Eldred. 'All of us. We were *brilliant*. It was worth it, every minute.'

When the Sister came in, they were all laughing.

Chapter Sixty-six

On the way home, Eldred said, 'If someone had a lot of money – if they sold an invention, for instance – and could afford the best medical treatment with the most sophisticated technology, anywhere in the world, could they be cured of anything?'

Mildred, who had been sitting in a stupor of tiredness, took his hand gently. 'No one could cure Keith, love,' she said.

'Not even God?'

'He doesn't seem to,' said Mildred.

'Do you think Jesus really healed people?' asked Eldred. 'Or is it a myth?'

'I don't know, love. Maybe he did.'

'Why doesn't it happen now?'

'Eldred, don't ask me these things. How am I supposed to know?'

'Do you think it was that Jesus was a special person?'

'Yes, probably that's it,' said Mildred. She had never worn these tight, high-heeled shoes for so long at one time. Her feet felt as though they would never revert to their normal shape; they would stay with the toes crammed together into a point for ever now.

'But why,' said Eldred, 'if God is good, would he listen to Jesus' prayers more than to anyone else's? I mean, that doesn't seem fair, does it? To have favourites?' As usual when he got no reply, he attempted to answer his question himself. 'Perhaps,' he said, 'we don't really pray. I mean, maybe people think they're praying but really they're just hoping for the best and thinking at the back of their minds, "This isn't going to work." Maybe that's it. What do you think?'

'Mm,' said Mildred, far away.

'So why,' said Eldred, 'doesn't he give us a few tips on how to pray? If we knew the words... no, that's not it. I'm sure it's not like that, or it would be like a spell, wouldn't it? Like magic. It can't be a question of knowing what words to say or what rituals to use. Mum? Mum?'

'Yes, dear.'

'What's the difference between prayer and magic?'

'Oh, Eldred!'

'I'm only asking.'

'You should know by now I'm not the person to ask, Eldred. Your poor mum is dim.'

He hunched his shoulders. 'You're not. I don't mind if you don't have all the answers. I just wanted your opinion.'

'What was the question again?'

'If prayer is different from magic, what makes it different?'

Mildred frowned. 'I suppose it must be God. Magic isn't anything to do with him, is it? He forbids it.'

'Oh, does he?' Eldred was interested. 'I didn't know that. You mean, wizards and witches and magicians – they're not working with him; they're on their own?'

'I suppose they must be. If he forbids magic, then he can't be with them, can he? Two more stations, Eldred. Get your ticket ready.'

'How do you know he forbids it, Mum? Mum, how do you know...'

'It's in the Bible,' said Mildred. She wanted to be at home, with her feet in a bowl of water, with Edgar making her a cup of tea. She felt as though she had been on a long journey into unknown territory and hadn't seen her husband for weeks.

'In the Bible? Have you read it, Mum?'

'Yes, dear.'

'All of it? It's huge! You don't read books!'

'Not all of it,' Mildred admitted. 'But we did a lot of it at school, and in Sunday school.'

'Were you taught about it by other people, though, or did you read it for yourself? Keith says you have to find out about God yourself first; you can't do it all second-hand; it's not scientific.'

'We were taught,' said Mildred, 'but some of us were interested and read a lot of it for ourselves.'

'Is it a good book?'

'It's not a book,' said Mildred. 'It's lots and lots of books, written at different times over thousands of years.'

'By people who had got to know God for themselves?'

'That's right. One more station, Eldred.'

'Who were they, though? And how did they get to know him, if they weren't taught second-hand but found out for themselves?'

'The early ones were all Jewish,' said Mildred, gathering up her handbag and carrier bag. 'They were prophets and religious leaders who told how to live the commandments in day-to-day life. Then the New Testament – that's the more recent books, about Jesus – was written by people who met him and tried to live like he did himself.'

'What's a prophet?' asked Eldred.

'Someone who listens to God.'

'Listens to God?' Eldred was agog. 'You mean, God talks?'

'Of course, dear,' said Mildred. 'How else would we have the ten commandments? Don't screw up your ticket like that, Eldred; the man won't be able to read the date on it.'

'Mum!' said Eldred. 'How long have you known all this?'

'All what, dear?'

'About God.'

'Always, I suppose,' said Mildred. 'It's something everyone knows, if they grew up Christian, isn't it?'

'Why didn't you ever tell me? How can you say that you're dim and you don't know anything, and all the time you knew all this and you never told me it?'

'I thought you'd learn it in school or something,' said Mildred. 'You do religion at school, don't you?'

'Oh, religion, yes,' said Eldred dismissively. 'But not this. We do myths and religious beliefs and religious practices, Hinduism, Buddhism, Islam and all that. Nobody tells us about God and how you get to know him, or if he really exists.'

The train stopped. Mildred took Eldred's arm with painful firmness as they got off. She was always afraid he might fall down the four-inch gap between the carriage and the platform and his foot would have to be amputated.

They were silent as they walked home. It was only as they reached the front gate that Eldred said, as if to himself, 'Talks to people?

You're sure about this? So what do you have to do to be a prophet? Mum?'

But Edgar was already opening the door.

'I was looking out for you,' he said. 'How did you get on?'

Mildred flung her arms around him. 'Oh, Edgar,' she said, 'you know I never tell you what to do, but let him go to that school, will you, love? I can't go through a day like today again!'

Chapter Sixty-seven

Louise phoned as Edgar and Eldred were sitting down to eat scrambled eggs on toast. Mildred was lying on the sofa, too tired to want a meal. She opened her eyes when the phone rang.

'I'll get it,' said Eldred.

'Eldred!' said Louise. 'How did it go?'

'All right, thanks,' said Eldred. 'It wasn't much like the Oprah Winfrey show, though. They said it was meant to be, but they didn't invite any experts and they didn't involve the audience nearly so much. And the presenters weren't nearly so shrewd. But it went okay.'

'Good,' she said. 'Did they ask you a lot of questions?'

'Yes,' he said. 'Do you want to speak to my dad?'

'No,' she said. 'You'll do. I've got some more good news. I've managed to set up an interview with that project manager from the German chemical company, the one who talked about your machine on the local news – remember?'

'I didn't actually meet him,' said Eldred. 'He just talked about me.'

'Right. Well, now I've arranged a meeting, and some of the press are interested. I don't know yet if we can get a TV crew to cover it too.'

Eldred didn't want to hurt her feelings, when she had been so helpful. He said cautiously, 'I think things have changed a bit, actually, Louise.'

'What do you mean?'

'I think my dad's going to let me go to another school.' He looked across at Edgar for confirmation. Edgar nodded.

'That's good news,' Louise agreed, 'but what does it change?'

'We won't need any more publicity,' Eldred explained, 'because the Head isn't going to make us pay the fees, just the uniforms and extras and things. And Mum has a job now, you see.'

From the sofa, Mildred, her eyes still closed, smiled peacefully.

'This isn't about your school fees, Eldred,' said Louise. 'It's about finding a buyer to develop your recycling process.'

'Oh, I know,' Eldred affirmed, 'but we won't need the newspapers and the TV people. I don't mean you, of course,' he added hastily. 'You're always very welcome.'

'Do you mean you don't want me to set up this meeting?'

Eldred hoped he was only imagining that Louise sounded annoyed with him.

'Of course I'd like to sell the machine,' he said, 'but do I actually have to meet the person? Couldn't he write to me? I mean, he talked about me before without meeting me, didn't he? It's the processing plant he's interested in.'

'No,' she said, 'it isn't. There's a difference between a company buying the rights to a new experimental product, which is a high risk and will involve them in major capital expenditure with no guarantee of the saleability of the results, and an individual project manager becoming intrigued by an innovative process developed by a nine-year-old boy. It gives the whole procedure an added bite.'

'You mean I'm like an added gimmick that might make him buy the patent from me, when he mightn't if it belonged to somebody else?'

'Right. They're bombarded with people trying to find a market for their inventions, Eldred. If you have a novelty value, don't knock it, use it, for God's sake. It could make all the difference between success and obscurity.'

'Oh, right,' Eldred said. 'Well, you'd better speak to my dad.'

'Wait a minute,' said Louise. 'What happened to all your

enthusiasm, Eldred? I'm doing this for you, you know. Don't you want to be a famous inventor at nine years old?'

'It would be nice,' Eldred assented. 'But what I'd like more than anything is to start at this new school. I don't mind missing time off school now, but when I go to the new one I won't have time for publicity; I'll be learning things. And if Mum has to take more time off to take me to places she might lose her job, and she doesn't want to.'

'I'll take you to this one,' said Louise. 'Tell your mum.'

Eldred sighed. 'Could I just meet the man?' he asked. 'Without all the cameras and the interviews? Or does he want publicity too?'

'Eldred,' said Louise, 'this meeting is meant to be mutually beneficial – that means it benefits everyone. Herr Wolfmann gets a bit of attention for his company and for himself, for being sharp enough to spot a valuable invention even when it originates from a child; you get a boost to sell your machine and maybe a market for your future inventions... see?'

'How about you?' said Eldred.

'Pardon?'

'You said mutually beneficial,' Eldred reminded her. 'How would it benefit you?'

'I get to set up the press conference,' said Louise.

'But how does that benefit you?' Eldred pursued.

'The German company will pay me to do it,' she said, after a slight pause, 'because I'm their contact with you. And I renew my contacts with the newspapers and magazines involved, so they're more likely to take a favourable look at the next article or idea I submit to them for publication.'

'Oh, I see,' Eldred said. He went quiet.

'So?' said Louise. 'Is the answer yes?'

'You'll have to speak to my dad,' said Eldred. 'I don't want to hinder your career or anything, Louise, and we're all very grateful indeed for what you've done...'

Edgar held out his hand for the phone. 'Give that to me.'

'Here's Dad,' said Eldred.

'What's the problem?' said Edgar into the receiver. He listened. 'Is this man serious,' he said, 'about buying the patent?'

Mildred sat up and watched him, as though trying to gauge from his face what was being said at the other end of the phone.

'Listen to me,' Edgar said. 'We're all grateful to you for arranging all this publicity for Eldred and his invention, but he's only a child and it's time he got on with his schooling. If he's made into a little celebrity, he won't be accepted by his new classmates, will he? It'll make it harder for him to settle in.'

Another silence.

'I see,' Edgar said, 'but we'll need to discuss this as a family. If Eldred's invention is as good as everyone seems to think, it will sell, won't it, with or without the publicity? What Eldred needs is to be left to get on with some proper schoolwork. Yes, I understand what you're saying. Of course, yes, of course. Tomorrow evening. Very well. After seven, then we'll have finished our tea. Goodbye.'

'What have you fixed?' asked Eldred.

'Miss Palmer is coming tomorrow evening to hear our decision.'

'I don't know if I want to see her,' said Eldred. 'I'm fed up with publicity. She only wants to get me to do more.'

Mildred took away his plate of cold, uneaten scrambled egg. 'A nice hot bath for you,' she said. 'You're overtired, Eldred. It's been a long day. You can have milk and ginger biscuits in bed.'

Eldred allowed himself to be comforted and led away. Even the inventor of an industrial process which had aroused the interest of an international company could get tired of the limelight and prefer privacy and ginger biscuits sometimes.

Chapter Sixty-eight

'The sooner he starts at that new school the better,' said Edgar. 'It'll get him out of the limelight and he can be a normal child.'

Mildred raised her eyebrows.

'More normal,' Edgar amended. 'They'll know how to deal with a bright child, at Abingdale. Mr Clinford didn't get annoyed with him, even when he asked all those questions and took books off the shelves and strewed them all over the floor, did he?'

'No,' said Mildred. 'But it won't be Mr Clinford teaching him. Shouldn't we ask to meet his class teacher, Edgar, before we decide?'

'We could do,' Edgar mused. 'Though I can't see that Eldred could be any worse off than where he is now. Why didn't he tell us earlier, about that Mrs Garcia? The woman sounds a menace – telling him to shut up in class, changing his grades to suit herself. Who does she think she is?'

'Maybe we didn't listen to him when he did tell us,' said Mildred. 'He did complain. We told him to have more respect for his teachers.'

'Nonsense,' Edgar said. 'I would never have told him that. The woman's not fit to teach, Mildred, if she can't give every child their due merits. I've a good mind to make a complaint to the school.'

'Oh, don't!' pleaded Mildred. 'You'd only cause Eldred embarrassment. But let's get him out of there before that programme gets shown on telly, or she really will make his life a misery.'

'He said something about Mrs Garcia? On TV?'

'He must have said something at the preliminary interview, Edgar, and the presenters asked him directly what happened at school when he came top of the class too often. He didn't know how to get out of answering; I could see he didn't want to answer. Then some people in the audience asked him about being bored in class, and what kind of things he was being taught, and they started to laugh.'

'Laughed at Eldred?'

'Not at him, no. They laughed because it seemed so ridiculous that he was drawing little pictures of Henry the Atom, or whatever it was, when he'd been answering complicated questions about the nuclear power process.'

'It is ridiculous,' said Edgar grimly. 'It's gone on long enough. We'll tell Mr Clinford we accept that place for Eldred at his school, Mildred. It's the best offer we're likely to have, isn't it? They might make him wait till next term to change schools, in any case.'

'We could insist that he doesn't,' said Mildred.

Edgar was surprised. 'Us? Insist? It's up to the school, Mildred!'

'Mr Clinford seemed keen to have him,' Mildred pointed out. 'He was quick enough off the mark, after Eldred was on the News.'

'What about his present school, though? They won't let him leave in the middle of a term, surely? We owe it to them to do things decently.'

'We don't owe them anything,' said Mildred.

Edgar looked at her. 'You know, you've changed,' he said. 'You never used to say boo to a goose.'

'It's different, standing up for yourself and standing up for a child,' Mildred said. 'You can do all kinds of things you wouldn't normally do.'

'Like mixing with TV people at a studio all day,' Edgar said. 'You won't be in any state to go to work tomorrow, Mildred, that's for sure. You'd better phone them, first thing in the morning.'

'I'm phoning nobody,' said Mildred. 'I'm going.' Seeing Edgar open his mouth, she said, 'Don't tell me I can't do it, Edgar. I can, and I'm going to.'

'Yes, dear,' he said meekly.

'I'll go and take Eldred his biscuits,' she said. 'I think I heard him letting the bathwater out. By the way,' she said, from the kitchen doorway, 'what took you so long to decide? About the school?'

'I wasn't sure,' said Edgar, 'if it might be better to wait and aim for the boarding school. The standards might be higher than at a local one.'

'Are you sure now,' said Mildred, 'that Abingdale's the best place for him? I mean, if they offered him a free place there, he might get other offers – even from one of those public schools.'

Edgar shook his head. 'What made me decide was you. It'd do no good to send him away from home, Mildred. You'd pine.'

She was shocked. 'You can't decide that because of me! He might be better off in one of those schools, surrounded by clever people who can answer all his questions. Every question he asks me, Edgar, I say, "I don't know." No wonder he's frustrated.'

'He'll get frustrated anywhere,' said Edgar, 'because he wants to learn everything about everything. All he needs is a school that'll show him how to find answers for himself; you heard what Mr Clinford said. But where will he find anyone, in boarding school, who'll make him hot chocolate or bring him biscuits in bed when he's upset? Think about that one, Mildred. He's still only nine years old.'

'I know,' she said. 'I know. But I'm still not happy about you making the decision because you think I'd pine away without him. That can't be right, love. You know I'd let him go, if it was for his good.'

'Nothing wrong with a bit of letting go,' Edgar conceded. 'At nine years old, a child needs a bit of freedom, I grant you. What he doesn't need is his parents letting him go, full time, to a lot of strangers.'

'I don't want to coddle him,' said Mildred fearfully. 'After all, in the circumstances, his birth being unusual and coming when we didn't expect...'

'No need to worry,' said Edgar robustly. 'He won't get spoilt. You can't get away from it, Mildred: there's people much better equipped to educate him than us, but they can't take the place of parents. The best parents Eldred could have are the ones he's got. It's meant to be like that.'

Mildred looked thoughtful. 'I suppose we didn't choose him,' she said, 'any more than he chose us. So maybe it is meant.'

Edgar gave her a wink. 'While you're being the perfect mother to our son,' he said, 'his dad wouldn't mind a cocoa. If you're too tired, I'll make it myself,' he added.

Mildred kissed the top of his head. 'I'm not the perfect mother,' she said, 'or the perfect wife, come to that, but cocoa is something I can manage.'

Chapter Sixty-nine

'Dear Keith,' wrote Eldred in the history lesson, while his fellow pupils were chewing the ends of their biros and wondering what to write and he had long finished, 'it was nice of you to write to me. What make is your computer? I'm glad you didn't have to stay long in hospital and you're feeling better now. Thank you for praying for me. I don't think anyone ever did that before. Maybe my mum.

'I did what you suggested and read the four gospels: Matthew, Mark, Luke and John. You were right: they don't agree on the details. There's quite a lot of it I don't understand. I wish you lived nearer so I could call round and you could explain it to me. I don't want to tire you but I would just like to ask you two questions. If you can't answer them, that's all right. What does it mean when Jesus says, "I am the way, the truth and the life"? Also, when he says, "If you forgive someone's sins they are forgiven and if you retain someone's sins they are retained," who retains the sins? The person who did the sin or the person who doesn't forgive them?

'Have you heard from Lulubelle? I had a postcard from Cheshire and she says the circus is coming down south. Wouldn't it be great if we could go and see the show? Then I could see you as well and we could have a good talk.

'My dad has told the headmaster of the new school they want me to go there as soon as possible. I can't wait to go. We have to go and meet my class teacher tomorrow at five o'clock.

'I'm writing this in class, the last lesson of the day, and I'm going to the library on the way home. I might have another read of those gospels and see if I understand any more of it. Sometimes if you read something over and over you see something new in it. What do you like to read? You said you had all the James Bond films on video. Which do you like best? Which was the one with the crocodiles in? Wasn't that wicked?

'Must go, write soon, lots of love, Eldred Jones.

'PS – What do you have to do to become a prophet? Do you know anyone God talks to? Has he ever talked to you?

'PPS – Sorry, just realized that's three more questions as well as the other two. If you can only answer one, can you make it the last one? Thanks. Eldred.'

In the reference library after school, rows of students sat hunched over the long table, elbow to elbow. Eldred, finding no room, sat on the floor and opened the New Testament. It fell open at a page and he started reading halfway down. There it was again! 'I am the way, the truth and the life.' Whose life, Eldred pondered? Everybody's life? Or the only life worth having – as when people lay back in the sunshine and said, 'Oh, this is the life!'? Or the source of life, like a river is a source of life to the ocean?

He tore out a page of his exercise book – near the end, in the hope that by the time Mrs Garcia discovered the theft Eldred would no longer be one of her pupils. With a blunt pencil, he started doodling. Sometimes it was easier to think on paper. He drew a river flowing into the sea, then scribbled it out. The image didn't seem right. Then he drew a tree with its roots in the water. Better. A bird hatching out of an egg. Getting warmer, he felt.

Then, from memory of a textbook found in the Sister's office in one of the women's wards in the hospital when he was five, he drew the female reproductive system and an egg in one ovary. He sketched a blur of travelling sperm and shaded one in.

Lying on his stomach to get a closer view, he re-drew the system with the next stage of progress, the moment of contact between the sperm and the egg. He drew an arrow pointing towards the fused elements and wrote in large capitals, THE MOMENT OF LIFE and then, I AM THE LIFE.

As he did, a strange sensation passed through him and he shuddered violently. He sat upright, looking around to see if anything had happened to anyone else, but they were all still writing steadily. It obviously wasn't an earthquake then, he reasoned, but something that affected only Eldred.

He bent over the paper again, and wrote, WAY, TRUTH, LIFE,

under the diagram. Then, without knowing why, he wrote, in very small letters, 'violence, rape, crime, womb, baby'.

It was coming back to him again, the way it had in the hospital, that terrible memory. Why now? Why wouldn't his mother explain to him what had been happening to her while her unborn child screamed and quivered and felt that oppressive weight of darkness all around it, a darkness so opaque that even when he had finally, after an eternity, been propelled down that long tunnel and into the light, his heart had refused to stop pounding and his lungs had refused to inflate?

What had happened that had affected him so badly that for five years of his life he had been unable to breathe for more than an hour at a time unaided, and he had thought that an oxygen mask was part of a child's normal clothing?

And what zeal to find out the truth had driven him, as a child who could barely walk, to begin his night-time forays for information, until finally, at the age of five, his researches brought him in contact with that article on pre-birth memories resulting in childhood trauma and impaired function of the pulmonary organs?

Eldred found he was on his feet, packing his bag, and heading for the indexes, but others were ahead of him. The queue at the information desk was even longer. In a trance, it seemed to him, he drifted towards the only source of information that seemed in low demand – the microfiche reader in the newspaper archive section. Someone had left a fiche in the machine. The image on the screen was out of focus.

Eldred adjusted the focus control and found himself looking at the front page of the local newspaper, dated ten years ago. He scanned the headlines and was about to move on when a familiar name caught his eye.

Police were appealing for information following the attack in West Grove municipal cemetery last week on a local woman, Mrs Mildred Jones.

Mrs Jones, aged thirty-eight, who had been married for eleven years and had no children, had been severely beaten, raped and left for dead. Mrs Jones could not identify her assailant and no witnesses had been present at the incident, which had occurred at around four-thirty on the afternoon of Thursday July 6th.

A battered grey Ford Escort had been parked near the entrance to the cemetery at about that time. Anyone who had seen it or had noticed anyone behaving suspiciously should contact the police immediately on the following number.

Chapter Seventy

They reached a compromise. Louise would set up a meeting with Herr Wolfmann and one of his colleagues. Eldred would be there, and Edgar. Mildred would not be required to attend. ('Your turn,' she told Edgar.)

Eldred would have a chance to talk about his invention and hear Herr Wolfmann's proposals on how to promote and market it, without the press being there. It would not, Louise promised, be anything like a chat show.

'A private business meeting,' she said. 'All right, Eldred?'

'All right,' he said. He was sorry he had been dismissive on the phone, and surprised at how pleased he was to see her when she arrived.

The press would be invited to come only after the meeting, when everything had been finalized. They would be free to ask questions of Eldred and Herr Wolfmann and, if everything had gone smoothly, photograph the senior European executive and the schoolboy inventor signing the contract together and shaking hands.

'That will be acceptable,' Edgar consented. 'But when that's done...'

'When it's finalized, I'll let you get on with your lives,' Louise promised. 'Are you looking forward to starting at the new school, Eldred?'

'I think so, yes. I expect I'll look forward to it more when I've met some of the people who'll be in my class. I feel moderately apprehensive about the prospect of approaching a whole classful of unknown faces,' Eldred said solemnly, 'though recently I have made a couple of new friends, quite easily as it happened, so perhaps my apprehensions are unfounded.'

'Perhaps so,' said Louise. 'Who are the new friends, Eldred?'

'Lulubelle and Keith. She's an acrobat in a circus; he's a boy who's had fifteen operations. And believes in God,' he added.

'The children from the TV show? You got on well with them, then?'

'Yes. Possibly because we are all a bit peculiar,' Eldred said.

'Aren't we all?' said Louise with a laugh. 'You, me, Lulubelle, and the human race.'

'You're not obviously peculiar,' observed Eldred.

'Thank you, Eldred,' said Louise. 'I hide it well. Now, I'd better let you good people have some peace. Thanks for inviting me, Mr Jones. Mrs Jones, thanks for the coffee and cake. You're quite happy with the arrangements for this meeting then, Eldred? No questions you want to ask me before I leave?'

'Well, there is one,' Eldred said.

Edgar groaned. 'Wouldn't you know it,' he said. His eyes strayed longingly towards the television screen. One of his favourite programmes was about to begin.

'About the meeting?' asked Louise.

'No. About whether you've heard God speak.'

She laughed again. 'I wasn't expecting that one! Yes, I suppose I have, once or twice. Not a booming voice from the sky or anything. An inner voice, I suppose you'd call it.'

'What did he say to you, Louise? If you don't mind me asking?'

'Oh, it was once when I wasn't sure what to do with my life, whether to marry someone I liked very much but hadn't known very long. He was waiting to hear whether he'd been offered an overseas job, when I first met him, and when he heard that he had and would have to leave within a month, he asked me to go with him and marry him. I was almost a hundred per cent certain I wanted to and it was right, but to be on the safe side I prayed.'

'And God told you something else?' Eldred prompted.

'Yes. I felt it was him, because it was actually the opposite of what I was telling myself, and I did hear a voice that time, quite clearly...'

'What sort of voice?' asked Eldred.

'Eldred, these are very personal questions you're asking,' Mildred chided. But she'd put down the *TV Times* and was listening. Edgar, embarrassed by this open talk about God, was fiddling with the volume-off button on the remote control but, intrigued despite himself, was also keeping an ear open for Louise's answers.

'A calm voice,' Louise said. 'Very reassuring, very certain.'

'And what did he say to you? Did he say, "Don't marry him"?'

'Not exactly, no. He said, "Where your treasure is, that's where your heart will be too."'

Eldred frowned. 'What does it mean?'

'It's a line from scripture, from one of the gospels. Jesus actually said it in the context of telling people not to hoard possessions in this life, because they'll keep you earthbound and prevent you from being free to enjoy the real treasures of heaven. But in the context of what was going on in my life at that time, what the word "treasure" conjured up in my mind was my heritage in the Church. I'd had good experiences of growing up in my Church – I'm Catholic – and this man I was thinking of marrying had had quite negative experiences of church people, so he was quite negative about my involvement in it.

'And I realized that if my heart still treasured the Church that had given such a lot to me, and I was giving my heart to him in marriage, then my heart would be divided, wouldn't it?'

'Wouldn't he have let you still go to your church?' asked Eldred.

'Oh, I expect he would; he wouldn't have considered it his business to tell me whether to go or not to go to church on a Sunday, but it involved much more than that. I had a whole set of values and priorities, taught to me by people within that Church, which on the whole I still agreed with and wanted to live by. If his view of the Church was so negative, then sooner or later his reaction to me would be negative too, because he couldn't treasure what I did. His heart would be in a different place from me.'

'Oh,' said Eldred, thinking. 'And I expect you might have discovered this, maybe after a couple of years, and you only didn't see it then because you hadn't had time to get to know what he thought about lots of things that might be quite important really but hadn't come up in conversation yet?'

'Precisely,' said Louise, smiling.

'So God gave you a shortcut, like a glimpse into the knowledge you would have found out for yourself but not in the time available to you to decide?'

'You could put it that way, Eldred, yes.'

'Would he talk to me, do you think? Do you have to have faith?'

'If he'd create you, Eldred, why wouldn't he talk to you? You take a continuing interest in your inventions, don't you? And they're just machines. Human beings are much more interesting to have a relationship with than machinery. Of course your Creator wants to stay involved in every detail of your life.'

'But only if you have faith?'

'No. He's equally interested in everybody. But to enjoy a relationship with him, you have to – maybe not have great faith, but give him the benefit of the doubt, at least. You can't get to know someone if you've convinced yourself he isn't worth knowing or doesn't exist.'

'No,' said Eldred. 'I can see that. But is he more interested in some things than other things? I mean, whether one of his children marries the right person for them is obviously important to him, isn't it, if he's meant to be the Father, like Jesus says? But what about, say, if somebody invents something and doesn't know who to trust with it, or someone goes to a new school and doesn't know which person might want to be friends with them, or if...'

Louise smiled at him. 'Eldred, if it's important to you, it's important to him.'

'Oh really? I didn't know that.' He thought for a moment, frowning. 'Yes,' he said. 'That is consistent.'

'I'll see myself out,' Louise said. 'Herr Wolfmann told me to tell you, by the way, Eldred, that he's not sure his English is up to the challenge but he's very much looking forward to meeting you.'

Chapter Seventy-one

They were worried about Grandad. It was unlike him to be depressed.

'Even you can't get through to him,' Andrew told Keith. Keith was in bed, having his afternoon rest, and Andrew, contrary to his mother's instructions, was sitting on his own bed in their shared room, talking to him.

'He's upset about Uncle Dan,' said Keith. 'It's natural.'

'I know. But why won't he talk to us? It's like he doesn't want to know us any more.'

'Perhaps it's the other way round,' said Keith. 'He feels ashamed, as if we wouldn't want to know him.'

'That's silly. Why would he think that?'

'How would you feel if the police were trying to contact your son in connection with a series of violent assaults?'

'Yes, but it's not Grandad's fault, is it?'

'He may not see it like that. He feels responsible. He brought him up.'

'He brought Mum up as well. She doesn't go round attacking people, does she?' said Andrew.

'No.'

'Keith,' said Andrew, after a few minutes. 'Do you know what made him like that? I mean, could we have helped him, do you think, and we didn't, while he was with us?'

'I don't know,' said Keith. 'I've thought about it a lot. The only thing I ever thought was strange about Uncle Dan was all the stories he told and the games he played with us.'

'We liked them, Keith! They were great! We used to think what a good uncle he was because he was always ready to play with us and tell all those stories.'

'Yes, but he seemed to believe them.'

'What d'you mean?'

'Well, I never thought anything of it when I was little. Like you said, he was really fun to have around. But when I started to grow out of stories and pretending to be rulers of the universe, it seemed to me that he hadn't.'

'Hadn't grown out of them?'

'Yes.'

'How has that got anything to do with assaulting people?'

'I don't know if it has, but I think it might have. If he couldn't tell the difference between the stories you tell to frighten yourself as a child, and reality; if he's living out different stories in his head all the time...'

'You mean, if he really believed he was Superman, come to save the world, and wasn't just acting it out to amuse us kids?'

'Yes. Or the scary stuff he used to like – curse of the werewolves and all those spooky things he pretended to be. He was always watching horror films, wasn't he?'

'I watched them with him. He used to laugh, all the way through. He never took them seriously, Keith.'

'No, but that worried me really. I mean, they were about people getting terrified out of their lives and threatened with grisly deaths, and murdered. They're meant to give people a shock – a thrill of fear, or whatever. Isn't somebody a bit sick if he finds it funny?'

'I never thought about it. I remember him as a really kind, funny person,' said Andrew. 'I can't imagine him attacking anybody. Can you?'

'No. But I can't imagine anybody doing that. I can't imagine what it must feel like inside, to want to do it or to feel compelled to beat up and rape some helpless stranger. But I suppose everybody who does must be somebody's uncle or son or brother, mustn't they? I mean, they're not a separate species from the rest of the human race.'

'Do you think he'd be different, if we saw him now, Keith? Would we see him walk in the door and think, "Oh, there's Uncle Dan," or would he seem like someone else?'

Keith was silent for a minute. Then he said, 'I think he'd seem different. He must be different, if he's done all that.'

'But maybe he was like that before, and we just didn't see it. So if we saw him again, maybe we'd just see nice Uncle Dan who told us stories and brought us presents...'

'No,' said Keith. 'I don't think so. He might have had a tendency to be violent, even when we knew him, and we didn't see it, as little boys. But he hadn't lived it out then; he still had a choice of whether to be Uncle Dan or whether to be a man who threw off the family's restraints and let his violence loose on other people, and at that time he was choosing to be the kind uncle. When he went away, he made the other choice. He's not Uncle Dan now. He's somebody who has to be caught and locked up, for his own safety and everyone else's.'

Andrew kicked Keith's wheelchair. 'Don't say that! You're as bad as Grandad, saying we'll all come to wish he was dead! To me, he'll always be Uncle Dan anyway.'

'That's fine,' said Keith. 'As long as it's the real Uncle Dan you keep loving, not the fantasy. We didn't know what he could do then. We do know now.'

Andrew scowled at him. 'That still doesn't make me want him to be dead.'

'Grandad didn't say he'd stopped loving Dan, did he?' Keith said. 'He said we might come to wish he'd died, instead of getting into what he has done. He's not disowning him, Andrew. He's saying he believes it would have been less harmful for Dan if he'd physically died, and maybe less of a tragedy even for his family, who've been dreading hearing that he's dead ever since he left. He doesn't want Dan to be dead, and he's not cutting him out of the family. But he wishes the rapist in him had never come to life.'

'You don't understand anything,' said Andrew angrily.

'I wasn't as close to him as you were,' Keith said. 'What did you like about him, Andrew?'

'He spent time with me,' said Andrew. He swallowed. 'He'd call me his best buddy – "Hey, best buddy, want to be Dracula's apprentice?" He'd dress up for it – black cloak, everything. He'd put his cloak over me and we'd fly off into the night, looking for a victim.' He hesitated. 'The victim was only Action Man or something, except once... once it was me. He put his fangs in and blindfolded me.' His voice shook slightly. 'He put his hands round my throat and then he bit me. Really. I mean, for real. I had to push him off me.' Tears collected in Andrew's eyes. He turned to leave the room.

'Listen,' said Keith, 'before you go. Can we talk about him again sometime?'

'Why? We'd only argue.'

'It doesn't matter if we don't agree. But agreeing not to talk about him, the way this family has been doing since he left, is like saying he is dead.'

'Yes, all right.'

'And Andrew... when I'm gone, will you do the same? Don't let everyone stop talking about me, for fear of upsetting anyone else?'

'Keith! I wish you wouldn't keep saying those things!'

'I'm not saying I'm going imminently,' said Keith. 'I might not die for a long time. But if everyone keeps pretending it's not going to happen, are they going to be able to change when it does? Or are you all going to start acting as though it hasn't happened?'

'We can hardly do that. Even though I think you're a pain in the bum, Keith, I am going to notice you're not around, you know!'

Keith laughed. 'Thanks. But seriously, it's dangerous to avoid talking about difficult things, isn't it? They just get driven underground.'

'Maybe that's what happened to Uncle Dan,' said Andrew sombrely. 'Maybe everyone did notice there was something not right about him and everyone was too nice to mention it – or too frightened. Is it all right to pray for him, do you think?'

'Of course it is. He must need it, if anyone does.'

'I can't pray for him to be found, though, Keith; I just can't.'

'Don't then.'

'Can you?'

Keith took a deep breath. 'Yes,' he said. 'I'm sorry, but I can't stop thinking about those women. I know we don't know them, but they're precious to somebody too, aren't they? They're somebody's aunt or daughter or something. Yes, I am praying that he gets caught, Andrew. Quickly.'

Chapter Seventy-two

Lulubelle's ambition now was to work towards being able to do what Lucia and Carmel did: reach the top of the pyramid unaided, by springing up from the trampoline, rather than being passed up from hand to hand.

She spoke to Mr Mannfield about practising jumping from the trampoline up to a platform. As she got better at it, the platform could be raised higher.

He was uncertain about the safety aspect. The platform Lucinda climbed up to, to reach the trapeze, was too high but could easily be lowered. But there needed to be a safety net all around it. He agreed to discuss it with Ian, the leader of the acrobatic troupe, and let her know. In the meantime, she could have time to practise on the trampoline, as long as the more senior acrobats weren't using it.

Lulubelle had been practising for an hour now, and she was fed up. Her trampolining wasn't bad at all; she could get the height, and had no trouble landing either back on the trampoline or on the ground. What she needed to practise was landing on a raised platform.

Arto was rehearsing, across the ring. He would easily lower the platform for her; he could do it on his own. But he couldn't climb up to it; even if he'd been agile enough, the rope ladder would have torn under his weight.

It was terrible to want to do something so badly and have to wait to get started, Lulubelle thought. How could she perfect a new technique, that she knew she could do if only she practised, when she couldn't even start the practice? If she got it right, as she felt in her bones she would, she wouldn't need a safety net around her anyway. Lucinda never used to use one, even for high wire. She did now, but she was older. Young, talented acrobats who appeared on TV shows shouldn't need such things.

There were props of various heights in the wings: tubs and stands used by the seals; step-ladders and towers used by the clowns. She could probably use one of those. She'd just have to work out the height she needed first.

She tugged on the cord that kept the rope ladder tied to one side, and let the ladder dangle to the ground, then started to climb it as she'd seen Lucinda do so many times. About fifteen steps up, she thought was probably the right height to jump, for starters. If she could find an object that height, that would do fine.

The hollow wooden tower would probably do. It was on castors; the clowns dragged it in and out, sometimes with one of them inside it, so it couldn't be too heavy to shift into the ring. With a bit of effort, she found she could do it. It was quiet in the Big Top this morning. Early morning was a good time. Apart from herself, there was only Arto, who as usual was totally absorbed in his practice.

He was rehearsing his act with the seesaw. He would call people from the audience – the heaviest adults – and sit four of them on the seesaw, going up and down. Then when everyone was laughing at the sight, he would lift the seesaw off its stand, balance it over his shoulder and walk off. It caused a riot.

Lulubelle loved to watch him. He made it appear so effortless. It was only now, seeing him practise it with weights instead of members of the audience, that you saw the hard work. Sweat ran into his eyes and blinded him, and the veins in his neck looked fit to burst. Relentlessly, he practised his craft, over and over again, till he could create the illusion that the heavily laden seesaw was feather-light.

But she had work of her own to do now; she couldn't stand here watching Arto. She positioned the tower near the rope ladder, climbed the ladder and swung herself over on to the top of the tower to assess its height. Yes, that should be about right.

She dragged the trampoline nearer, pacing out the distance between it and the tower. Then, marking out a starting point a good length back from the trampoline, she launched herself towards it in a series of handsprings, landed squarely in the centre of the trampoline and shot upwards towards the top of the tower, landing neatly on her feet and flinging out her arms for balance.

'No problem, Lulubelle!' she said aloud. Safety net, indeed! This tower was as safe as houses, perfectly stable, and her judgment and balance were good. 'Now,' she told herself, 'let's try it with a somersault in the uplift.'

Grabbing the rope ladder, she swung herself down. Out of the corner of her eye, she saw one of the maintenance men come into the ring, through the performers' entrance tunnel. She might have to be quick, if she wanted a few more practices. The men didn't like the props to be moved, sometimes, if it got in the way of something they were doing. She hoped he was here to work on the seats or the rigging, which would keep him out of the ring and avoid him asking her what she was doing. So she ignored him instead of turning to wave hello as she normally would have done, and hoped he'd ignore her in return.

This time she was more confident, running from the scuff-mark she'd made as her starting point. The handsprings were stronger, higher, and her launch from the trampoline more energetic, giving her the force for one perfect somersault in the air before landing, arms out, on the tower.

Something touched her hand. Flinching, she saw him hanging on the rope ladder, his arm stretched out towards her, touching her hand. He was grinning. The teeth either side of his front two were filed into points. He was wearing the anorak hood with his blue jacket. The hood was red.

Lulubelle screamed, wrenched her arm away, and pulled backwards. As he went to step from the rope ladder on to the tower, she threw herself sideways, off the tower and down to the ground, landing on her back and lying still, at an awkward angle with feet and hands splayed out, like a ragdoll carelessly flung down by a child who had outgrown it.

Chapter Seventy-three

'Dear Lulubelle,' wrote Eldred, upstairs in his room at home, 'I have so much homework since I started at Abingdale School that this will only be a short note. I don't have time to write letters in lessons any more because Mr Dabrowski – that's my class teacher – has set me a project. So if I finish my work before the others, I have to get out my project and do some more work on it. It's really good, though.

'The first week, I started a project on aviation but I got bored with that because all the good information was in one book and there didn't seem much point in just copying it out. So I asked him if I could change and he said I could, and now I am doing a project on prophets. So far, I am looking at books on (or by) Mohammed, Buddha, Mahatma Gandhi, and the prophecies of Isaiah foretelling Jesus Christ. Do you know anything about them or any other really spectacular prophets?

'I hope you get this before the circus leaves Snelcombe. I've written a note on the envelope asking the Post Office to forward it if you've moved on, if they know where Mannfield's Circus has gone.

'Things are happening with my organic waste recycling plant. You remember I told you Louise had set up a meeting with a German businessman, and I had an uneasy feeling he might not be the right person to sell the rights to? Well, Louise said it was okay to pray about anything that was important to you, so I prayed about that and asked Keith to as well, and he prayed too.

'The next day Louise phoned and said Herr Wolfmann – that's the businessman – had been called back to Germany by his company, so the meeting and press conference had to be called off. And the day after that, Bruce Mackeson phoned (the farm manager who gave me lots of useful information which helped me perfect the design of the machine) and said he and some other farmers had got together a consortium to bid for the machine and develop it, and I would be one of the partners and not only be paid for the rights but share in the profits it will make.

'Louise wasn't sure this was better at first, because she thought Herr Wolfmann's company would be annoyed with her, but when I told her I'd prayed for Herr Wolfmann to go away if he wasn't the right person, she laughed and said it must be okay, and it served her right for telling me I could talk to God about anything I liked and he'd answer me, and she'd be more careful who she told that to next time. So we're going ahead with Bruce Mackeson, and Louise has decided to come in as a partner too.

'How is your practising going for the new move you mentioned – the handsprings leading to the trampoline jump to the platform? It must be hard to judge the distances accurately. How long do you have to practise for every day?

'Must go, lots of love, write when you can, love Eldred.

'PS – Keith was asking if I'd heard from you. He hasn't been well again. Can you send him another postcard soon? Lots of love, E.J.

'PPS – By the way – I hope you don't mind me asking – does it ever bother you that you don't know who your father might be? You don't think your mother hates him, do you?'

'He hardly touched his tea again,' said Mildred.

'Wants to get on with his homework,' Edgar said. 'He'll be all right when he settles down at this school. At least he's not bored all day now.'

'I hope he's not fretting for his old friends,' said Mildred. 'I said he could go to the park and meet them for football after school but he said he was tired. You don't think something's troubling him, do you? Edgar?'

'What? No, of course not, Mildred; don't fuss. If he says he's tired, he's tired, that's all. Only natural, starting at a new school, two years ahead of his age and all, and in the middle of a term.'

'I hope you're right,' she said thoughtfully. 'I'll just pop upstairs and see if he wants anything.'

'Leave him to finish his homework,' Edgar said. 'He'll be down in five minutes, most likely, to watch The Bill.'

As Mildred hesitated, the phone rang. Edgar didn't move.

'Eldred!' Mildred shouted up the stairs, covering the receiver in her hand. 'It's for you.'

'Who is it?' Eldred shouted back.

'It's that girl. Lulubelle.'

Eldred hurtled down the stairs and snatched the receiver out of Mildred's hand. 'Lulubelle! I was just writing to you. How are you?'

'Fed up,' said Lulubelle. 'I hurt my back; I've been lying on a board for a week.'

'Is it bad? Can't you move?'

'It's better than it was. I had some physio. But I'm sick I can't rehearse. Did I tell you I had this new move, with a mini-trampoline?'

'Is that how you got hurt?'

'Yes, mistimed it and landed awkwardly. I'll probably have to lie flat for another week.'

'That's sad for you,' said Eldred. 'I can't imagine you keeping still. Have you got any books?'

'Only school stuff and I don't feel like it,' she said.

'I could send you some books,' said Eldred. 'What kind do you like?'

'I don't really,' she admitted. 'I like comics best.'

'Shall I send you some comics, then?'

'Mum got me all this week's,' she said. Her voice was flat, unlike the Lulubelle he knew.

'I've got some old ones,' he said. 'I'll ask Mum to post them tomorrow on her way to work. Are you still in Snelcombe?'

'Yes, but not for much longer. You couldn't come up and see me, Eldred, could you?'

He was distressed. 'I wish I could, but I don't see how. Mum goes on night shift from Friday, and she's working the weekend.'

'Oh, that's all right,' said Lulubelle. 'I thought you probably couldn't. I have to go now, Eldred. I sneaked out to use the phone but the money's going. You will send me the letter you were writing, won't you, even though you've spoken to me?'

'Yes, of course I will.'

'Post it tomorrow,' she said, 'even if it's not finished, okay?'

'Okay,' he said, but she had been cut off.

'How is Lulubelle?' asked Mildred.

'Injured,' he said. 'If someone gets up and walks when they're meant to be lying flat, would they make a back injury worse?'

'I expect so, yes,' said Mildred. 'Would you like a chocolate biscuit while you watch The Bill?'

'No, thanks,' said Eldred. 'I'm going to add a bit to a letter. Then I'll probably go to bed,' he said.

'It's very early! Are you tired again, Eldred?'

'No,' he said listlessly, 'not really.' He left the room.

'There is something wrong,' said Mildred. 'I'm sure of it.'

'Nonsense,' said Edgar. 'We all get a bit tired from time to time. You take it easy yourself, Mildred, if you're going to start these night shifts. Any chance of a cup of tea before the programme starts?'

Chapter Seventy-four

Eldred awoke with a start as Mildred pulled him upright in bed and hugged him. It was pitch dark, the middle of the night.

'What...?' he said groggily.

'You were screaming your head off,' Mildred told him. 'Did you have a bad dream?'

'Oh,' he said, remembering. 'Lulubelle. She was in a wheelchair, like Keith.'

'Well, it was only a dream,' said Mildred. 'Lulubelle's a survivor; her back will get better all right. Go back to sleep now.'

'No,' he said, holding on to her. 'Don't leave me.'

'What's wrong?'

'Nothing,' he said. 'Just don't go yet. Talk to me.'

'Eldred, it's two o'clock in the morning. Your father's asleep.'

'Talk to me for a little while,' he pleaded.

'We'd wake him up, Eldred. He has to work in the morning. And you've got school.' She looked at his face and relented. 'Put your dressing-gown on and come downstairs then. Want some hot chocolate?'

'Yes, please. Wait for me,' he added urgently, as she reached the door. 'Don't go down without me.'

'What is this?' Mildred scolded, in a whisper. 'A big boy like you!'

Downstairs, she turned on the lamp and the electric fire. 'Sit there,' she said, 'and keep warm', but he followed her into the kitchen.

She didn't say another word until he was curled up beside her on the sofa and had eaten two biscuits. Then she patted his shoulder and said, 'Something's bothering you, isn't it?'

'No,' said Eldred.

'Is it the kids at school?'

'No, they're fine.'

'Have you made any friends?'

'Yes.'

'Has anyone said any more about you not having all the proper uniform yet?'

'No.'

'And how are you getting on with Mr Dabrowski?'

'Fine. He's nice.'

'Oh, that's good. How about your old schoolfriends, Eldred? Do you miss them?'

'Sometimes. I saw most of them at the park last week, though, so it's not too bad.'

'Mm.' Mildred was running out of inspiration. 'Well, you can see a bit more of them at half-term, can't you? And have one of your new friends to play if you want to. Are any of them interested in computers?'

'Yes, most of them.'

'You know your father spoke to Mr Dabrowski last week?'

'Yes, you said.'

'He's very pleased with your work. He said in all his years as a teacher he's never known a child work like you.'

'Yes,' said Eldred. 'Dad told me.'

There was silence. Mildred cleared her throat. 'You would tell me, wouldn't you,' she said, 'if something was bothering you?'

Eldred drank his hot chocolate.

'Anything at all,' Mildred said. 'Any time. I'd far rather know.'

He drained the mug and put it down.

'Right, then,' said Mildred, after a few more minutes during which Eldred stared at the fire and said nothing. She stood up and switched the fire off. 'Back to bed now.'

'No,' said Eldred. The bright electric bar faded from red to dull brown.

Mildred sat down again. 'Come on, Eldred,' she said. 'It's very late, love. If there is something worrying you, tell me, but if not then go back to bed. You won't have another bad dream now.'

'Anything?' said Eldred.

'Pardon?'

'You said anything,' he reminded her. 'I could say anything, any time.'

'Of course you can, love? Who else can you tell, if not your mum?'

'It's not something to tell,' said Eldred. 'It's more a question.'

Mildred yawned and put her hand to her mouth. 'Go on then, but you know what I'm like with questions, even when it's not two o'clock in the morning!'

'Not that kind of question,' he said.

She waited, stifling a second yawn. She could feel her eyelids drooping.

'Who is my father?' said Eldred.

'What?' said Mildred. 'You know who your father is, Eldred. What is this?'

'Who is he?'

'What do you mean, who is he? Dad. Edgar Jones.'

'He isn't the one who raped you though, is he?'

Mildred's mouth dropped open. Her face changed colour.

'I saw an old newspaper page,' said Eldred. 'It said you didn't see the man's face. It wasn't Dad, was it?'

'Oh my God,' said Mildred. 'Where? Where did you find this, Eldred?'

'In the library. On microfilm.'

Mildred put her head in her hands.

'I'm sorry,' said Eldred. He caught hold of her hands and held them. 'I didn't mean to upset you.'

'When did you see it?' she asked.

'A few weeks ago.'

'A few weeks! Why did you keep it to yourself?'

'Why did you?'

'I didn't see any reason why you should know, Eldred. It's all in the past.'

'But was it Dad who raped you?'

'Of course it wasn't him, Eldred. How could you think such a thing?'

'Who was it?'

'I don't know. I don't want to know. Some yobbo. Probably drunk or on drugs or mental. He kept laughing. They didn't catch him.'

'Is he my father, then?'

'No,' she said. 'No.'

'Did you know you were pregnant with me?'

'What? When?'

'Did you know, Mum?'

'Do you mean, how long afterwards did I find out?'

'No. I was there already, wasn't I?'

She hesitated, not looking at him. 'Oh,' she said, 'yes, I expect so. I don't remember the exact dates now. It was so long ago, Eldred. It needn't concern you.'

'But I was there, wasn't I?' he said. 'I remember it happening.'

'Oh, Eldred, of course you don't!'

'I do,' he said, 'only I didn't know what was going on. It was really scary. I remember being born as well.'

'That's impossible. You've got a vivid imagination.'

'No. People often remember being born, and have memories from being in the womb as well. I've read about it.'

'You read too much,' she said sharply. 'If you hadn't gone reading and prying into what didn't concern you, this wouldn't have come out. It had nothing to do with you, nothing at all.'

'But I was there too,' he insisted. 'It happened to me as well, inside you.'

'It didn't!' she said, exasperated. 'You weren't conceived until that moment!'

As the words slipped out, she clapped her hands over her mouth, horrified at herself.

Eldred froze. 'So he isn't my dad,' he said. 'Edgar Jones.'

'Don't talk about him, like that, by his name! He's not some stranger, Eldred!'

'He's not my father, though,' Eldred said. His voice was toneless.

'He is,' she said. 'He is.'

He turned on her, tears welling up in his eyes. 'You keep contradicting yourself! I don't believe you! The article said you'd been married eleven years and had no children. If you weren't pregnant when it happened, then it must have been that man – unless it was Dad who raped you. Was he there or wasn't he?'

'Listen,' said Mildred. 'Listen. Stop crying. Do you want me to tell you what happened?'

He nodded.

'You're sure you want to know?' she said. 'All right, then.'

Chapter Seventy-five

'It was my father's anniversary,' said Mildred. 'He'd died three years before. I went to put some flowers on his grave. Edgar was at work;

I hadn't told him I was going there. I thought I'd be home long before he was.

'I'd filled up the flower vase with water – there was a tap there, in a corner of the cemetery, behind some trees – when somebody jumped on me. I hadn't seen anyone there; I was completely off-guard. I only got one glimpse of him before he hit me in the face and I couldn't see any more. I couldn't even say what he looked like, except that he seemed youngish and he wore a red anorak hood with a blue jacket. I hadn't the breath to scream. I shouldn't be telling you this. You're only a child.'

'Go on,' said Eldred.

'He raped me,' said Mildred. 'Several times. I went unconscious. When I came round, he'd gone. It was getting dark. It was summer, so it must have been quite late.'

'The article said it happened at about four-thirty,' Eldred said. His voice was very quiet.

'Yes,' said Mildred. 'I lay there a long time. They close the gates of the cemetery before sunset.'

'Were you there all night?' Eldred asked. He was crying.

'Nearly. Your father found me at about five in the morning.'

'How did he get in?'

'Climbed over the gates.'

'How did he know where to look?'

'He didn't,' she said. 'But he'd looked everywhere else. He phoned everyone we knew, he contacted the police, then he spent all night out on the streets, going everywhere I ever went. When he passed the cemetery, he remembered my father had died in the summer time and he thought it might be worth a try. He ran up and down every avenue until he found me, behind the trees.'

Eldred broke into sobs. Mildred tightened her arm round him.

'He picked me up,' she said, 'and carried me as far as the gates. He climbed back over the gates and flagged down a passing car – there were one or two going by, even at that time in the morning. He got the driver to phone an ambulance and the police. They broke open the gates.

'He went with me to the hospital and sat by my side all the rest of the night, all day and all the next night. He never let go of my hand and never left me, except to go to the toilet. He didn't eat or drink.'

'It wasn't him, then,' said Eldred.

'I told you,' said Mildred. 'He would never do that to me.'

'No, I mean, it wasn't him who... who germinated me. Why did you call me a name that was a mixture of yours and his? Did you want to pretend?'

'No,' said Mildred. 'There was no pretence.'

'Then why...?'

'Eldred, this isn't easy for me. Let me tell it in my own way, will you? I'll come to that in a minute. Let me think.'

'Okay,' he said. 'Sorry. Go on.'

'When I went home, I was weak – in mind as well as in body. I went for whole weeks without knowing what day it was. I couldn't remember anything. I don't mean just that I couldn't remember the attack, though I couldn't; it was no good the police asking me questions; my mind was a blank. But as well as that, I couldn't remember to do things. Edgar did the shopping. I cooked, but I'd forget. I'd put something in the oven for two hours then find I hadn't lit it. Or I'd put sausages under the grill and come in to find them in flames.

'I chain-smoked. People told me it was bad for the baby, but I couldn't stop myself. It's probably what made your lungs bad.'

Eldred shook his head. 'No,' he said. 'It wasn't that.'

'I couldn't bear to talk to anyone,' continued Mildred. 'The neighbours were kind, and the few friends we had, but whenever they visited I couldn't wait till they went home again. I'd watch their mouths moving and hear the sounds coming out, but I couldn't make sense of the words.'

'Frightening,' said Eldred.

'You would think so,' said Mildred, 'but I wasn't frightened so much as numb. I'd lost all my feelings. I knew who Edgar was, of course, but I couldn't feel anything towards him. He was another person in the house, but he didn't seem like my husband. I didn't feel connected to him, or to anyone. I felt like I was on another planet – or everyone else was.'

'How long did it go on like that?' asked Eldred.

'Until you were born,' said Mildred. She went silent.

'I do remember being born,' Eldred said. 'Truly. It was like coming down a dark tunnel, a very long way, and then a bright light at the end.'

'Yes,' said Mildred. 'That's what it must have been like, all right.'

'Were you scared to look at me?' asked Eldred. 'In case I looked like him or something?'

'No,' Mildred said. 'You see, you were the light at the end of the tunnel for me too. When you came out, you brought me with you. I don't know what happened, but something lifted. Edgar could see it too. He said I looked at him and saw him again for the first time in nine months.'

'What about when he saw me?' Eldred said fearfully.

'Oh,' said Mildred, 'when the nurses had wrapped you up and given you to me to hold, you know what he did?'

'No, what?'

'He took you from me. He took you in his arms and he held you and looked at you and he said, "Hello, son." Then someone brought me a cup of tea and when I'd drunk it, he said, "You go to sleep." And when I woke up, I'd been moved down to the ward, and he was sitting there beside me – just like he had before, after the attack, only this time he was holding you, still holding you against his chest.

'That's why I'm telling you, Eldred; that's who your dad is, and you'd better believe me, because it's the truth. If anyone could think that God gives a gift like fatherhood to some pervert who would rape a woman when she's defenceless, they're very wrong. He saves that gift for the one who earns it. That's why you're called after us both, Eldred – because you're his, just as much as mine.

'That other man, he threw away his sperm the way he was throwing away his life, and he probably thought he'd thrown my life away as well. I must have looked more than half dead.

'But something must have brought me through it, Eldred, to give birth to you. You were the one good thing to come out of all of it. You, and your father caring for me – caring for both of us. I know he doesn't show his feelings easily, but he has loved you from the first moment.'

'But why does he say things like, "You get this talent from me, son," if he knows there's no genetic inheritance? He is pretending, isn't he?'

'The first time he said that kind of thing, maybe he was,' said Mildred, 'or maybe not. It may not be genetic, but children often do take on a resemblance to people who are close to them.'

Eldred pondered this. 'Like people come to look like their dogs? Or the dogs come to look like them?'

Mildred smiled. 'I don't know about that. Maybe we did pretend for a while, Eldred, that you were his in blood as well, or maybe we just wished so much for it that it became real.'

'How?'

'To be honest, I think by now we'd both forgotten. It's Edgar's name on the birth certificate. We didn't see it as lying, though I suppose it was. I don't know, love. We'd wanted a child for so long and nothing happened; we'd had such plans, such dreams, that gradually faded as the years passed. Then when we discovered I was pregnant, of course it was a shock, because of the way it had come about. But I honestly don't think it ever occurred to us not to see you as ours – Edgar's as well.'

Eldred nodded his head. 'Yes,' he said, 'but he must have wished it never happened.'

'We both wished that,' said Mildred softly. 'Of course we did. But we never once wished we hadn't had you.'

'Not like that!' Eldred blurted. He hammered his eyes with his fists. 'I came from hell!'

'No,' said Mildred. 'I don't know, love, if it's really like you said – if you remember something happening. I don't know if it's possible for a child to have something carved on its memory right at the very minute it's conceived. I suppose, if what happened was strong enough, that could be. What I do know is, yes, I went through hell and, whether you knew it or not, you came with me. But you also brought me out of it, Eldred.'

'It wasn't worth it, though,' he said. 'Not all that, that you went through.'

She turned his face to look at her. His eyes were screwed up and puffy and his cheeks were blotched.

'Oh yes, it was,' she said.

Chapter Seventy-six

Keith was off school with bronchitis. The antibiotics upset his stomach, and his breathing was more laboured when he lay down, so he was sitting in his wheelchair in the dining room, within easy reach of the downstairs toilet. His mother had carried the television in there.

'I'm only in the kitchen,' she said, 'and I'll leave the door open, and the hatch too, so call if you want anything.'

So he was there, within sight of the front door, when Grandad came. He saw his mother open the door and saw Grandad, without a word, step in and put his arms round her. They stayed like that for a long time. Finally, he let her go.

'It's over,' he said. 'They've got him.'

'Is he in prison?'

'In hospital. Up north somewhere, a seaside resort. I'll have to go up there.'

'I'm coming with you.'

'No, don't come. You have to stay here with Keith. It's just as well.'

'Is he badly hurt?'

'In intensive care.'

'Oh God. Come in, come in properly, Dad, and tell me.'

'I should go,' he said, 'straight away.'

'You can't go in this state, Dad; you're shaking like a leaf. Let me phone Frank at work. He'll drive you.'

'No, no, I can't ask that.'

'Of course you can, for God's sake! Look at all you've done for us, for Keith. Sit in the kitchen while I phone him.'

'No,' he said. 'You'll need him here with you. I've phoned for the times of the trains. There's one in an hour. You can phone me a taxi from here, if you will.'

Grandad walked past the open door of the dining room, not seeing Keith in there. His footsteps were shuffling and his head was lowered. He seemed to have aged ten years, during this last week or two.

Keith thought his mother had forgotten him too. She returned from the phone in the hall and went straight to the kitchen, without a glance at him through the open door. She had left the serving hatch open. Keith would be able to hear every word. He felt as though he was eavesdropping and didn't know whether he should call out and remind them he was there, but that seemed an intrusion too. He pressed the remote control to turn the sound down on the television, partly to avoid disturbing them, and partly because he really wanted to hear; it might be the only way he would know. His parents were still prone to protect him from unpleasant truths.

'What happened?' his mother asked.

'He attacked some young girl, in a fairground or some such place.'

Keith could hear his mother's sharp intake of breath. 'Oh no! Is she okay?'

'She fell from a height and injured her back, but she'll be all right. She's been treated for shock.'

'How did Dan get hurt? Did he fall as well?'

'He was up some tower or something. A man threw a beam at him and knocked him off.'

'A beam?'

'That's what they said. A great beam of wood. Hit him in the back of the head, knocked him out and knocked him to the ground. The police were called, at the same time as the ambulance. It was when he got to the hospital that they realized he was the man they'd been pursuing. They didn't know he'd gone that far north; he'd been sighted in another town and then they'd lost track of him. They reckon there are years' worth of unsolved crimes to his name.'

There was silence.

Then his mother said, 'What state is he in?'

'He hasn't regained consciousness. They're not sure whether he will. The police want to know if we want to press charges against the man who threw the beam at him.'

'What do you think, Dad?'

'No,' he said. 'How can we? Defending some young girl? No.'

'What do they want you to go up there for? To identify him?'

'No, they've got fingerprints and enough other evidence to be sure. They know who he is. They're not asking me to go; they just came to let me know what had happened, that's all. We don't have to do anything.'

'So you don't have to go?'

'I have to go,' said Grandad. 'Not for them. For myself.'

'Why, Dad? Why put yourself through it? He might not even wake up.'

'He might. If he heard his dad's voice.'

'Is that what you want?'

'I don't know,' said Grandad. Keith flinched at the pain in his voice.

'Why?' his mother said. 'He left us a long time ago. Wouldn't it be better to leave him now, where he is? He can't come to any more harm now. Why do you have to go – all that long journey, on your own?'

'Because,' said Grandad harshly, 'he's my son.'

Chapter Seventy-seven

Eldred never understood why his mother jeopardized her job, and almost lost it, by cancelling her shifts over half-term, nor why his father took unpaid leave from work. He was all right now, he assured them. He wasn't upset any more. He even felt relieved, now he knew the truth. There was no need for all this.

Even on the train, he was trying to persuade them that they didn't have to do this for him. Edgar and Mildred smiled and persisted. It was a treat they all needed, Edgar said, a bit of light relief. 'Do us all good. Get your mother away from her slaving and give you a break from the studying. What better way of giving the brain a rest?'

The weather was against them, dismal and wet. As soon as the rain stopped, it started again.

The bed-and-breakfast proprietors in Garton-on-Sea expected them to be out of their room by 10 a.m. and to stay out all day from then on.

The breakfasts were lukewarm, the egg yolks solid as chalk, the bacon limp.

The museum was a poor refuge, even from driving rain. The cafés were crowded and the babies always screamed.

But once a day, every day for three days, they entered a world of magic: a world of seals who balanced stacks of plates on their noses, of lions who opened and never closed their jaws around a live man's head, of clowns with mouths as red and wide as a pillarbox, who tripped each other up and coated each other with foam and threw buckets of water.

Horses adorned like royalty danced like ballerinas, to the astonishment of the Joneses and the rest of the audience. Trapeze artists locked arms in mid-air, high above their heads and swung back and forth, performing heart-stopping feats. A strongman ('the size of our garden shed,' whispered Edgar), lifted a whole seesaw-load of people over his shoulder and carried them round the ring.

There were balloons and bubbles, smoke and dry ice, lights and laser beams, music and drumrolls, laughter, screaming and noise, and tumultuous applause.

But undoubtedly the highlight of the show was Lulubelle – Lulubelle recovered from her injury, as supple and assured as ever before, twisting and leaping and turning, contorting her small lithe body into impossible shapes, balancing her whole weight on one slim hand, standing upright and leaning her head slowly backwards till she was folded in half and the dangly earrings with the bells she had rung with her toes now reached down to the backs of her knees.

But the best part, thought Eldred, was her new trick: the lightning succession of hand-springs in decreasing circles round the ring, culminating in a leap on to a small trampoline, which projected her like a missile on to a high platform, where she stood triumphantly waving and smiling. And when she turned in the direction where Eldred sat with his parents, Mr and Mrs Edgar Jones, she looked right down at them and blew a kiss.

It wasn't for everyone; it was just for him. Only one other member of the audience, on the very last night of the circus's stay in town, merited such favouritism and that was a pale skinny boy draped awkwardly across a wheelchair, who smiled and hooted in the wings.